'The plot, however clever, is not the main attraction. Hill is a masterful writer, quirky and intelligent and his characters – not just the principal duo – are drawn with a depth rare in crime fiction. And, astonishingly, 21 books into the Dalziel and Pascoe saga, I have yet to feel he's repeating himself'
The Times

'Hill is one of England's finest crime writers and this is one of his best novels. A fitting send-off (if, indeed, a send-off it is) for Andy Dalziel'
Glasgow Herald

'The plot twists and turns to a climax that has you on the edge of your seat'　*Woman*

'Hill keeps us in suspense throughout the entire book . . . it's a gripping read which displays Hill's brilliant characterization and dialogue and his skilful plot structure'　*Sunday Telegraph*

'More than just a well-constructed mystery featuring some clever twists and turns; it's also a very human story about loyalty and vengeance, shot through with a wicked and irreverent humour'　*Yorkshire Post*

'His energy, wit and erudition are astonishing . . . he can still see off most of his rivals' *Daily Telegraph*

By the same author

Dalziel and Pascoe novels

A CLUBBABLE WOMAN
AN ADVANCEMENT OF LEARNING
RULING PASSION
AN APRIL SHROUD
A PINCH OF SNUFF
A KILLING KINDNESS
DEADHEADS
EXIT LINES
CHILD'S PLAY
UNDERWORLD
BONES AND SILENCE
RECALLED TO LIFE
PICTURES OF PERFECTION
ASKING FOR THE MOON
THE WOOD BEYOND
ON BEULAH HEIGHT
ARMS AND THE WOMEN
DIALOGUES OF THE DEAD
DEATH'S JEST-BOOK
GOOD MORNING, MIDNIGHT
A CURE FOR ALL DISEASES
MIDNIGHT FUGUE

Joe Sixsmith novels

BLOOD SYMPATHY
BORN GUILTY
KILLING THE LAWYERS
SINGING THE SADNESS
THE ROAR OF THE BUTTERFLIES

FELL OF DARK
THE LONG KILL
DEATH OF A DORMOUSE
DREAM OF DARKNESS
THE ONLY GAME

THE STRANGER HOUSE

THERE ARE NO GHOSTS IN THE SOVIET UNION

REGINALD HILL

DEATH OF DALZIEL

HARPER

Harper
An Imprint of HarperCollins*Publishers*
77–85 Fulham Palace Road, London W6 8JB

www.harpercollins.co.uk

This paperback edition 2009

First published in Great Britain
by HarperCollins*Publishers* 2007

7

A catalogue record for this book
is available from the British Library

ISBN-13: 978-0-00-731322-8

Typseset in Meridien by Palimpsest Book Production Ltd,
Grangemouth, Stirlingshire

Printed and bound in Great Britain

For the peacemakers
whichever god's children they are

What, old acquaintance? Could not all this flesh
Keep in a little life? Poor Jack, farewell . . .
Death hath not struck so fat a deer today.

Shakespeare *Henry IV* Part 1,
Act V scene iv

A Knight of the Temple who kills an evil man
should not be condemned for killing the man
but praised for killing the evil.

St Bernard of Clairvaux,
Liber ad milites Templi

Part One

Some talk of ALEXANDER
And some of HERCULES;
Of HECTOR ...

Anon, 'The British Grenadiers'

1

mill street

never much of a street

*west – the old wool mill a prison block in dry blood
brick its staring windows now blinded by boards its
clatter and chatter a distant echo through white haired
heads*

*east – six narrow houses under one weary roof huddling
against the high embankment that arrows southern
trains into the city's northern heart*

few passengers ever notice Mill Street

never much of a street

*in winter's depth a cold crevasse
spring and autumn much the same*

*but occasionally
on a still summer day*

with sun soaring high in a cloudless sky
Mill Street becomes
desert canyon overbrimming with heat

2

two mutton pasties and an
almond slice

At least it gives me an excuse for sweating, thought Peter Pascoe as he scuttled towards the shelter of the first of the two cars parked across the road from Number 3.

'You hurt your back?' asked Detective Superintendent Andy Dalziel as his DCI slumped to the pavement beside him.

'Sorry?' panted Pascoe.

'You were moving funny.'

'I was taking precautions.'

'Oh aye? I'd stick to the tablets. What the hell are you doing here anyway? Bank Holiday's been cancelled, has it? Or are you just bunking off from weeding the garden?'

'In fact I was sunbathing in it. Then Paddy Ireland rang and said there was a siege situation and you were a bit short on specialist manpower so could I help.'

'Specialist? Didn't know you were a marksman.'

Pascoe took a deep breath and wondered what kind of grinning God defied His own laws by allowing Dalziel's fleshy folds, swaddled in a three-piece suit, to look so cool, while his own spare frame, clad in cotton jeans and a Leeds United T-shirt, was generating more heat than PM's Question Time.

'I've been on a Negotiator's Course, remember?' he said.

'Thought that were to help you talk to Ellie. What did yon fusspot really say?'

The Fat Man was no great fan of Inspector Ireland, who he averred put the three effs in offi-cious. If you took your cue and pointed out that the word only contained two, he'd tell you what the third one stood for.

If you didn't take your cue, he usually told you anyway.

Pascoe on the other hand was a master of diplomatic reticence.

'Not a lot,' he said.

What Ireland had actually said was, 'Sorry to interrupt your day off, Pete, but I thought you should know. Report of an armed man on premises in Mill Street. Number 3.'

Then a pause as if anticipating a response.

The only response Pascoe felt like giving was, Why the hell have I been dragged off my hammock for this?

He said, 'Paddy, I don't know if you've noticed, but

6

I'm off duty today. Bank Holiday, remember? And Andy drew the short straw. Not his idea you rang, is it?'

'Definitely not. It's just that Number 3's a video rental, Oroc Video, Asian and Arab stuff mainly . . .'

A faint bell began to ring in Pascoe's mind.

'Hang on. Isn't it CAT flagged?'

'Hooray. There is someone in CID who actually reads directives,' said Ireland with heavy sarcasm.

CAT was the Combined Anti-Terrorism unit in which Special Branch officers worked alongside MI5 operatives. They flagged people and places on a sliding scale, the lowest level being premises not meriting formal surveillance but around which any unusual activity should be noted and notified.

Number 3 Mill Street was at this bottom level.

Pascoe, not liking to feel reproved, said, 'Are you trying to tell me there's some kind of Intifada brewing in Mill Street?'

'Well, no,' said Ireland. 'It's just that when I passed on the report to Andy . . .'

'Oh good. You have told him. So, apart from not feeling it necessary to bother me, what action has he taken?'

He tried to keep the irritation out of his voice, but not very hard.

Ireland said in a hurt tone, 'He said he'd go along and take a look soon as he finished his meat pie. I reminded him that 3 Mill Street was flagged, in case he'd missed it. He yawned, not a pretty sight when he's eating a meat pie. But when I told him I'd already followed procedure and called it in, he got abusive. So I left him to it.'

'Very wise,' said Pascoe, also yawning audibly. 'So what's the problem?'

'The problem is that he's just passed my office, yelling that he's on his way to Mill Street so maybe I'll be satisfied now that I've ruined his day.'

'But you're not?'

A deep intake of breath; then in a quietly controlled voice, 'What I'm not satisfied is that the super is taking what could be a serious situation seriously. But of course I'm happy to leave it in the expert hands of CID. Sorry to have bothered you.'

The phone went down hard.

Pompous prat, thought Pascoe, setting off back to the garden to share his irritation with his wife. To his surprise she'd said thoughtfully, 'Last time I saw Andy, he was going on about how bored he's getting with the useless bastards running things. He sounded ripe for a bit of mischief. Maybe you ought to check this out, love, before he starts the next Gulf War single-handed. Half an hour wouldn't harm.'

None of this did he care to reveal to Dalziel.

'Not a lot,' he repeated. 'So perhaps you'd like to fill me in.'

'Why not? Then you can shog off home. Being a clever bugger, you'll likely know Number 3's CAT flagged? Or did Ireland have to tell you too?'

'No, but he did give me a shove,' admitted Pascoe.

'There you go,' said Dalziel triumphantly. 'Since the London bombings, them silly sods have put out more flags than we did on Coronation Day.

Faintest sniff of a Middle East connection and they're cocking their legs to lay down a marker.'

'Yes, I did hear they wanted to flag the old Mecca Ballroom at Mirely!'

A reminiscent smile lit up Dalziel's face, like moonlight on a mountain.

'The Mirely Mecca,' he said dreamily. 'Had some good times there in the old days. There were this lass from Donny. Tottie Truman. Her tango could get you done for indecent behaviour –'

'Yes, yes,' interrupted Pascoe. 'I'm sure she was a charming girl vertically or horizontally –'

'Nay, ho'd on!' interrupted the Fat Man in his turn. 'You shouldn't be so quick to put folk in boxes. It's a bad habit of yours, that. Tottie weren't just a bit of squashy flesh, tha knows. She had muscle too. By God, if they'd let women throw the hammer she'd have been a gold medallist! I once saw her chuck a wellie from halfway at a rugby club barbecue and it were still rising as it went over the posts. I thought of wedding her, but she got religion. Just think of the front row we could have bred!'

It was time to stop this trip down memory lane.

Pascoe said, 'Very interesting. But perhaps we should concentrate on the situation in hand. Which is . . . ?'

'That's the trouble with you youngsters,' said Dalziel sadly. 'No time to smell the flowers along the way. All right. Sit rep. Foot-patrol officer reported seeing a man in Number 3 with a gun.

Passed on the info to a patrol car who called in for instructions. So here we are. What do you make of it so far?'

The Fat Man had moved into playful mode. It's guessing-game time, thought Pascoe. Robbery in process? Hardly worth it in Mill Street, unless you were a particularly thick villain. This wasn't the commercial hub of the city, just the far end of a very rusty spoke. The mill itself had a preservation order on it and there'd been talk of refurbishing it as an industrial Heritage Centre, but not even the Victorian Society had objected to the proposed demolition of the jerry-built terrace to make space for a car park.

The mill project, however, had run into difficulties over Lottery funding.

Right wingers said this was because it didn't advantage handicapped lesbian asylum seekers; left wingers because it failed to subsidize the Treasury.

Whatever, plans to demolish the terrace had gone on hold.

The remaining residents had long been rehoused and, rather than have a decaying slum on their hands, the council encouraged small businesses in search of an address and office space to move in and give the buildings an occupied look. Most of these businesses proved as short-lived as the rathe primrose that forsaken dies, and the only survivors at present were Crofts & Wills, patent agents, at Number 6 and Oroc Video at Number 3.

All of which interesting historical analysis

brought Pascoe no nearer to understanding what they were doing here.

Losing patience, he said, 'OK, so there might be a man with a gun in there. I presume you've some strategy planned. Or are you going to rush him single-handed?'

'Not now there's two of us. But you always were a bugger for the subtle approach, so let's start with that.'

So saying, the Fat Man rose to his feet, picked up a bullhorn from the bonnet of his car, put it to his lips and bellowed, 'All right, we know you're in there. We've got you surrounded. Come out with your hands up and no one will get hurt.'

He scratched himself under the armpit, then sat down again.

After a moment's silence Pascoe said, 'I can't really believe you said that, sir.'

'Why not? Used to say it all the time way back before all this negotiation crap.'

'Did anyone ever come out?'

'Not as I recall.'

Pascoe digested this then said, 'You forgot the bit about throwing his gun out before he comes out with his hands up.'

'No I didn't,' said Dalziel. 'He might not have a gun and if he hasn't, I don't want him thinking we think he has, do I?'

'I thought the foot patrol reported seeing a weapon? What was it? Shotgun? Handgun? And what was this putative gunman actually doing?

Come on, Andy. I left a jug of home-made lemonade and a hammock to come here. What's the sodding problem?'

Even diplomatic reticence had its limits.

'The sodding problem?' said the Fat Man. 'Yon's the sodding problem.'

He pointed toward the police patrol car parked a little way along from his own vehicle. Pascoe followed the finger.

And all became clear.

Almost out of sight, coiled around the rear wheel with all the latent menace of a piece of bacon rind, lay a familiar lanky figure.

'Oh God. You don't mean . . . ?'

'That's right. Only contact with this gunman so far has been Constable Hector.'

Police Constable Hector is the albatross round Mid-Yorkshire Constabulary's neck, the long-legged fly in its soup, the Wollemi pine in its outback, the coelacanth in its ocean depths. But his saving lack of grace is he never plumbs bottom. Beneath the lowest deep there's always a lower deep, and he survives because, in that perverse way in which True Brits often manage to find triumph in disaster, Mid-Yorkshire Police Force have become proud of him. If ever talk flags in the Black Bull, someone just has to say, 'Remember when Hector . . .' and a couple of hours of happy reminiscence are guaranteed.

So, when Dalziel said, 'Yon's the sodding problem', much was explained. But not all. Not by a long chalk.

*   *   *

'So,' continued Dalziel. 'Question is, how to find out if Hector really saw a gun or not.'

'Well,' mused Pascoe. 'I suppose we could expose him and see if he got shot.'

'Brilliant!' said Dalziel. 'Makes me glad I paid for your education. HECTOR!'

'For God's sake, I was joking!' exclaimed Pascoe as the lanky constable disentangled himself from the car wheel and began to crawl towards them.

'I could do with a laugh,' said Dalziel, smiling like a rusty radiator grill. 'Hector, lad, what fettle? I've got a job for you if you feel up to it.'

'Sir?' said Hector hesitantly.

Pascoe wished he could feel that the hesitation demonstrated suspicion of the Fat Man's intent, but he knew from experience it was the constable's natural response to most forms of address from 'Hello' to 'Help! I'm drowning!' Prime it as much as you liked, the mighty engine of Hector's mind always started cold, even when as now his hatless head was clearly very hot. A few weeks ago, he'd appeared with his skull cropped so close he made Bruce Willis look like Esau, prompting Dalziel to say, 'I always thought tha'd be the death of me, Hec, but there's no need to go around looking like the bugger!'

Now he looked at the smooth white skull, polished with sweat beneath the sun's bright duster, shook his head sadly, and said, 'Here's what I want you to do, lad. All this hanging around's fair clemmed me. You know Pat's Pantry in Station

13

Square? Never closes, doesn't Pat. Pop round there and get me two mutton pasties and an almond slice. And a custard tart for Mr Pascoe. It's his favourite. Can you remember all that?'

'Yes, sir,' said Hector, but showed no sign of moving off.

'What are you waiting for?' asked Dalziel. 'Money up front, is that it? What happened to trust? All right, Mr Pascoe'll pay you. I can't be standing tret every time.'

Every tenth time would be nice, thought Pascoe as he put two one-pound coins on to Hector's sweaty palms, where they lay like a dead man's eyes.

'If it's more, Mr Dalziel will settle up,' he said.

'Yes, sir . . . but what about . . . *him*?' muttered Hector, his gaze flicking to Number 3.

Poor sod's terrified of being shot at, thought Pascoe.

'Him?' said Dalziel. 'That's what I like about you, Hector. Always thinking about other people.'

He stood up once more with the bullhorn.

'You in the house. We're just sending off to Pat's Pantry for some grub and my lad wants to know if there's owt you'd fancy. Pastie, mebbe? Or they do grand Eccles cakes.'

He paused, listened, then sat down again.

'Don't think he wants owt. But a nice thought. Does you credit. It'll be noted.'

'No sir,' said Hector, fear making him bold. 'What I meant was, if he sees me moving and thinks I'm a danger . . .'

'Eh? Oh, I get you. He might take a shot at you. If he thinks you're a danger.'

Dalziel scratched his nose thoughtfully. Pascoe avoided catching his eye.

'Best thing,' said the Fat Man finally, 'is not to look dangerous. Stand up straight, chest out, shoulders back, and walk nice and slow, like you've got somewhere definite to go. That way, even if the bugger does shoot, chances are the bullet will pass clean through you without doing much harm. Off you go then.'

Up to this point, Pascoe had been convinced that the blind obedience to lunatic orders which had made the dreadful slaughter of the Great War possible had died with those millions. Now, watching Hector move slowly down the street like a man wading through water, he had his doubts.

Once Hector was out of sight, he relaxed against the side of the car and said, 'OK, sir. Now either you tell me exactly what's going on or I'm off back to my hammock.'

'You mean you'd like to hear Hector's tale? Why not? Once upon a time . . .'

Hector is that rarity in a modern police force, a permanent foot patrol, providing a useful statistic when anxious community groups press for the return of the old beat bobby. The truth is, whether behind the wheel or driving the driver to distraction from the passenger seat, a motorized Hector is lethal. On a bike he never reaches a speed to be dangerous, but his resemblance to a drunken giraffe, though contributing much to the mirth of Mid-Yorkshire, does little for the constabulary image.

So Hector plods; and, plodding along Mill Street that day, he'd heard a sound as he passed Number 3. 'Like a cough,' he said. 'Or a rotten stick breaking. Or a tennis ball bouncing off a wall. Or a shot.'

The nearest Hector ever comes to precision is multiple-choice answers.

He tried the door. It opened. He stepped into the cool shade of the video shop. Behind the counter he saw two men. Asked for a description, he thought a while then said it was hard to see things clearly, coming as he had from bright sunlight into shadow, but it was his fairly firm opinion that one of them was 'a sort of darkie'.

To the politically correct, this might have resonated as racist and been educed as evidence of Hector's unsuitability for the job. To those who'd heard him describe a Christmas shoplifter wearing a Santa Claus outfit as 'a little bloke, I think he had a moustache', 'a sort of darkie' came close to being eidetic.

The second man ('looked funny but probably not a darkie' was Hector's best shot here) seemed to be holding something in his right hand which might have been a gun, but it was hard to be sure because he was standing in the deepest shadow and the man lowered his hands out of sight behind the counter when he saw Hector.

Feeling the situation needed to be clarified, Hector said, 'All right then?'

There had been a pause during which the two inmates looked at each other.

Then the sort-of-darkie replied, 'Yes. We are all right.'

And Hector brought this illuminating exchange to a close by saying with an economy and symmetry that were almost beautiful, 'All right then,' and leaving.

Now he had a philosophical problem. Had there been an incident and should he report it? It didn't take eternity to tease Hector out of thought; the space between now and tea-time could do the trick. So he was more than usually oblivious to his surroundings as he crossed to the opposite pavement with the result that he was almost knocked over by a passing patrol car. The driver, PC Joker Jennison, did an emergency stop then leaned out of his open window to express his doubts about Hector's sanity.

Hector listened politely – he had after all heard it all before – then, when Jennison paused for breath, off-loaded his problem on to the constable's very broad shoulders.

Jennison's first reaction was that such a story from such a source was almost certainly a load of crap. Also there were only five minutes till the end of his shift, which was why he was speeding down Mill Street in the first place.

'Best call it in,' he said. 'But wait till we're out of sight, eh?'

'I think me battery's flat,' said Hector.

'What's new?' said Jennison, and restarted the car.

Unfortunately his partner, PC Alan Maycock, came from Hebden Bridge which is close enough to the Lancastrian border for its natives to be by Mid-Yorkshire standards a bit soft in every sense of the term, and he was moved by Hector's plight.

'I'll get you through on the car radio,' he said.

And when Jennison dug him viciously in his belly, he murmured, 'Nay, it'll not take but a minute, and when they hear it's Hec, they'll likely just have a laugh.'

As a policeman, he should have known that the rewards of virtue are sparse and long delayed. If you're looking for quick profit, opt for vice.

Instead of the expected fellow constable responding from Control, it was duty inspector Paddy Ireland who took the call. As soon as he heard Number 3 Mill Street mentioned, he gave commands for the car to remain in place and await instructions.

'And then the bugger bursts in on me like he's just heard the first bombs dropping on Pearl Harbour,' concluded Dalziel. 'Got me excited, till he mentioned Hector. That took the edge off! And when he said he'd already called it in, I could have wrung his neck!'

'And then . . . ?' enquired Pascoe.

'I finished me pie. Few minutes later the phone rang. It were some motor-mouth from CAT. I tried to explain it were likely all a mistake, but he said mebbe I should let the experts decide that. I said would this be the same experts who'd spent so much public money breaking up the Carradice gang?'

Pascoe, the diplomat, groaned.

* * *

18

Six months ago CAT had claimed a huge success when they arrested fifteen terrorist suspects in Nottingham on suspicion of plotting to poison the local water supply with ricin. Since then, however, the CPS had been forced to drop the case against first one then another of the group till finally the trial got under way with only the alleged ringleader, Michael Carradice, in the dock. Pascoe had his own private reasons for hoping the case against him failed too – a hope nourished by Home Office statements made on CAT's behalf which were sounding increasingly irritated and defensive.

'What's up with thee? Wind, is it?' said Dalziel in response to Pascoe's groan. 'Any road, the prat finished by saying the important thing was to keep a low profile, not risk alerting anyone inside, set up blocks out of sight at the street end, maintain observation till their man turned up to assess the situation. Why're you grinding your teeth like that?'

'Maybe because I don't see any sign of any road-blocks, just Maycock smoking a fag at one end of the street and Jennison scratching his balls at the other. Also I'm crouched down behind your car with the patrol car next to it, right opposite Number 3.'

'Who need road-blocks when you've got a pair of fatties like Maycock and Jennison? And why move the cars when anyone in there knows we're on to them already? Any road, you and me know this is likely just another load of Hector bollocks.'

He shook his head in mock despair.

'In that case,' said Pascoe, tiring of the game, 'all you need do is stroll over there, check everything's OK, then leave a note for the CAT man on the shop door saying you've got it sorted and would he like a cup of tea back at the Station? Meanwhile . . .'

It was his intention to follow his heavy irony by taking his leave and heading for home and hammock, but the Fat Man was struggling to his feet.

'You're dead right,' he said. 'You tend to fumble around a bit, but in the end you put your white stick right on it, as the actress said to the short-sighted cabinet minister. Time for action. We'll be a laughing stock if it gets out we spent the holiday hiding behind a car because of Hector. Where's yon bugger got with my mutton pasties, by the way? We were mad to trust him with our money.'

'My money,' corrected Pascoe. 'And you misunderstand me, I'm not actually suggesting we do *anything* . . .'

'Nay, lad. Don't be modest,' said Dalziel, upright now. 'When you've got a good idea, flaunt it.'

'Sir,' said Pascoe. 'Is this wise? I know Hector's not entirely reliable, but surely he knows a gun when he sees one . . .'

As a plea for caution this proved counter-productive.

'Don't be daft,' laughed Dalziel. 'We're talking about a man who can't pick his nose unless someone paints a cross on it and gives him a mirror. If he heard owt, it were likely his own fart, and the bugger inside were probably holding a take-away kebab. Come on, Pete. Let's get this sorted, then you can buy me a pint.'

He dusted down his suit, straightened his tie, and set off across the street with the confident step of a man who could walk with kings, talk with presidents, dispute with philosophers, portend with prophets, and never have the slightest doubt that he was right.

Interestingly, despite the fact that little in their long relationship had given Pascoe any real reason to question this presumption of rightness, the thought crossed his mind as he rose and set off in the footsteps of his great master that there had to be a first time for everything, and how ironic it would be if it were Ellie's tender heart that caused him to be present on the occasion when the myth of Dalziel's infallibility was exploded . . .

At this same moment, as if his mind had developed powers of telekinesis, Mill Street blew up.

3

intimations

Ellie Pascoe was asleep in the garden hammock so reluctantly vacated by her husband when the explosion occurred.

The Pascoe house in the northern suburbs was too far from Mill Street for anything but the faintest rumour of the bang to reach there. What woke Ellie was a prolonged volley of barking from her daughter's mongrel terrier.

'What's up with Tig?' Ellie asked yawning.

'Don't know,' said Rosie. 'We were playing ball and he just started.'

A sudden suspicion made Ellie examine the tall apple tree in next-door's garden. Puberty was working its rough changes on her neighbour's son and a couple of times recently when the summer heat had lured her outside in her bikini, she'd spotted him staring down at her out of the foliage. But there was no sign, and in any case Tig's nose pointed south towards the centre of town. As she followed his fixed gaze she saw a long way away a faint smudge of smoke soiling the perfect blue of the summer sky.

Who would light a fire on a day like this?

Tig was still barking.

'Can't you make him shut up?' snapped Ellie.

Her daughter looked at her in surprise, then took a biscuit off a plate and threw it across the lawn. Tig gave a farewell yap, then went in search of his reward with the complacent mien of one who has done his duty.

Ellie felt guilty at snapping. Her irritation wasn't with the dog, there was some other cause less definable.

She rolled out of the hammock and said, 'I'm too hot. Think I'll cool down in the shower. You OK by yourself?'

Rosie gave her a look which said without words that she hadn't been much company anyway, so what was going to be different?

Ellie went inside, turned on the shower and stepped under it.

The cool water washed away her sweat but did nothing for her sense of unease.

Still nothing definable. Or nothing that she wanted to define. Pointless thinking about it. Pointless because, if she did think about it, she might come up with the silly conclusion that the real reason she was taking this shower was that she didn't want to be wearing her bikini if bad news came . . .

* * *

Andy Dalziel's partner, Amanda Marvell, known to her friends as Cap, was even further away when Mill Street blew up.

With her man on duty, she had followed the crowds on the traditional migration to the coast, not, however, to join the mass bake-in on a crowded beach but to visit the sick.

The sick in this instance took the form of her old headmistress, Dame Kitty Bagnold who for nearly forty years had ruled the famous St Dorothy's Academy for Catholic Girls near Bakewell in Derbyshire. Cap Marvell had ultimately made life choices which ran counter to everything St Dot's stood for. In particular, she had abandoned her religion, divorced her husband, and got herself involved in various animal rights groups whose activities teetered on the edge of legality.

Yet throughout all this, she and Dame Kitty had remained in touch and eventually, rather to their surprise, realized they were friends. Not that the friendship made Cap feel able to address her old head by her St Dot's sobriquet of Kitbag, and Dame Kitty would rather have blasphemed than call her ex-pupil anything but Amanda.

A long and very active retirement had ground Dame Kitty down till ill health had finally obliged her to admit the inevitable, and two years earlier she had moved into a private nursing home that was part of the Avalon Clinic complex at Sandytown on the Yorkshire coast.

At her best, Dame Kitty was as bright and sharp as ever, but she tired easily and usually Cap was alert for the first signs of fatigue so that she could start ending her visit without making her friend's condition the cause.

This time it was the older woman who said, 'Is everything all right, Amanda?'

'What?'

'You seemed to drift off. Perhaps you should sit in this absurd wheelchair while I go inside and order some more tea.'

'No, no, I'm fine. Sorry. What were we saying . . . ?'

'We were discussing the merits of the government's somewhat inchoate education policy, an argument I hoped your sudden silence indicated I had won. But I fear my victory owes more to your distraction than my reasoning. Are you sure all is well with you? No problems with this police officer of yours, whom I hope one day to meet?'

'No, things are fine there, really . . .'

Suddenly Cap Marvell took her mobile out.

'Sorry, do you mind?'

She was speed-dialling before Kitty could answer.

The phone rang twice then there was an invitation to leave a message.

She opened her mouth to speak, closed it, disconnected, and stood up.

'I'm sorry, Kitty, I've got to go. Before the mobs start moving off the beaches . . .'

This effort to offer a rational explanation produced the same sad sigh and slight upward roll of the eyes brought by feeble excuses for bad behaviour in their St Dot days.

'OK, that's not it. Sorry, I don't know why,' said Cap. 'But I've really got to go.'

'Then go, my dear. And God go with you.'

Normally this traditional valediction would have won from Cap her equivalent of the old headmistress's long-suffering expression, but today she just nodded, stooped to kiss her friend's cheek, then hurried away across the lawn towards the car park.

Dame Kitty watched her out of sight. There was trouble there. Despite the bright sun and the cloudless sky, she felt it in the air.

She stood up out of the wheelchair which the staff insisted she should use on her excursions into the gardens, gave it a whack with her stick, and began to make her slow way back to the house.

4

dust and ashes

Later Peter Pascoe worked out that Dalziel had probably saved his life twice.

The Fat Man's car which they'd been sheltering behind was flipped into the air then deposited upside down on the pavement.

If he hadn't obeyed the Fat Man's command to follow, he would have been underneath it.

And if he hadn't been walking in the lee of that corpulent frame when the explosion occurred . . .

As it was, when some slight degree of awareness began to seep back into his brain, he felt as if every part of his body had been subjected to a good kicking. He tried to stand up but found the best he could manage was all fours.

The air was full of dust and smoke. Like a retriever peering through the mist in search of its master's bird, he strained to penetrate the swirling veil of motes and vapour. An amorphous area of orangey red with some consistency of base gave him the beginnings of perspective. Against it, marked by its stillness in the moving air, he made out a vague heap of something, like a pile of earth thrown up alongside a grave.

He began to crawl forward and after a couple of yards managed to rise off his hands into a semi-upright crouch. The shifting coiling colour he realized now was fire. He could feel its heat, completely unlike the gentle warmth of the sun which only an hour ago he'd been enjoying in the green seclusion of his garden. That small part of his mind still in touch with normality suggested that he ought to ring Ellie and tell her he was all right before some garbled version of events got on to local radio.

Not that he was sure how all right he was. But a lot all righter than this still heap of something which he was now close enough to formally identify as Andy Dalziel.

He had fallen on to his left side and his arms and legs were spread and bent like the kapok stuffed limbs of some huge teddy bear discarded by a spoilt child. His face had been shredded by shards of glass and brick, and the fine grey dust sticking to the seeping wounds made him look as if he were wearing a kabuki mask.

There was no sign of life. But not for a second did Pascoe admit the possibility of death. Dalziel was indestructible. Dalziel is, and was, and for ever shall be, world without end, amen. Everybody knew that. Therein lay half his power. Chief constables might come and chief constables might go, but Fat Andy went on for ever.

He rolled him over on to his back. It wasn't easy but he did it. He brushed the dust away from his mouth and nose. He definitely wasn't breathing. He checked the carotid pulse, thought he detected a flutter, but a combination of his dull fingers and Dalziel's monolithic neck left him in doubt. He opened the mouth and saw there was a lot of debris in there. Carefully he cleared it away, discovering in the process what he hadn't known before, that Dalziel had a dental plate. This he tucked carefully into his pocket. He checked that the tongue hadn't been swallowed. Then he cleared the nostrils, undid the shirt collar, and put his ear to the mighty chest.

There was no movement, no sound.

He placed his hands on top of each other on the chest and pressed down hard, five times, counting a second interval between.

Then he tilted the head back with his right hand under the chin so that the mouth opened wide. With the thumb and forefinger of his left hand, he pinched Dalziel's nose. Then he took a deep breath, thought, I'm never going to hear the end of this, pressed his mouth down on to those great lips and blew.

Five times he did this. Then he repeated the heart massage and went through the whole process again. And again.

Once more he tried the pulse. This time he

was sure there was something. And the next time he blew into the mouth, the chest began to rise and fall of its own volition.

Now he began to arrange Dalziel in the recovery position. This was a task to daunt a fit navvy with a block and tackle, but finally he managed it and sank back exhausted.

All this seemed to take hours but must have consumed only a few minutes. He was vaguely aware of figures moving through the miasma. Presumably there were sounds too, but at first they were simply absorbed by the white noise which the blast had filled his ears with. Another hour passed. Or a few seconds. He felt something touch his shoulder. It hurt. He looked up. PC Maycock was standing over him, mouthing nothings, like a fish in a glass tank. He tried to lip read and got, 'Are you all right?' which hardly seemed worth the effort. He pointed at Dalziel and said, 'Get help,' without any assurance that the words were coming out. Maycock tried to assist him to his feet but he shook his head and pointed again at the Fat Man. He stuck his little fingers in his ears and started to prise out the debris which seemed to have lodged there. This, or perhaps the simple passage of time, improved things a little, and he began to pick out a higher line of sound which he tentatively identified as approaching sirens.

Time was still doing a quickstep. Slow, slow, quick, quick, slow. In the slow periods he felt as if sitting here in the post-blast smog watching over Fat Andy was all he'd ever done and all he was ever likely to do. Then he closed his eyes for a fraction of a second and when he opened them the smog had thinned and paramedics were stooping over Dalziel's body and firemen were going about the business before the ruined terrace. Where Number 3 had been there was nothing but a flame-filled cavity, like hell-mouth in a morality play. The Victorian entrepreneurs' shoddy building materials had offered little resistance to the blast. This was perhaps one of those instances of a Bad Thing eventually turning out to be a Good Thing, which divines through the ages had educed as evidence of God's Mysterious Purpose. If the walls of Number 3 had shared any of the massive solidity of the viaduct wall against which the terrace rested, the blast would have been directed straight out. As it was, Numbers 2 and 4 were in a state of complete collapse, and the rest of the terrace looked seriously shell shocked.

They were attaching all kinds of bits and pieces to the Fat Man. But not, so far as Pascoe could see, a crane. They'd need a crane. And a sling. This was a beached whale they were dealing with and it would take more than the puny efforts of half a dozen men to bear him back to the life-supporting sea. He tried to say this but couldn't get the words out. Didn't matter. Somehow these supermen were proving him wrong and managing to get Dalziel on to a stretcher. Pascoe closed his eyes in relief. When he opened them again he found he was looking up at the sky and moving. For a second he thought he was back on his hammock in his garden. Then he realized he too was on a stretcher.

He raised his head to protest that this was unnecessary. The effort made him realize it probably was. Ahead he could see an ambulance. Beside it stood an all too familiar figure.

Hector, the author of all their woes, his face a cartoonist's dream of uncomprehending consternation.

As the medics slid the stretcher into the vehicle, he held out both his hands towards Pascoe. In them were two paper bags, partially open to reveal a pair of mutton pasties and an almond slice.

'Sir, I'm sorry, but they were out of custards . . .' he stuttered.

'Not my lucky day then,' whispered Peter Pascoe. 'Not my lucky day.'

5

the two Geoffreys

Andre de Montbard, Knight of the Temple and right-hand man to Hugh de Payens, the Order's Grand Master, was fishing in the dull canal at the far end of Charter Parker. He sat on a canvas stool, his back against a plane tree, his rod resting on a fork made from a wire coat-hanger. The sun had vanished behind the warehouses on the opposite bank but the air was still warm and the sky still blue, though darkening towards indigo from the azure of the afternoon. His float bobbed in the wake of a passing narrow boat and the helmsman gave a half apologetic wave.

A man walking his dog paused and said, 'Anything biting?'

'I think I felt a midge.'

'Oh aye? Just wait half an hour and you'll need a mask. Cheers.'

'Cheers.'

As the man moved away, he passed the two Geoffreys strolling slowly along the tow path.

Geoffrey O stooped to pat the dog but Geoffrey B didn't look in the mood for chit-chat. As well as the shared name, they both wore black pants, trainers and T-shirts. But there any claims to being a matching pair ended, thought Andre. Odd relationship. Shrinks would have a field day with it. Useless twats. What do you call a shrink treading on a land mine? A step in the right direction. Himself, he'd always been an effects man, bugger causes. And the effect here had been to make them ripe for knighthood.

Performance was another thing. Soon as he'd heard things had gone a bit pear-shaped, he'd started anticipating how they'd react.

His guess was, Geoff B headless chicken, Geoff O heartless wolf.

He knew he'd got it right even before Geoff B opened his mouth.

When they reached him, they paused as if to ask how the fish were biting. At least that was the impression Geoff O gave, smiling down at him pleasantly. But Geoff B couldn't manage a smile. He unslung the small rucksack he was carrying over his shoulder and dropped it by the empty catch basket. As he did so, he brought his face close to Andre's and hissed with barely controlled anger, 'What the hell was all that about? A communications post, you said, a bit of gear maybe, but not a fucking powder magazine.'

Andre looked at him steadily till he straightened up.

Then he said, 'Bad intelligence. It happens. Hugh says sorry. But look on the bright side. It certainly made a bang!'

'Jesus Christ!' exclaimed Geoff B. 'It put two cops in hospital. One of them critical, the news says.'

Andre shrugged and said, 'My info is the stupid sods were grandstanding. If they'd followed instructions and stood off . . .'

'Is that supposed to make me feel better? I'm giving notice, if one of them dies, that's me finished, understand?'

You're finished anyway, son, thought Andre. One strike and out. Returned to unit.

Geoff O spoke before he could respond.

'Was the cop who came into the shop one of those injured?'

Andre flickered an approving smile. No bother there. First rule of combat: be prepared for collateral damage. Can't get your head round that, might as well stay home.

He said, 'That would have been tidy, but no, he wasn't. Seems he hasn't come up with much of a description, though, so I don't think we need worry too much about him.'

'For God's sake!' exclaimed Geoff B, determined not to let go of his anger. 'Is that all you're concerned about? Whether there was a witness?'

Andre looked at him coldly.

'Mebbe you'd be more concerned if you'd been the one he clocked,' he said.

That shut the bugger up. He pressed on, 'Anyway, the cop showing up didn't stop you from opting to go ahead, did it?'

In the planning the bugger had needed to act like he was in charge, so now let's see if he could carry the can.

Geoff O rescued him, saying, 'I made sure he didn't get a good look at me.'

'Course you did. Clever thinking. But sometimes being clever's not enough. You've got to be lucky too. Word is that Constable Hector who wandered into the shop is half a loaf short of a picnic and would have trouble giving a good description of himself. So no problem there. In fact, things could be a lot worse. Mission accomplished, so let's keep our fingers crossed and hope the cops don't die.'

Geoff O said, 'I presume you're holding back the press release.'

Andre nodded approval of the move from personal feelings to practicalities.

'Yes. Hugh agrees that a cop on the critical list isn't what we want associated with our opening statement. Shame. Really starting with a bang that would have been. Still, what me and Archambaud have got planned should to make 'em sit up and take notice.'

'Need any help?' asked Geoff O.

Definitely getting a taste for it, thought Andre. Enthusiasm was good. Impatience might be a problem. Needs watching?

He said, 'No, it's sorted. Don't worry. We're just starting. Lots of work for an energetic youngster. Just be patient. Good intelligence, careful planning, that's what makes for successful ops.'

Geoff B snorted incredulously, but that was to be expected. It was Geoff O's disappointed frown that Andre focused on.

He said, 'War's like fishing. Hours of empty fucking tedium punctuated by moments so crowded they burst at the seams. Learn to enjoy the emptiness. Now, I'm going to pack up before these fucking midges chew my face off. I'll be in touch.'

He rose and began to reel in his line.

Geoff B said, 'Tell Hugh, if that cop dies, I'm out. I'm serious.'

'Let's hope the poor sod makes it then,' said Andre indifferently. 'See you.'

The couple started to walk away. Geoffrey O glanced back. Andre gave a conspiratorial wink but got nothing in return.

Didn't bother him.

What did bother him was the weight of the discarded backpack.

He checked no one was close then opened it.

Like he'd thought, one weapon missing.

He looked after the two Geoffreys. No prize for guessing which one had hung on.

He recalled a training sergeant once saying to him, 'You've earned yourself a big kiss for keenness, a big bollocking for stupidity. Which do you want first, son?'

He smiled, dropped the backpack into his basket, slung it over his shoulder, gathered up the rest of his gear and set off along the tow path.

6

blue smartie

Peter Pascoe was still having trouble with time.

He opened his eyes and Ellie was there.

'Hi,' he said.

'Hi,' she said. 'Pete, how are you?'

'Fine, fine,' he said.

He blinked once and her hair turned gingery as she aged ten years and put on a Scottish accent.

'Mr Pascoe. Sandy Glenister. Feel up to a wee chat?'

'Not with you,' said Pascoe. 'Sod off.'

He blinked again and the face rearranged itself into something like a Toby jug whose glaze had gone wrong.

'Wieldy,' said Pascoe. 'Where's Ellie?'

'At home making Rosie's tea, I expect. She'll be back later. How are you doing?'

'I'm fine. What am I doing here? Oh shit.'

Wield saw Pascoe's face spasm with remembered pain as he answered his own question.

'Andy, how's Andy?' he demanded, trying to push himself upright.

Wield pressed the button which raised the back of the bed by thirty degrees.

'Intensive Care,' he said. 'He's not come round yet.'

'Well, what do they expect?' demanded Pascoe. 'It's only been . . a couple of hours?'

His assertion turned to interrogation as he realized he'd no idea of the time.

'Twenty-four,' said Wield. 'A bit more. It's four o'clock, Tuesday afternoon.'

'As long as that? What's the damage?'

'With Andy? Broken leg, broken arm, several cracked ribs, some second-degree burns, multiple contusions and lacerations from the blast, loss of blood, ruptured spleen, other internal damage whose extent isn't yet apparent –'

'So, nothing really serious then,' interrupted Pascoe.

Wield smiled faintly and said, 'No, not for Andy. But till he wakes up . . .'

He left the sentence unfinished.

'Twenty-four hours is nothing,' said Pascoe. 'Look at me.'

'You've been back with us a lot longer than that,' said Wield. 'Bit woozu maybe with all the shit they pumped into you, but making sense mostly. You don't think Ellie would have taken off if you'd still been comatose?'

'I've spoken with Ellie then?'

40

'Aye. Don't you remember?'

'I think I recall saying hi.'

'Is that all? You'd best hope you didn't make a deathbed confession,' said Wield.

'And there was someone else – ginger hair, Scots accent, maybe the matron. Or did I dream that?'

'No. That would be Chief Superintendent Glenister from CAT. I was there when she turned up.'

'You were? Did I say much to her?'

'Apart from "sod off", you mean? No. That was it.'

'Oh hell,' said Pascoe.

'Not to worry. She didn't take offence. In fact, she's sitting outside in the waiting room. You've not asked what's wrong with you.'

'With me?' said Pascoe. 'Good point. Why am I in here? I feel fine.'

'Just wait till the shit wears off,' said Wield. 'But they reckon you were lucky. Contusions, abrasions, few muscle tears, twisted knee, couple of cracked ribs, concussion. Could have been a lot worse.'

'Would have been if I hadn't had Andy in front of me,' said Pascoe grimly. 'What about Jennison and Maycock?'

'Joker reckons he's gone deaf but his mates say he were always a bit hard of hearing when it came to his round. Their cars are a write-off though. Andy's too.'

'What about Number 3? Was there anyone in there?'

'I'm afraid so. Three bodies, they reckon. At least. They're still trying to put them together. No more detail. The CAT lads are going over the wreckage with a fine-tooth comb, and they're not saying much to anyone – and that includes us. Of course, they've got a key witness.'

'Have they? Oh God. You mean Hector?'

'Right. Glenister spent an hour or so with him. Came out looking punch-drunk.'

'Hector did?'

'No. He always looks punch drunk. I mean Glenister. I'd best let her know you're sitting up and taking notice.'

'Fine. Wieldy, do a check on Andy, will you? You know what they're like in these places, getting good info's harder than getting your dinner wine properly *chambré*.'

'I'll see what I can do,' said Wield. 'Take care.'

He left and Pascoe eased himself properly upright in the bed, trying to assess what he really felt like. There didn't seem to be many parts of his body which didn't give a retaliatory twinge when provoked, but, ribs apart, nothing that threatened much beyond discomfort. He wondered if he could get out of bed without assistance. He had got himself sitting upright and was pushing the bed sheet off his legs preparatory to swinging them round when the door opened and the ginger woman came in.

'Glad to see you're feeling better, Peter,' she said, 'but I think you should stay put a wee while longer. Or was it a bed pan you wanted?'

'No, I'm fine,' said Pascoe, pulling the sheet back up.

'That's OK then. Glenister. Chief Super. Combined Anti-Terrorism unit. We met briefly earlier, you probably don't remember.'

'Vaguely, ma'am,' said Pascoe. 'In fact I seem to recall being a bit rude . . .'

Glenister said, 'Think nothing of it. Rudeness is good, it needs a working mind to be rude. I'd just been interviewing Constable Hector for the second time. I couldn't believe the first, but it didn't get any better. Is it just shock, or is that poor laddie always as unforthcoming?'

'Expressing himself isn't his strongest point,' said Pascoe.

'So you're saying that what I've got out of him is probably as much as I'm likely to get?' said Glenister. 'His descriptions of the men he saw are, to say the least, sketchy.'

'He does his best,' said Pascoe defensively. 'Anyway, surely it'll be DNA, fingerprints, dental records, that are going to identify the poor devils in there?'

'Aye, we should be able to find enough of them for that,' said Glenister.

She was mid to late forties, Pascoe guessed, full figured to the point where she fitted her tweed suit comfortably but if she didn't cut down on the deep-fried Mars Bars, she'd soon have to upsize. She had a pleasant friendly smile which lit up her round slightly weather-beaten face and put a sparkle into her soft brown eyes. If she'd been a doctor he would have felt immensely reassured.

Pascoe said, 'You'll want to debrief me, ma'am.'

Glenister smiled.

'Debrief? I see you're very with it here in Mid-Yorkshire. Me, I'm too old a parrot to learn new jargon. A full written report would be nice when you're up to it. All I want now is a wee preliminary chat.'

She pulled a chair up to the bedside, sat down, produced a mini-cassette recorder from the shoulder bag she was carrying, and switched it on.

'In your own words, Peter. All right to call you Peter? My friends call me Sandy.'

Trying to work out if this were an invitation or a warning, Pascoe launched into an account of his part in the incident, with some judicious editing, in the interest of clarity and brevity he told himself.

'That's good,' said Glenister, nodding approval. 'Succinct, to the point. Just what I need for the record.'

She pressed the off button on the recorder, sat back in her chair and took a tube of Smarties out of her shoulder bag.

'Help yourself,' she said. 'So long as it's not blue.'

'No thanks,' said Pascoe.

'Wise man,' she said. 'I started on the sweeties when I stopped the ciggies. When I realized five bars of fruit-and-nut a day were going to kill me as surely as forty fags, I tried to go cold turkey and that nearly had me back on the nicotine. Now I treat myself to a Smartie whenever the urge comes on. Just the one. Except if it's a blue one. Then I can have another. God knows what I'll do now they're stopping the blue ones.'

She gave him that attractive smile, mocking herself. She really should have been a doctor, thought Peter. With a bedside manner like this, she could have sold urine samples at a guinea a bottle.

'Now let's stray off the record, Peter,' she said, popping one of the tiny sweets into her mouth (a yellow one, he noticed) and settling herself more comfortably into her chair. 'Just you and me. Thoughts and impressions this time. And maybe just a wee bit more detail. For a start, why were you really there?'

'I told you. Inspector Ireland rang me and I went to assist.'

'And why did Paddy Ireland ring you?'

'Because of my negotiating experience, I suppose,' said Pascoe. But even as he spoke he was registering the *Paddy* as a gentle reminder that Glenister had already interviewed the inspector.

'And because I think he felt that, as the video shop had been flagged by you people, Mr Dalziel might be grateful for some assistance,' he added.

'And was he?'

'I think so.'

'But he hadn't contacted you himself?'

'He wouldn't care to disturb me on my day off,' said Pascoe.

'A most considerate man then. I gather he even offered to obtain refreshment for the people inside Number 3.'

So she knew about the bit of knockabout with the bullhorn. Hector. Or Jennison. Or Maycock. Why wouldn't they describe exactly what had happened? Even if they'd tried to play it down, they'd have been easy meat for this bedside manner.

He said, 'Yes, Mr Dalziel did try to make contact with anyone who might be inside the shop.'

'Who "might" be? You had doubts?'

'Our information seemed a bit vague.'

'Vague? Not quite with you there. Foot patrol sees an armed man in Number 3. Reports it to the car-patrol officers who pass it on to the duty inspector who alerts the station commander. Don't see where the vagueness lies. All by the book so far.'

'Yes, and that's the way it continued,' said Pascoe firmly. 'Knowing that the property was flagged, Mr Dalziel made sure your people were alerted then proceeded to Mill Street as instructed.'

'As instructed?' Glenister chuckled.

Chuckling was a dying art, thought Pascoe; genuine chuckling that was, not just that pretence of suppressed mirth which politicians still use to make or, more often, avoid a point. But Glenister's chuckle was the real McCoy.

'My understanding of his instructions,' continued the superintendent, 'is that he was told to withdraw any police vehicles from Mill Street, establish blocks at its ends, maintain observation from a distance, and make no attempt to approach Number 3. Which bit of his instructions would you say Mr Dalziel followed, Peter?'

'I don't know because I've only your say-so that that's what they were,' retorted Pascoe, consigning to the recycle bin what the Fat Man had told him as they squatted behind the car. 'But, if we're portioning out responsibility, what I'm certain your instructions didn't contain was any reference to the fact that there was enough explosive in the place to blow up the whole bloody terrace! But I guess you didn't know that, else why would it only have a bottom-level flagging?'

Glenister shook her head and said sadly, 'You're so right, Peter. We should have known that. But you're completely wrong if you think I'm here to offload blame. Wrists will be slapped at CAT, have no fear. If your Mr Dalziel got it wrong, then we got it wrong just as much, and he's paid a far higher price. I hope he comes through but the signs aren't good. So the only person I've got who can give me a close-up account of what took place is you. All I want is to be absolutely sure about everything you saw during your time outside Number 3 Mill Street.'

'That's easy,' said Pascoe. 'From my arrival to the explosion, I saw absolutely no sign of life in the house, or anywhere else in the terrace. Full stop.'

'Fine, that's good enough for me,' said Glenister, standing up and offering her hand. 'We'll talk again when you're back on your feet. I hope that will be very soon.'

'But can't you tell me what you think happened in there?' demanded Pascoe, holding on to the hand.

Glenister hesitated, then said, 'Why not? I hear you're a discreet man. In fact you might turn vain if you knew how highly you're rated. Quite the blue Smartie yourself.'

She smiled at her joke. Pascoe gave her a token flicker and said, 'So?'

'We had the shop flagged as a meeting place, at best a casual message centre, for a group who showed little inclination to move from dialectic to destruction. At some time in the past few days a decision must have been taken to upgrade it to a storehouse for explosive in preparation for an event. We had some non-specific intelligence that something big was being planned in the north.'

'Like blowing up Mill Street?' said Pascoe incredulously. 'Not exactly the Houses of Parliament, is it?'

'I said Number 3 was just the storehouse,' said Glenister. 'Though it won't have escaped your notice that the terrace backs on to the embankment carrying the main London line, and your

48

fair city is being honoured with a royal visit the week after next. Be that as it may, suddenly there is a large quantity of explosive on site, harmless enough when being handled by experts. But, as I say, the group who had hitherto made use of the shop were anything but experts. Your Constable Hector disturbed them, your Mr Dalziel made them panic. Perhaps they were simply trying to conceal the explosive more thoroughly and something went wrong. Or perhaps when they saw you and Mr Dalziel moving forward, they weighed a long night in an interview room with you against an eternity in Paradise with a martyr's promised *houris*. Either way, boom!'

She gently disengaged her hand, which Pascoe now realized he'd been clinging on to like an ancient mariner eager for a chat.

'You take care of yourself now, Peter,' said Glenister. 'The Force can't spare its blue Smarties in these troubled times. I hope you're back at work really soon.'

She went out of the room. Pascoe stared at the closed door for a while, then shoved back the sheet and swung his legs on to the floor. He was surprised to find how weak this simple movement left him and he was still sitting on the bed, nerving himself to test his knee, when Wield came in.

'Where do you think you're going?' demanded the sergeant.

'I'm going to see Andy.'

'Not now you're not,' said Wield.

Something in his tone alerted Pascoe that the sergeant wasn't just coming the nurse-substitute.

'Why? What's happened?' he demanded.

'I asked the ward sister to check how Andy was doing in Intensive Care,' said Wield. 'She was talking to someone there when all hell broke loose at the other end of the phone. Pete, his heart stopped. They've got the crash team working on him now, but from what the sister said, it's not looking good. Pete, we need to face it. This could be the end for Fat Andy.'

7

dancing with death

Andy Dalziel is in the Mecca Ballroom, locked in a tango with Tottie Truman from Donny.

He feels as light as a feather. His feet hardly seem to be in contact with the floor, his muscles responding to every modulation of the music as if the notes were vibrating along his arteries rather than through his ears. And he can feel the blood pulsing through Tottie's veins in a perfect counterpoint to his own rhythms as they move inexorably towards that blissfully explosive moment of complete fusion . . .

But not on the dance floor! It's all a question of timing. In search of delay, he makes his mind step back and take in his surroundings.

The Mirely Mecca has changed a lot since his last visit which was . . . he can't recall when. Never mind. The ceiling's higher now and the soaring windows, spring-bright with coloured glass, wouldn't disgrace a cathedral. The walls are lined with long tables, covered in white linen cloths on which rest a royal banquet of everything he loves – on one table crowns of lamb, barons of beef, loins of pork ridged with crackling, honey-glazed hams; on another roasted geese, Christmas turkeys, duck with cherries, pheasant adorned with their own feathers; on a third whole salmon, pickled herring, mountain ranges of oysters and mussels. Yet another is crowded with desserts: bread-and-butter pudding, rhubarb crumble, Spotted Dick, and his childhood favourite, Eve's Pudding.

And there, by a table laden with bottles of every kind of malt whisky he'd ever tasted, stands Peter Pascoe, an open bottle of Highland Park in one hand and in the other a king-size crystal tumbler full to the brim which he is holding out in smiling invitation . . .

Later, lad, he mouths. Later. First things first. Dance till the music reaches its climax, then straight out of the door into that dark alcove at the end of the corridor to reach his and hers . . .

After which, being a gentleman, he'll wait a decent interval of mebbe a minute and a half before heading back inside for another helping of Eve's Pudding . . .

But just as he begins to wonder if he can hold out any longer, the music changes, accelerating from the sensuous pulse of the tango into the mad whirl of a Viennese waltz. His muscles obey the new commands effortlessly though his mind wonders what the fuck the band leader's playing at. Round and round and round he spins, till the high walls and coloured windows and laden tables retreat to a blur of Arctic whiteness and Tottie's body, which during the tango had been a comfortable armful of warm softness moulding itself ever closer to his, begins to feel like a sackful of old bones.

Now he too is beginning to feel tired, as if age and exertion and all the excesses of a life spent in mad pursuit of God knows what are at last catching up with him. He wants to rest. Surely Tottie would want to sit this one out too? He nuzzles his lips against her ear to whisper the suggestion, but he can't find it. The cheek pressed against his no longer feels soft and warm but cold and hard and smooth.

He moves his head back to look into his partner's face. Instead of the lustrous brown bedroom eyes of Tottie Truman, he finds himself peering into the deep shadowy sockets of a skull whose toothy leer and vacant gaze have something familiar about them.

Then recognition dawns.

Dalziel laughs.

'Hector, lad,' he cries. 'I always said tha'd be the death of me, but I never meant it so literal!'

The skeletal figure does not reply but its grip tightens round the Fat Man's broad frame and he finds his weary legs being urged into an even wilder dance which feels as if it will only end when those bony arms have squeezed out of him everything that makes up the life force – sun and wind and air and rain, good grub and mellow whisky, light and laughter – and whirled what little remains away into some icy eternity.

For a moment he is lost. He, the great Dalziel, who on his day has danced from dusk to dawn and then washed down the Full British Breakfast with a tumbler of whisky, has no strength to resist as Death, or Hector, bears him off to oblivion.

Then at the very point of submission, something happens.

New resolve seems to course through his weary limbs like an electric shock. Then another, even stronger. A third . . . a fourth . . . a fifth . . .

Sod this for a lark! he thinks. I'll give this bugger a run for his money afore I let him dance me off my feet!

Pressing Death or Hector even closer to his chest, he rises on to his toes and goes whirling round the room, once more the leader not the led, faster and faster, till he leaves the wild music trailing in his wake. And this time, instead of blurring out his surroundings, the speed of the dance seems to bring them back into focus. First the high windows with their multi-coloured lights, and then white-clothed tables laden with provender, and finally he becomes aware that the brittle bones in his arms are once more clothed in the warm and yielding flesh of Tottie Truman from Donny.

8

blame

'He's stable now, but it was a close-run thing,' said Dr John Sowden. 'With anyone else I'd have called it after the fifth shock. But I looked down at the fat old bastard lying there and I thought, I'm not going to risk being haunted by you! And I gave him one more go.'

Dr Sowden was an old acquaintance of the Pascoes, a relationship which had started way back in a close encounter with Andy Dalziel under suspicion of causing death by drunk driving.

'And that did the trick?' said Ellie Pascoe.

'It started his heart beating again. Which is something, but don't get your hopes up. He's only back to where he was. Still showing no sign of regaining consciousness. And we've no idea what state he'll be in if and when that happens. You, Peter, on the other hand are looking remarkably spry, considering.'

'So when can I go home?' said Pascoe. 'I feel fine.'

It was almost true. The anxiety caused by the

news about Fat Andy, the relief at hearing they'd got him back, and the pleasure of having Ellie sitting on his bed, had seemed to combine as a sort of tonic. John Sowden ought to be showering praise on him for his resilience rather than pursing his lips.

'Let's see how you are in a couple of days,' said the doctor dismissively. 'Ellie, nice to see you again. Make sure he behaves himself.'

He went out.

'John ought to brush up his bedside manner, don't you reckon?' said Pascoe.

'I think he's a bit worried there may be some delayed emotional reaction,' said Ellie carefully.

'He's been talking to you, has he? Don't tell me he actually used those tired old words post-traumatic stress disorder!' Pascoe laughed harshly. 'Listen, if ever I start feeling sorry for myself, I just have to think of Andy lying up there in a coma.'

Ellie took his hand and squeezed it.

'I know, I know,' she said. 'I often wished the earth would open up and swallow the fat bastard, but it's almost impossible to imagine a world without Andy, isn't it?'

'Not almost,' said Pascoe. 'You said you'd seen Cap. How's she taking it?'

'Hard to say. She once told me that the only worthwhile thing she learned at St Dot's Academy was to deal with crisis and catastrophe by not letting it mark your upper crust. While us plebs scream and shout and run about, people of Cap's class maintain an even keel and look to the practicalities.'

Pascoe smiled at 'us plebs'. Ellie's family were irremediably petit bourgeois despite all her efforts to downgrade them to acquire street cred in the class war. By contrast Cap Marvell, while making no effort to deny her upper-class background and education, had been much more successful in her efforts to disoblige her old connections. Having a secret weapon like Andy Dalziel you could produce at will can't have been a disadvantage either.

Pascoe liked her in a cautious kind of way. She was good for Dalziel emotionally and intellectually and, one presumed, physically, but her readiness to strain the law in pursuit of her animal rights causes was a ticking bomb for a working cop. On the other hand it struck him as one of God's better jokes that after many years of heavy-handed jesting about Ellie's unbecoming behaviour as a political activist, Dalziel should find himself hoist with the same petard.

'What are you grinning at?' demanded Ellie.

'Just smiling with pleasure at having you here,' he said.

'I hope so. I can't stay long. Rosie's rehearsal finishes at seven.'

Pascoe shuddered. Public performances by the school orchestra in which his daughter played the clarinet were bad enough. He couldn't bear to think what a rehearsal must sound like.

'Didn't she want to visit me?' he asked plaintively.

'Of course she did. But no point in traumatizing the kid. I wanted to be sure you weren't going to be too much of a shock to the system, so I told her the hospital had banned child visits till tomorrow.'

'I'll be coming home tomorrow,' protested Pascoe. 'I really do feel fine, no matter what the amateur psychiatrists say.'

'Let's wait and see what John says,' said Ellie. 'They may need to do more tests.'

'You know me,' said Pascoe confidently. 'Show me a test, I sail through it.'

'Yeah? Well let's try this one,' said Ellie.

She leaned forward and kissed him long and hard, at the same time slipping her hand beneath the bed sheet.

After about thirty seconds she pulled back and said, 'Yes, you seem to be making firm progress.'

'Better than you imagine,' said Pascoe rather hoarsely. 'Test me again.'

'I think once is enough at this stage in your convalescence,' she said primly.

'You reckon? Do you think the NHS trains its nurses in this technique?'

'Yes, but you need BUPA for that. By the way, that nice matronly woman with the Scottish accent, who is she exactly?'

'Sandy Glenister? She's a Chief Super from the anti-terrorist unit.'

'I thought that's what she said, but I wasn't paying too much attention.'

'So what did you talk about?'

'I don't know. You, I suppose.'

'Me?' said Pascoe, alarmed. 'What did you tell her?'

'What do you think I told her?' retorted Ellie indignantly. 'Where you've stashed all that drug money you've stolen? I was upset, believe it or not, and she was kind.'

'Yes, I'm sorry,' said Pascoe placatingly. 'She does seem very kind. All the same, better check your purse and change your PINs.'

Ellie smiled the smile of a woman confident that no one of either sex could sweet-talk her out of anything she didn't want to give.

'I'd better go,' she said, looking at her watch. 'Last time I was late picking Rosie up from rehearsal, I found her sitting on the school wall, playing her clarinet. There was some change on the ground in front of her, but I suspect she'd put it there herself.'

'Pity,' said Pascoe. 'Nice if she could be self-supporting. Give her my love. And tell her I'll see her tomorrow.'

'Yeah. Pete, what shall I tell her about Andy? I think she needs to know how bad things are, just in case . . .'

'In case what?' snapped Pascoe. 'Sorry. Tell her the truth; that's what we've always tried, isn't it? But keep it cool, yes?'

'Sure,' she said. 'By the way, they gave me what was left of your clothes. I went through your trouser pockets before I dumped them. Found a dental plate.'

'It's Andy's,' he said. 'Clean it up, will you? He'll want it when . . .'

His voice creaked into silence.

'I'll clean it,' said Ellie, stooping to kiss him. 'Now I've got to dash. But you won't be lonely. I think I spotted another visitor lurking.'

She grinned as she spoke and a few moments later Pascoe realized why. The door slowly opened and a dolorous visage appeared, its brow puckered with uncertainty, like a sheep contemplating a gap in the hedge which separated its field from a busy motorway.

'Hector,' he said. 'Nice of you to visit. Or are you just looking for the lavatory?'

He was surprised to hear himself make the joke. Usually he made a conscious effort not to join in the friendly piss-taking which Hector provoked among his colleagues.

Maybe somewhere deep inside, or not so deep, I blame him, he thought. If it hadn't been for Hector, none of this would have started. Or if someone else had started it, then perhaps Dalziel would have taken it more seriously. Or . . .

He pushed the thoughts aside and forced a smile.

'Come in then,' he said. 'Have a seat.'

Slowly Hector advanced. Like many lanky men, he walked with his head held low and thrust forward, as if to distract attention from his height. At moments of maximum uncertainty, which were many, the posture was so exaggerated that he put Pascoe in mind of those men whose heads do grow beneath their shoulders that Desdemona seemed to find a turn-on. Dalziel, less literary but in his own way just as poetic, had once said to him, 'For God's sake, straighten thyself up, lad. You look like someone's hung your tunic on a coat hanger with you still in it!'

Perched on the edge of the chair, he stared fixedly at Pascoe.

'So,' said Pascoe heartily. 'And how are things down at the factory? I mean, the Station. The Police Station.'

It was as well to be precise in your intercourse with Hector.

'OK,' said Hector. 'I mean, everyone's dead worried about you and Mr Dalziel, but.'

'Are they? Well, you can tell them I'm doing fine. And the Super, well, we'll just have to wait and see.'

There followed a long silence and Pascoe was thinking about bringing the visit to an end with a plea of fatigue when Hector burst out, 'Is it true he's going to die, sir?'

'I hope not,' said Pascoe, touched by the degree of concern shown. 'But I'm afraid he is very ill. Look, Hector, you shouldn't blame yourself . . .'

'Blame who, sir?' said Hector, screwing up his eyes in the effort of concentration.

Whoops, thought Pascoe. Got that wrong, didn't I. Whatever's bothering Hector, it's not a sense of guilt.

'Blame anyone,' he said. 'It's no one's fault. Just one of those awful things that can happen to anyone.'

Hector nodded vigorously, very much at home with the concept of awful things that could happen to anyone but which for some reason were more likely to happen to him.

'I gather you've been talking to Mrs Glenister,' Pascoe went on; then, observing a familiar blankness spreading across Hector's face, he added, 'Chief Superintendent Glenister from the anti-terrorism unit.'

'Glenister?' said Hector. 'Joker said her name were Sinister. Her who speaks funny?'

Deafness clearly hadn't affected Constable Jennison's love of a laugh, thought Pascoe, for which I suppose we ought to be grateful.

'Yes, she does. It's called a Scottish accent. That's Mrs Glenister all right. I hope you were able to help her.'

'Oh yes,' said Hector, very positive. 'Kept on asking about the men I saw in the shop. Asking and asking. I started getting a bit confused but Mrs Sinister – sorry, Mrs Glenister – said not to worry as the men I saw must have got blown up anyway. Then she helped me with my report.'

'That was nice of her,' said Pascoe. 'And it's nice of you to come visiting. But I'm a bit tired now, Hector . . .'

He paused and started counting to fifty. Dropping a hint to Hector was like turning on an old-fashioned wireless. You had to wait for the valves to warm up.

At forty-six, Hector stood up and said, 'I'd best be going.'

He took a step towards the door. then turned back.

'Nearly forgot,' he said. 'Brought you this –'

Out of the depths of his tunic jacket he took a paper bag which he placed carefully on the bedside locker. Then he set off again, this time reaching the door before he halted once more.

'Sir,' he said. 'I hope Mr Dalziel doesn't die. He's been very good to me.'

Then he was gone, leaving Pascoe only a little less amazed than he would have been if the angel Gabriel had popped in to tell him he'd been chosen to have a baby.

He settled back into his pillows to contemplate the nature of the Fat Man's goodness towards Hector, noticed the paper bag on his locker, reached out and picked it up.

It contained, rather squashed but not beyond recognition, a custard tart.

'Oh shit,' said Pascoe.

And suddenly for some reason beyond reason, the barrier he'd been erecting both consciously and unconsciously between himself and the events in Mill Street crumbled like the walls of Number 3, and when the nurse looked in to check that all was well, she found him with his face buried in his pillow, sobbing convulsively.

Part Two

The Days that we can spare
Are those a Function die
Or Friend or Nature – stranded then
In our Economy
Our Estimates a Scheme –
Our Ultimates a Sham –
We let go all of Time without
Arithmetic of him –

Emily Dickinson, 'Poem 1184'

1

a tidy desk

On the third day, there were many in Mid-Yorkshire not normally noted for their religious fervour who would have been unsurprised to hear that Dalziel had taken up his hospital bed, hurled it out of the window, and walked away.

But in an age of digital TV and the mobile phone, commonplace miracles have gone out of fashion, so the day dawned and departed with the Fat Man still comatose.

Pascoe, on the other hand, did manage to rise and limp away, not through divine intervention, but by dint of nagging Dr John Sowden into discharging him, though only on the strict understanding that he took a minimum of seven days convalescent leave.

On his second day home he announced his intention of dropping in at work to see how things were going.

Ellie's objections were forceful in expression and wide in range, starting with medical diagnostics and ending with reflections on his mental stability. When she paused for breath, Pascoe said, 'You're absolutely right, love. About everything. Only, I feel that, here at home, I'm not pulling for Andy. I know it's daft, and me going back to work isn't going to make the slightest difference. But somehow it feels like it might.'

Ellie said, 'You and your daughter, you're both mad. But you'd better go. It's going to be bad enough if the fat bastard dies without you feeling personally responsible.'

In her mind, Ellie had already given up on Dalziel and was gathering her strength to deal with the aftermath of his death. She did not doubt it would be traumatic, like losing a . . . Here her imagination failed her. Like losing what? No human simile fitted. Humans went. It was their nature. You grieved. You got on with living. But Dalziel, when he went it would be like losing a mountain. Every time you saw the space where it had been, you'd be reminded nothing was for ever, that even the very majesty of nature was only smoke and mirrors.

If anything she was more worried about her daughter than her husband. Peter knew that his reaction was daft. OK, he still went ahead, but he knew. Rosie, by contrast, had reacted to the news of Uncle Andy's coma with apparent indifference. When Ellie had gently tried to make sure she understood the seriousness of the situation, she had reversed the roles and with the patience of mature experience addressing childish uncertainty replied. 'Uncle Andy will wake up when he wants to, don't you see?'

Ellie had promised herself when Rosie was born that she would never be anything but completely honest with her daughter. Often her resolution had been strained close to breaking point, but she'd always tried. Now she nodded and said, 'Let's hope so, love. Let's hope so. But he is very ill and we've got to face it: maybe he's so ill that he wouldn't want to wake up, and he'll just die. I'm sorry.'

Her words clanged dully in her own ears, but Rosie's expression didn't change.

'That doesn't matter,' she exclaimed. 'He'll still wake up when he's needed.'

Like King Arthur, you mean? thought Ellie. Or, perhaps more aptly, the Kraken?

But she said no more. What else was there to say but the clichés of comfort? And the time for them, though close, had not yet arrived.

So, leaving behind a wife absolute for death and a daughter buoyed up by a sure and certain hope of resurrection, Peter Pascoe returned to work.

Determined to conceal any evidence of debility, as he approached the CID suite he took a deep breath which proved rather counterproductive, sending a spasm of pain through his rib cage that made him momentarily let up on the effort of will necessary to control his left knee.

Thus the first sight his junior colleagues had of him, he was limping, wincing and breathing hard. Edgar Wield followed him into his office and said anxiously, 'Pete, you OK? I thought you were laid up for a week at least.'

'Bloody quacks, what do they know?' said Pascoe roughly. 'Right, Wieldy, bring me up to speed.'

'Not a lot's changed,' said the sergeant. 'Three more break-ins up on Acornboar Mount; spate of credit-card fraud – looks like someone's recording PINS; couple of muggings; an affray outside the Dead Donkey –'

'Jesus, Wieldy!' interrupted Pascoe. 'That's not what I'm worried about. Someone blew up half a street, three dead, Andy lying in a coma, that's the only case I'm interested in. So what's the state of play there?'

Wield shrugged and said, 'Sorry, out of our hands. You'll need to talk to CAT. Dan's told us to co-operate fully. So far that's meant pointing Glenister and her men towards the best pubs and restaurants.'

Dan was Chief Constable Dan Trimble.

'So he's had his arm twisted,' said Pascoe. 'Two can play at that game.'

He reached for the phone.

Wield said, 'Actually, he's here. In Andy's room, I think . . .'

'Andy's room? What the hell's he doing in there?' demanded Pascoe.

'Well, he is the chief constable . . .' began

70

Wield, but he was speaking to Pascoe's back as the DCI headed out of the door.

He didn't bother to knock when he reached Dalziel's office but burst in.

'Peter!' said Sandy Glenister, her round farmer's-wife face lighting up with a welcoming smile. 'Good to see you. We were just talking about you, weren't we, Dan?'

'Er, yes. But I wasn't expecting . . . Shouldn't you still be on sick leave?' said Chief Constable Trimble.

Glenister was sitting in Dalziel's extra-large chair behind a desk which was as clear and tidy as Pascoe could recall seeing it. Trimble was sitting opposite her so that he had to twist round to look at the newcomer.

'I'm fine, sir,' said Pascoe shortly. 'Couldn't lie around when there's so much to do. Who have we got heading up the Mill Street investigation, sir?'

'That would be me, I think,' said Glenister.

'No, I meant from our side,' said Pascoe.

'Our side? I hope that's what I'm on too.' She smiled.

'Sir?' said Pascoe, addressing himself pointedly to Trimble.

The Chief eyed him speculatively, decided to make allowances and said, 'Peter, in view of the national security aspects of the business, I think it's reasonable that we follow Home Office guidelines and let the specialists deal with the investigation –'

'Sir!' interrupted Pascoe. 'There's been a major

incident on our patch, we've got bodies, Mr Dalziel's in a coma, the people of Mid-Yorkshire, our constituents, will be expecting their own police force to provide answers. The local media will want to see faces they know, not listen to the meanderings of some imported spin doctor. Our own men need to feel they're involved instead of being sidelined by a bunch of –'

'Enough, Chief Inspector!' said Trimble, rising.

He wasn't a very big man, but even Dalziel grudgingly allowed that, when he wanted, Trimble could be quite formidable. Clearly he wanted now.

'Decisions have been made. Your job when you return officially to work will be to follow and to implement them. I'm sure that Chief Superintendent Glenister will keep you informed of progress, on a need-to-know basis, of course . . .'

'You mean there may be things relating to criminal activity in Mid-Yorkshire that I don't need to know?' exclaimed Pascoe incredulously. 'Has there been a change of government or what?'

Trimble went fiery red. But before he could reply, Glenister said, 'Hey, come on, you two! My da used to say that the English were a cold, unfeeling race, no passion. He should be here now! Dan, Peter's quite right. I'd feel the same in his position. Home Office guidelines! What do those wankers know about life at the sharp end, eh? And I could do with all the help I can get. Why don't you leave me and him to get acquainted and work out a modus operandi?'

The chief constable thought for a moment, during which his cheeks cooled to their normal healthy glow.

'That sounds reasonable,' he said. 'But if you should decide that in your estimation the chief inspector needs to rest for the full term of his prescribed convalescence, just let me know.'

He left.

Pascoe said, 'You and the Chief seem to be very close.'

'Oh yes, we go way back, me and Dan,' said the woman. 'Started out together in the days of auld lang syne.'

And now, thought Pascoe, Dan's chief constable and you're chief super which, making allowances for what Andy called the handicap of tits and twat in the police promotion stakes, puts you several lengths ahead. Definitely one to watch.

She stood up and came round the desk to his side.

'Anything new on Mr Dalziel?' she asked.

He shook his head.

'Well, while there's life . . . Sorry if that sounds banal but, at times like this, there's no gap between banal and pretentious. I found that out when I lost my man. Banal's sincere; pretentious means they don't give a damn.'

'Your . . . man, was he job?'

'Oh yes. Funny really. We'd been married seven years. I was at the point where I really had to decide, kids or career. Then I woke up one morning realizing I could have both. Just as me and Colin would share the kids, so we'd share his career, which looked set to be glorious. It all seemed so obvious. I'd never felt so happy. And that of course was the day it happened.'

She fell silent. Pascoe didn't ask what happened. Her motives for telling him this much were obscure. If she wanted to tell him more, she would.

After a while he said, 'I'm sorry.'

'Thank you. So am I. On the other hand, if it hadn't been for that, I wouldn't be here now. Peter, why don't you sit there?'

She indicated the chair behind the desk which she'd just vacated.

'If anyone should keep this seat warm, it's you,' she said. 'I've got an Ops room down the corridor. Dan asked me if I'd sit in here if I had any spare time. With his two best CID officers out of the frame, I think he wants someone senior to make sure things keep ticking over. I didn't much care for the idea, but, like I say, he's an old friend . . .'

She smiled the smile of someone who finds old friends hard to refuse.

In fact, guessed Pascoe, what she was probably doing was checking through Andy's files to see if there was anything there which tied in even remotely with the events in Mill Street. She'd be lucky. Dalziel's system of paperwork was sibylline.

Left to himself he would have been reluctant to take over the Fat Man's seat, but now he refused to play coy.

He sat down, looked around and said, 'Someone's been tidying up.'

'Me, I'm afraid. The way I work. Set things in order, then you'll see what they mean. Your Mr Dalziel, from all accounts, belongs to the opposite school. Ignore chaos and ultimately its meaning will come looking for you.'

'I think rather he had . . . has . . . the ability to set things in order in his mind, but reckons that chaos has its meaning too,' said Pascoe.

'Meaning now I've put stuff where it ought to be, he won't be able to find a thing,' she laughed. 'Anyway, here's the deal, Peter. You'll have full access to my Ops room. I'll have full access anywhere I care to go in CID. I'll consult with you first before using anything I think may be relevant. And I expect you to return the courtesy.'

Seated at Dalziel's desk, it occurred to Pascoe that the proper response would be to say he didn't take kindly to folk offering to do him favours on his own CID floor, but he swallowed the words and said as mildly as he could manage, 'That sounds reasonable. Why don't we stroll along to your Ops room now and you can bring me up to speed?'

He rose, went to the door, opened it, and stood there to usher her out.

For a moment she looked slightly non-plussed at the speed with which he was moving things along, then gave him the open matronly smile again and moved through the doorway.

The CAT Ops room bore the Glenister trademark. It was as tidy and well organized as she'd left Dalziel's desk. Three computers had been set up on a trestle table at the far end. Not a spare inch of power cable showed. On a wall-board were pinned six photos, three showing the remains found in the ruins of Mill Street, each connected to a headshot of a man, two of them distinctly Asian in colouring and feature, the third less so. Beneath each photo was a name. Umar Surus, Ali Awan, and Hani Baraniq.

'Surus and Awan are positive ID's,' said Glenister. 'We have dental records and, in Awan's case, DNA. Baraniq isn't positive yet but we're eighty per cent sure.'

'You've shown these pics to Hector?'

'Naturally. Could be his "sort of darkie" was Awan, and the other possibly Baraniq, though he's even vaguer there. I've tried to push him beyond "sort of funny, not so much a darkie", but no luck. I hope we never have to put poor Hec up on the witness stand.'

She spoke with a smile.

Pascoe thought, Two minutes on our patch and already she's making our jokes.

He said, 'Look, what Hector doesn't see is most things. But what he says he does see, you can usually rely on. His shortcomings are verbal rather than optical.'

This wasn't just a knee-jerk Hector-might-be-an-idiot-but-he's-*our*-idiot reaction. Pascoe had once spotted Hector sitting on a park bench, note-book open on his knee, eyes fixed on a pair of sparrows dining on a discarded cheeseburger.

'Making notes in case you have to arrest them, Hec?' he'd enquired jocularly as he came up behind.

Hector had reacted as if caught committing an indecent act, jumping up so fast he dropped his pencil stub, all the while regarding Pascoe as if he carried a flaming sword. At the same time, he was ripping the page out of his notebook, but not before Pascoe glimpsed what looked like a sketch of the two birds.

'Can I have a look?' Pascoe had asked.

With great reluctance Hector had handed the sheet over.

Smoothed out, it revealed what proved to be a lively and accurate depiction of the feeding sparrows.

'Please, sir, you won't tell anyone, please,' said Hector tremulously.

'This is good,' said Pascoe, returning the sketch. 'I didn't know you could draw, Hec.'

'But you won't tell anyone,' repeated the constable anxiously.

It now struck Pascoe that it wasn't being reported for misuse of his official notebook that bothered Hector so much as the idea of his colleagues knowing that he drew pictures. Everyone needs a secret, he thought. Most of us have too many. But if you've only got the one, how precious must that be.

'Of course I won't,' he said. 'Carry on, Constable!'

And he'd kept his word, not even sharing Hector's secret with Ellie.

So he certainly wasn't going to be specific with Glenister, who said doubtfully, 'If you say so, Peter. Now, is there anything else we can bring you up to speed on?'

'Maybe . . .'

He went to the computer table and tapped the shoulder of the operator who looked to have least happening on his screen.

'Could you bring me up the Mill Street SOCO file?' he said.

The man glanced up at him, blank faced. Blank was the right word here. He had a regularity of feature which made you think android. His mirror and photographic images were probably indistinguishable. In his thirties, Pascoe guessed, but metro-thirties rather than up-north-thirties. The jacket draped over the back of the chair and his open-necked shirt said bet-you-can't-afford-me loud and clear. His blond hair had more gel in it than Dalziel would have let pass without some crack about an oil change. And he had eyes the colour of slate and just as hard.

The eyes held Pascoe's for a moment then the man turned to look at Glenister.

Pascoe also turned to face her, his head cocked to one side, his lips pursed in exasperation, his eyebrows raised interrogatively.

She said, 'Listen in, laddies. This is DCI Pascoe. What he asks for, you give him. No need to come running to me like I'm your mam and you need your nose wiped. OK?'

'Yes, ma'am,' the other two responded with a crispness born, Pascoe guessed, of past refusals by their boss to hear anything that wasn't loud and clear, but the blond's only response was to bring up the file. He then rose and offered Pascoe his chair.

Glenister said, 'Peter, meet Dave Freeman. He has been known to speak.'

A smile touched Freeman's lips without getting a grip and he said, 'Hi.'

'And hi to you too,' said Pascoe, sitting down.

Though not in the same super-league as Edgar Wield, who it was rumoured could hack into Downing Street to check out what anti-wrinkle cream the PM used, Pascoe regarded himself as premier division, IT-speaking. As he gingerly accessed the file and realized just how extensive and comprehensive it was, the sense of an audience made him a touch nervous and he found himself bogged down in photos, both still and moving, of the rubble. He lingered here a while as if this were where he wanted to be before moving on to his real goal, a lengthy list of every recognizable item recovered from the ruins.

After scrolling through it twice, he asked, 'Where's the gun?'

'Sorry?' said Freeman at his shoulder.

Pascoe got in a bit of payback, blanking him for a second before swivelling round in search of

Glenister who he discovered had moved across to the wall-board.

'Where's the gun?' he said. 'Hector reported that one of the men he saw had a gun. There's no gun mentioned here.'

'Peter,' said the woman, 'despite your admirable loyalty to Constable Hector, you've admitted yourself that, when it comes to detail, he's not the most reliable of witnesses. In fact, wasn't it Hector's involvement that made Mr Dalziel so sure there was no man with a gun on the premises that he took the reckless action he did?'

Reckless. Shit on Dalziel, shit on Hector, in fact, shit on Mid-Yorkshire policework generally. He thought he was getting the message.

He stood up and said, 'Thanks, Dave,' to Freeman.

'Any time, Pete.'

Pete. Was this kid his own rank? Or just a cheeky sergeant?

Neither, the answer came to him. The C in CAT stood for combined. Freeman was a spook. Did Trimble know that Glenister had imported non-police personnel into the Station? Of course he did! Pascoe answered himself angrily. He was getting as paranoid as Andy Dalziel about the security services.

Glenister was observing him as if his reactions were scrolling across his forehead.

He went up to her and said brusquely, 'So what's the state of play now?'

'Complex. We're working backwards and forwards at the same time, trying to trace where all this explosive we didn't know about came from, and what it was they planned to do with it. I'll tell you what I'll do, Peter. I'll get your PC linked to our network here so you'll have everything at your fingertips and not need to wear a hole in the corridor running along here every time you need an update. But do drop in any time you need to. For obvious reasons we need to have a bit of a firewall between us and the rest of the Station. But as far as you're concerned, you're fireproof. And I'm hoping it will be two-way traffic. Anything you think may help, don't hesitate. You're the man on the spot. Your input could be invaluable.'

It was an exit-cue if ever he'd heard one.

But for all her vibrantly sincere assurances, as Pascoe returned to his own office he felt less like a protagonist with big speeches still to come than an attendant lord, fit to swell a progress or start a scene or two.

In fact it occurred to him as his ribs twinged and his knee began to ache that at the moment he didn't actually feel fit enough even for those walk-on roles.

And when Edgar Wield looked in twenty minutes later and found him half slumped across his desk, he made no protest as the sergeant escorted him down the stairs to the car park and drove him home.

2

show business

Archambaud de St Agnan said, 'Aren't we too close?'

'For what?' said Andre de Montbard. 'He's used to being followed. That's what makes it so easy.'

Ahead of them, the silver Saab turned right into a long street of tall Edwardian houses and came to a halt after about fifty yards. Andre pulled the black Jaguar into the kerb some three car lengths behind.

The driver of the Saab got out. He was a tall, athletically built man with shoulder-length hair and a lean intelligent face with a neat black moustache beneath an aquiline nose. Pausing beneath a street lamp to look back at the Jaguar, he put his hands together and made a small perfunctory bow before running lightly up the steps, inserting a key and vanishing through the door.

'Cheeky sod,' said Andre. 'Thinks he's bullet proof. He's due a reality check.'

He got out, opened the back door and took out a sports bag.

'You OK?' he said to Archambaud who hadn't moved.

'Yeah. Fine.'

Andre said, 'Listen, it's OK to be scared. Really. Ones I always looked for were the ones who didn't look scared first time out. Remember what they did to your uncle, OK? All you've got to do is give him a tap, I'll be taking care of the serious stuff. Crap yourself if you must, so long as you don't freeze, OK?'

Managing a smile, Archambaud said, 'I'll try to avoid both.'

'So let's do it.'

They walked quickly along the pavement and climbed the steps of the house. Andre glanced down the list of names by the bell-pushes, selected the one marked Mazraani and pressed.

After a short delay a voice came over the intercom.

'Gentlemen, how can I help you?'

'Just like a quick word, sir,' said Andre.

'By all means. Won't you come up?'

They heard the wards of the door lock click open.

'See? Easy.'

They went inside. There was a lift but Andre ignored it and set off up the stairs.

The flat they wanted was on the second floor. They rang the bell. When the door opened, they went in. There were two men in the room, which was conventionally furnished with a sofa and easy chair, a hi-fi system from which, turned well down, came the voice of a woman singing in Arabic, and heavy oak dining table with four matching chairs. The tall man from the Saab was standing in front of the table, facing them. The other man, in his twenties with a wispy beard, sat in the easy chair. He was smoking a richly scented cigarette and avoided eye contact with the newcomers.

'Evening, Mr Mazraani,' said Andre to the tall man. 'And this is . . . ?'

'My cousin, Fikri. He's staying with me for a few days.'

'That's nice. Anyone else in the flat?'

'No. Just the two of us,' he replied.

'Mind if we check that? Arch.'

Archambaud went out of a door to the left. After a few moments he came back into the living room and said, 'Clear.'

'So now we can perhaps get down to what brings you here. Won't you introduce yourselves? For the tape?'

Mazraani's voice was bland and urbane. He seemed almost to be enjoying the situation, by contrast with the other man who looked resentful and apprehensive.

Andre said, 'Certainly, sir. I'm called Andre de Montbard, Andy to my friends. And my colleague is Mr Archambaud de St Agnan. He's got no friends. And this lady singing is, I'd say, the famous Elissa? Compatriot of yours, I believe? Gorgeous girl. Lovely voice, and those big amber eyes! I'm a great fan.'

He moved to the hi-fi and turned up the volume, using his index knuckle.

Then he set his sports bag on the table, unzipped it, reached inside and took out an automatic pistol with a silencer attached.

A look of disbelief touched Mazraani's features but the seated man did not even have time to register fear before Andre shot him between the eyes from short range.

'Sorry about that, sir, but we wanted to talk to you privately,' said Andre. 'So why don't you just relax and we'll have that drink.'

Horror at what he'd just seen had paralysed Mazraani. He stood there looking down at the body, blinking now and then as if trying to clear the image from his vision, his mouth open but no words coming out.

Andre nodded at his companion, who looked almost as shocked as Mazraani.

'Wake up, Arch!' snapped Andre.

The man called de St Agnan gave a twitch, then reached into his pocket, took out a leaden cosh and swung it against Mazraani's neck with tremendous force. He gave a choking groan and sank to his knees.

'There, that wasn't difficult, was it?' said Andre. 'And unless my nose has got stuffed up, you've not even crapped yourself yet. Now it's show time.'

He went back to the sports bag and took out a video camera which he passed to Archambaud.

Next came a black hood with eye-holes which he pulled over his head, then a pair of long latex gloves which he put on.

Now he took out a length of polished wood, about two and half feet long, like the extension butt of a snooker cue. And finally he drew forth a bin-liner from which he took a gleaming steel cleaver blade, six inches deep and eighteen inches long, with a threaded tail of another eight inches which he screwed into the end of the wooden butt.

Mazraani was trying to rise. Archambaud raised the cosh again but Andre said, 'No need for that, Arch. Here, sir, let's give you a hand.'

He placed one of the dining chairs on its side in front of the stricken man, then pushed him forward so that his head rested over the chair back.

'Just get your breath, sir,' said Andre. 'Arch, you ready?'

'Do we really need this . . . ?' said Archambaud uneasily.

'Main point of the exercise. Just point the fucking thing and try to keep it steady.'

He pushed the tall man's long hair forward over his head to leave the neck clear, grasped the polished wood of the butt and raised the glistening blade high above his head.

'You rolling?'

'Yes,' said Archambaud in a low voice.

'Then here we go!'

The blade came crashing down.

It took three blows before the severed head fell on to the carpet.

'All that practise with logs, thought I'd have done it in one,' said Andre. 'You OK?'

Archambaud managed a nod. He was pale and shaking but he still held the camera pointed at the body.

'Good man,' said Andre.

He wiped the blade on the bearded man's robe before unscrewing it from the handle and dropping it into the bin-liner, which he replaced in the sports bag.

'Now all we need are the credits then we're out of here.'

From the bag he took a cardboard tube about eighteen inches long out of which he pushed a paper scroll. This he unrolled to reveal it was covered with Arab symbols. After checking it was the right way up, he held it before the camera for thirty seconds.

'OK,' he said, replacing the scroll in the tube 'You can turn that thing off now. Time to go. You touch anything out there?'

'Just the door handles and I wiped them.'

'Great,' he said, removing the hood and dropping it into the bag. 'We make a good team. Morecambe and fucking Wise, that's us. In fact, let's see . . .'

He looked at his watch.

'Four minutes thirty since we came through the door. I gave us five, and I was only expecting one of them. Now that's what I call show business!'

3

walking the dog

After his first attempt to get back to work, Pascoe spent the next two days in bed. On the third he was feeling recovered enough to insist that he was only going to spend another day on his back if Ellie joined him, which she did, purely on medical grounds, she said, which in fact turned out to be true as she cunningly contrived to leave him so exhausted that when he woke again, it was the morning of the fourth day.

He appeared so much better that Ellie had few qualms about letting him take their daughter's dog Tig out for a stroll after lunch.

'You won't be taking the car?' she said.

'Of course not. I'm going for a walk, remember?' he retorted.

Satisfied that this amounted to an assurance he wasn't going anywhere near Police HQ, she waved him goodbye before heading into her 'study' to get on with some very necessary work on her second novel.

(If asked – which few people dared – how things were going, Ellie would reply that it was one of the great myths of publishing that the most difficult thing of all was to follow up the success of a universally acclaimed first novel. No, the really difficult thing was to produce a second novel after your first had attracted as much attention as a fart in a thunderstorm.)

Now she re-immersed herself in her book, confident that all she needed to do here to produce a bestseller was apply the same subtle understanding of human nature that she had just demonstrated in her management of her husband.

Meanwhile, two streets away, Pascoe was climbing into a car driven by Edgar Wield, who wasn't happy.

'Ellie's going to kill me when she finds out,' he said.

'Relax. She'll not find out,' said Pascoe confidently.

Wield didn't reply. In his experience there were two people who always found out, and one of them was Ellie Pascoe.

The other was still lying in a coma.

'So what's Sinister Sandy up to?' said Pascoe.

'Oh, this and that,' said Wield vaguely.

Pascoe looked at him suspiciously.

'Start with this, then move on to that,' he ordered.

'Well, she plays her anti-terrorist stuff pretty close, that's understandable,' said Wield. 'But with

89

us being a bit short-handed at the top, it's been a real help her being an old mucker of Desperate Dan's. She keeps well back from the hands-on stuff, of course – says it's our patch, so it should be our call – but when it comes to structuring organization and paperwork, she's really got on top of things. Now it's not just Andy who knows what's going off, it's the lot of us.'

Pascoe's suspicions were thickening by the second. Praise from Wield on matters of organization was praise indeed. Well, he was entitled to call it like he saw it. But that crack about Dalziel came close to high treason.

He said, 'You sound like you're a convert, Wieldy. Hey, you didn't tell her I rang this morning, did you?'

'What do you think I am?' said Wield, hurt. 'Anyway, she had to drive down to Nottingham. The Carradice trial's started and she's involved.'

'Involved in the great cock-up, is she?' said Pascoe not without satisfaction. 'God, and she's the one calling the shots in our investigation!'

They drove the rest of the way to their destination in silence except for the excited panting of Tig, who always insisted on having a car window open sufficiently for him to stick his snout out. Basically a terrier, he condescended to treat most humans as equals on condition they fed him, played games to his rules, and took him on adventurous walks, all that is except Rosie Pascoe, whom he had elected Queen of the Universe.

Now as the car came to a halt the little dog tried to squeeze the rest of his body through the narrow gap in his eagerness to explore what to him was new terrain.

'So here we are,' said Wield. 'What do you want to do?'

'Just take a look,' said Pascoe. 'No harm in that, is there?'

They were parked at the end of Mill Street. The rubble of the wrecked terrace had not yet been cleared away and barriers had been set up at either end of the street. A PC Pascoe recognized as a probationer called Andersen regarded them suspiciously till Wield wound down the window and waved.

'Taking their time, tidying up,' observed Pascoe. 'That down to Glenister?'

'I suppose. But the Council Works Department are still assessing damage to the viaduct wall. Word is it looks OK and they're starting running trains over it again with a ten miles per hour speed restriction. The diversions were causing absolute chaos.'

'So bad folk noticed, you mean?' said Pascoe. 'What about our royal visitant?'

'Coming by chopper. What he prefers anyway.'

'I see the papers are taking it as read that his train was the target,' said Pascoe.

'Keeps them happy,' said Wield. 'Glenister says she's keeping an open mind.'

'So you have been chatting about the case?' said Pascoe.

'Like I said, she's approachable. And the PC in your office is on the CAT network, like she promised.'

'Very cosy. Have you managed to check how many no-go areas are built in?'

'Jesus, Pete,' protested the sergeant. 'She's falling over herself to keep us happy. You think I'm going to help matters trying to trip her up? Even if she does hold back a bit, I bet not even Trimble's got the clearance you need to know all that CAT stuff.'

'I'm sure you're right,' said Pascoe shortly. 'So let's go and take a look before young Andersen there follows orders and shoots us.'

They got out and went towards the barrier.

Andersen greeted them with a smart salute, then took out his notebook.

'No need for that,' said Pascoe smiling. 'This is sort of unofficial official. Must be a bit boring for you, just hanging around here.'

'Doesn't seem much point to it,' agreed the youngster disconsolately.

'Not to worry,' said Pascoe. 'As long as you're appreciated where it matters, eh? I'll have a word with Mr Ireland, see if he can't find you something a little more testing.'

'Thanks very much, sir,' said Andersen, delighted.

'You really going to start telling Paddy Ireland how he should deploy his men?' said Wield as they walked towards the ruined terrace.

'I may suggest diplomatically that there are better ways of nurturing youthful enthusiasm than giving it all the most boring jobs,' replied Pascoe.

Wield gave a grunt which was in itself a masterpiece of diplomacy, conveying the message *You must be out of your tiny mind* without getting close to a definably insubordinate phoneme.

Pascoe wasn't paying attention anyway. He was recalling that day, so close still yet feeling as if it belonged in the historical past, when he'd risen from behind the car and taken those last few steps in the wake of Dalziel.

The wake of Dalziel. Not the best omened of phrases.

He shook it out of his mind and concentrated on the collapsed terrace into which Tig was already plunging with great delight, sending up clouds of white dust.

'Any traces of asbestos?' he asked, suddenly alarmed.

'No, you're OK,' said Wield, glancing in a plastic folder. 'Don't think expensive fire-retardant materials had much appeal for the guys who built houses like these.'

'That Jim Lipton's report you've got there?' said Pascoe.

Lipton was the Chief Fire Officer.

'That's right.'

'What about the CAT stuff? If I know them, they wouldn't be happy till they got their own experts in to second-guess the local yokel.'

'Tried to access it, but they've got a firewall even Jim 'ud find it hard to chop down,' said Wield.

'So you have been checking!' said Pascoe, thinking that IT protection that kept Wield out had to be serious gear.

'Only because I didn't want to draw attention, this visit being so accidental.'

'Quite right,' said Pascoe. 'So what's Jim say?'

'The way this place was built, the blast reduced it to matchwood, which was very handy for the fire. Site of the big bang was definitely Number 3. Relatively small amount of damage to the viaduct wall suggests that if it was their intention to plant the explosive there, they hadn't yet started their excavation.'

'Anything on the explosive?'

'Not from Jim. Not his bag. But it was definitely Semtex.'

'Your friend Glenister tell you that?'

'No, I got chatting to one of her officers. Nice lad.'

Pascoe raised his eyebrows and said, 'Wieldy, I hope you remembered you're a happily married man.'

The sergeant and his partner, Edwin Digweed, had taken advantage of the new legislation formalizing same-sex relationships soon after it came into force. The Pascoes and Dalziel had attended the ceremony, which was a quiet affair. The party which followed in their local pub, the Morris, was far from quiet, but, rather surprisingly in view of

Wield's profession, neither ceremony nor celebration caused the least ripple of interest in the local media. Surprisingly, that was, to everyone except Pascoe. He'd expressed the hope to Dalziel that, despite the two Eds' declared determination to live their lives as they wanted, there'd be no intrusive media presence. The Fat Man had replied, 'Shame. I were looking forward to seeing our Wieldy as Bride of the Month in *Mid-Yorkshire Life*. But mebbe you're right. I'll have a word.'

It was generally believed that if Dalziel *had had a word*, news of the death of Little Nell would not yet have reached Mid-Yorkshire.

'Get anything else from this nice lad?' enquired Pascoe.

'Nay. Sandy Glenister came along just then and he were off like a linty.'

'So much for her open sharing policy.'

'I think you've got her wrong,' said Wield. 'She answers all my questions, or if she doesn't, she tells me why. She reckons they were probably setting up a detonator device and something went wrong.'

'It certainly went wrong for Andy,' said Pascoe grimly.

'It started going wrong before that,' said Wield. 'It started going wrong when he decided not to follow instructions.'

'Got that in one of your cosy chats, did you?' snapped Pascoe.

Wield did not acknowledge the question but

after a short silence said gently, 'Pete, what exactly are we doing here?'

What indeed? thought Pascoe. It was a desolate scene. The hot sunny spell was long gone, the temperature was distinctly unsummerish, clouds scudded overhead on a gusty wind which picked up handfuls of ash and created little dust-devils in the gloomy cleft formed by the looming mill and the railway viaduct. To explain he was here because of some crazy notion that only by finding out exactly what had happened in this place could he hope to keep Andy Dalziel alive would make him sound positively doolally.

He said, 'A crime was committed here. That's my job, investigating crime.'

It came out more pompous and dismissive than he intended.

Wield said, 'So you're going to do your great detective act and sift through the ashes and find a clue the CAT team missed?'

The open sarcasm was no more than he deserved, thought Pascoe.

Trying to lighten things, he said, 'No, I'll leave that to Tig. What have you got there, boy?'

Tig, a great snapper up of unconsidered and often insanitary trifles, came to them like his own ghost, covered in white dust and carrying something in his mouth.

Pascoe stopped to accept the gift, wincing as his ribs reminded him that they might be ignorable when he was dallying with his wife, but at all other times, they could still crack a sharp whip.

It was a piece of plastic, fused into a bolus by the intense heat of the fire.

'One of the videos, I expect,' said Wield. 'The report says there was hardly anything left identifiable.'

Pascoe threw it away, which was a mistake. Tig went after it with a delighted yelp, raising an even denser cloud of dust and ash. He was going to need a thorough brushing before he came in sight of Ellie.

'We've got company,' said Wield.

'Shit,' said Pascoe.

A car had drawn up by the barrier. Out of it stepped a blond-haired elegantly suited figure he recognized as Dave Freeman, Glenister's attendant spook.

He came towards them, a faint smile on his too regular face.

'Hi,' he said. 'Nice to see you up and about again, Pete.'

Pascoe resisted an urge to come over regimental and insist on his rank,

'Just out for a stroll, Dave. With my daughter's dog.'

On cue, Tig, having retrieved his bit of plastic melt-down, returned to wag his tail at the newcomer. Pascoe was childishly pleased to see some of the ash thus redistributed drift on to Freeman's immaculate shoes.

'And you're out for a stroll too, Sergeant?' the

CAT man said to Wield, who Pascoe noted had slipped the plastic folder under his shirt.

'Sir,' said the sergeant.

Wield's *sir* coming from a face as expressionless as a quarry wall was so neutral it could have been Swiss.

'How about you, Dave? What brings you here?' enquired Pascoe.

'Just here to see the site clearance people get a start. Sometimes a JCB can uncover something a finger search has missed.'

'You think you might have missed something?' said Pascoe with ironic incredulity.

'It happens. We can only try to be less fallible than the opposition,' said Freeman.

'What's that,' said Pascoe, 'CAT calendar quote for July?'

Even Wield looked slightly surprised at this heavy-handed mockery.

'One thing you did miss, sir,' he came in quickly. 'Or mebbe it's me that's missed it. But looking through the file I didn't see any mention of the keyholder at Number 6.'

'Number 6?' said Freeman.

'Yes, sir. The only other premises in the terrace still occupied. Crofts & Wills, patent agents.'

They all looked towards Number 6. The blast from Number 3 had ripped Numbers 4 and 5 apart but hadn't been quite strong enough to bring down the gable of the end house, which was presumably made of sterner stuff than the internal separating walls. The fire which followed the blast had done its best but there was still a good fifteen feet or so of blackened brickwork standing.

'Someone checked them out,' said Freeman off-handedly. 'Seems they were going out of business and had cleared their office that weekend. Lucky break. For them, I mean.'

'Funny place for a Patents Agency, Mill Street,' observed Pascoe.

'Indeed. Could be that's why they went out of business,' said Freeman.

Pascoe didn't reply but set out towards the end of the terrace.

'Shouldn't get too close to that wall,' called Wield. 'Doesn't look very safe.'

Pascoe ignored him. Like a child determined to demonstrate its independence, he went right up to the derelict wall and peered through the gap where a door had been blown out, its aluminium frame still hanging drunkenly from its hinges. Here he had a view down the whole length of the terrace to the matching wall of Number 1 which, having only one intervening house to cushion the blast, had taken a harder hit and at its highest point rose no more than five feet from the ground.

What the fuck am I doing here? Pascoe asked himself. What is it I expect? That those little swirls of dust and ash raised by Tig will shape themselves into the wraith of one of the poor bastards who blew himself up here? And even if that did happen, what would I want to ask him?

He turned away and rejoined the other two. As he did so, two trucks, one of them carrying a JCB, came rolling up to the barrier.

'Here come the horny-handed sons of toil,' said Freeman. 'No rush though, Peter. First thing they'll do is erect a canvas hut and get a brew going, so plenty of time to complete your examination of the site.'

He's taking the piss, thought Pascoe.

He said, 'Right, Wieldy. Let's be off,' and with a curt nod, he set off to the car.

'Seems a nice enough guy,' said the sergeant falling into step.

'You reckon? Your type, is he, Wieldy?'

'Could be he's a bi-guy,' said Wield equably. 'But if you mean, do I fancy him, then no. All I meant was, he's polite and helpful. You don't agree?'

'He's a spook,' said Pascoe. 'Probably a prick too. It's a condition of service.'

He got into the car. Tig followed dustily, dropping his lump of melted plastic on to the floor and taking his place at the open window.

'Where now?' said Wield. 'Back home?'

'Not with Tig in this state. He needs a swim in the river, so drop me by the park.'

He reached down to pick up Tig's trophy, intending to drop it out of the window, but as he retrieved it, he felt something move inside. He raised it to his ear and gave it a shake. It rattled. Wield glanced at him.

'Thinking of taking up the maracas?' he asked.

'Only if I can hold a rose between my teeth,' said Pascoe, pocketing the piece of plastic. 'Wieldy, sorry about what I said. About you and Freeman and Glenister, I mean.'

'No problem, long as you let me take a picture of you with the rose.'

'You'll be the first, I promise you that!'

The two men smiled at each other. Wield removed the file from under his shirt and passed it over to Pascoe. Tig barked joyously at a passing starling.

Behind them, in Mill Street, Dave Freeman talked into his mobile phone.

1

dead men don't fart!

Andy Dalziel is floating uneasily above Mid-Yorkshire.

His unease derives not from his ability to defy gravity, which seems quite natural, but his fear that someone below might mistake him for a zeppelin and shoot him down.

Not that England is currently at war with anyone likely to use zeppelins.

On the other hand what lies directly beneath him does look a bit like a bomb site.

It occurs to him that this might be exactly what it is. Hard to identify even the familiar from above, but isn't that the old wool mill . . . and over there the railway line with a no-man's land of desolation between . . . ?

And don't the spirits of the dead come back to haunt the place where they passed away?

But he'd shaken off Death, hadn't he?

A starling circles him twice, then settles on his shoulder.

'Watch what you're doing up there,' says Dalziel, squinting at it. 'I'm not a fucking statue.'

The bird's beady eyes fix on his. With its smooth gleaming head hunched down between its folded wings, it reminds him of . . . Hector!

'Sod off!' commands Dalziel. 'I'm not dead!'

The bird's gaze communicates an indifference worse than mockery.

The Fat Man feels his gut twist and tauten.

The pressure becomes intolerable.

He breaks wind.

The relief is huge and more than physical.

'Dead men don't fart!' he cries triumphantly.

The starling rises from off his shoulder and flutters before his face as though contemplating sinking its arrowhead beak into his eyes.

Dalziel breaks wind again, this time with such force he gets lift-off and accelerates into the bright blue yonder like a Cape Canaveral rocket. Soon the startled starling is nothing more than a distant mote, high above which an overweight, middle-aged detective superintendent at last realizes the Peter Pan fantasy of his early childhood and laughs with sheer delight as he tumbles and soars between the scudding clouds of a Mid-Yorkshire sky.

5

age of wonders

The following day, Pascoe was back at work.

Ellie, as omnivident as Wield had feared, did not take long to find out about the expedition to Mill Street.

She'd been too deeply immersed in her writing to pay much heed when Pascoe and Tig returned from their walk. A swim in the river had removed all the ashy evidence from the dog's coat and Ellie's creative absorption had given Pascoe plenty of time to brush the tell-tale dust from his shoes and turn-ups. But when she came down from Parnassus to find him in the garage, carefully sawing a bolus of melted plastic in half, her suspicions were instantly roused and a very little application of that wifely knife, deep questioning, soon probed the truth out of him almost at the same time as he probed a small lump of impacted metal out of the plastic.

'Wait till I see Edgar!' she threatened, her anger evidenced by her use of the sergeant's first name instead of the usual Wieldy.

'Not his fault,' said Pascoe loyally. 'I'm his superior officer. I ordered him.'

'Hah!' said Ellie, conveying her low estimate of the authority of orders from such a tainted source. Then, sensing that her husband was less concerned about her wrath at the discovery of his perfidy than he ought to be, she said, 'So what have you got there?'

'I would say it's probably a bullet,' said Pascoe, holding the distorted sphere of metal to the light. 'From a gun.'

'I know where bullets come from.'

'I'm sure you do. But this is a rather special gun. It's invisible to a CAT's eye, you see. Of course, it might just be a metal spool in a cassette, melted by the heat.'

She detected that this rider owed more to superstition than to doubt.

'So what does it mean?' she said.

'I've no idea. But it could prove something which in the past only the most fanciful of speculators have even dared hint the possibility of. Hector might have got something right. What's for tea?'

Next morning he was up at his normal time. Ellie like a master tactician knew when protest was pointless and fed him his breakfast without comment, except to say as he kissed her goodbye, 'Pete, you're not going to do anything silly, are you?'

'Good Lord, no,' he said. 'This could be evidence. I'll hand it over to Glenister.'

But not, he added silently to himself, before

I've made sure it really is evidence!

Which was why his first call was not at the Station but at the Police Laboratory, where he made it monosyllabically clear to Tony Pollock, the head technician, that he didn't want it done soon, he wanted it done now.

As a life-long Leeds United supporter, Pollock was well equipped to deal with whatever crap life could hurl, but even he remarked to his assistant, 'With that fat bastard in a coma I thought we might get a bit of peace and quiet from CID.'

'Aye,' said the assistant. Adding, not unimpressed, 'Never would have thought the DCI knew words like that.'

The result was what Pascoe had hoped for, what he'd expected.

He found Sandy Glenister once more sitting behind Dalziel's desk.

'Peter!' she said with the warm smile. 'I wondered if we'd see you today. Dave mentioned seeing you in Mill Street and he thought you looked really well.'

'Yes, I'm feeling much better,' said Pascoe. 'Look, something a bit odd. My dog was rooting around in the debris . . .'

He contrived to suggest that Tig had carried the melted plastic all the way home and chewed the bullet out of it.

'Interesting,' said Glenister. 'Probably nothing, but if you leave it with me, I'll have our people check it out at the lab.'

106

'Been there, done that, got the report,' said Pascoe. 'Definitely a bullet. In fact almost certainly 9 x 19 mm NATO parabellum, possibly fired from a Beretta semi-automatic pistol, 92 series.'

He opened his briefcase, took out the evidence bag containing the bullet and the envelope containing the lab analysis and set them neatly on the desk before her.

She looked down at them but didn't touch them.

'I see,' she said slowly. 'Well, you have hit the ground running, haven't you? So what do you make of it?'

She hadn't invited him to sit but he did so now while it was still a matter of choice rather than necessity caused by his dicky knee.

'It's obvious. A gun was fired, Hector heard the shot, the round finished up in one of the video cassettes. The big question is, what happened to the gun?'

Glenister sat back and steepled her fingers against her nose. Then she opened her hands and put them behind her head, the movement raising her pompion breasts in a manner which Pascoe had to make an effort not to find distracting.

She smiled at him and said, 'Perhaps the big question should be left till we've looked at the wee ones. Firstly I'll need to get our CAT experts to confirm the findings of your local technicians. No reflection on their ability, you understand, but we've all got our specialisms . . . Having established it is a bullet, I will want them to look at this piece of plastic you say it came out of. You still have it, I take it?'

'Yes, it's at home . . .'

'So you didn't take it to your lab? Perhaps as well. Our people prefer to start from scratch without having to contend with any damage earlier, less subtle attempts at examination might have made.'

Pascoe thought of the rusty clamp in his garage and the rather blunt hacksaw he'd used to get the bullet out.

'And if they confirm it's a bullet in a melted video cassette . . . ?' he asked.

Then we must ask how and when it got there. There may be no way of confirming it was fired from a gun on those premises on the same day as the explosion . . .'

'It fits with what Hector heard!'

'Oh aye. Hector!' she said mockingly.

Pascoe again found himself reacting to this knee-jerk dismissal of the constable.

He said, 'Look, just because Hector's pre-digital doesn't mean he doesn't function. He's managed to identify one of the men he saw, hasn't he? OK, description-wise he's no great shakes, but find the right picture and he could still pick out the other.'

His fervour seemed to impress Glenister.

'You know your own men best, Peter,' she said. 'All right. Let's say he did hear a gunshot and that this is indeed the bullet that was fired. This brings us to what you call the big question: Where's the gun? Well, you've supplied one answer, you and your dog.'

'You mean it might have been missed?'

'This was,' said Glenister lowering her hands to touch the evidence bag. 'We sifted the debris thoroughly, of course, but what we were looking for were indications of the nature of the explosion, the kinds of explosive used, their possible source. Plus, of course, body parts, remnants of clothing et cetera that could help identify the men killed. If there were a gun at or near the centre of the explosion, it could simply have disintegrated and its fragments been distorted unrecognizably by the subsequent heat.'

'Unrecognizably? Not very likely, is it?' exclaimed Pascoe. 'Not unless your people aren't as finicky as we like to be in Yorkshire.'

'Peter,' she said gently, 'you've done well, but before you slag off the efforts of others, don't forget it was a stroke of sheer luck that put you on this track. I'll find where the council are dumping the debris and make my people go over it again. OK?'

Before he could respond, the door was pushed open and Freeman said, 'Sorry, didn't know you had company. Sandy, we need to speak.'

Glenister gave a little frown. Maybe she objected to Freeman's rather peremptory tone in the presence of a native. Who was it held the whip hand in this weird twilight zone the CAT people inhabited? Pascoe wondered.

She said, 'Can it wait a moment, Dave?'

'No.'

Well, that was certainly the sound of a whip-crack, thought Pascoe.

Glenister said, 'Peter, let's continue this later, all right?'

'Why not? I'll see if I can fit you in,' he said. 'Dave, good to see you again.'

He left, closing the door firmly behind him and resisting a strong temptation to press his ear to the woodwork.

Instead he went to see Wield and put him in the picture about the bullet.

His reaction was familiar.

'So Hector could've been right. Had to happen! What's Sandy going to do?'

'Fuck knows,' said Pascoe. 'Get her own examination done, then probably kick the whole thing into touch if it doesn't fit her agenda.'

'Pete, you've got to wait and see,' protested Wield. 'Like I told you yesterday, she really seems to be treading eggshells to make sure we don't feel sidelined.'

'You reckon? Well, I think pretty soon you're going to hear a great deal of crunching underfoot. Something's happened, and us being on the need-to-know list is even less likely than Hector getting things right. And if you'd care to bet on that, I'll just run home and get the deeds of the house!'

A man who had left a garden hammock to get

blown up on an English Bank Holiday should have learned to distrust certainties.

Fortunately Wield didn't take the bet. Fifteen minutes later Pascoe got a summons to the CAT Ops Room. When he arrived he was met by men coming out carrying computer equipment. Inside he found Glenister talking animatedly into the scrambler phone. As he approached she finished speaking and handed the receiver to one of her men who unplugged the phone and put it into a box.

'You're moving out?' said Pascoe.

'Yes, we're on our way. Wouldn't have been long anyway, we were just about done here, but something's happened. What do you know about Said Mazraani?'

'Just what I've seen and read. Lebanese academic, teaches at Manchester, good looking, talks well, dresses smart, claims high-level contacts throughout the Middle East. In other words, all the right qualifications for getting on the talking-head shows whenever they want an apparently rational Muslim extremist viewpoint. What the papers called the acceptable face of terrorism until he blotted his copybook with Paxman.'

This had been the previous month, after the kidnapping and videoed execution of an English businessman called Stanley Coker. Mazraani had been trotted out to give an insight into the motives and mindset of the kidnappers, a group calling themselves the Sword of the Prophet. He prefaced

111

his remarks with a fulsome expression of sympathy for the dead man's family, which he repeated when asked if he unreservedly condemned the killing. 'Very nice of you,' said Paxman. 'But do you condemn the killing?' Again the verbiage, again the question. And again, and again. And never a direct answer came.

Next day the papers went to town, led as always by the *People's Voice*.

The *People's Voice*, the youngest and fastest-growing of the tabloids, was in fact not so much the voice of the people as the rant of the slightly pissed know-it-all in the saloon bar who isn't fooled by government statements, legal verdicts, historical analyses, or forensic evidence, but knows what he knows, and knows he's right!

The *Voice* headline screamed

BEHEADING HOSTAGES IS OK!

(so long as it's done in the best possible taste)

'That's the one,' said Glenister. 'Well, barring miracles, he's done his last talking-head show. For the past two days there's been a rumour that Al Jazeera had received a tape showing an execution, a beheading. But not a Western hostage this time. A Muslim.'

'So? In Iraq they've shown little compunction about killing their own.' Then it came to him what she was saying. 'You don't mean . . . ?'

'This morning the BBC, ITV and Sky all received

112

copies of what is presumably the same tape. Yes, it's definitely Mazraani. He hadn't been seen in any of his usual haunts for several days. We sent a team to visit his flat in Manchester. They were told to be discreet but there was already enough of a smell to bother the neighbours. He was in there, him and his head, quite close but not touching. Plus another man not known to us.'

'Jesus!' exclaimed Pascoe. 'Was he beheaded too?'

'No. Shot. They want me back over there now. Mazraani was on my worksheet.'

'This sounds like big trouble,' said Pascoe.

'More than you can imagine,' she said grimly.

'Well, thanks for bringing me up to date . . .' he began.

'That's not why I sent for you,' she interrupted. 'It will be in the papers anyway. Al Jazeera have said they're going to broadcast today. No, what I wanted to say, Peter, was I've asked Dan Trimble if I can take you with us. He says fine, if you feel up to it.'

Pascoe was gobsmacked and made no attempt to hide it.

'But why . . . ?' he managed.

'Peter, I can't be certain, but I've got a feeling there might be some link with what happened here. Being as involved as you are usually means that judgments get blurred, corners cut. But from what I've seen, I get the impression it's just tightened your focus, heightened your responses. If

113

there are any connections, could be you're the one most likely to sniff them out. So what do you say? Couple of days can't hurt, and you'll only be an hour or so's drive away.'

Pascoe hesitated, finding this hard to take in. He was given a breathing space by the appearance of Freeman, who gave Glenister a file and Pascoe a flicker of those cold eyes before disappearing.

'You say you've cleared this with the Chief?' he said. 'What about your bosses?'

'They're fine with it.'

He found himself reluctant to accept the unanimity of this vote of confidence.

'And Freeman? I bet he jumped for joy.'

'Not the jumping kind,' she said with a smile. 'Though in fact it was Dave who put the idea in my head. You've made a big impression there.'

This got zanier.

He said, 'I'll need to talk to . . . people . . .'

'Your wife? She struck me as a sensible woman. I'll have a word if you like, assure her I'll take good care of you.'

Pascoe smiled.

'No, I'll take care of that,' he said.

'That's a yes then. Good. Go and get packed.'

As Pascoe moved away he wondered what Glenister would have said if he'd told her that what really worried him was the prospect of admitting to Wield that he'd got it absolutely wrong.

The sergeant didn't gloat. That wasn't his thing, but he surprised Pascoe by saying, 'Pete, watch your back out there.'

'Watch my back? It's Manchester I'm going to, Wieldy, not Marrakesh.'

'So? There's funny buggers in Manchester too,' said Wield. 'You take care.'

Part Three

Awhile he holds some false way, undebarr'd
By thwarting signs, and braves
The freshening wind and blackening waves.
And then the tempest strikes him; and between
The lightning bursts is seen
Only a driving wreck,
And the pale Master on his spar-strewn deck
With anguish'd face and flying hair
Grasping the rudder hard,
Still bent to make some port he knows not where,
Still standing for some false, impossible shore.

Matthew Arnold, 'A Summer Night'

1

Lubyanka

Manchester is monumental in a way that no other northern town quite manages. You can feel it flexing its muscles and saying, I'm a big city, better step aside. The building which housed CAT had all the family traits. It was solid granite, its tall façade as unyielding as a hanging judge's face. Carved into a massive block alongside a main entrance that wouldn't have disgraced a crusader's castle were the words THE SEMPITERNAL BUILDING.

'Tempting fate a bit, aren't you?' said Pascoe as he and Glenister approached.

She laughed and said, 'Not us. It was a Victorian insurance company. Went bust during the great crash so they paid for their hubris. It's been used for lots of things since then. We took it over three years ago. Most of your new colleagues refer to it as the Lubyanka, the Lube for short. Whether that's tempting fate or not, we've yet to see.'

They went into a wide foyer which looked conventional enough until you noticed that further progress could only be made through security gates with metal detectors, X-ray screening, and large men in attendance. There were almost certainly cameras in operation too, thought Pascoe, though he couldn't spot them. Perhaps they were hidden among the summer blooms which filled what looked like an old horse trough standing incongruously at the foyer's centre.

At the reception desk, Pascoe was issued with a security tag with a complex fastening device.

'Don't take it off till you're leaving,' said Glenister. 'They're self-alarmed the minute you pass through the gate. Removal anywhere but the desk sets bells ringing.'

'Why would I want to take it off?'

'Why indeed? It's to stop anyone taking it off you.'

She said it without her customary smile. Necessary precaution or just self-inflating paranoia? wondered Pascoe.

They went straight into a room with twenty chairs set in four rows of five before a large TV screen. Pascoe and Glenister took seats in the second row. He glanced round to see Freeman in the row behind. Was this indicative of a pecking order? And if so did they peck from the front as in a theatre or from the rear as in a cinema?

As if in answer, the man sitting directly in front of him turned round and smiled at him. Pascoe recognized him instantly. His name was Bernie Bloomfield, his rank was commander and the last time Pascoe saw him, he'd been giving a lecture on criminal demography at an Interpol conference. If he hadn't pursued a police career, he might well have filled the gap left by that most sadly missed of British actors, Alastair Sim.

'Peter, good to see you again,' said Bloomfield.

For a moment Pascoe was flattered, then he remembered his security label.

'You too, sir,' he said. 'Didn't realize you were in charge here.'

'In charge?' Bloomfield smiled. 'Well, in this work we like to keep in the shadows. How's my dear old friend Andy Dalziel doing?'

'Holding on, sir.'

'Good. I'd expect no less. A shame, a great shame. Andy and I go way, way back. We can ill spare such good men. But it's a pity it was one of your less indispensable officers who was first on the scene, Constable . . . what was his name?'

'Hector, sir,' said Glenister.

'That's it. Hector. From what I read, we're likely to get more feedback from the speaking clock. "Sort of funny and not a darkie", isn't that the gist of his contribution?'

There was a ripple of laughter, and Pascoe realized that their conversation had moved from private chat to public performance. He felt a surge of irritation. Only here two minutes and already he was having to defend Hector in front of a bunch of sycophants who clearly felt very superior to your common-or-garden provincial bobby.

Time to lay down the same markers he'd already put in place with Glenister.

He said with emphatic courtesy, 'With respect, sir, as I've told the superintendent, I think it would be silly to underestimate Constable Hector's evidence. While it's true that in his case the picture may take a bit longer to come together, what he does notice usually sticks and emerges in a useful form eventually. What he's given us so far has proved right, hasn't it? In fact, with respect, isn't most of what we know about what happened in Mill Street that day down to Hector rather than CAT?'

This defensive eulogium, which in the Black Bull would have had colleagues corpsing, reduced the audience here to silence. Or perhaps they were simply waiting to see how Bloomfield would deal with this uppity newcomer who'd just called him silly and his unit inefficient.

The commander gave Pascoe that Alastair Sim smile which indicates he knows a lot more than you're saying.

'That's very reassuring, Peter,' he said. 'Or are you just being loyal?'

'Never back down,' was the Fat Man's advice. 'Especially when you're not sure you're right!'

Pascoe said firmly, 'Loyalty's nothing to do with it, sir. You find us a live suspect and I'm sure you'll be able to rely on Hector for identification.'

'I'm glad to hear it. Now I think it's time to get our show on the road.'

122

He rose to his feet and let his gaze drift down the rows.

'Good day to you all,' he said. 'What you are about to see is a tape played on Al Jazeera television earlier today. It isn't pretty, but no point closing your eyes. Some of you will need to see it many times.'

He sat down and the lights dimmed.

The tape lasted about sixty seconds, but even to sensibilities toughened by a gruelling job as well as by general exposure to the graphic images shown most nights on news programmes, not to mention the computer-generated horrors of the modern cinema, the unforgiving minute seemed to stretch for ever.

There was no soundtrack. Someone said 'Jesus!' into the silence.

After a long moment, another man stood up in the front row. Fiftyish, balding, wearing a leather patched jacket, square-ended woollen tie and Hush Puppies, he spoke with the clipped rapidity of a nervous schoolmaster saying grace before he is interrupted by the clatter of forks against plates. His label said he was Lukasz Komorowski.

'This is without doubt Said Mazraani. His body was found in his flat this morning with the head severed, preliminary examination suggests by three blows as illustrated in the video clip. The chair, carpet and background in the tape sequence correspond precisely with what was found at the flat. There was a second body in the flat. This belonged to a man called Fikri Rostom who, as you will hear, Mazraani introduced as his cousin. Rostom, a student at Lancaster University, was shot in the head.'

He paused for breath.

Glenister said, 'What's the writing say?'

'It says *Life for life, eye for eye, tooth for tooth, hand for hand, foot for foot, burning for burning, wound for wound, stripe for stripe.*'

He paused again, this time like a schoolmaster waiting for exegesis. Pascoe knew it was biblical, probably Old Testament, but could go no further. Andy Dalziel would have given them chapter and verse. He claimed his disconcerting familiarity with Holy Writ had been acquired via a now largely neglected pedagogic technique which involved his RK teacher, a diminutive Welshman full of *hwyl* and *hiraeth*, boxing his ears with a leather-bound Bible each time he forgot his lesson.

Pascoe found himself blinking back tears at the same time as Glenister said, 'Exodus 21.'

Commander Bloomfield twisted in his chair to look at her.

'I'm glad to see we're not yet a completely godless nation,' he murmured. 'Do go on, Lukasz.'

Komorowski resumed at a slightly slower pace.

'Verses 23 to 25; the language is Arabic and the source is a tenth-century translation of the Bible by Rabbi Sa'adiah ben Yosef who was the gaon, or chief sage, of the Torah academy at Sura. The Torah is an Hebraic word meaning the revealed will of God, in particular Mosaic law as expounded in the Pentateuch, which is the first five books of the Old Testament of which Exodus is the second . . .'

He paused again.

'Tell us something we don't know,' murmured Glenister.

Clearly they educated kids differently in Scotland, thought Pascoe.

Komorowski resumed, 'Below we find the words *In memory of Stanley Coker*. Coker, you will recall, was the English businessman taken hostage and subsequently beheaded by the Prophet's Sword group. The flat and the bodies are currently being examined. Full reports will be issued as soon as they are available. Preliminary post-mortem findings confirm the timetable indicated by our tapes. The bullet recovered from Fikri Rostom was a nine millimetre round almost certainly fired from a Beretta 92 series semi-automatic pistol.'

Pascoe turned to look at Glenister, who continued to stare straight ahead.

'I have the tape here which gives us the timings,' continued Komorowski. 'Mazraani, even if he had not discovered the exact location of our listening device, always assumed he was being overheard. Indeed, as you will hear, he refers to our tape. So he always took the precaution of playing masking music. Here is what we have.'

He raised his index finger and a recording started to play.

First sound was of a door being opened.

'Tape activated by arrival, we guess, of the alleged cousin,' said Komorowski.

Music began to play, then a female voice began to sing.

'Elissa, the Lebanese singer,' said Komorowski. 'Fikri seems to have been a fan. We can run on here I think.'

The tape gabbled forward then slowed again to normal speed.

'Fifteen minutes on, the door opens again, Mazraani arrives, beneath the music we can hear greetings being exchanged,' said Komorowski. 'Then the music is turned up louder, suggesting that what they say next they do not wish to be overheard. AV are not hopeful of extracting anything useful from this portion of the tape but will continue to try. A minute later . . . here it comes . . .'

The singing suddenly sank to a low background and a click was heard.

'The intercom. Our killers have rung the door bell downstairs,' interposed Komorowski rapidly.

Now a voice spoke, educated, urbane.

'Gentlemen, how can I help you?'

'Mazraani,' said Komorowski.

'Just like a quick word, sir.'

This voice, even though distant and tinny through the intercom, had the unmistakable flat force of authority.

'By all means. Won't you come up?'

The sound of a door being opened then a pause, presumably to wait for the newcomers to make their ascent.

'Evening, Mr Mazraani. And this is . . . ?'

The voice of authority again. Northern. Presumably a linguist could get closer.

'My cousin, Fikri. He's staying with me for a few days.'

That's nice. Anyone else in the flat?'

'No. Just the two of us.'

'Mind if we check that? Arch.'

Doors opening and shutting.

'Clear.'

A third voice. Lighter, tighter. Holding on to control?

'So now we can perhaps get down to what brings you here. Won't you introduce yourselves? For the tape?'

The urbanity came close to mockery. Poor bastard, thought Pascoe. He thinks he's just got the law to deal with.

'Certainly, sir. I'm called Andre de Montbard. Andy to my friends. And my colleague is Mr Archambaud de St Agnan. He's got no friends. And this lady singing is, I'd say, the famous Elissa? Compatriot of yours, I believe? Gorgeous girl. Lovely voice and those big amber eyes! I'm a great fan.'

And now the singing was turned up to a volume even higher than before.

Lukasz Komorowski let it run for a moment then made a cut-off gesture and the tape stopped.

'During the next couple of minutes we believe the killings took place. First the shooting, then the beheading. The killers leave. At eight thirty-nine the Elissa CD stops. Five minutes later the recording stops too and is not reactivated until our team enter this morning. Right. Questions? Observations?'

Glenister began to say something but Pascoe cut across her. Make his presence felt. Show the bastards he wasn't here just to make up the numbers.

'Mazraani said "Gentlemen", plural, when he answered the intercom. Like he knew there was more than one of them.'

'Your point being . . . ?'

'My point is it suggests he'd spotted them earlier.'

'Very likely. Mazraani must have got used to being followed. Even if he didn't see anyone, he'd assume they were there.'

'Meaning he'd think these two were yours?'

'Possibly,' said Komorowski dismissively. 'Thank you, Mr Pascoe. Sandy . . .'

But Pascoe wasn't done.

'Then why the hell weren't they?' he demanded.

'Sorry?'

'Why weren't there any of your men around? OK, I gather you'd managed to lose track of Mazraani earlier that day. I'd have thought the obvious thing to do was put someone on watch outside his flat. At least that's the way we'd have done it back in good old-fashioned Mid-Yorkshire CID, despite our staffing problems.'

128

Komorowski put his hand to his mouth as though to inhibit an over-hasty reply and looked down at Pascoe with a speculative gaze. Presumably he was high enough up the pecking order on the Intelligence half of CAT to feel he didn't need to take crap from DCIs. Pascoe noticed with distaste that his fingernails were cracked and none too clean.

Commander Bloomfield twisted his long frame in his chair and smiled at Pascoe.

'If I didn't know you were one of Andy Dalziel's boys, I think I'd have guessed,' he said. 'Thing is, Peter, despite all this crisis talk, we're desperately short of manpower here in CAT. Probably in real terms even shorter than you doubtless are in your good old-fashioned CID. Result: we're continually re-assessing priorities. The chaps on Mazraani lost him. Procedure is report it in, return to base for reassignment. As for watching the flat, why waste men when we've got a bug inside? Soon as the tape was checked and we became aware there was activity, we'd have had someone round there.'

'So when was the tape checked?' asked Pascoe.

Bloomfield glanced at Komorowski.

'Midnight that night,' said the man.

'So you sent a surveillance team round then?'

'Well, no,' admitted Komorowski. 'There'd been no further activation of the tape after the CD finished playing, so it was assumed the flat was now empty.'

'While actually it was full of dead people,' said

Pascoe. 'And didn't whoever checked the tape out wonder who these two guys – what did they call themselves . . . ?'

'Andre de Montbard and Archambaud de St Agnan,' said Glenister, who was looking at Pascoe with the gentle smile of a mother proud of her prodigious son,

'. . . which to anyone but the brain-dead sound suspiciously like assumed names – didn't he wonder who this pair were?'

Komorowski now looked like a schoolteacher cornered by a smart-arse pupil.

'Or,' Pascoe went on relentlessly, 'did he make the same error as Mazraani and assume they were official, maybe because he'd got used to working in an environment where the right hand doesn't always know what the left is doing?'

A silence followed this question, and in Pascoe's eyes answered it too.

Then Freeman spoke from behind him.

'Lukasz,' he said, 'if Pete here's quite finished . . .'

Pascoe glowered round at him. Teacher's pet, he thought. Get your boss off the hook, earn brownie points.

He said, 'I'm done. For now.'

'Thanks,' said Freeman. 'Lukasz, these weird names the killer gave – or rather, the man we assume is the killer gave – do we have anything on them?'

'Yes, as a matter of fact we do,' said

Komorowski. 'But first I should draw your attention to an e-message every newspaper, TV news centre and news agency received two days ago. It read: *It would appear that a new order of knighthood has been founded on earth.*'

He paused as if inviting identification.

When none came he said, 'Don't worry. Of the great intellects who run our press, only one recognized it, and that, curiously, was the sports editor of the *Voice*. He was intrigued enough to mention it to the paper's Security correspondent, who passed it to us. We put it on file with a question mark. Now I think the question mark can be removed.'

He paused again and Bloomfield said, 'In your own time, Lukasz.'

'Thank you, Bernie,' said Komorowski, as if taking the remark at face value. 'In fact this is a translation of the opening words of St Bernard of Clairvaux's *Liber ad milites Templi*, written at the request of his friend, Hugh de Payens, to define, justify and encourage a new order of knights Hugh and a few others had just founded. These were the Knights Templar, whose initial function was to protect the many pilgrims travelling to Jerusalem. Although the First Crusade had seen the establishment of new Christian states in the region, it was still a dangerous place for the unwary pilgrim, who provided an easy target both for religious zealots and for common thieves. Rapidly, however, the new Order outgrew its founding purpose and evolved into an independent fighting force dedicated to

131

driving the infidels out of the Holy Land. Eventually it became so powerful that it had to be crushed by the very powers of Western Christendom whose values it was formed to defend. But it is its beginnings not its ending that concern us here.'

He paused again and looked around as though anxious for approval.

Bloomfield said, 'Good, good. And your point, Lukasz?'

'Besides Hugh de Payens there were eight other founder members of the order, all French noblemen,' said Komorowski. 'One is unknown, possibly Hugh Count of Champagne who was de Payens' liege lord. Two are known only by their Christian names: Rossal and Gondamer. The names of the others are Payen de Montdidier – incidentally, the fact that Payen here and its plural form in the name of the Order's founder look like medieval forms of modern *paien*, pagan, seems to be a coincidence.'

Another pause, another glance around as if looking for comment or contradiction. There was none, unless an audible sigh from Bloomfield could be interpreted as either.

'Now where was I?' said Komorowski. 'Oh yes. Montdidier. Then there are two Geoffreys: de St Omer and Bisol. And finally, and for our present purpose, most significantly, there is a knight called Archambaud de St Agnan, and a future Grand Master of the Order whose name is Andre de Montbard.'

2

a pale horse

Hugh de Payens was galloping his grey stallion across a wide green meadow under an ancient castle's beetling walls. On either side ranks of armed men held their eager mounts under strict control, their restless hooves rising and falling on the same spot, their heaving breasts creating a dark ripple of muscle that ran as far as the eye could see. Cuirasses glinted in the bright summer sun, pennants bearing lions, bears, griffins and dragons, rampant, courant, couchant, fluttered above them, and high over all floated the broad banners which on a lily-white ground bore the symbol of their purpose and their faith, the red cross.

Then a little bell rang and in a trice the castle became an insubstantial ruin, the mounted men and their flags vanished, leaving the rider hacking gently along the edge of a field on a placid grey mare with nothing for company but a few un-curious cows.

He reined in, took out a mobile, accessed

Messages and found a single capital **X**.

He erased it and urged his mount forward into a spinney of beech trees slimming into willow as he approached a narrow but deep and fast-moving stream. On its bank he came to a halt and slackened the rein so that the horse could crop the long grass.

He speed-dialled a number.

'Bernard.'

'Hugh.'

'De Clairvaux.'

'De Payens.'

Silence. He counted mentally.

one thousand two thousand three thousand

Dead on three seconds the other voice spoke.

Anything less, anything more, and he would have switched off, removed the SIM card, cut it in half with the pair of electrical wire strippers attached to his belt, and hurled the pieces and the phone into the stream.

'Hugh, the loose end, there's been a suggestion it might not be so harmless as we thought. I wonder if it wouldn't be as well to tie it up. Discreetly, of course.'

A moment's silence then Hugh said, 'I'm not sure I like the sound of that. It's not what we're about.'

'Of course it isn't. But in the field sometimes the choice is between collateral damage and protecting our own. Or, let's not be mealy-mouthed, protecting ourselves.'

'Our structure protects us.'

'There are always links. You know me. Andre knows you. The Geoffreys know Andre.'

'I hope you trust my discretion. I trust Andre. And he says the Geoffreys are reliable.'

'Are they? From what you reported of Bisol's reaction to Mill Street, I would have doubts.'

'He's concerned about the injured policeman. Removing another as damage limitation isn't going to make him feel any better.'

'Properly done, no reason why he should ever know, is there? Look, I don't like this any more than you do, but I know how easily things can unravel. I've already had to put one nosey policeman on a tight rein. The loose end in question seems to be accident prone, so it shouldn't be too difficult to remove him without arousing either suspicion or further agitating Bisol's tender conscience. From what you say of him, I imagine Andre would take it in his stride. I leave it with you.'

The phone went dead.

Hugh switched off. His patient horse, alert to signals, raised its head, then resumed cropping the grass as its rider made no movement but sat in thought for a while.

Finally he activated his phone once more, texted an X, and disconnected.

A few moments later the phone rang.

'Hugh.'

'Andre.'

'De Payens.'

'De Montbard.'

one thousand two thousand three thousand

'Andre, how are you? I've just been talking to Bernard. There's a little job which sounds very much your cup of tea . . .'

3

kaffee-klatsch

Two days after Pascoe had gone west, Ellie Pascoe and Edgar Wield met outside the Arts Centre. Wield knew it wasn't by chance when Ellie, uncomfortable with deception, over-egged her look of surprised pleasure.

She wants to talk about Peter, he guessed, but is worried about looking disloyal.

'How do, Ellie?' he said before she could speak. 'Fancy a coffee at Hal's?'

He saw he'd stolen her line, and she'd been married to a detective long enough to work out why by the time they climbed up to the mezzanine café-bar in the Arts Centre.

With relief, because she hated masquerade, she took this as an invitation to cut straight to the chase as soon as they'd got their coffee.

'Have you heard from Peter?' she asked.

'Aye.'

'And what's he say?'

'This and that,' he answered vaguely. 'Have you not heard yourself?'

'Of course I have,' she said indignantly. 'He rings me every night.'

Every night seemed a large term for the two nights Pascoe had been away.

'Rings me during the day,' said Wield. 'Don't expect he misses me at night.'

They smiled at each other like the old friends they were.

'So what's he talk to you about?' said Ellie.

'That and this,' repeated Wield. 'Work stuff. You know Pete. Thinks the place is going to fall apart if he's not there to keep an eye on things.'

Ellie saw that he might have opened things up for her, but he had his loyalties too. This was her call.

She said, 'I'm a bit worried about him, Wieldy. More than a bit. A hell of a lot. I think he's got really obsessive about this bomb investigation.'

'Came close to killing him,' said Wield. 'Enough to make you both obsessive.'

'Meaning, how clear's my own judgment here?' interpreted Ellie. 'Wieldy, if you can put your hand on your heart and tell me he's fine, that'll do the trick for me.'

He drank his coffee. His face was as unreadable as ever, but Ellie knew because she'd known it from the start that she wasn't going to hear much for her comfort.

He said, 'Wish I could. But it's not so odd that

I can't. Being close to something like Mill Street doesn't just go away. I reckon it shook Pete up more than he'll admit. Since it happened, he's definitely not been himself. Trouble is, from what I've seen of him, what he's trying to be is Andy Dalziel. The way he deals with people, the way he talks, even, God help us, the way he walks, it's like he feels he's got to fill in for Fat Andy. But likely you'll have noticed?'

'I noticed something,' said Ellie unhappily. 'But he's a great bottler-up. Stupid sod imagines he's protecting me and Rosie by clamping down the hatches. He said an odd thing when he went back to work that first time. He said he felt he had to, as if him not being there would lessen the chances of Andy recovering. A sort of sympathetic magic.'

'Very like,' said Wield. 'Look, luv, I don't think you should worry too much. Either Andy'll make it and we'll all get back to normal, or he won't, and we'll all get back to normal then too, only it'll take a bit longer and normal will have changed.'

She'd wanted honesty before comfort. This sounded to her reasonably close to the former and a long way short of the latter.

She said, 'I just wish he hadn't gone to Manchester. I suppose we should be grateful to Sandy Glenister for seeing how much it meant to him to stay involved, but I don't really see how he can be of any use to those CAT people across there . . . What?'

Wield knew that in the innermost reaches of his mind he had grunted sceptically, but he was certain that nothing in his larynx had uttered even the ghost of an echo of that grunt. Also he had the kind of face which made the Rosetta Stone seem as easy to read as the back of a cornflake packet. 'Watch his left ear,' advised Andy Dalziel. 'It doesn't help, but it means you don't have to look at the rest of his face.'

Yet despite all this, perhaps because over the years he and Ellie Pascoe had got very close, and in matters relating to her family she was supersensitive, somehow the grunt had reached her ears telepathically.

'I said nowt,' he said.

She said nowt too, which made her point very effectively.

'All right,' he said, pushed another step towards honesty. 'I reckon maybe Mrs Glenister didn't take Pete with her team just so he could help pursue their investigations over there, she took him to make sure he wasn't sticking his nose in back here.'

'But why should she do that? I thought she'd fallen over herself to make sure Mid-York CID were fully involved?'

'Oh aye, she did,' agreed Wield. 'I'm not suggesting owt sinister. It's just that, once you get into Security, you've got to tread very carefully. It were all right long as she were around, but likely she could see Pete were so obsessive, he wasn't going to stop picking away at things just because the CAT team had moved on.'

Ellie sipped her cappuccino. It left a smudge of creamy brown foam along her lip. She had the kind of strong facial structure which age only improved and the kind of figure which only strong will power in the matter of cream dough-nuts and buttered crumpets kept this side of orientally voluptuous. Looking at her, Wield thought of the old gay joke – *doesn't it sometimes make you wish you were a lesbian?*

She licked her lip and said, 'This have anything to do with that bullet Tig found? Pete seemed to think that was a bit of a mystery.'

'A mystery susceptible of more than two explanations can hardly be deemed mysterious,' said Wield.

He caught Pascoe's intonation so perfectly that Ellie laughed out loud.

'That's what he decided, was it?' she said.

'He certainly got his two explanations,' evaded Wield. 'Look, Ellie, I really don't think there's owt much to worry yourself about. Give it time. He'll be back soon – when he rang through yesterday he said he felt he were superfluous to requirements . . .'

'Hanging around like a yard of foreskin at a Jewish wedding, was how he put it to me,' said Ellie.

Wield grinned.

'Me too.' Another one from the wit and

wisdom of Fat Andy, I think. Anyway, like I say, he'll be back in a day or two. And when he is, there's such a backlog of stuff piling up, he'll not have time to worry about owt else.'

'I hope you're right, Wieldy,' said Ellie. 'But all this Templar stuff in the papers today do you think that it could be connected with the Mill Street explosion?'

The papers had all been running the Mazraani killing on their front pages for a couple of days now. Several of them had used blurry images taken from the video, though none had gone so far as to show the severed head. The *Voice* had gone as far as showing the moment of first impact, and the same paper had come closest to expressing approval of the killing with the headline NOW IT'S YOUR TURN!

Reaction in the Muslim community, already heated by news of the murders, was brought to boiling point by this and other ultra-nationalist responses. A protest march to the *Voice* offices in Wapping might have caused a riot if a strong police presence had not prevented right-wing youths from getting closer than shouting distance to the Muslim marchers. Thwarted of its hoped-for images of violence, the *Voice* had compensated with a front-page photo of the protesters under the headline

RIGHT TO DEMONSTRATE? YES!
But where were they when Stan Coker died?

142

It was only today, however, that the media had made the connection between the cryptic message about the 'new knighthood' and the Manchester killing. CAT had kept the lid on the contents of its audio tape, but a second message to the media reading, *If the State cannot protect us, then we must look to those who can*, signed *Hugh de Payens, Grand Master, The Order of the Temple*, had let the cat out of the bag, and already there'd been some speculation about a possible connection with the Mill Street bombing.

'Possible, but far from sure,' said Wield. 'But as far as Pete's coming home's concerned, I don't see it making any difference. He's a man who likes to be useful. If them daft buggers are just letting him tread water, he won't want to hang around.'

He spoke reassuringly but he was holding back and, despite his best efforts, he suspected Ellie knew it. He'd lied about only hearing from Pascoe at work during the day. Last night he'd taken a call on his mobile at home. Pascoe had made it clear he believed there was a connection between Mill Street and the beheading. He'd concluded by asking the sergeant to check out a couple of things, accompanying the request with the exhortation, 'And do it in person, eh, Wieldy? No phoning from the Station.'

Wise precaution or paranoia? Wield didn't know, though he had his concerns and they were more about Pascoe's state of mind than the behaviour of CAT.

But you didn't tell an old mate – much less his wife – you thought he might be off his chump till you were absolutely certain, and he'd been on his way to deal with the first of these requests when Ellie ambushed him.

It was only a short walk to the Fire Service Headquarters. It looked like being a wasted walk when the Chief Fire Officer's secretary told him her boss was in a meeting. Then her face split in a grin and she added, 'But he'll be glad of an excuse to get out of it, that is if your business is urgent, Sergeant Wield?'

'Oh yes,' Wield assured her solemnly. 'Life and death.'

Five minutes later, Jim Lipton, the CFO, appeared.

'Wieldy, lad,' he said. 'You're a life-saver. Another two minutes with those plonkers and there'd have been such a case of spontaneous combustion, I'd have had to put myself out! A cup of coffee?'

The two men were old acquaintances, full of respect for each other's expertise. But even respect has its boundaries. Under the tutelage of his partner, Edwin Digweed, Wield had come to admit that Hal's espresso was a cut above Camp, but he'd needed no tuition to recognize the awfulness of firehouse coffee which, according to Pascoe, was the direct opposite of Instant, having been on the boil so long there might be grounds in there coeval with Conopios.

144

'No thanks. Just had some,' he said.

'Then let's get down to business, What brings you?'

'It's about the Mill Street explosion,' he said. 'Sorry, that a problem, Jim?'

There are two kinds of Yorkshire face: the one which gives nowt away, not even when the ferret down its owner's trouser leg wakes up and goes looking for breakfast, and the one like the giant screen at an international match.

Lipton's was the latter. It showed every emotion and, if you pressed the right buttons, gave a re-run in close-up.

'It's just yon Scots lass said I weren't to talk about this to any bugger except her.'

'Oh *her*,' said Wield. 'She's been called back to Lancashire. Likely they'd forgotten how to load the dishwasher.'

This racist and sexist slur was enough to re-assure Lipton, who relaxed, sipped his coffee with every sign of pleasure and said, 'So what do you want to know? Not that there's owt I've not put in my report. You'll have seen my report?'

'Oh aye,' said Wield, pulling a copy out of his pocket and waving it negligently. 'Couple of things not in here, 'cos there's no reason for them to be. You mention that you and the housing officer checked out the terrace eighteen months ago when the council's plans for pulling it down went on the blink. Recommendation – not fit for domestic habitation, but OK for commercial use.'

'Aye, a bit of arm-twisting went on there,' said Lipton.

'You reckon there was a fire-hazard?'

'I reckoned the whole place *were* a fire-hazard!' corrected Lipton. 'The council promised to check out the electrics and give the woodwork a fire-retardant treatment. But like spraying your knickers with insect repellent at the Mayor's Christmas Dance.'

In local government mythology, the Mayor's Christmas Dance made the Ball of Kirriemuir sound like a revivalist meeting.

'How about the roof space?' asked Wield casually. 'Were the dividing walls solid brick or just lath and plaster?'

'Don't be daft! Neither, 'cos there were no dividing walls, just a common roof space. Fire got up there in Number 1, it 'ud be paying a visit on Number 6 quicker than a fit lad could run along the pavement!'

'Terrible,' said Wield. 'They should have listened to you, Jim.'

'Nay, fair do's,' said Lipton. 'What happened there, nowt I recommended would have made a difference. Explosion like that were going to flatten the place and kill every bugger in it, the fire were just an optional extra.'

'Aye, it must have been some bang,' agreed Wield. 'I had a look myself, me and one of the Scottish woman's team. There were a door at the side of Number 6, looked a good strong security door, metal frame. I noticed it were hanging off its hinges. That would be the blast that blew it open, I suppose? Or did your boys mebbe open it when they were making things safe?'

'No, it were the blast. I noticed it myself.'

'But a door like that, two dead locks it had, if they'd been shot home . . .'

'They weren't,' said Lipton promptly. 'Can't have been locked either. That's why it flew open when the blast hit it. Probably that's what helped the walls stay up. The way Mill Street terrace were built, yon wall was ready to tumble like Jericho if the doorway hadn't given the blast an escape route.'

Wield stayed a few minutes longer, chatting about this and that, and giving an update on Andy Dalziel's progress.

'That's what really showed me what a big explosion this was,' said Lipton as the sergeant left. 'Any bang that could bowl yon bugger over must've been a real stunner!'

It was funny, thought Wield as he walked away. To a large section of the population of Mid-Yorkshire 'the threat of the terrorists in our midst', as the local paper had so unimaginatively put it, was exponentially increased by the possibility that their midst had had Andy Dalziel permanently removed from it.

He glanced at his watch. Getting on for lunch, but first he had to visit the morgue. That should put an edge on his appetite. Sometimes as he sat in the cosy living room of the cottage he shared with Edwin, listening to his beloved Gilbert and Sullivan, he found himself counting the days to retirement.

It was a long count. There were still years to do before he could metaphorically swap his truncheon for a poppy or a lily.

Whistling the sergeant's song from *The Pirates of Penzance*, he walked his mystic way up the steep hill that led to the Central Hospital.

4

burglary

By the end of his second day in Manchester, Peter Pascoe had had enough.

During the initial video show and briefing, he'd felt he was on the front line. But on arrival at the Lubyanka early the next morning, he'd been directed to a stuffy cellar where two agents who on first sight looked young enough to be students on Work Experience had invited him to join them in trawling through Intelligence files in search of anything that might link to this self-styled new Order of Templar Knights.

By the end of the day, he had reached several conclusions.

Firstly, his new colleagues were not quite as young as they looked, with the one called Tim (dark-haired, medium build, with a round, melancholy face) senior to the one called Rod (blond, blue-eyed, slim, with a fresh lively face which readily broke into a smile). Secondly, though apparently rather light-hearted in their approach to their work, in fact they took it very seriously. And thirdly, that however seriously Tim and Rod took it, from his point of view it was a complete waste of time.

The following morning he had spent another hour in the cellar, then gone in search of Glenister. When he announced his intention, Rod grinned at Tim and Tim frowned at Rod, but they gave him directions without comment. A couple of minutes later he was standing before a door with the superintendent's name on it. There was no reply to his knock, so he tried the handle. It was locked. Frustration made him rattle it violently. Behind him he heard a dry cough. He turned. Lukasz Komorowski was standing there. In one hand he carried a plastic bottle, in the other a pair of scissors. Probably just about to give a seminar on how to kill an enemy agent using objects you'd find in the conventional kitchen.

'She is out,' said the man in his precise voice. 'That is why her door is locked.'

Feeling foolish, Pascoe said, 'So when will she be back?'

'Not till late afternoon, I would guess. She is in Nottingham. Crisis management.'

'You mean, the demonstrations?'

Fuelled by the lurid tabloid stories about the Templars and their 'execution' of Mazraani, there had been demonstrations and counter-demonstrations outside the courthouse where Michael Carradice aka Abbas was being tried.

Komorowski said, 'No, we do not do crowd control, Mr Pascoe. The crisis is in the way the trial is progressing.'

'Things going badly, are they?' said Pascoe.

'Depends how you look at it,' said Komorowski. 'From our point of view, very badly. From yours, however, perhaps not so bad?'

Shit! thought Pascoe, taken aback. These people . . . do they know everything?

When Carradice and his so-called gang had been arrested, Ellie had said, 'Interesting. Mum's mum was a Carradice and she came from Nottingham.'

'Oh God,' said Pascoe. 'Don't tell me we're related to a major terrorist!'

'You're always saying my relatives are dull,' said Ellie. 'I'll check with Mum.'

Pascoe had thereafter read the background articles on Carradice with some slight unease. Even without a personal connection, it was a story to make anyone uneasy.

After taking a degree in Art History at Nottingham University, Michael Carradice had decided that back-packing round the world was a better option than finding a job. He had set off in company with his girlfriend. Eight months later she returned alone, saying that Michael had grown increasingly weird during their trip, so weird that finally she'd packed up her bags one night while he slept and headed for the nearest airport.

Nothing was seen and little heard of Carradice

for almost another year until he turned up at the British Embassy in Jakarta, a convert to Islam, heavily bearded and calling himself Abbas Asir, and demanded that these changes of name and appearance be recorded in a new passport. The best the embassy could do was to offer him documentation sufficient to get him back to the UK where the Passport Office could more easily deal with his altered status. At this he became threateningly abusive. After he left, the interviewing official, foreseeing nothing but trouble from this source, had an unofficial word with a colleague in the Department of the Interior. Early the following morning, Carradice found himself picked up, declared undesirable, and put on a plane to the UK with a speed that immigration officials in London could only marvel at.

This got a bit of publicity, not all of it unsympathetic. Then Carradice had dropped out of the public eye for eighteen months, though it now appeared CAT had always had him in their sights. Their interest was formalized into Operation Marion. After many weeks of surveillance and undercover work, CAT felt the moment had come to strike. The house in Nottingham which Carradice shared with half a dozen other young Muslim men was raided, the inmates arrested and a large amount of material removed, including, it was alleged, literature and chemicals relating to the manufacture of ricin.

Simultaneously across the city another ten

Muslims were arrested. The news headlines were full of the terrorist plot which could have resulted in the death of thousands of Nottingham's citizens by poison in the water supply.

Sensitivity to the libel laws made most papers tone down their rhetoric as the cases against the alleged conspirators began to fold. Only the *Voice* refused to back off, declaring that dangerous men were being set free not because they were innocent but 'because our antiquated English law has more loopholes in it than a crocheted cardie'.

In the end, Carradice was the only one sent for trial. It was at this point that Ellie had come back to Pascoe and said, 'I was right. Mum says yes, these are Gran's Carradices. But not to worry. They're so far removed, they might as well be Chinese. Mum says the last time she had contact with any of them was when I was thirteen and a carload of them called in as they were passing, and I was given a baby to hold, and he peed all over me. Mum thinks he was called Mick. Funny if it was him.'

'Pissing cousins not kissing cousins, then,' said Pascoe.

So distant a connection was hardly a connection at all, he told himself, but he took great care not to let any hint of it reach his colleagues' ears. Police humour can be heavy and abrasive. Andy Dalziel was the greatest danger. He had a nose for little secrets which could have earned him a fortune as a scandal-sheet journalist.

But now Pascoe was realizing that even the Fat Man was a mere tyro alongside the CAT people.

He took a deep breath and forced a smile. With his shabby schoolmaster appearance and manner, Komorowski was a man it would be easy to disregard. Easy but foolish. Pascoe was still in the process of filling in the complex sudoku of CAT's power structure, but he had a strong suspicion that this man was far from a cipher.

He said, 'You know what they say about choosing friend and relatives.'

'Indeed.'

The man seemed to want to add something, but was having difficulty finding the words.

Finally he said, 'It wasn't my intention to offend you or show how clever we are by mentioning the relationship, Mr Pascoe.'

'That's all right then.'

'I just thought it might ease your mind. Stop you worrying if we knew, and whether it made any difference if we did.'

'Difference to what?' said Pascoe, a little off balance but still suspicious.

'To our degree of trust in you. Absolute trust requires absolute knowledge.'

'And I've passed the test?'

'Absolutely.' Now Komorowski smiled. The smile was like a shaft of sunshine lighting up a distant valley. It revealed the young man he once had been. Smooth out the creased leathery skin, add a mop of jet-black hair, and what you had was a very attractive piece of goods with the added allure of just a whiff of Eastern European exoticism.

Pity about the dirty fingernails.

His gaze must have dropped for now Komorowski held up his bottle and scissors.

'My other job,' he said. 'The building is surprisingly full of plant life, some of which I confess I have introduced myself: a couple of window boxes, and you may have noticed the trough in the foyer. Also many people bring in house plants to add a little colour, then forget about them and neglect them. It's the British way. So I've appointed myself head gardener to the Lubyanka.'

'Good Lord,' said Pascoe, feeling ashamed of his prissy thoughts about personal hygiene when all that the man's hands displayed was a love of good honest earth. 'I hope they pay you well.'

'The job takes me away from my own lovely garden for far too much of the time,' said Komorowski. 'This is a small compensation. *Il faut cultiver* and all that. Anything I can ever do to assist you, Mr Pascoe, just ask.'

Pascoe watched him walk away.

A friend, he thought. I've found a friend. I think.

He returned to the cellar where his new colleagues greeted him once more without comment and for the rest of the day he worked steadily, conscientiously and unfruitfully through the files. Perhaps this truly was important work. He didn't know. And he didn't care. It wasn't providing him with any good reason for giving up the comforts of home.

Midway through the afternoon, there was a diversion. The phone rang. Rod answered it. What he heard made him look serious for a moment. He said 'Good Lord. Right. On it already.'

He put the phone down and said, 'Someone's tried to off Sheikh Ibrahim.'

Sheikh Ibrahim Al-Hijazi was Imam of a Bradford mosque who ever since the 7/7 bombings had been a regular tabloid target. He had long been known for his extreme views, and though he never openly condoned the actions of terrorist groups, he never condemned them either. He had a band of devoted followers, mostly young men, at his mosque. Several of them had been investigated under suspicion of complicity in terrorist acts, but the nearest any had come to a formal charge was when one of them had been arrested in Pakistan and subsequently vanished into American custody. Al-Hijazi was personable and articulate and so far had displayed great dexterity in staying just the right side of all the laws, old and new, under which the tabloids howled for his head. His reaction of measured outrage to the Mazraani killing had been expressed in terms which were perfectly reasonable and perfectly calculated to send the right-wing press into a spasm of apoplectic indignation.

'What happened?' demanded Pascoe, excited

at the possibility of there being some real police-work here for him to get his teeth into.

In fact the story turned out to be almost dull. The Sheikh had left the mosque after the *Zuhr* or midday prayer to keep an appointment in Huddersfield some twenty miles away. As the car eased its way into the traffic flow on a nearby main road, the passengers heard a sharp crack as though a passing vehicle had thrown up a stone which had hit the side. The driver hadn't stopped, but when they reached their destination he had checked the paintwork for damage. What he found was a small hole punched through the cover of one of the rear lights. And closer exam-ination revealed a bullet lodged inside.

'We'll get a look at it eventually, but first reports from Bradford suggest it's from a small-calibre pistol, fired at almost the limit of its range,' concluded the young man.

'Not the kind of weapon you'd expect a well-organized assassination team to use at a distance,' said Pascoe. 'Any claim being made? By these Templars, for instance?'

'Not a sound so far,' said Rod cheerfully. 'But it's early days. Meanwhile, just in case there is any connection, they want us to put the details into our search profile.'

So, thought Pascoe, no excitement, just another layer of dull futility.

At five thirty he was back at Glenister's door but he found it still locked.

Frustrated, he turned away and saw the superintendent coming through the door at the far end of the corridor, deep in conversation with Freeman.

When she noticed him she didn't look delighted but she summoned up a smile as she approached and greeted him.

Close up he could see that she looked worn out, but he stamped hard on the little flutter of sympathy.

'Can I have a word, ma'am?' he said, formally.

'I'm a bit stretched, laddie,' she said. 'Could it wait till morning?'

'No,' he said. 'It could not.'

Freeman gave him a get-you look.

'A few seconds then. Dave, I'll be with you shortly.'

She unlocked her door and he followed her into the office. She didn't sit down herself, nor invite him to sit.

'So how can I help you, Peter?' she asked.

'You can find me something useful to do,' he retorted.

'But you are doing something extremely useful . . .'

He snorted. His wife was a very good snorter, Dalziel could snort for Denmark, even Wield who rarely let any uncensored emotion escape had been known to aspirate expressively, but the snort hadn't figured much in the sonic range of a man sometimes referred to by his fat boss as Pussy-Foot Pascoe, the Tight-Rope Dancer.

Now, however, it emerged as if he'd been a snorter from birth; equine rather than porcine in nature, it was true, but powerful and unambiguous for all that.

'Useful? I've spent time more usefully reading Martin Amis,' he sneered. 'If you really want to marginalize me, why don't you just send me to the seaside and ask me to count grains of sand?'

Glenister looked concerned.

'Peter, I'm sorry, but in fact that's what a lot of our work here feels like. You get used to it. The first five years are usually the worst.'

She gave the sweet maternal smile she could have sold to a renaissance artist sketching his next *Madonna and Child*. He responded with the this-is-no-laughing matter-these-are-my-feelings-you're-crapping-on grimace he'd learned from his daughter.

Freeman stuck his head round the door. The bastard had probably been listening.

'Sandy, Bernie's just buzzed me. He's waiting . . .'

'On my way. Sorry, Peter,' said Glenister, urging him through the door, 'I'd like to talk more, but when master calls . . . Tell you what, you look a bit tired. We mustn't forget what you went through. Why don't you take tomorrow morning off, have a lie-in, take a stroll around, see the sights? Let's meet for a sandwich at the Mozart, one o'clock, and then we can work out how best to put that mighty brain to work, eh?'

He watched her as she hurried away down the

corridor. He felt excluded. Not that there was any reason he should be included in what was presumably a debriefing on the Carradice trial, or a briefing on the Sheikh Ibrahim assassination attempt, but at the moment the building felt like it was full of doors which were firmly shut against him.

Then it occurred to him that there was one door not firmly shut. Glenister had forgotten to lock her office.

If they were going to treat him as a sort of licensed intruder, maybe it was time to start acting like one.

The corridor was empty. He pushed open the door and went back inside.

He had no idea what he hoped to find. Maybe some file or memo relating to himself and what they were really doing with him here. But what he was really doing was obeying another of Dalziel's dicta: 'Whatever chances the good Lord gives you, take 'em, and ask questions later!'

He recalled once being shown into Dan Trimble's office with Dalziel. The Chief would be along in a minute, his secretary had assured them. The second the door closed behind her, Dalziel had started opening desk drawers. Catching sight of Pascoe's disapproving expression, the Fat Man had grinned and recited, 'How doth the little busy bee improve each shining hour. Hello, what have we here?'

All he'd had was a bottle of twelve-year-old Glen Morangie, from which he'd taken a generous slug before his early-warning sensors had sent him back to his chair, ready to greet Trimble with a broad smile of welcome a few seconds later.

I could do with a drink, thought Pascoe.

He started on the desk drawers. There were only three, two shallow, one deep. The deep one was locked. The shallow ones produced nothing more interesting than a selection of pencils and some chocolate biscuits. Smarties were never going to be enough for a woman of her build, specially with the promised demise of the blue ones.

He looked at the deep drawer. In for a penny, in for a pound. From his wallet he extracted a small leather envelope containing various slim pieces of metal. Many CID officers carried such a piece of kit, which had usually been offered in evidence during a burglary case and then somehow not returned to the police store. So far the most felonious use Pascoe had put it to was removing a wheel clamp one dark and stormy night when there wasn't a taxi to be had for two hours.

Compared to a clamp, this lock was a doddle.

The drawer, despite its depth, contained nothing more than a slim plastic file, but this turned out to be potential treasure. Across the cover in Glenister's bold hand were scrawled the words *Mill Street*. There were about a dozen sheets inside, paper-clipped together in five or six sections. No time for more than a glance now. Every second he stayed here put him in danger of discovery. For all he knew, given the paranoid nature of the establishment, he was already being filmed!

He selected two sections of two sheets, one containing the explosive-analysis report that not even the electronic legerdemain of Edgar Wield had been able to extract, while the other had something to do with the examination of the bodies taken from Number 3.

He took the sheets to the fax machine standing by the wall and ran them through the copy facility. Then, after carefully using his handkerchief to wipe his prints off everything he'd touched, he replaced the file, relocked the drawer, and made his escape.

As he deposited his security badge at the desk in the foyer and headed for the exit, he felt as if he were trailing visible clouds of guilt. He didn't relax till he reached his hotel room. Even here his sense of safety might be delusive. It was, after all, CAT who'd booked him in. But at least, he told himself as he plucked a bottle of Becks from the mini-bar and settled down in the deep soft armchair, they weren't penny pinching.

It took little more than a glance at the explosive analysis to convince him he'd need a friendly technical eye to make any sense out of it.

He turned to the second pair of sheets.

This was more accessible. It contained everything about cause of death and identification factors that he'd heard verbatim from Glenister in her briefings. But there were references to other findings and their attendant hypotheses which after a while he realized must have been contained in a separate report. So far as he could make out, it had something to do with position of limbs and examination of mouth cavities.

The thought that this too might have been in the plastic file made him annoyed for not taking more time to check while he'd had the chance. At least he'd been clever enough to instruct Wield to have a quiet chat first with Jim Lipton, the CFO, then with Mary Goodrich, the pathologist at Mid-Yorkshire Central into whose care the burnt corpses had been placed for a short while before CAT whisked them away. Pity that the Head of the Path Department, 'Troll' Longbottom, had been away on vacation. Troll was an old mate of Dalziel's and the personal link would have made him co-operative. Goodrich was new in the job. Her appointment as Longbottom's assistant was her first big career step, leaving her very susceptible to the kinds of pressure CAT had probably exerted upon her.

On the other hand, Edgar Wield had a definite way with women. Andy Dalziel had no problem analysing it.

He's bent as a lavatory brush, he's got a face like that battered old teddy bear most women love more than their kids, and he could sell a fish a bicycle.

Pascoe smiled at the memory as he helped himself to another Becks. Yes, Wieldy would get to the bottom of things. He'd warned the sergeant not to ring till evening. In the Lubyanka walls had ears. But any moment now . . .

His phone rang. He checked the caller display. He was right.

'Wieldy,' he said. 'You come upon your hour, bearing good news, I hope.'

'Don't know about that,' said the sergeant. 'I spoke to Jim Lipton like you said.'

Wield filled him in on his conversation with CFO.

'Excellent,' said Pascoe. 'If you got as much out of Goodrich, I may have to pay the bribe and make you a lord.'

Wield, happy to hear his friend sounding so like his old self, wished he could continue the good work, but there was no point wrapping it up.

He said, 'Sorry. Got nowt there. Turned up unannounced like you suggested. She didn't look busy, but soon as she got a whiff what I were talking about, she suddenly became far too busy to talk. When I pressed her, I got a reminder that I was nowt but a sergeant and mebbe ought to have a word with my superiors afore I bothered her again.'

'Stuck-up cow!' said Pascoe. 'And I thought she was OK the only time I met her.'

'Nay, Pete,' said Wield. 'I reckon she's running scared. She's been seriously warned off talking about the Mill Street bodies.'

'Yeah? I'd have liked to see them warn Troll

Longbottom off. He'd have got so mad, he'd have called a press conference.'

'Maybe. But being mad only lasts till bedtime. Being scared is what's waiting for you when you wake up alone in the middle of the night.'

There was a personal note here that Pascoe on another occasion might have wanted to examine more closely, but at the moment he had no time for distractions. At least this confirmed his reading of the CAT report. There really was something to hide.

'So, anything else, Wieldy?' he said.

'Not really. No change on Andy. And I saw Ellie this morning. We bumped into each other and had a coffee.'

'*Bumped* like a real shunt, or like on the dodgems?' said Pascoe suspiciously.

'I think she was glad to have a chat,' said Wield. 'I reckon she's worried about you. We all are. Pete, where the hell is all this going?'

'I'm just earning my pay, Wieldy. Which incidentally wouldn't run to staying in this place. I've got a bathroom bigger than our sitting room!'

Wield, recognizing this as a cut-off, said, 'Listen, Pete, don't get too used to the high life. We've got Ernie Ogilby sitting in Andy's office. If you could solve crimes by studying traffic flow, we'd have the best clear-up rate in the UK!'

'Inspector French solved a lot by studying train timetables,' said Pascoe.

'French? Don't know him. What's his patch?'

'The past,' said Pascoe. 'They did things differently there. Cheers.'

He put the phone down, wondering what had brought Inspector French into his mind. It was years since he'd read any of the books.

He went downstairs and enjoyed his excellent dinner. He didn't mind dining alone in a restaurant. There was an infinity of entertainment to be derived from working out the relationship between and back-stories of the other diners.

Afterwards he took a turn round the block then went up to his room, climbed into his emperor-sized bed, imagined what it would be like if Ellie were there to explore it with him, rang her and shared his imaginings, remarked but did not remark upon the fact that she didn't mention her meeting with Wield, then switched on the TV and watched one of those English heritage movies which drifts like a slow cloud across a summer landscape till at some point indistinguishable from any other point he mingled with the movie and fell fast asleep.

5

all the way home

'Hugh.'

'Bernard.'

'De Clairvaux.'

'De Payens.'

one thousand two thousand three thousand

'Hugh, have you heard? Someone took a pot-shot at the Sheikh.'

'Yes, it was on the news. Nothing to do with us, unless of course we've inspired some right-thinking but inept copy-cat.'

'A copy-cat using one of Andre's guns, from the look of it.'

'*What?*'

'It's not absolutely sure. The round our persistent friend Pascoe dug out of Mill Street was very badly damaged, but what few scorings were detectable coincide precisely with those on the Sheikh's bullet. Can Andre be freelancing?'

'Not his style. Also, if he'd decided to grandstand, the Sheikh would be dead. But I'll check it out.'

'Do. Al-Hijazi is on our list, but after this he's likely to take a lot more care. Another possibility is one of the Geoffreys.'

'Perhaps. But Andre's well trained. All weapons back to the armourer. Certainly with Bisol so uptight about the wounded pig, I doubt if he's going to go around blasting off wildly.'

'Perhaps not. Talking of pigs, anything yet on that other one?'

'Yes. Word is he'll be going wee-wee-wee all the way home tomorrow morning.'

6

an urban fox

Adolphus Hector woke up.

They say Fortune picks its favourites, but it also picks its fools. Hector had been on its hit-list ever since his premature birth and instant christening.

What caused his mother to pick the name Adolphus is not known. Perhaps some passing imp of mischief whispered it in her ear as the hospital chaplain asked her what she would like to call her son. Certainly the newborn had seemed such a weak and ailing child that no one present felt the name had other than a soteriological significance.

Perhaps the child's early arrival had caught his fairy godmother out too. Arriving at the christening too late to dispense the traditional baptismal presents, all she'd managed to slip under his pillow was the one gift without which all the others are useless anyway.

The instinct for survival.

Despite all pessimistic prognoses, Adolphus refused to die. When against all the odds he reached school age, he rapidly discovered the disadvantages of being called Adolphus. So when the first of many moves took him to a new school where his second name was assumed to be his first, he bore the mockery of *its* silliness with equanimity. At least Hector, as one kind teacher pointed out, was a hero and could be shortened to the very acceptable Hec, while Adolphus shrank only to the even less desirable Adolf.

If these bailiff-inspired moves were bad for his education, they did at least mean he was able to carry the lessons taught by peer persecution from one institution to the next. He even learned to hide the only skill he had that got within spitting distance of a talent, which was making recognizable portrait sketches in pencil. A child psychologist might have identified this as being associated with a relatively mild form of autism, but he rarely stayed anywhere long enough to be more than a flicker on a psychologist's laptop screen. Resenting equally his fellow pupils' efforts to involve him in producing caricature or pornography, and his teachers' efforts to persuade him to sketch subjects of their choice, he soon learned to conceal this tiny talent also. So it remained hidden and unexplored, personal, private, and a comfort only to himself.

Perhaps this ability to catch significant detail on paper was part of his equally hidden talent for survival. Like his pencil, it was a blunt instrument, consisting of little more than the capacity to select what was useful from what anyone said to him and ignore the rest. His choice of career arose from the baffled flippancy of a careers master who said, 'I don't know what to recommend, Hector. A life of petty crime, perhaps, only you're not qualified. Maybe you should try for the police!'

So he did. And his application, coming at a low point in recruitment figures, was accepted even though his academic qualifications were at the stretch-mark of minimal, his verbal skills were risible, and his self-presentation swung between the ridiculous and the pathetic. Marked down as a certain failure the instant most instructors set eyes on him, this certainty in fact protected him. Being convinced that the rigours of the course would by themselves cause him to drop out, they took no positive steps to get rid of him. This showed that they missed the essence of Hector. Show him the door and he would have gone. But not being shown the door he took as a positive, and not even being knocked back to redo most of his courses with the following intake could make him relent his first avowed intent to be a policeman. Eventually, in a prefiguration of his subsequent career, like a persistent mouse who survives both trap and poison, he ceased to be a pest in the college and became something of a pet. No one wanted to be known as the man who gave the coup de grâce to Hector.

And so, to everyone's amazement except his own, eventually he passed out of the training course and into Mid-Yorkshire legend.

That morning, as always after waking, Hector lay in bed for five minutes precisely. Then he arose. He did not need an alarm clock any more than a bird. He was on early turn this week, and this was the time he got up on earlies, and he would have been bewildered by any suggestion that he might awake earlier or later than he did.

Thirty minutes later, washed, fed and clothed, he opened the front door of the terrace in which he rented a bed-sitter with kitchenette and shared bathroom, and stepped out on to the pavement of the narrow suburban street which some civic ironist had christened Shady Grove. Despite the absence of trees, birds were singing as yet unchallenged by traffic noise, and at the end of the long terrace the tail of an urban fox, on its way home after a pretty successful night scavenging the discarded take-away trail from the Chinese chippie half a mile away, flounced round the corner.

The air held promise of another glorious summer day and Hector, not insensitive to natural impulses, had a Monsieur Hulot spring in his step as he strode along the pavement.

At some point he heard a car behind him, some distance away and travelling slowly, but unusual enough at this hour for Hector's well-tuned ear to detect it. Ahead at a T-junction, Shady Grove joined a slightly busier street with the equally unlikely name of Park Lane. At the junction, Hector turned as always to cross the Grove and proceed along the Lane. Normally this did not involve a pause, just a right turn of almost military precision, but today, aware of the car, he halted on the pavement to check its position.

It was a black Jaguar, only about twenty yards away now, but as it had come to a halt it offered no danger. Indeed, he saw the driver behind the tinted glass smile at him and gesture him to cross with a gloved hand.

He nodded acknowledgement and stepped out on to the roadway.

The car engine roared, the wheels span, rubber burned, and in a moment far too short for even a mind far sharper than Hector's to register alarm, the Jaguar had covered the twenty yards and flipped him so high into the air, it passed beneath him before he came crashing to the ground.

The car braked, slewing to a halt across Park Lane. The driver looked back at the inert figure through his rear window. It twitched. He engaged reverse gear. But before he could start reversing, a milk float came into view at the far end of Shady Grove.

Banging it into first, he sent the Jag racing away down Park Lane.

7

Sauron's eye

Across the Pennines in Lancashire, which hates to be outshone in any way by its eastern neighbour, the day dawned with the same bright promise that had greeted Hector.

Back in Yorkshire, such promises were usually kept, and when, after allowing himself an extra hour in bed, Pascoe finally strolled out of his hotel in search of the sights Glenister had advised him to see, he ignored Manchester's reputation for meteorological fickleness and didn't bother to carry a coat.

He was still looking for the first of the promised sights when a totally unharbinged volley of rain sent him diving into a doorway in search of cover.

He found himself at the entrance of what turned out to be a second-hand bookshop. Prominent in its dusty window display was a hefty leather-bound volume entitled *The Templar Knights*. The rain showing little sign of abating its attack, he went inside. At a rickety table sat a Woody Allen look-alike immersed, not too happily, in entering figures in a ledger. To Pascoe's request to take the book from the window he replied with the perfunctory nod of one whose mental addition has been interrupted.

Pascoe did a quick skip through the volume. An introductory chapter gave the background to the Order's foundation in a style even more pedagogic than Lukasz Komorowski's. The sumptuously illustrated book then went on to describe how the Order evolved into a fighting force of such wealth and resource, it came to be seen as a threat by many European states. The vows of poverty and obedience were self-evidently shattered, and rumour alleged that the vow of chastity was even more comprehensively disobeyed by acts of what were coyly described as 'unnatural congress'.

'Very nice volume that,' said a voice which was so George Formby that Pascoe had difficulty ascribing it to Woody Allen.

'Yes, indeed,' he said. 'How much is it?'

'Think I've marked it up at one seven five. You're not trade, are you?'

'Oh no,' said Pascoe, taken aback. 'Bit rich for my blood, I'm afraid.'

'I could let me arm be twisted for one fifty.'

'No, really, it's the subject matter I'm interested in more than the volume.'

'Oh yes?' said the man sniffily. 'Lot of interest

in that kind of stuff since that geezer Tom Brown became all the rage.'

'Dan Brown, I think you mean.'

'Do I? Anyway, result is there's any amount of paperbacks come out on the Templars and such like; there's a box over there, one quid fifty each or three for a fiver.'

'I think your mathematics may have gone astray,' said Pascoe smugly.

'Don't think so. Folk daft enough to buy three ought to pay more,' said the man.

Unwilling to be relegated to this group, Pascoe said, 'Actually, I do do a bit of collecting. Crime novels. I inherited several first-edition Christies a few years back, and I try to fill in the gaps when I can.'

'Is that right? Sorry, don't think I've anything of the old lady's that might interest you, but I do have a Freeman Wills Crofts. *Death of a Train*. First edition, Hodder and Stoughton 1946, fine, with a fine jacket, just a couple of tiny nicks, nothing more. Snip at two fifty. Like a look?'

He didn't wait for an answer but, something in Pascoe's reaction clearly giving him hope of a sale, he went to fetch the volume.

Pascoe stared down at the picture of a locomotive and a railwayman which formed the cover design, but what he was really looking at, and what had caused him to react, was the name. Or rather the names. Particularly in conjunction with the title.

Freeman. Wills. Crofts.

Death of a Train.

The firm of patent agents at Number 6 Mill Street had been Crofts & Wills.

And of course there was Dave Freeman . . .

Coincidence? What was it the Gospel According to St Andy said?

Bump into your best mate coming out of the Black Bull, that's coincidence. Bump into him coming out of your wife's bedroom, that's co-respondence.

'Yes, it's a really nice volume,' said Woody Allen, mistaking his raptness for interest in the book. 'Could cut my own throat and do it for two.'

'No, I'm sorry, I'm really just a Christie man,' said Pascoe. 'Thanks anyway.'

Pausing only to purchase a paperback on the Templars from the bargain box (which as an act of atonement the proprietor clearly rated on a par with Becket's murderers dropping a couple of groats into the poor box as they left the cathedral), he resumed his drift round the city. A shaft or two of watery sunlight tried to lure him into the middle of a park, far from shelter, but he was too smart for that and when the next downpour came, he was only a dash away from the Café Mozart where Glenister had arranged to meet him. There was a good hour to go before the appointment, but his bad leg was twingeing and a sit-down with a drink seemed very attractive.

The place had gone for an old-fashioned Central European feel – waiters with long aprons, newspapers in wooden holders, lots of urns and ferns to hide behind, the air filled with Viennese waltz muzak which probably had Mozart turning in his pauper's grave.

Spooks must feel very much at home here, he thought as he helped himself to a *Guardian*, sank into a low sofa, and ordered a coffee.

The thought seemed to act as a conjuration.

'Pascoe, that you? Thought it was.'

He looked up to see Bernie Bloomfield staring down at him. Perhaps the lowness of his seat exaggerated the man's height, but he felt like a wandering hobbit who has inadvertently attracted the attention of Sauron's distant eye. At a more accessible level he could see Lukasz Komorowski loitering in the background.

'Hello, sir,' he said.

Bloomfield folded himself on to the sofa and became Alastair Sim again.

'How are you, Peter?' he asked solicitously. 'Looking a bit peaky, if you don't mind me saying. That was a terrible ordeal for you. You sure you're over it?'

'I'm fine, sir,' said Pascoe firmly.

'Good, good. And Andy Dalziel, anything new there?'

'Not yet.'

Komorowski, he noted, had found another table and was examining a potted fern with a phytographic intensity, or perhaps he was just checking for concealed mikes.

'Never despair. If I know my Andy he'll open

178

his eyes one of these days and start demanding to know what's been done about finding the bastards that put him there.'

'And we'll be able to give him the good news that they're all dead,' said Pascoe.

'That's right. Regrettably, of course.'

'Regrettably?'

'No intelligence from dead bodies, Pascoe. I'm sure you understand that. Andy certainly would.'

'Yes sir. Though he might find it a bit harder to understand why Dave Freeman had been allowed to set up a covert surveillance operation in Mill Street without tipping him the wink. He's very territorial.'

If Bloomfield had reacted with Alastair Sim's expression of polite bafflement, Pascoe would have had a lot of backtracking explanation and apology to do.

Instead he didn't know whether to feel pleased or fearful when the man nodded and murmured, 'Sandy told you about that, did she?'

Finessing the commander might be clever, but he doubted if it was wise. And a direct lie was certainly a folly too far.

'I half worked it out myself, sir,' said Pascoe with cautious ambiguity. 'Crofts & Wills. Not the smartest of cover names.'

'One of young Dave's whims. He quite likes Willis and Hardy too. I must have a word with him. But before you start getting hot under the collar, remember I'm still a cop. I know how

179

important to morale these things are, so it's rule number one on my watch: the local force must always be kept in the loop. On a need-to-know basis, of course. In this instance, Dan Trimble needed to know, but for the moment Andy didn't.'

'Mr Trimble knew about Number 6 but didn't tell the super?' said Pascoe, unable to hide his surprise which came close to amazement. He'd always had a lot of respect for the chief constable. Whether this news increased it or reduced it, he wasn't yet sure.

'It was very low key at that stage. Oroc Video was rated as nothing more than a talking shop, then we got a hint it might be changing up. Crofts and Wills was really just a precautionary cover in case we later needed to set up a real surveillance op.'

'And there was no one there when the explosion happened?'

'No, thank God. Bank Holiday, remember? Someone going in and out of a patents agency would have looked distinctly odd, wouldn't it? Of course, the minute we'd made it fully operational, the Mill Street flagging would have been upgraded and all relevant senior officers in Mid-Yorkshire would have been notified.'

'But it hadn't been upgraded yet, because Wills, or was it Crofts, happened to miss a huge delivery of Semtex?'

'It wasn't all that huge in terms of sheer bulk, Peter. Nothing that couldn't have passed for a couple of boxes of videos. But, yes, missing it was unfortunate.'

'*Unfortunate?*' echoed Pascoe derisively. 'You really shouldn't be so hard on Crofts, or was it Wills, sir? Maybe the stuff had been delivered on an earlier Bank Holiday. Or a Sunday. Do CAT teams get Sundays off too?'

Long before he finished, the old Pascoe diplomat in him was whispering *cool it!* but his voice was drowned by the new Dalziel thunder.

Bloomfield rose slowly.

'I understand why you feel upset, Pascoe. This is a bad business and I'm sorry you got sucked into it, but no one's to blame here, except the enemy. Talk of poor intelligence, or instructions not being followed, just confuses the issue. If the worst happens and Andy dies, I'd like him to be remembered as a hero. Enjoy your stay with us. I'm sure you can make a contribution.'

He rested his hand lightly on Pascoe's shoulder, then went to join Komorowski, who was already drinking coffee and eating a large cream cake with a fork.

Whoops, thought Pascoe. Really got the eye of Sauron on me now. Maybe I should have kept my mouth shut like a wise little hobbit.

Bloomfield took a seat with his back to Pascoe's table. As Komorowski poured him coffee from a tall cream-and-blue glazed pot with a metal top, the commander took out a mobile and keyed a number.

Pascoe raised the *Guardian* and started to read an article about pollution. Government policies were ineffective, it claimed. Opposition suggestions, it mocked, were idiotic. What was needed, it implied, was someone as wise as the article's author who had answers to problems the politicians hadn't even got questions for.

Plonker, thought Pascoe. He looked for the sport section. It was on a separate holder. Perhaps they couldn't find wood strong enough to bear the weight of a whole newspaper these days. The commander, he noted, had finished his call.

He'd only managed a couple of paras when his own phone rang.

It was Glenister.

'Peter,' she said. 'Sorry, but I can't make our date. Something's come up.'

I bet it has, thought Pascoe.

'Oh yes? Anything I can help with?'

'I wish. On my way to Nottingham. The wheels are coming off in the Carradice trial.'

Great! thought Pascoe. Having a condemned terrorist in the family wasn't a pleasant prospect. He kept the relief out of his voice as he said, 'What's happened?'

'One of our witnesses has done a runner, some of our best evidence has been declared inadmissible, and the defence are pressing for a dismissal. I think they'll get it. Time for damage limitation.'

While your boss is relaxing with a *Kaffee mit Schlag*, thought Pascoe. Why wasn't he on the job?

182

Because damage limitation puts you in the fall-out area, came the answer.

Glenister was still talking.

'Look, laddie, no reason for you hang around here over the weekend. I'm sure that lovely wife of yours is missing you like hell. Why don't you head back to sunny Yorkshire this afternoon, take the weight off your feet? I'll be in touch Sunday evening, first thing Monday at the latest. Got to rush now. Bye.'

Pascoe put the phone back in his pocket. Komorowski glanced his way and said something to Bloomfield, who turned, smiled and nodded encouragingly, as if he had overheard what Glenister had just said.

Probably didn't need to. OK, no reason to doubt Glenister was on her way to Nottingham, but he suspected the idea to send him back to Yorkshire came from somewhere a lot closer.

Sauron was doing a bit of damage limitation after all.

There was little resentment in the thought.

How could he resent a manoeuvre which sent him home to the people he loved most in the world?

8

now it's safe

At three o'clock that afternoon in Nottingham Crown Court after a series of delaying tactics that would have made Fabius Cunctator seem impetuous, the prosecution finally admitted defeat and shortly afterwards Abbas Asir, né Michael Carradice, stepped down from the dock a free man.

As George Stainton, his solicitor, shook his hand, no emotion showed on what could be seen of his client's face behind a vigorous black beard which, extending halfway down his chest, made his stocky body seem even shorter.

A court official approached and courteously invited Mr Asir to accompany him to go through the formalities of processing him out of the system and returning to him the personal possessions removed when he was taken into custody some six months earlier.

'I'll step outside and keep the media happy,' said the lawyer. 'You're sure you want to talk to them, Abbas?'

Carradice nodded.

'You will be careful what you say? Mustn't give the buggers any excuse to take you back into custody.'

The two men parted.

Stainton went out of the main entrance of the court building to be greeted by a media pack which began howling and yelping when they saw he was alone.

'Mr Asir will join me shortly,' he assured them. 'Yes, he will be happy to answer questions. Meanwhile, if I may offer my own reactions to the trial and its outcome . . .'

He began a carefully rehearsed statement in which the terms *dodgy intelligence, rule of law, police state, historical freedoms, free speech etc, etc,* occurred frequently, in fact rather more frequently than rhetoric demanded as his client's non-appearance obliged him to recycle his declaration of human rights to fill in the time.

The pack members, scenting a deception, were beginning to snarl once more.

Finally the solicitor excused himself and went back into the building.

The court official who had approached them earlier assured him that the formalities of release had been completed at least ten minutes ago. His last sighting of Mr Asir had been as he left the room, presumably heading to the main entrance to celebrate his freedom.

Stainton could only speculate that his client had

changed his mind about meeting the gentlemen of the press and found another way out of the building. Doubting if he could persuade these same gents that he hadn't been party to the deception, and realizing that even if he succeeded all he would be doing was making himself look a fool, the solicitor decided his best option was to follow his client's example.

Several of the more persistent pack members were already waiting for him at his office and in the end he had to tell his switchboard not to accept any more calls unless they were certain of the identity of the caller.

He rang home to warn his wife. She told him rather irritably that there were already journalists camped outside the gate with a few bolder ones poking around in the greenhouse and the garden, clearly suspecting that Asir might have taken refuge there.

He told her not to speak to them and when he finally headed home it was with some natural trepidation at the prospect of the welcome he was about to receive both outside and inside his house.

But to his surprise and relief as he drove into the pleasant dormer village where he lived, he could spot no sign of alien life around the gateway of his mock-Georgian villa, and his wife confirmed that ten minutes earlier they had all suddenly got into their cars and headed off with much burning of rubber.

'I told you not to worry,' he told her rather

pompously. 'The good thing about our media is that, like children, they have a very short attention span. All that it takes to soothe away the pain of a disappointment is the promise of another bigger treat. Now I think I've earned a large G and T.'

As he busied himself preparing the drinks, his wife turned on the television to catch the early-evening local news programme.

'Oh, look, George,' she said. 'Isn't that the mere?'

As ardent birdwatchers, one of the attractions of their house for the Staintons was its proximity to a large reservoir with a thriving population of both resident and visiting waterfowl.

'There's something going on there,' said Mrs Stainton. 'I do hope they're not disturbing the greylags.'

Stainton turned to look at the picture. The camera was panning over crowds of people on the reedy banks of the reservoir. He recognized some of them. The disappearance of the reporters was now explained. He'd been right about the promise of a bigger treat and here they all were, thronging the banks in anticipation of it.

The sound was turned down low but he thought he caught the name Carradice and suddenly he felt a vague unease. He took a sip from his glass, topped it up with gin and went to sit down next to his wife.

'Turn up the volume, will you?' he said.

The commentator was explaining, clearly not for the first time, that every main media outlet had received a message suggesting that anyone concerned about the outcome of the Carradice trial should go to the reservoir where they might find something of interest.

The camera now moved to give a shot out across the water.

About sixty yards from the edge floated what looked like an inflatable rubber dinghy with a short mast and a loosely hanging sail. A motor boat full of uniformed policemen was speeding towards it. But the camera was quicker, zooming in close.

There seemed to be something in the dinghy, but its alignment in relation to the camera made it hard to be certain what. Then a puff of breeze swung the vessel round.

'Look at those poor grebes,' said his wife indignantly as birds rose from the surface to avoid the motor boat speeding through them.

'Oh shit,' said the solicitor.

Lolling in the dinghy with one arm trailing in the water was a man, his mouth agape, his eyes wide and staring. He had a thick black beard that stretched halfway down his chest.

The camera moved slowly up the mast, which turned out not to be a real mast but an oar or paddle propped upright. And the sail wasn't a real sail but some sort of banner with words printed on it, illegible until another puff of wind straightened it out above the reservoir's dark blue water, revealing it as the kind of swallow-tail guidon that might have fluttered above a troop of medieval knights galloping into battle. The resemblance didn't end there. At the broad end of the pennant in bright red was painted the cross of St George.

Alongside it were some words, block capitals in black. It took a little time for the camera and the wind to make these readable, but when they were, the solicitor emptied his gin and tonic in a single gulp.

NOW IT'S SAFE!

Part Four

A man that looks on glasse,
On it may staye his eye,
Or if he pleaseth, through it pass . . .

George Herbert, 'The Elixer'

1

the shock of recognition

Andy Dalziel is having an out-of-body experience.

How he knows this is different from dancing with Tottie Truman in the old Mirely Mecca or tumbling like a pigeon in the bright air high over Mid-Yorkshire, he isn't sure, but that small core of awareness which preserves the self even in the wildest dreams and the scariest nightmares detects the difference.

Perhaps it's the fact that he can see himself? A man doesn't dream himself, does he? And if you can see your own body, then it is self-evident that you are out of it.

The body in question lies supine on a bed. It has tubes and wires connected to it. What it is doing there the Dalziel consciousness floating above it has neither the capacity nor the inclination to enquire, but it does have the critical power to remark that it's not a pretty sight. If anything, it reminds him of the carcase of a beached whale he once saw near Flamborough.

And that had been dead three days.

A couple of nurses are working on the hulk, cleaning it, anointing it, checking the inlets and outlets of the various tubes. Their purpose he has no curiosity about, but he feels sorry that such a pretty pair of lasses should have nothing better to do with their time than administer to this slab of unattractive flesh.

He moves away. It's easy. No need to fart this time, no question of effort, hardly even of volition. This is very different from the pigeon-tumbling which his dream self so enjoyed. Then his fecund fancy created for himself the physical delight of flight – air streaming over the limbs like water over a swimmer, the exhilaration of the swoop, the serenity of the soar – just as the same fancy recreated the voluptuous softness of Tottie Truman's flesh . . .

Now however there is no physicality. Flesh was that hulk on the bed. Good riddance to it.

He drifts through other rooms full of beds on which lie men and women in all sorts of conditions, some comatose, some in pain, some sitting upright, bright-eyed and impatient for their time of escape, some with visitors whom they find delightful, debilitating or downright depressing in equal proportions.

And then he penetrates into a small ward with only two beds in it, one empty, one occupied by a figure who looks strangely familiar.

He hovers above it, trying to arrange those

sleep-blanked features into a pattern with a name.

Suddenly the eyes open wide.

The woken face makes identification easy.

But there's something more, something unexpected in those eyes, something which shocks Dalziel.

They belong to Constable Hector, and they look as if they're actually seeing him.

He doesn't wait to check this out but flees like a ghost at daybreak back to the welcome unconsciousness of the beached whale.

2

Rule Five

If being in your friends' thoughts is truly a form of survival, then Andy Dalziel needn't have had any fears, for hardly a minute went by without someone somewhere in Mid-Yorkshire having occasion to think of him.

Some thought of him with affection, with tears, even with prayer. Others with a quiet satisfaction that one great obstacle to their hopes and dreams had been removed. The triggers of memory were many and varied. The drawing of a pint of beer, a simple turn of phrase, the distant slamming of a door, the shadow of a cloud drifting across a hillside, a dog lying in the sun and scratching itself contentedly.

And sometimes it was a situation that brought into the minds of those who knew him best one of those philosophical truths with which the Marcus Aurelius of Mid-Yorkshire from time to time condescended to improve their lives.

Such a maxim popped into Peter Pascoe's mind

on his return home that Friday evening.

According to the Great Sage Dalziel, the fifth rule of marriage was, *Never give your wife a surprise she doesn't know about.*

'The first four rules,' he'd gone on to explain, 'aren't allowed to be writ down, else no man would ever get married.'

Pascoe had broken Rule Five by deciding to turn up at home unannounced. Alongside a conventional male fantasy of the possible delectable consequences of taking Ellie unawares, he had a good rational reason for his decision. There were things he needed to do in Mid-Yorkshire and he didn't know how long they might take. To ring Ellie and say, 'Hello, darling, I've got the rest of the day off so why don't you slip into something comfortable like our bed, I'll be back as soon as I can,' was one thing. To ring and say, 'Hello, darling, I've got the rest of the day off but there's stuff I want to do which I rate more important than heading straight home,' was quite another.

As his various diversions occupied several hours, his decision seemed quite a wise one as he pulled into his driveway at shortly after six. The evening stretched out invitingly before him. There'd be only the two of them. Friday night was stopover night. Rosie and a couple of classmates were spending it with their friend Mandy Pulman whose mother Jane was taking them ice-skating in the morning, thus guaranteeing the long lie-in he was hoping would prove necessary.

He opened the front door quietly. Tig came to meet him. Happily he greeted everyone silently except for Rosie, and Pascoe rewarded his restraint with a pat on the head. The downstairs rooms were unoccupied but he heard a sound upstairs. This got better. Perhaps she was having a shower. Or taking a nap. His fantasy was in full flight now and he tiptoed up the stairs, anticipating melting into her dream as the rose blendeth its odour with the violet. Ahead was the bedroom door, ajar. Gently he pushed it open.

Ellie was sitting at her dressing table, applying lipstick. She saw him in the glass. Those rich dark eyes and those deep incarnadined lips rounded in surprise.

She said, 'Oh shit.'

This wasn't quite the greeting he'd hoped for, but creeping up on her had been pretty infantile so he made allowances, which was easy as she looked gorgeous.

'Sorry,' he said. 'Should have rung, but here I am anyway.'

He went to her and they kissed. It was a pretty good kiss, but it didn't feel like it was going anywhere.

He said, 'Had a hard day, love?' he hoped sympathetically, as she pulled away and started repairing her make-up.

'Not really. Peter, it's great to have you home, but I've just arranged to go out.'

'Oh,' he said. 'Can't you unarrange?'

'No, not really. Sorry, but this is big. They want me on *Fidler's Three*. Tonight.'

Fidler's Three was the current big-hit television talk show. Each week its host, Joe Fidler, invited three guests to join him in a different venue to discuss matters of current interest before a participating audience. *Fidler's Three* had two gimmicks that made it very popular. First, no politicians, journalists or A-list personalities were permitted on the panel. Second, at the start of each show a list of debating clichés scrolled down the screen starting with the old favourites – *level playing field, at the end of the day, with great respect, hard-working families, etc* – then moving on to the latest arrivals. Guests undertook to make a donation of fifty pounds to a charity of Fidler's choice each time they used any of these, a slip marked by a recorded voice crying, 'Order! Order!' above a cacophony of zoo sounds which were the signal for audience participation in the form of a barrage of multi-coloured ping-pong balls hurled at the offender.

Fidler himself was a personable young man who'd been a New Labour MP till 'the sheer meaningless gab of it' had driven him to resign and spend more time with his money by becoming a TV personality. He claimed that the only qualification needed by his guests was that they should be articulate and opinionated, but usually there turned out to be some kind of linking theme to his choice.

'A bit short notice, isn't it?' said Pascoe.

'Well, it's Ffion, actually,' said Ellie.

'Ah.'

Ffion Lyke-Evans was the press officer in charge of the publicity for Ellie's novel. Pascoe had met her at a signing in Leeds. Delayed, he'd entered the almost empty store twenty minutes late. Seeing Ellie's solitary figure sitting alongside a wall of unsold books, her desperate eyes giving the lie to her insouciant smile, he might have stolen quietly away if a seductive Welsh voice hadn't lilted into his ear, 'Hello, sir. Come for the signing, have you? It's a lovely book, you won't be able to put it down.'

She talked a good book, Pascoe had to admit. She was young and attractive, with long black hair, huge dark eyes, lips to suck men's souls with, and a winningly mischievous smile. Once Pascoe identified himself, she offered him twenty-five convincing reasons for the absence of punters. Pascoe was unpersuaded but noticed that Ellie, the arch-sceptic, hung on every spellbinding word uttered by the Welsh witch.

Her faith had been blunted a little by the subsequent silence of all branches of the literary media, but still, if invited to share a joke at Ffion's expense, she would insist the girl knew her job. And, despite his ingrained scepticism, Pascoe, whenever he spoke to Ffion, always found himself momentarily infected by her merry optimism.

Today it seemed all Ffion's skills had been put to the test. She had contrived to get one of her authors domiciled in the north-east on to *Fidler's Three* and had made the long journey north to smooth his path and calm his nerves. Then, just as she arrived in Middlesbrough, her mobile rang and she was told he couldn't make it, having been summoned to the sickbed of a near and dear relative.

Faced with the prospect of Joe Fidler's fury and the loss of her own credibility, she'd thought quickly. First she rang Ellie and explained the situation. Ellie's first novel launch hadn't been her finest hour, she admitted, which was why, she went on with scarcely a breath, she'd been really excited at this God-given chance to make up for past failings by offering Fidler Ellie's name.

'Not tentatively,' she told Ellie. 'TV doesn't do tentative. I told them you're wise, witty, and wacky, opinionated, assertive and articulate, and that you are a definite rising star, the next George Eliot, Virginia Woolf, Agatha Christie . . .'

'Agatha Christie?' queried Ellie indignantly.

'I could see they hadn't heard of the others,' said Ffion. 'So they're not surprised they haven't heard of you! But they're desperate to have you. Can you come?'

'Try to stop me!'

'Great. Grab a taxi and get yourself up here pronto! See you!'

Ffion Lyke-Evans broke the connection and punched in Joe Fidler's mobile number. She didn't think she'd been dishonest. In her job a simple temporal reorganization was a long way from a lie.

What would have been stupid was to sell Ellie to Joe and then discover she was on holiday. Of course if Fidler said, 'No way!' she'd have to ring Ellie back and invent a reason for disappointing her, but dealing with authors' disappointments was the first thing they taught you at publicist school. Anyway, she was sure that she had the arguments to persuade Fidler to accept Ellie as substitute.

'Hi, Joe,' she said. 'It's Ffion. Listen, I've got some rather bad news and some incredibly good news . . .'

And Peter Pascoe, cynical though he was about anything connected with the media, could not bring himself to voice any doubts when he saw that Ellie regarded this as incredibly good news too.

'So I can't ring back and tell Ffion I can't do it after all, can I?' she concluded.

'No, of course not,' he agreed. 'Who are the other guests, by the way?'

'No idea. No one knows who the three are going to be till show-time, not the audience, not even the guests. Which is good. No one will know I was a second choice!'

'And they'd find it hard to believe anyway,' he said gallantly.

She mouthed him a kiss.

'Thank you kindly,' she said. 'It's really great to know you'll be here when I get back. By the way, did you hear about Hector?'

'No. What's he done now? Got the Nobel Prize for Brain Surgery?'

'Not funny. The poor sod got knocked over this morning. Hit and run. Wieldy told me this afternoon when he rang to see how I was. He's OK, though.'

She told him the story.

'Poor bastard,' said Pascoe. 'If I'd known. I could have looked in on him earlier.'

'Earlier?'

'Yes,' said Pascoe, mentally kicking himself. 'I called in at the hospital to see how Andy was.'

It was, like the best lies, only half a lie. He had certainly called at the hospital, but his enquiry about the Fat Man had been an afterthought made on the internal phone.

Ellie, though susceptible to her press officer's blandishments, had been a detective's wife long enough to have developed a sensor for evasions.

'Funny no one mentioned Hector,' she said.

'I was hardly there a moment,' he said. 'I was in a hurry to get home, remember?'

Oh, you'll pay for this in the next life, he thought. In fact, as the door bell rang, he acknowledged he was paying for it now.

'That will be my taxi,' said Ellie. 'Just think what that's going to cost the bastards. They must really want me! Listen, Pete, it's just struck me, why not come along? I'm sure they can find you a seat in the audience.'

Pascoe thought about it then shook his head.

'No,' he said, 'I've done enough travelling for one day and I'm pretty bushed. I'll just sit here and watch a bit of telly. I expect I'll fall asleep. There's never anything interesting to see on a Friday night, is there?'

She gave him a hard jab in the ribs.

'Don't wait up,' she said. 'I can always wake you if I want anything. Which I wouldn't be surprised if I do.'

'I'll take that as a promise,' he said.

They smiled at each other lovingly. Then Pascoe spoiled it by saying, 'Ellie, be careful if Fidler tries to get you talking about the terrorist threat, that kind of thing . . .'

'Because of my connection with you, you mean?' said Ellie. 'Pete, why can't you get it into your head that in most people's eyes I'm not defined by the fact that I'm married to a cop? They value me for what I am, what I do. And I made it quite clear to Ffion when my novel came out that I didn't want any reference to the fact that you were a cop. OK, she may have hyped me up a bit to get me on the show, but it's Eleanor Soper the novelist they're interested in, not Ellie Pascoe the demure little policeman's wife!'

'Hey, when do I get to meet *her*?' said Pascoe. 'Sorry. You're dead right, of course. It was a silly thing to say. Put it down to resentment at not being able to get any closer to you than ten million other people this evening.'

'Ten million? Is that all?' said Ellie. '*Ciao!*'

She was smiling again, so that was all right.

And he'd deserved the reproach, thought Pascoe

as he watched the taxi pull away. He was just going to have to get used to having a celebrity wife. Eventually.

Back in the house, Pascoe made himself a sandwich, opened a can of lager and sat down in front of the telly. There was still an hour and a half to go before *Fidler's Three*.

He picked up the phone and rang Wield.

'Hi, it's me,' he said. 'I'm home.'

Briefly he explained, then said, 'Ellie told me about Hector. What happened?'

'Sounds like he did his usual trick of stepping off a pavement without looking.'

'Yes. Hard to blame the driver.'

'You can blame the bastard for not stopping,' said Wield. 'A milkman found Hector unconscious.'

'How did he know? Sorry. Ellie says he's OK though.'

'Yes. If it had been serious I'd have rung you. He's bruised and battered but mostly unbroken. They were worried about brain damage – don't say a thing – but eventually they realized that what they'd got was normal and unhooked him from all the life-support stuff. Can't recall a thing, of course. The milkman saw a car pulling away, black he thinks, powerful, maybe a Jag. Paddy's had his boys doing house-to-house in case anyone heard or saw owt. Anyway, are you back with us for good, do you think, or have you made yourself indispensable in Manchester?'

'Who knows?' said Pascoe. He would have

liked to talk things over with Wield, but he found
he was too paranoiac to trust his own home
phone.

He said, 'Let's meet for a jar tomorrow, Wieldy.
The Feathers, early evening, suit you? Meanwhile,
don't forget to tune in to *Fidler's Three.'*

'Wouldn't miss Ellie for worlds,' said Wield.

If I'd got home an hour earlier, there wouldn't
have been anything to miss, thought Pascoe
glumly.

He opened his briefcase and took out the slim
file in which he was recording his very unofficial
investigation into the Mill Street explosion. He
started making notes of his afternoon's work in
an effort to assess whether it got anywhere close
to being worth the loss of his wife's company.

He wasn't betting on it.

3

Hectoring

Pascoe's first port of call on returning to town had
been the Civic Centre. In the Housing Office there
he had talked to a woman called Deirdre Naylor
whom he knew from the PTA at Rosie's school.
She had obtained for him details of the renting
out of Number 6 Mill Street to Crofts & Wills. He
had bluffed Bloomfield into an admission, but that
wasn't worth the air it was spoken on without
concrete evidence to back it up. Whether he'd
ever reach a point where such evidence would
be needed, he'd no idea, but it made sense to get
it while he could, and in person, not by phone.

The rental had begun only five weeks before
the explosion. He read through the correspon-
dence and examined the contract.

'Didn't strike anyone as strange that a patents
agency should want office space in such a locality?'
he said.

'Why?' she asked. 'Not the kind of business that
has people tramping in and out all day, I shouldn't

have thought. So they just wanted an address and somewhere cheap. Do you reckon they were up to something, Peter?'

He shook his head.

'Not really,' he said. 'Just having a bit of bother tracking them down to check a couple of things out after the explosion.'

She looked at him doubtfully then said, 'You could just have rung us.'

He gave her his most charming smile and said, 'Just happened to be passing so I thought I'd save the ratepayers a few bob.'

It didn't sound all that convincing, but to his surprise she smiled back and it occurred to him that she might be imagining this was personal. A good-looking woman in her thirties, she was bringing up her boy alone and, with her extrovert manner and curvaceous figure, she was probably used to being a far from obscure object of desire.

'Can I take copies of this stuff?' he said.

'Of course you can. Always happy to co-operate with the Law,' she said. 'How's Ellie? Haven't run into her at the PTA for a while. We usually have such good crack.'

Mention of Ellie was good. It told him that, while she didn't object to a bit of friendly flirtation, he'd be out of his mind to imagine she'd dream of really getting involved. Which was a relief.

And also, just looking at things hypothetically of course, a touch disappointing.

From the Centre he'd gone to the forensic lab where he'd talked to Tony Pollock, the technician who'd checked the Mill Street bullet. He showed him the CAT technicians' report on the round recovered from the body in Mazraani's flat. Pollock looked at it for a moment then said, 'Am I authorized to see this?'

'If I'm authorized then you are too,' said Pascoe firmly.

Pollock grinned as if he saw right through this prevarication.

'Good enough for me,' he said. Privately he'd always regarded Pascoe as a bit of a prancing pony that it amused Dalziel to toss the odd sugar lump to. Now it was dawning on him that you didn't run in harness with the Fat Man unless you could pull your weight. And punch it too.

Unasked, he did a quick comparison of the Manchester results with his own and confirmed that, while the same make of gun had almost certainly been used, the rounds had come from different weapons.

'Something else I'd like you to take a look at,' said Pascoe.

He handed over the CAT analysis of the Mill Street explosive.

'Same authorization as before?' enquired Pollock mockingly.

'Definitely.'

As he read the stolen paper, the technician frowned.

'What?' said Pascoe.

'This stuff about the detonator, you'll have read it?'

'I started but gave up when they abandoned standard English, which is why I'm asking you what it all means. I do know that the theory is they were preparing a detonator and they'd got the timer wrong or something and blown themselves to bits.'

'Aye, but from what this lot says, it doesn't look like a mechanical timer device were being used here. They reckon it was a remote-control job using a telephone signal.'

'So?'

'Lot harder to go wrong. Would need someone to dial the number by accident after you'd got the thing set up. Why'd they be mucking about with detonators though when they'd not even got the hole dug in the viaduct, if that was what they were after?'

'Conclusion?'

'They weren't thinking of blowing up the viaduct, not when they were playing around with this. That would mebbe explain why they found traces of two types of Semtex.'

'There are different types?'

'Same stuff, basically. Like ale. But different brewers produce different brews.'

Pascoe digested this, then said, 'So the man working on the detonator explosive got his personal supply from a different source?'

Pollock said, 'I think you're getting a bit confused about detonators, if you don't mind me saying so.'

'Not in the least. In fact, you're probably understating my condition. Words of one syllable might come in useful.'

'Right. In Mill Street there were a big lump of explosive and a little lump. The little lump was what this remote-control detonator were stuck into. You're talking like you think the whole of the little lump were a detonator.'

'Didn't it set the big lump off?'

'Oh yes. But that's not to say that's what it were meant to do. We're calling it a little lump, but that's comparative. By itself it wouldn't have wrecked the whole terrace but it would certainly have wrecked any room it went off in. As it happened, the room it went off in already contained the big lump, so the little lump acted as a detonator for the big lump, but that was likely accidental.'

Pascoe said, 'In other words, it was a separate bomb.'

'Aye, that's probably the easiest way of thinking of it,' said Pollock.

'Using explosive differently sourced from what was in the big lump,' mused Pascoe. 'Anything about the possible source?'

'Which one?'

'The little lump. From what I understand, they're pretty certain they know the original source of the big lump because they'd intercepted a consignment of exactly the same type at the start of the year.'

Pollock sighed and said, 'Think you're getting confused again, Mr Pascoe.'

'Am I?'

'Aye. What you say's right enough, but it's the little lump whose provenance they know all about. They're still working on the big lump.'

Pascoe's mind was racing. Was this significant or was he simply desperate to find significance? Wield's conversation with his 'nice lad' had been interrupted by the superintendent before he could reveal that there'd been two types of Semtex involved at Mill Street, and Glenister had not thought fit to share this information with the sergeant in their subsequent cosy co-operative chats. Arranged like that, it looked significant, but he'd spent too many hours in court to trust appearances.

He said casually, 'If you had access to a big lump of Semtex, how easy would it be to slice off a little lump without drawing attention?'

'Depends on how big and how little and how much attention was being paid.'

'But the actual slicing, any problems there?'

'No. It's pretty inert stuff.'

Pollock was now regarding Pascoe with grave suspicion.

In an effort to put him at ease, Pascoe said, 'So, getting back to the report, what you're saying is, the bomb that went off, the small lump with the detonator in it, was made from Semtex of exactly the same type as a shipment the security forces had intercepted a few months earlier?'

He could tell his effort at reassurance had met with only limited success.

Pollock chewed this over for a moment then said, 'No. I'm saying nowt.'

'I mean, the report is saying it?'

Pollock smiled. Not a friendly smile but the faintly mocking smile of a hard-nosed Yorkshire-man who's listened to your sales pitch and isn't going to buy.

He took out a large grey handkerchief and carefully wiped round the edges of the sheets of paper. Then, still holding them in the cloth, he handed them back to Pascoe.

'Report? What report, sir?' he said.

Pascoe had lived in Yorkshire long enough to know the end of a lane when he saw one.

'You must have misheard me,' he said. 'Who mentioned a report? But thanks for your help anyway.'

'Don't follow you,' said Pollock, who'd retrieved the bullet analysis and was busy giving that the handkerchief treatment too. 'You've asked me nowt and I've told you nowt. And I'll thank you not to tell any bugger different, Mr Pascoe, else I might have to resort to words of one syllable again. Now, I've got work to do.'

He turned and left.

He's right, thought Pascoe, feeling reproached.

You shouldn't get other people involved in your mess unless they knew what they were getting into. Which, as he still had little idea what he himself might be getting into, was rather hard to explain.

It was now he rang the Central to check that Mary Goodrich was around. On reaching the hospital, he parked in space allocated to the Senior Gynaecological Consultant, who he knew would be on or about the ninth green at this time on a Friday.

He found Goodrich in her office and was greeted by the welcoming smile which was the response of most young women to Pascoe in the boyish-charm mode which came so naturally to him. But the moment he mentioned Wield's visit, her face blanked over and she said, 'Wield? Oh yes, the ugly one. Yes, he did call, but things were so hectic . . . in fact, I'm still up to my eyes, so unless it's urgent . . .'

She was trying to usher him through the door. Not so long ago it might have worked, but now the only effect was that Pascoe felt himself inflating into Mid-Yorkshire's version of the Incredible Hulk.

He stood before her planted as firm as a full-grown tree and said heavily, 'All right, luv, so you're too busy to talk to the police about the Mill Street corpses? In that case, it'll be a doddle dealing with the gents of the press when they come looking for the medical spokesman who's the source of the information they're shortly going to get.'

'Is that some sort of threat?' she said wonderingly.

Pascoe held up his forefinger.

'Is that a finger?' he replied.

He could tell she was thrown by his manner and trying to reconcile it with the gently amiable Pascoe she'd encountered previously.

'So what kind of information might that be?'

'Information about the mouth-box contents and about the disposition of the corpses' limbs,' he said.

That got her interest.

She said, 'If you know so much, why do you need to come here bullying me?'

Sensitive to the justified accusation, he said, 'Look, I'm sorry about that, but I've just got the outline, what I need are the details. OK, I'm pretty sure you've been advised not to discuss the matter with anyone else, but that hardly applies to me, does it?'

He saw at once he'd made a mistake.

When the CAT people warned her off, they'd probably been very precise. Talk to no one, and no one included everyone in Mid-Yorkshire CID. The consequence of disobedience had been made clear. She was young, her career was just taking off. Step out of line here and the whole fascinating area of Home Office-sponsored forensic pathology would be closed to her. At best she might be allowed to confirm that corpses from the geriatric ward hadn't received a helping hand in passing though death's door.

She believed the CAT people in their threats. By relaxing his manner, all he'd done was confirm her instinct that he didn't have it in him to carry his threat through.

He took out his mobile and dialled.

'Give me Sammy Ruddlesdin, will you? Thanks, I'll hold.'

He said to Goodrich, 'You know Sammy? The *News*'s ace reporter. Loves a good story, especially one he can sell on to the nationals.'

'So what's the story you've got for him?' she said, still unimpressed.

'Mill Street bombings. Examination of the corpses. Findings concealed. Was there more going on here than a simple accident among some cack-handed terrorists?'

'Sounds a good story,' she said.

'It gets better when I tell him I got the basic facts from the only person to examine the bodies before the security services whisked them away,' he said.

'And I'll deny it,' she said spiritedly. 'Why believe you and not me?'

He smiled a smile he'd learned from Dalziel.

'Because I'm an honest upstanding cop that Sammy's known for a long long time and from whom he's never had an iota of dud information. Because we sometimes have a drink together and we trust each other. Because you've only been here two minutes and you're young and you're a woman. Anyway, it doesn't matter what Sammy believes, does it? Your friends in security – was it a nice young chap called Freeman, by the way? – they'll have no problem believing the story because it will give them me as well as you, and they'll be only too delighted to get me by the short and hairies. They'll just fuck your career up as an afterthought.'

She was regarding him with bewildered loathing.

'But if they can harm you as well, then why –?'

'Why?' he interrupted. 'Because whatever happened in Mill Street has left someone very important to me lying in a coma and God knows if he's ever going to come out of it, and I'm not going to rest till I find out why. Not the probable story, or the official story, but the truth, the whole truth and nothing but the fucking truth. Sammy, hi, Peter Pascoe here. Yeah, I'm fine. Listen, Sammy, can you hold on just a second?'

He pressed the phone to his chest and looked at Mary Goodrich.

She said, 'So what do you want to know?'

Once she'd made up her mind to talk, she gave the facts in a detailed orderly manner that Edgar Wield would have approved of.

Two of the bodies had been completely blown apart by the explosion and the fragments roasted by the fire till not much was left but bone. She reckoned it would take days of slow and detailed examination to get any meaningful results from them. The vagaries of blast are such, however, that one body had more or less held together though it had suffered equally from the heat of the fire. This was where Goodrich had concentrated her attention in the couple of hours she had before the CAT removal men arrived. In particular she'd started making notes on the jaw, because she reckoned that dental identification was going to be the best bet. All her notes had been removed, but she recalled being surprised by the amount of ash in the mouth cavity.

'Why should that surprise you?' enquired Pascoe. 'I reckon I had to be hosed down when they got me to hospital, and I wasn't in the middle of it.'

'It was the nature of this ash,' she said. 'Tongue, plate, all the soft-tissue stuff had been burnt off or melted down. But mixed in with the fatty residue you'd expect there was this fine ash. Like you might get if you burned cloth. And there was a fragment of what looked like thread between one of the incisors and the canine next to it.'

'What makes you think it was the remains of cloth?' he asked.

'I've examined fire victims before,' she said.

'But never found anything like this in their mouths?'

'No.'

'The thread you found in the teeth, what happened to it?'

'I handed it over to your *friends*,' she snapped. 'Why not ask them?'

He ignored this and said, 'So what about the disposition of the limbs?'

'In most cases when a body is recovered from a serious fire, there is a characteristic foetal configuration of the torso and limbs. You've probably seen it. In this case, though the legs had come up towards the chest in the typical manner, the arms for some reason hadn't come forward but seem to have remained behind the back.'

'You mean, as if there'd been something preventing the natural forward movement? As if the arms had been tied behind the back, for instance? With a gag in the mouth producing the cloth ash?'

'That's your area of expertise, not mine,' she said. But he could tell that she'd made the speculation.

'Yes, it is,' he said. 'Anything else you can tell me?'

'Apart from go screw yourself? No.'

It would have been nice to let her have the last word, but for her sake as well as his own, he couldn't do that. She was mad now. Mad enough maybe to open her mouth to someone who might open their mouth to someone . . .

For both their sakes, he needed to remind her what Wield had told him.

Being mad only lasts till bedtime. Being scared is what's waiting for you when you wake up alone in the middle of the night.

He took a step towards her.

'Then hear this,' he said. 'You were warned before to keep quiet. I'm warning you again. This time I'd listen.'

As he left her office, he felt powerful, positive. But within half a dozen steps he felt so guilty that it was all he could do to stop himself from turning round to apologize.

Even now, sitting in his own living room, the memory made him feel bad. Hectoring bright young women didn't come easy to him.

Hectoring . . .

He let himself be diverted by the word.

How had Hector, the great hero, the personification of Trojan nobility, declined by the seventeenth century into a contemptuous term for a swaggering bully? Was it the same in any other language, or was it only the English with their tabloid instinct to look for feet of clay who deconstructed old heroes thus?

Not that a swaggering bully was the term's lowest deep, not in Mid-Yorkshire anyway. He tried to imagine a confrontation between Prince Hector in all his pomp and Constable Hector in all his pathos. It would have made stepping in front of a car seem like a friendly embrace! Ultimately, however, it was the pathetic constable not the proud prince he might have to use to buttress the still flimsy hypothesis he was erecting on the ruin of the Mill Street terrace.

Don't do Hector down, he reproved himself. Somehow, whenever the earth stopped shaking and the dust settled, Hector was still there. Maybe someone up there liked him enough to steer him clear of harm. After all, Homer tells us that the Olympians all had their favourites whom they did their best to protect. He recalled enviously how Paris, who started it all, having lost a titanic battle with the vengeful Menelaus, had found himself lying at the cuckold's mercy, till suddenly Aphrodite whirled him away from the battlefield and deposited him alongside his gorgeous mistress in his own scented bedroom.

So it was with Troy very much in his mind that Pascoe fell asleep on the sofa, but he did not dream of battles. Instead his punning subconscious placed him on the sinking *Titanic* from which he looked shoreward to where Helen, looking very like Ellie, stood topless on one of the towers of Ilium.

1

Troy

Hector too was preoccupied with Troy.

Of course his tutelary spirit, who dwelt a little lower than Olympus, hadn't managed to whirl him away from danger and deposit him in a scented bedroom with the loveliest woman on earth. On the other hand, Hector was very willing to settle for a hospital bed and a bunch of sympathetic nurses.

On first arrival in hospital they'd placed him in Intensive Care and he awoke to find himself sprouting a variety of wires and tubes. His first words being a request for his breakfast, the doctors had feared there might be serious head trauma as well as the various bruises and breakages already diagnosed, but when X-rays showed no brain damage and his visiting colleagues confirmed normalcy, they had removed him from IC, transferred him to a small side ward, and given him a tranquillizing shot.

Here he had slept the sleep of the drugged for some hours.

Opening his eyes and seeing Dalziel floating under the ceiling might have put another man into shock, but for Hector it was simply a mild surprise.

This acceptance of whatever happened without any inclination to analyse either an event or his own reactions to it was an essential element of the talent for survival that was the sole gift of his tutelary spirit. It meant that, as the growing Hector made his pinball progress from one disaster to another, he never absorbed the damage into himself by dwelling on it.

If Hector had analysed his vision (which of course he didn't), he might have said that it wasn't so much that he actually *saw* the Fat Man floating above him, it was more that he felt as he would have felt had he in fact seen this phenomenon. But though not a shock, the surprise itself was enough to wake him to full consciousness, and after a few moments he sought for and found a bell-push which summoned a nurse to whom he reiterated his earlier demands for solid food.

A doctor was consulted. On the basis that, if Hector had suffered any significant internal injury, his reaction to the insertion of a hospital meat pie would be as good a diagnostic tool as anything, he gave the go-ahead. When Hector survived and asked for another, he was downgraded even further off the critical list.

Replete, he lay back in bed, and this was where Troy came in. His mind, usually a comfortable blank in moments of repose, turned into a screen on which strange images were being played.

He saw a figure he recognized as himself emerge from a small copse to stand on the edge of a white plain stretching to infinity. He glanced to his right. About twenty yards away stood a chariot just like the chariots they used in *Troy*, one of his favourite videos which he'd watched only a couple of nights ago. The only difference was that it was pulled not by a horse but by some sort of cat the size of a horse.

The charioteer raised the visor on his helmet and Hector was a bit disappointed to see it wasn't Brad Pitt. But whoever it was smiled at him and with a gauntleted hand motioned him to continue to advance.

Hector managed a nod of acknowledgement and took a step forward.

And that was that. No sense of impact, flying through the air, hitting the ground. He opened his eyes and found himself in bed and the picture was simply cut off.

But it was easy to replay it. All he had to do was close his eyes again. He did this two or three times in the hope that it would move on, then he found himself distracted by a sudden burst of activity in the room.

A nurse explained that, because he was so much improved and they were really short of space, they were moving another patient into the room. This turned out to be a man in late middle age with no outward sign of his condition. He showed little interest in his roommate but brusquely supervised the positioning of a small TV set at his bedside. Hector could see the screen at an angle but there was no disturbing noise as the man was listening through a headset.

Normally a devotee of TV so long as the programmes contained a maximum of action and a minimum of talk, Hector felt too tired to be envious. He fancied a little sleep, but irritatingly, every time he closed his eyes, the sequence with the cat-drawn chariot still kept running.

It did occur to him to wonder if there might not be something of memory in it. If so, he knew he ought to pass it on to his colleagues. But he couldn't see a way to share his vision without its oddities leaving him open to professional mockery. Just because he was used to mockery did not mean he was inured to it. Hector was proud of being a policeman. In a low orbiting life, getting through the training course and surviving his probation period marked points of apogee. Much of his hesitancy in reporting and giving evidence derived from a desire to be sure he got it right, and if in the end he'd adopted the maxim *When in doubt, leave it out*, the fault lay as much in the attitude of colleagues as in himself.

His assertion, which Pascoe had found so amazing, that Dalziel had been good to him, derived principally from a sense that the Fat Man didn't single him out. Yes, he made him the butt of his jokes, but then he made everyone the butt of his jokes, even the perfect Pascoe. Yes, he laid on the tongue-lashings with great vigour, but when did he ever hold back? Yes, he treated everything Hector said with great caution fading into outright scepticism, but at least he always insisted on hearing that everything. 'Don't tire thy brain out trying to separate wheat from chaff,' he'd once said. 'Tell me the lot, son, and I'll do the sorting.' And on another never to be forgotten occasion Hector had overheard him bellow at a DI who'd fallen short of the Fat Man's high standards, 'Thinking for tha self, were you? By God, I'd sooner have someone like Hector who knows his limitations than buggers like you who fancy they're twice as clever as they really are!'

So there it was. If Dalziel were around it would be easy. He'd let him know about the chariot sequence running through his mind and rest happy that the Fat Man would do the sorting.

But he wasn't around, except in the sense that his body was lying unresponsively in a nearby ward and his spirit might be floating equally unresponsively beneath the ceiling. So the sorting was down to Hector.

He opened his eyes and tried to let his sideways glimpse of the TV screen blot out the chariot. To his surprise there was a face on it he thought he recognized. Could be wrong – he was used to being wrong – and the angle made things look sort of squashed and long at the same time. But the face definitely had a look of DCI Pascoe's missus.

He shifted his position to try to get a better view and the other patient glanced angrily towards him like one of those guys on a bus who don't like you reading their newspaper over their shoulder.

He turned away and closed his eyes and tried to sink into an imageless sleep.

He was almost there when suddenly he was jerked back to the surface by an exclamation from the other bed.

'Bloody hell!' cried the grumpy man. 'Did you see that? Did you see that?'

Someone with a greater mastery of repartee might have responded, 'No, because when I tried to see it, you gave me a piss-off look!'

But for Hector even *esprit d'escalier* required a staircase like Mount Niesen's.

He sat up in bed and looked towards the other patient.

He too was sitting bolt upright, staring aghast at his now blank TV screen.

'What?' said Hector.

'Did you not see it? You should have seen it! Is this what they call reality TV then – shooting buggers dead afore your eyes? Nurse! Nurse! Bloody hell!'

5

fiddle-de-dee

Talking of tutelary spirits, there is one – much overworked – whose job it is to save men from sins of omission which involve forgetting birthdays and anniversaries and other significant events in the lives of their loved ones. Its intervention can take many forms from an efficient secretary to a reminder stapled to your Y-fronts by a distrusting wife.

In Pascoe's case it took the form of Tig jumping on to the arm of the sofa and starting to lick his idle servant's eyes open.

Pascoe awoke with a jerk. It took a moment to realize the folly Tig had saved him from. In reward he opened the French window to let the dog out then switched on the TV set. The timing was close. The opening titles of *Fidler's Three* were just coming to an end, and here was young, cool Joe Fidler himself, immaculately casual in a designer sports shirt and crotch-clinging trousers.

'Hi!' he cried, his mouth curving to show teeth

from which gleamed a light that never was on sea or land. 'My guests tonight are local lad, Maurice Kentmore . . .'

The screen filled with the face of a man in his late thirties with tousled brown hair, candid blue eyes and a determined jaw, smiling rather nervously at the camera.

'. . . whose family have been farming at Haresyke Hall in the lovely dale country near Harrogate for at least five generations.'

Hardly local to Middlesborough then, thought Pascoe. But doubtless, to these southern media types, Yorkshire was like Watford, with fewer take-aways.

'Which makes you a bit of a local squire, is that right, Maurice?' continued Fidler.

'Oh I wouldn't say that.'

'But you do host the local village fête on your land, don't you? I know that because you asked me for a plug at dinner. So anyone in search of nice day out for gran and the kids, look no further than the village fête at Haresyke Hall near Harrogate tomorrow, Saturday. There you are, Maurice. You can slip me the fiver later.'

Funny face, pause for laughter. If you didn't laugh at Fidler's jokes, you probably found your car clamped, thought Pascoe.

'Maurice is a man of many talents,' resumed Fidler. 'Keen mountaineer, expert horseman, he is also a powerful and influential voice in the National Farmers' Union and the Countryside Alliance. Nor does he hesitate to put his principles into practice. During the 2001 foot-and-mouth outbreak, he resisted attempts to slaughter his livestock when his land came within the designated distance of a confirmed infection. Despite the authorities' calculations being proved wrong, Maurice was put on trial for threatening behaviour with a firearm, but was triumphantly acquitted. If he'll go to those lengths to protect his rare-breed pigs, I shouldn't care to cause offence to his friends and family.'

Another knowing grimace, another laughter pause.

'Alongside him,' resumed Fidler, 'we have another man who has triumphed against adversity, Kalim Sarhadi, who comes from Bradford.'

The name rang in Pascoe's ears like a warning bell.

Sarhadi was in his late twenties, slim built, darkly handsome. He grinned broadly at the camera, lounging at ease in his swivel chair. (Fidler liked swivels, it was said, because they permitted his guests to really get in each other's faces.)

The presenter continued, 'Eighteen months ago Kal was in Pakistan, visiting relations, when he got picked up by the security police. After a week of isolation and assault, he was interviewed first by three Americans, then by two Englishmen, none of whom ever identified himself and all of whom claimed to believe he was a terrorist. Happily for Kal, back home a huge campaign orchestrated by the editor of the *Bradford News* put such a fire-cracker under the backside of our beloved leader that finally the government intervened and, after a month of incarceration, Kal was finally released.'

Yes, it was that Sarhadi. Shit, thought Pascoe.

'Very active in that campaign was his fiancée, Jamila, who is in the audience tonight. Yes, there she is. Give her a big hand.'

A camera focused on a young Asian woman sitting at the back. For a moment she looked confused and turned to a slightly older woman sitting next to her, who squeezed her arm reassuringly. Then, recovering, she smiled and waved her hand to acknowledge the applause. She was very pretty but it was her companion Pascoe's eyes were drawn to. With a narrow almost emaciated face whose pallor was accentuated by jet-black hair cropped so short it might almost have been painted on, her striking looks would not have been out of place on a wall painting in an Egyptian tomb.

The camera returned to Fidler, who said, 'I think you said it's a week tomorrow that you'll be giving up your freedom again, Kal?'

'Right!' said Sarhadi. 'Only this time I won't be asking for the British consul!'

Laughter and applause. As it died, Fidler resumed, 'My final guest is novelist Eleanor Soper from Mid-Yorkshire.'

Ellie's face appeared. Pascoe thought she looked gorgeous, but then he always did. He tried to telepath his advice, which was, Don't trust this smarmy bastard an inch!

'Ell's debut novel exploded on the literary scene last year. She has been described as one of the most exciting new talents to emerge in recent years. Her book stares modern issues and dilemmas right in the face and, from what I hear of Ell, she's not afraid to do exactly the same. If that's right, Ell, you've come to the right place!'

Ellie winced – whether at the hype, which had more fiction in it than her book, or at the paring of her name wasn't clear – then managed a modest smile.

Fidler went on, 'Boy and girls, you'll soon have your chance to find out what my guests are really made of, but first let's have a big hand for tonight's *Fidler's Three!*'

The audience broke into enthusiastic applause. They were seated in a tight, gently raked semi-circle before the panellists. There wasn't even a table separating them. The front row could have leaned forward and patted them on the knee. *On my show there's nowhere to hide!* was another of Fidler's proud boasts.

To start with, everything seemed fine. Fidler got the ball rolling by asking Kentmore how many politicians he'd trust to tell a cow from a cabbage. Kentmore talked eloquently of what he saw as the real problems of the rural economy. The audience began to join in. Pascoe suspected that, like the PM at Question Time, Fidler planted questions. A

scruffy young man looking too like a hunt sabo-
teur to be true tried to start the old fox-hunting
debate running, but Kentmore brushed it aside.

'Personally, if I get bother from a fox, I shoot
it. Never saw any reason to risk my neck or my
horses' legs galloping around over rough ground
chasing the damned things.'

Applause, and Ellie, who looked as if she was
getting wound up for her anti-blood-sport rant,
subsided.

Encouraged by the applause, Kentmore went
on, 'In fact, now that hunting foxes with dogs has
been banned, I reckon we could solve the problem
by substituting, say, journalists – except the poor
dogs might find them rather unpalatable.'

Ellie was nodding again, but Kalim Sarhadi
shook his head violently and said, 'All right for you
to make jokes about journalists, Maurice, but if it
weren't for them lads on the *Bradford News* and all
their mates, I reckon I'd be chained to a wall with
a hood over my head in Guantanamo Bay now.'

Kentmore looked discomfited but Fidler
rescued him by asking, 'Just in case anyone out
there hasn't heard your story, Kal, could you tell
us what happened to you?'

Pascoe had heard the tale before but it still
made uncomfortable hearing. Sarhadi had been
walking down a street in Lahore when he spotted
a familiar face. It belonged to a young man called
Hasan Raza who'd gone to the same school.

'We weren't mates or owt, but we sat down

in a caff and had a coffee. He were keen for news from home. When I asked what he were doing in Lahore, he got all vague. Then this car drew up outside, two big guys got out and next thing we were in the back and being driven away.'

What had happened now seemed to be clear. Raza was a terrorist suspect the authorities had had their eyes on for some time. The sight of him talking to a new contact from the UK provoked the security police to move in. When their fairly primitive interrogation techniques produced no results, they called in their American counterparts, who at least didn't get directly physical. Then the British interrogators arrived.

'Was that because the Yanks were beginning to believe you?' asked Fidler.

'Nay, I think it were 'cos they couldn't understand a word I were saying,' said Sarhadi, very broad Bradford.

That got a big laugh, after which he finished his story, stressing his conviction that it was only the publicity pressure back home that got him released.

'Kal, how much do you think the fact that your mother is English helped get public support for that campaign?' asked Fidler.

Sarhadi gave him a long cool stare.

'Me dad's English too. Might be different down south, but up here that's what we call folk who were born in England and work in England and pay their taxes in England.'

Big cheer. Fidler grinned and said, 'Whoops.

Sorry, Kal. Forgot you were a straight-speaking Yorkshireman. So, in the same spirit, did the fact that your mam is white make a difference to the level of public support?'

'No idea,' said Sarhadi. 'I were chained up in a cellar, remember?'

'Of course. Terrible. Sir, you've got a question?'

A fat man near the back stood up and said, 'I'm sorry for what happened to you, lad, but fair do's, you lot don't do yourself any favours, do you? Look at all these riots the papers are full of –'

'Hold on there,' interrupted Fidler. 'Demonstrations, I think you mean.'

'You call 'em what you will, looked like bloody riots to me. And what about yon Raza, your mate, he really is a terrorist, right? So you can't blame the cops when they saw the two of you so chummy together jumping to the wrong conclusion, right?'

'If you'd been kicked so hard in the balls you were pissing blood into a rusty bucket for a fortnight, you'd mebbe want some bugger to blame!' declared Sarhadi. 'Just like the lads on them demos want to know who's to blame for murdering them two innocent Muslims in Manchester. As for Raz, till he's had a fair trial, he's just an ordinary British citizen like you and me, and our government should be protecting him, not apologizing for yon mad bastard George Bush and his mates.'

'Strong words,' said Fidler. 'Just how much did your experience radicalize you?'

235

'If you mean it's turned me into an extremist, you're dead wrong,' said Sarhadi. 'But it did make me see it weren't enough just to keep my nose clean and get on with my own concerns. It made me start thinking about what being a Muslim really meant.'

'Yes, and as I understand it, this means you've become much more active in your local mosque at Marrside. The mosque your friend Raza attended, right? And isn't Sheik Ibrahim Al-Hijazi, who has been so forthright in his condemnation of the quote foot-dragging police investigation unquote into the Manchester killings, the Imam there?'

'What are you trying to say, Joe? That we're all terrorists at Marrside?'

'No, of course not. But Sheikh Ibrahim's views are well known, aren't they?'

'Aye, like the Archbishop of Canterbury's. And if every churchgoer who disagreed with him walked out, where'd that leave the C of E?'

'Are you claiming to be a force for moderation then, Kal?'

'No. I'm just like most other young Muslims in Marrside: a British citizen trying to live his life by following the laws of his country and the laws of his religion.'

'And if they clash?'

'Properly interpreted, they don't clash.'

'I think Sheikh Ibrahim might give you an argument there. Incidentally, is he going to your wedding?'

He was a clever bastard, thought Pascoe with reluctant admiration. He was managing to use Sarhadi to represent the Muslim both as victim and villain.

'Why shouldn't he be?' said Sarhadi angrily. 'Look, Joe, you want to have a barney with Sheikh Ibrahim, mebbe it's him you should have invited on to the show.'

'Funny you should say that, Kal,' said Fidler with the self-satisfied smirk of the chat-show host who has got his guest to provide a desired cue. 'We did invite the Sheikh, but after the report of the alleged attempt on his life earlier this week, his people came back to us with questions about security. Naturally we gave the assurances we offer all our guests, but it seems they weren't enough for the Sheikh and he withdrew.'

Not having much luck with your guest list this week, thought Pascoe. Presumably Fidler had hoped to engineer a public confrontation between Sarhadi and the Sheikh.

'Perhaps,' continued Fidler, 'what he was really worried about was whether he could get away without falling into the cliché trap. So far we've done rather well, but you've all got your weapons of mass destruction ready, just in case?'

The audience laughed and waved the plastic bags full of coloured ping-pong balls which they received as they entered the broadcast hall.

Ellie tried to speak but Fidler ignored her. Saving her for something else? wondered Pascoe uneasily, as the halogen smile beamed on Kentmore again.

'Maurice, you've had your problems with the Law,' said the presenter. 'Do you think we have strong enough laws to control extreme political agitation?'

'We elect people to make our laws,' said the farmer shortly. 'If we don't like them, then we should elect somebody else.'

'That's pretty reasonable of you, Maurice, considering what happened in your own family,' said Fidler.

Turning to speak directly to the camera with the serious sympathetic face of a man offering condolence to a bereaved neighbour, he went on, 'Some of you may recall that Maurice's younger brother, Flight Lieutenant Christopher Kentmore, was one of the earliest British casualties during the invasion of Iraq.'

Kentmore turned pale with shock, then fury. He hadn't been expecting this. Suddenly the true reason why he'd been invited to join the panel was obvious. Which left . . .

Ellie beware! Pascoe tried to telepath.

Fidler, leaving Kentmore to simmer, was already turning to her.

'Nowadays nearly everyone has some link, close or distant, to the modern terrorist threat. Ell, I know you use your maiden name on your book jackets, but wasn't your husband, DCI Pascoe, one of the victims of the recent terrorist explosion in Mid-Yorkshire? Happily not the most seriously injured. In fact, I believe he's back at work. But are his hands too tightly tied by the very laws he upholds? And what about you, Ell? How do you feel about the kind of people who nearly made you a widow?'

It was blindingly obvious now how Ffion had managed to get unknown Ellie with her unimpressive literary track record on to the show.

You treacherous cow! thought Pascoe. You with your double effs!

At least now it shouldn't take a Dalziel to tell Ellie what the other one stood for.

He waited anxiously for her response. A blank *no comment* was probably safest, but Ellie wasn't the no comment type. He gritted his teeth and waited for the explosion.

But despite his great love and admiration, he could still underestimate his wife.

She leaned forward, very serious and said, 'Well, all other things being equal, Joe, at the end of the day, all the police want is a level playing field . . .'

Chaos erupted. The speakers blasted out a chorus of zoo screeches over which a parliamentary voice bellowed, 'Order! Order!' Klaxons blared, lights flashed, audience members screamed, 'Cliché! Cliché!' and stood up to hurl their multi-coloured ping-pong balls at Ellie, who sat unflinching beneath the barrage.

'Oh Ell, Ell!' cried Fidler. 'This is serious money time! OK, folks, settle down, thank you, I think we've shown the dreaded clichés exactly what we think of them . . .'

The shower of balls diminished to a trickle and the audience began to subside. But a woman in the front row remained on her feet, her hand still in her plastic bag.

'You don't fool me,' she was yelling. 'You deserved all you got, you murdering bastard! You're just like the rest on 'em at yon mosque, you and that Sheikh. You send other bastards out to do your dirty work, but you're just as bad. They should lock every last one of you up and throw away the key!'

It was Sarhadi directly in front of her that she was shouting at, not Ellie.

Her hand came out of the bag. In it was a gun.

For a fraction of a second Pascoe thought, This is another of Fidler's plants!

Then he saw the presenter's face. Even the make-up couldn't hide the pallor of terror. His lips moved but nothing came out. He tried to push himself backwards but only succeeded in sending his swivel chair spinning round and round till he was bound fast by his own microphone wire.

The gun came up. It was pointed at Sarhadi, who stared at it in a disbelief which hadn't yet had time to dissolve into fear.

Someone screamed. To the left and right of the woman the people best placed to intervene opted for self-preservation and flung themselves side-ways.

And Ellie began to rise from her seat.

To Pascoe's sagacious eye, she didn't look like she was thinking of diving for cover or making a run for it.

'No!' he yelled. 'Don't be stupid! No!'

He hadn't yelled at a screen like this since he was a kid at a Saturday-morning picture club.

And now, as if offended, the screen he was yelling at went completely blank.

6

Kilda

For the next five minutes Peter Pascoe exercised the greatest degree of control he had ever called upon.

He did nothing.

Every instinct screamed at him to react. The loudest and most lunatic scream urged him to jump into his car and start driving north. Pointless! It would take an hour even breaking every speed limit.

Nearly as loud and on the surface more sensible was the scream telling him to grab the phone and start ringing. Ellie's mobile first, then the TV station, then Middlesbrough police, then his own CID office, then . . .

What stopped him was the certainty that Ellie, knowing he was watching, would ring him as soon as she could. He didn't even dare risk using his mobile in case that was the button she hit. As for ringing her mobile, she'd have it switched off because of the broadcast and, when it got switched on again, it would be to ring him.

He knew this beyond all doubt, but it wasn't a comfort. It meant if she didn't ring, she couldn't.

Five minutes, he told himself. He'd give her five minutes.

He sat there staring at the screen.

An announcer appeared. She began to apologize for the break in transmission as if it had been caused by a simple power failure. Why was she smiling faintly? he wondered. Perhaps she hated Joe Fidler and hoped he'd been shot in the mouth. Then her face became serious and she said they were going over to the newsroom for an update on the body-in-the-reservoir story that had broken earlier. The picture changed to some kind of lake with a rubber dinghy floating in it. An announcer was saying, 'Police have not yet confirmed the rumour that the body has been identified as that of . .'

Impatiently Pascoe switched the set off. There was only one story he wanted to hear about. Surely that was five minutes now? He checked his watch. Only four! It felt like an hour. He watched the second hand sweep round and started to count down.

Twenty . . nineteen . . . eighteen . . .

Of course, if she didn't ring it meant nothing . . .

. . . fifteen . . . fourteen . . . thirteen . . .

She could be simply too preoccupied taking care of someone . . .

. . . ten . . . nine . . . eight . . .

Or her battery could be flat . . .

. . . six . . . five . . . four . . .

Or she'd left her phone in the make-up room . . .

. . . three . . . two . . . one . . .

She was dead.

He knew it with a certainty beyond the reach of logic.

She wasn't ringing because she couldn't ring because she was lying sprawled on the floor of the TV studio with the life-blood oozing out of her body.

The sense of loss was so huge, so stifling of all his senses, that he didn't realize for some little time that the phone was ringing.

He snatched it up.

'Peter?'

'Oh Jesus. Are you all right?'

'Yes, I'm fine. Nothing to worry about, really.'

'You're not dead . . . sorry . . . I'm babbling . . . I thought you might be . . . you're not hurt at all, are you sure?'

'Of course I'm sure. One of the first things they taught me at nursery school. Really, love, I'm fine.'

'Thank God. What about the others?'

'All fine, no problem. It was just a sort of air pistol, one of those gas-powered things. She got one pellet off, hit Joe Fidler in that tight-stretched crotch, very poetic. He says he's OK, which is just as well as I couldn't see anyone rushing to offer first aid.'

'And you're really all right? God, when I saw you getting up with your Superwoman look on . . .'

'No need to have worried. Before I could get to my phone booth, Maurice had done the deed. Real action-man stuff. No, I shouldn't mock, he was very brave. Fast, too. If it hadn't been for him, Kal would have got the pellet straight in the face. Listen, love, would you ring Jane just in case she was watching, or worse still, letting Rosie watch 'cos I was on.'

'Good thinking,' said Pascoe. 'I take it that's the end of the show now?'

'For me, certainly. Not before time either. Now I know exactly how Ffion got me on. I can see her on her mobile. She's probably selling my story to the tabloids. You might like to retain a good homicide brief. I'll be back soon as I can. Love you. Bye.'

'Love you too. Bye.'

He rang off. His mobile was ringing.

It was Wield.

'Pete, I were watching *Fidler's Three . . .*'

'Ellie's fine,' said Pascoe. 'She just rang to tell me.'

'That's grand,' said Wield. 'I waited a few minutes before ringing 'cos I knew you'd want the lines free.'

That was Wield, a mind for all seasons. In Pascoe's opinion he was one of the best cops in Mid-Yorkshire if not in the whole country. Sticking at sergeant had been his own choice, at first because he didn't want his gayness to become a promotion issue, and latterly, since setting up home with Edwin Digweed, because he had no desire to take any step which might disturb his domestic happiness.

In an unprejudiced society, he'd have been Commissioner by now, thought Pascoe.

He relayed Ellie's account of events.

'God knows what was bugging this woman,' he concluded. 'Thank God she could only lay her hands on an air pistol.'

'I've a mate in the Middlesborough mob,' said Wield. 'I'll give him a ring later when they've had time to get things sorted. As for the pistol, don't underestimate them. Close range, one of them gas guns can put a pellet through your eye right into your brain. In fact, if it hits soft tissue anywhere, it can do real damage.'

'I know,' said Pascoe. 'But I reckon Ellie would still have had a go even if it had been a Kalashnikov. Fortunately, that guy Kentmore seems to have been on the ball. I reckon I owe him a drink . . . sorry, Wieldy, got to go. The house phone's ringing.'

It was Jane Pulman.

'Peter, has Ellie been on the television tonight?'

'Yes, she has, but she's OK . . .' Then with sudden alarm, 'Why are you asking? Is it Rosie?'

He'd guessed right. The four girls were in one bedroom which had a TV set in it. They'd been allowed to watch a video, then Jane had looked in to make sure the set was off and the girls in bed.

'But you know kids,' she said. 'They must have switched it on again, spotted Ellie, then something happened, something with a gun, right?'

The girls had tried to convince themselves that it was just part of the show, like the ping-pong balls, but Rosie had been so agitated that in the end Mandy, Jane's daughter, had decided to put her hand up and admit to her mother they'd been watching, and ask for reassurance.

'Let me talk to her,' said Pascoe. 'No, better still, I'll get Ellie to ring and talk to her.'

He put the phone down, and rang Ellie's mobile.

'Hi, Pete,' she said, sounding rather breathless. 'It's chaos here. Place is full of cops and reporters. I wish I'd twisted your arm to come. Maurice has got his sister-in-law here and Kal has got Jamila, his fiancée. Lovely girl, you probably saw her on the box. They've stuck us all together in this side room where we've got to wait till we've made our statements. Fortunately it's the same room they had the pre-show refreshments in so we're not short of booze and snacks. God knows when I'll get away . . .'

He interrupted her to explain why he was ringing.

'I'd better ring Jane straight away, before the battery goes in my mobile,' she said. 'See you later, love. Don't know when, but no need to worry, I'm being well looked after. Bye!'

He switched the TV back on to catch the news and was irrationally put out to find the incident on *Fidler's Three* rated only third place behind the body-in-the-reservoir story and a plane crash in Canada. But as he began to take in the details of the reservoir story, his attention was fully engaged.

Though there was still no official confirmation, observers were absolutely definite that the dead man was Michael Carradice aka Abbas Asir, found not guilty a few hours earlier on terrorism charges. And now a leak from the police said it was suspected he'd died of ricin poisoning.

'Shit!' said Pascoe.

This was tragic. It might also be trouble. With Carradice's acquittal, he'd hoped that Ellie's connection with the man could remain a sleeping dog. But now, especially if this turned out to be a Templar killing, the press would be all over it.

He returned his attention to the news, which had moved on to the Canadian air disaster with the inevitable speculation about possible terrorist involvement. In this case it seemed most unlikely, but it didn't stop the 'experts' from stirring the pot.

Then at last it was the incident on the Fidler show. By comparison with the preceding items this was presented in a straightforward factual way with very little comment and a surprisingly small amount of film footage.

I'm on the wrong channel! Pascoe told himself.

Over the past couple of decades the great British

public, once so phlegmatic and passive, had learned that fortitude might be the virtue of adversity but it doesn't get you money in the bank. Now many thousands who might have difficulty spelling the words *psychological trauma* had no problem understanding its value. A twenty-first-century Dunkirk would see the lines of rescued men heading first not for home or hospital but to their lawyers' offices, there to be reunited with their loved ones already queuing up to make a claim for compensation.

The channel's lawyers would have advised, Play this down or you'll play the eventual bill up!

But their rivals would have no such inhibition.

He switched to another news programme and found he was right.

But along with a lack of inhibition, there was also a lack of footage, though to some extent they turned this to their advantage, giving the impression through the words of eye-witnesses of something close to the gunfight at the OK Corral.

Despite his superior knowledge, that was what it felt like to Pascoe too.

The next couple of hours dragged by. He tried to get through to Ellie again, but either her phone was switched off or the battery had gone. Presumably she was on her way home now, otherwise he was sure she'd have found some way of letting him know.

When his phone rang he snatched it up, certain it would be Ellie, but it was Wield's voice he heard.

'Is Ellie back yet?' he asked.

249

'No, but she should be on her way.'

'Good. Thought you might like an update on what I've got out of my chum in Middlesborough. They've got the whole thing on tape. Cameras kept rolling even after they cut off transmission. That guy Kentmore was the hero of the hour, moved like lightning, got himself between Sarhadi and the gun, then disarmed the woman. And of course he didn't know it wasn't a real pistol. So a real hero.'

'For which, much thanks. What's the SP on the woman?'

'Only son worked in London. Got caught in one of the tube bombings. Died in hospital three months later. Since then anyone east of Spurn Head has been her perceived enemy. Also she's a *Voice* reader.'

When its fellow tabloids fell into line behind the *Bradford News*'s pro-Sarhadi campaign, it was inevitable that the *Voice* should break ranks.

Coincidence? Maybe not! had been its headline over a photo of an under-fifteen soccer team with Sarhadi and Raza, heads ringed, standing next to each other. *Once team mates, always team mates?* it went on. *No smoke without fire?* And upon this flimsy base it had built *a provable case which needs to be answered!*

When complaints were made to the Press Complaints Commission, the *Voice* hid behind its question marks and offered a single-sentence apology in small type above the small ads.

'So it's just some poor deranged woman

250

looking for someone to blame, that it?' said Pascoe.

'Looks like it. There could be a question of how she got on the front row. All three of the panel said they'd noticed her looking a bit agitated from the start. Fidler said he noticed nothing, but one of his producers admitted they check the audience out on CCTV before the show and decide who's going to sit at the front.'

'So if you're a bit wild-eyed and foaming at the mouth, you get put within striking distance of the panel? Nice. They ought to sack that bastard!'

'Don't be daft, Pete. Tonight's do has probably doubled his ratings. Give my love to Ellie. We still on for tomorrow evening?'

'Yeah. Cheers!'

He hung up, opened another beer and settled down once more to wait.

All logic told him Ellie was fine, but it was still a huge relief finally to hear her key in the front door.

He rushed into the hall to greet her.

As he folded her passionately in his arms, over her shoulder he saw she wasn't alone. A man and a woman stood behind her on the threshold, making a big thing of examining the elegant 'Pompon de Paris' climbing up the porch pillar.

The man he recognized as Maurice Kentmore, Ellie's fellow panellist. The woman was familiar but it took him a second to realize it was the woman who'd been sitting next to Sarhadi's fiancée. In the flesh she looked even more striking.

Emaciation merely underlined her elegant facial bone structure and made her dark eyes seem huge. Against the blackness of her cropped hair the pallor of her skin seemed to glow.

'Peter, this is Maurice Kentmore,' said Ellie as she broke away. 'And Kilda '

'Maurice's sister-in-law,' said the woman, offering her hand. Her voice had the faintest hint of an Irish accent. Her grip was firm, her palm dry but chilly.

'There wasn't a car booked for me because I was a last-minute job,' explained Ellie, 'and getting a taxi in Middlesbrough on a Friday night's like getting a plumber on Christmas day. Then Maurice offered a lift, even though it's well out of his way.'

'Glad to help,' said Kentmore. 'Now, it's late, so perhaps we should leave you . . . .'

'Don't be silly. A drink's the least we can offer you,' said Ellie.

'Yes, please come in,' urged Pascoe with an enthusiasm over-egged by his private hope that they'd insist on being on their way.

'Well, just for a minute then,' said Kentmore.

As Pascoe ushered them in, he said to Ellie, 'You got through to Rosie?'

'Yes, she was really worried. We spoke till my battery gave out. I convinced her I wasn't dead, but not much more. She says she's coming home in the morning.'

'But I thought Jane was taking the whole gang of them ice-skating.'

'Not our daughter. She's a real doubting Thomas, won't be happy till she sees for herself I'm not in a wheelchair. Sorry, Maurice. The joys of family life, eh?'

'It's understandable that she's concerned,' said Kentmore.

'Drinks?' said Pascoe.

Kentmore and Ellie had Scotches. The woman had a vodka on the rocks, grimacing when he offered her tonic. Pascoe had another lager.

He said, 'Quite a night.'

'Not what I was expecting, and I don't just mean the lady with the gun,' said Kentmore. 'I made it quite clear when they invited me that my brother's death was a no-go area. I gather Ellie got ambushed too.'

'Bloody right, I did,' said Ellie. 'Ffion even pretended to have completely forgotten Pete was a cop when I reminded her that I didn't answer questions on his job.'

Kilda glanced at Pascoe and raised her thin black eyebrows.

'Good to see naïvety isn't a gender thing, eh, Peter?' she murmured, shaking her glass to produce the tinkle of ice undulled by liquid.

He returned her smile and refilled her glass. When he looked at Ellie he saw, unsurprised, that she didn't take kindly to being called naïve, even when she definitely had been. Or maybe, he told himself smugly, she just didn't care to see him exchanging smiles with a sexy young woman, which

Kilda in her skinny and bony way definitely was.

Kentmore said, 'I read about the explosion. Good to see you didn't take any long term-damage, Peter, but Ellie was saying your boss is still very ill.'

'Yes,' said Pascoe, more brusquely than he intended.

'Sorry, didn't mean to intrude,' said the man, finishing his drink. 'Think we should be moving.'

'No, look, have another drink,' said Pascoe, pushing the bottle forward as he recalled that not only had this guy also been through a traumatic experience, but his intervention had probably stopped Ellie from flinging herself on the gun-toting woman. 'I don't mean to be rude. It's just that there's nothing to tell. Andy, that's my boss, is in a coma. Nobody knows if he'll come out of it, or, if he does, what condition he'll be in.'

He thought he spoke calmly, but Kilda reached across to him and gently squeezed his hand. Kentmore poured himself more whisky, which he drank as if he needed it. As if in sympathy, the woman helped herself to another large vodka.

Ellie said, 'I wonder what drove that poor woman to do something so crazy.'

'Some close personal loss, I'd guess,' said Kilda. 'It drives different people to different things.'

She spoke dispassionately, you might almost have said uncaringly if you didn't know about her own loss, thought Pascoe. What had it driven her to? Drink, was the obvious answer.

254

He said, 'Yes, you're right.'

He saw no problem in passing on what Wield had told him about the woman, confident that every detail of her life would be splashed across the papers tomorrow.

When he finished, Kentmore nodded and said, 'Yes, I noticed her earlier and thought she looked a bit disturbed. Didn't expect a gun, though.'

Ellie said, 'If Fidler wanted a panel with some strong personal slant on the terrorism question, maybe the bastard got his researchers to make sure some of the audience were affected too.'

'I'd put money on it,' said Pascoe.

'It's terrible, using people like that,' said Kentmore angrily.

'I did try to warn you about shows like Fidler's,' murmured Kilda, whose glass seemed to be filling itself.

'Yes, you did,' said Kentmore, frowning. 'But I was foolish enough to believe my views on agriculture were enough to make me prime-time television fodder. Silly me. Ellie, Peter, I think we should be heading off. Many thanks for your hospitality.'

He hesitated then took a card out of his wallet and set it down on the table.

'Look, it would be nice to keep in touch, if you like, that is. In fact, as I was telling Ellie earlier, doing a bit of touting for custom, it's our local village fête tomorrow . . .'

'Yes,' said Pascoe, seeing where he was heading.

'I heard Fidler giving it a plug. Weather forecast sounds good. I hope you have a lovely day.'

But Kentmore was not to be diverted.

'They always have it on one of my fields,' he went on. 'From what you were saying, your little girl's going to miss out on her skating treat. I know it's not the same, but the organizers always go out of their way to give the kiddies a good time. So, just a thought, we're no distance really, Haresyke, just the far side of Harrogate. If you felt like a breath of country air . . .'

'What a nice idea,' said Ellie. 'We might just do that, mightn't we, Peter?'

She spoke with a degree of enthusiasm which seemed to go beyond politeness.

'Yes. Sounds great,' he said.

His own effort at enthusiasm must have fallen short because Kilda Kentmore grinned slyly at him, then finished her drink and leaned forward to brush her ice-chilled lips against his cheek, murmuring, 'Thanks for the drink. Good night, Ellie.'

Ellie shook Kentmore's hand and said, 'Thanks for the lift, and everything.'

'My pleasure. Goodnight.'

'Well, you seem to have made a hit there,' said Ellie after their guests had left.

'He seemed a nice enough guy,' said Pascoe.

'I wasn't talking about the guy but Miss Stolichnaya. Weird relationship.'

'You find a nice guy taking care of his dead brother's widow weird?'

'Still taking care a couple of years on I find weird. But you're right, he is rather nice. For a land-owning, Tory-voting, peasant-oppressing country squire, that is. Maybe it would be fun to drive down and take a look at him in his natural milieu – what do you think? And at lean and thirsty Kilda too, of course.'

'Kilda,' said Pascoe. 'Interesting name. Rings a bell.'

'She is, or was, a fashion photographer. Dropped out after she lost her husband, I gather. But maybe you recall it from a few years back when you were drooling over the lingerie adverts in the glossy mags.'

'Could be. But isn't there a saint called Kilda?'

'Wrong,' said Ellie, one of whose less attractive traits was combining snippets of esoteric knowledge with a love of being right. 'True, it's the name of a barren windswept island in the Outer Hebrides whence all life has fled, but in fact there never was an actual saint called Kilda. So a sort of pseudo saint. Fits in most respects, so far as I can see.'

Women beware women, thought Pascoe. Time to move on. But subtly.

'Talking of lean mean women,' he said, 'how did things end between you and F-Fiona? Did you pull one of her two f-faces off?'

'Don't be silly. I offered her a deal. Either I strangled her there and then or she undertook to get my next book the biggest exposure since Harry Potter.'

'I presume she's still breathing? I think you'll do very well in the media business, love. You've got the right twisted mind for it.'

'You reckon? So how would your nice straight mind react if I said let's take this bottle of Scotch upstairs and finish it in bed?'

Pascoe stood up and said, 'I feel a twist coming on.'

7

in the mood

On Saturday morning two nurses were straining their backs cleaning and rearranging Dalziel.

'Much more of this and they'll be finding a bed for me,' complained one of them, a little blonde with the face and figure of a well-fed angel. 'How long before they switch this bugger off?'

Her friend, used to excursions into the macabre as an escape route from the everyday horrors of their job, replied, 'Could be they're keeping him going till they find someone in need of a big heart. With his weight, he must have a huge one.'

'Not just his heart,' said the first nurse, looking down. 'Wonder if I could get that transplanted on to my Steve? Mind you, with his weak knees, he'd probably fall over every time he stood up!'

Dalziel, could he have heard the exchange, might have enjoyed a good laugh. Unfortunately he isn't having an out-of-body experience today. In fact he is very much in body, awareness reduced to a pinprick of dim light in a black box at the bottom of the deepest shaft of an abandoned mine. There is nothing in this awareness that could be called memory, not even of the most generalized kind – rain in the grass, light on the land, sun on the sea – no sense of anywhere else, not even really a sense of *here* and *now*, just the thinnest membrane of differentiation between pinprick and darkness.

And the only choice remaining is when to let the pressure of the dark pop the membrane and go out, go out, beyond all doubt . . .

The blonde nurse said, 'Right, that's Fatty done. No, hang on. Best put the music back on else his girlfriend will be looking for someone's arse to kick.'

Cap Marvell's mini-disc frequently got switched off, sometimes because a cleaner wanted the power point, sometimes because a consultant didn't like competition with the sound of his own voice, sometimes because a member of staff simply found *Swinging with the Big Bands* even *pianissimo* set his teeth on edge, but mainly because very few people believed it served any function other than to bolster delusional hope.

But delusion was not a term anyone cared to use in face of Cap Marvell's very real anger, so now the strains of 'In the Mood' played by the Dorsey Brothers' Orchestra stole forth once more, crept into the Fat Man's ear and sent its brassy brightness spiralling down into the darkness.

A couple of seconds later a momentary respondent syncopation of the hitherto regular notes of the heart monitor might have interested the nurses, but by now they were out of the door and on their way to their next angelic assignment.

8

without fear or favour

On Saturday morning Pascoe, as a result of what had been very much an in-body experience, woke late.

Ellie's side of the bed still bore her warm imprint and he rolled into it as he ran over the events of the previous night. After their initial frantic bout of love-making, Ellie had confessed how frightened she'd been at the sight of the gun and he had told her how he had felt in those long minutes after the screen went blank. Then they had lain silent in each other's arms for a long while, clinging to each other less like lovers than a pair of lost children in a dark forest who can face any terror except the terror of being alone.

The bedroom door opened. He looked towards it, smiling, expecting to see Ellie come in bearing coffee and croissants.

She came in, but coffee-less. And she didn't return his smile.

'I just heard the news. They've murdered Mike. Did you know about this?'

Who's Mike? he wondered, but happily before he could articulate the question his brain answered: Michael Carradice, aka Abbas Asir, suspected terrorist.

He sat up and said, 'There was something on the news about a body, his name was mentioned but nothing definite. Has it been confirmed it's him?'

'Oh yes. Why didn't you say something?'

'I had other things on my mind, remember?'

'Like sex, you mean?'

He didn't reply but regarded her gravely till she grimaced and said, 'Sorry. I know . . . I'm just so . . . shit, I don't know what I am. This is England, isn't it? But there's bombs going off, people getting their heads chopped off and waving guns around on the telly, and now this . . . What's happening, Pete?'

He reached out his hand and drew her down on to the bed beside him.

'I don't know, but I'm going to find out,' he said. 'What else did the police say?'

'Just that they confirmed the body was his. The reporters kept on asking about cause of death. Everyone's saying it was ricin poisoning, but the spokesman wouldn't confirm this. I put the telly on and I saw the shot they took of the dinghy he was in, and the banner. *Now it's safe.* Pete, they're saying they've heard from those Templar lunatics who beheaded Said Mazraani. He was acquitted, and they murdered him just the same.'

'They probably murdered him because he was acquitted,' said Pascoe sombrely.

'And what are your Manchester chums doing about it?' she demanded, pulling away from him. 'Or do they reckon this is just someone doing their dirty work for free?'

'I'll be sure to ask next time I see them,' said Pascoe. 'Now maybe we ought to get ourselves decent before Jane turns up with our daughter.'

He walked through a quick shower and got dressed. He could smell coffee being brewed downstairs. He picked up his mobile and dialled the Lubyanka. When the phone was answered he identified himself and asked if Lukasz Komorowski was in.

His thinking was simple. To anyone else he might have to explain his interest in Carradice, or risk them putting their own interpretation upon it.

To his surprise he got put through instantly.

'Hi,' he said. 'Didn't know if you'd be there.'

'Why wouldn't I be?' said Komorowski. 'How is your wife, by the way?'

'You saw the show?' wondered Pascoe.

'No. Not my thing. But I heard about it.'

I bet, thought Pascoe.

'She's fine. But this Carradice business coming on top of it . . . Look, I know this is personal, but if there's anything you can tell me, I'd appreciate it.'

'No problem,' said Komorowski. 'With acquittal very much on the cards, naturally we arranged surveillance. We had men in place. In addition we'd put a trace on him, a bug in the heel of his shoe. While he was being processed out of the system, his solicitor was telling the press his client would be joining him shortly to answer their questions. But of course he didn't. The bug told us he was still in the building. When we went looking we found his shoes on top of a lavatory cistern. We assumed this had all been part of a ruse concocted by his brief so that he could leave via one of the other exits. His lawyer denied it, but we were unpersuaded till we got the news that his body had been found in a dinghy floating on a Nottinghamshire reservoir. Cause of death: poisoning. Not ricin as everyone's saying – that would have taken much longer. A massive injection of diamorphine. Quicker. And kinder, though I doubt if that played much part in their thinking.'

'Shit. I gather there's been a message from the Templars.'

'Oh yes,' said Komorowski. 'All the main TV companies and most of the national papers. As before. *Where the Law fails, we will provide justice,* that sort of thing. It will, I fear, resonate with a lot of people.'

'A lot of *Voice* readers, certainly,' said Pascoe.

'*Voice* readers? Isn't that an oxymoron?'

Pascoe could sense the faint smile on the man's lips.

'Look, thanks a lot for being so open with me,' he said. 'It's not that there was ever any close connection between my wife and Carradice, you understand . . .'

'Of course,' said Komorowski. 'I'm glad you felt able to ring. In fact, if you hadn't, I was going to ring you.'

'You were?' said Pascoe, surprised. 'Well, thanks even more.'

'I must confess my motives were mixed,' said the man. 'Concern for your wife's feelings coming a little behind a more professional concern. The distant connection between Mrs Pascoe and the dead man is of course of no interest to anyone of sense, but the tabloids would seize upon it with great glee. Headlines like *I married a terrorist's auntie, says bombed bobby* would not, of course, bring down the government, but they could be deeply embarrassing. And in pursuit of a good story, these people are without scruple. No one is safe: colleagues, friends, family – children are particularly vulnerable.'

'Yes, OK, I know all this, but there's no reason why it should get out. Is there?'

'We live in an age of leaks, Mr Pascoe,' said Komorowski gloomily. 'Even the secrets we take to the grave with us aren't safe from the scavengings of biographers and obituarists. As for reasons, malice has its reasons that reason wots not of. But I'm probably taking too dark a view here. If you and Mrs Pascoe keep your heads beneath the parapet for a while, I'm sure the Carradice story will soon go the way of all copy.'

Am I being warned here or threatened? Pascoe asked himself.

He said, 'Was Carradice definitely guilty?'

'If it's any consolation, yes, he was. Beyond all doubt, except for the kind that defence lawyers cultivate like delicate orchids in the hot-house of our courts. Will you be returning to us on Monday?'

'Superintendent Glenister is going to ring me tomorrow,' said Pascoe.

'I see. Whatever, I'm sure we will meet again. Don't hesitate to ring if I can be of any further assistance. Goodbye.'

He rang off. From downstairs Ellie's voice called, 'Coffee's getting cold!'

In the kitchen he said, 'Sorry. I got talking on the phone.'

He passed on what Komorowski had said in full.

Ellie said, 'I thought the CAT spooks tended to keep you at arm's length?'

'And now here's one falling over himself to be friendly. Yes, I noticed that too.'

'And do you believe him?'

'Which bit of him?'

'Let's start with the bit about Mike being definitely guilty.'

'He seemed very sure.'

'It was people like him that were sure about weapons of mass destruction in Iraq.'

'That doesn't mean they're always wrong.'

'No. But it doesn't make any difference anyway. Does it?'

He knew what she was saying but he still said, 'What?'

'Mike was murdered. What he might or might not have been guilty of is irrelevant. He was murdered, end of story. Right? Or now you've been told he was definitely guilty, does this make it some sort of justified homicide in your book?'

'No, of course not,' said Pascoe irritably. 'An unlawful killing is an unlawful killing. It's up to the courts to take account of motive and circumstance. Without fear or favour. That's the way the judiciary operates in trying cases. And that's the way the police operate in investigating them.'

'And that's what you're doing in regard to the Mill Street explosion, right?'

'I'm sorry?' said Pascoe, thinking, Christ! and I thought I'd kept this under wraps! Could she have got a hint from Wieldy? Not likely, but how else . . . ?

'You're not letting it alone, are you, Peter?'

'It nearly killed me. It may have killed a very good friend,' he proclaimed. 'I'm sorry if I seem a bit obsessive about it. I'll try to put it out of my mind in future, shall I?'

It was bluster, aimed at winning space to think. Some time soon he would have to share his doubts and theories about what had actually happened in Mill Street, but he'd have preferred Edgar Wield to be the first to run his cool unblinking gaze over them.

Next moment he realized he no longer had a choice.

Ellie said, 'There was a file behind a cushion on the sofa.'

Oh shit. His private investigation file which events last night had put right out of his mind.

He said, 'You read it?'

'Stuff you find down the sofa is common property, house rule, remember?'

A rule which on occasion had provided a useful way of giving Rosie a bit of extra pocket money when an open advance would have breached strict economic policy.

'So?'

'So let's not beat about. Do you really think Mill Street wasn't just a dreadful accident but something more sinister? Or is this just a neurotic symptom of PTSD?'

'I don't know,' he said. 'It sounds a bit crazy, I know, but what's happened to Carradice and to Mazraani sounds crazy too, and we know that's really happened.'

'Yes, but whoever organized those killings wants the world to know about it. There's been no message relating to Mill Street, has there?'

'No, but it could be they're a bit reluctant to admit to doing something which not only killed three terrorists but also blew up two policemen, maybe killing one of them.'

That brought silence. Pascoe drank his cooling coffee and crumbled a soggy croissant. This was not in any respect the breakfast he'd expected.

Ellie said softly, 'Pete, are you sure you know what you're getting into here?'

'You mean if I've spotted there are inconsistencies, so have the CAT investigators, and why aren't they saying anything? Oh yes, I've looked down that road and I'm still not sure where it leads.'

'No,' said Ellie. 'I hadn't thought of it, but it just makes things worse.'

'What then?'

'It's what we were talking about before, only a lot more personal. I mean, if the explosion hadn't put Andy in a coma and come close to killing you, would you be so bothered about it? Even if you spotted inconsistencies. Three terrorists killed. Who cares? CAT want to call the shots. Dan Trimble is happy they should. Would you, in those circumstances, have started stirring things up and getting yourself noticed?'

'In those circumstances, the guys who did this would have wanted the world to know, so there wouldn't have been a problem,' declared Pascoe triumphantly. But it was merely a debating point and they both knew it.

He couldn't resist following it up with another.

'Anyway, it's not two minutes since you were getting aerated because you thought the death of Carradice might get downgraded because people thought he was a terrorist. So why are you down on me for trying to get at the truth about Mill Street?'

'I'm not down on you,' she said. 'I just know how much you'll beat up on yourself when you realize it's revenge you're after more than justice.'

'Oh yes? And is it simply justice you want for Carradice, or does being related come into it?'

'I held him in my arms, Pete.'

'He peed on you.'

'Rosie almost washed me away till I got the hang of it,' she said.

'He's not Rosie,' he said, half angrily.

'I expect he was to someone. The same. You know what I mean.'

He began to see what was really bugging her. She believed in giving their daughter her own space to develop along the lines of her own personality. But what if after all their love, all their care, one of those lines led to an end as unforeseeably sad as Mick Carradice's?

He looked for words to say, reassurances to offer, which wouldn't sound empty and banal. But she wasn't done with him yet.

'That CAT stuff in your folder about the bodies, there were some notes attached you'd written yourself. Where did they come from?'

He'd no intention of letting her know he'd burgled Glenister's office to get the original file but saw no reason to hide the fact that he'd talked to Mary Goodrich.

'And they'd really put the frighteners on her to keep her mouth shut,' he concluded, wanting to underline CAT's suspicious behaviour. As so often, her response leap-frogged his intention to a point he didn't really want her to reach.

'Oh yes? If she was so frightened, then why did she talk to you?'

'She's a good citizen,' he said lamely.

She was on him in a flash.

'You mean you found a way to make her talk even more frightening than CAT's to keep her quiet? What did you use, Pete? A cattle prod?'

He was saved from having to mount what was at best going to be a retreating defence by a sudden fanfare of barking from Tig as he leapt out of his basket and ran into the entrance hall. Only the imminence of Rosie provoked this response. Not that it meant she was at the door, just that she was less than a mile away and getting closer. It was of course impossible for the dog to know this, but he was never wrong.

I live in a house where everyone knows more than I do, thought Pascoe. And in some cases more about me too.

He said, 'End of our quiet weekend.'

'I didn't notice it had started,' said Ellie.

And if the media pack get wind of your relationship with Carradice, you'll be amazed at how much worse it can get, thought Pascoe. Suddenly home seemed not the best place to be.

'Tell you what,' he said. 'All this stuff about

terrorism and bombs and assassinations makes the thought of good old-fashioned traditional country entertainment seem rather attractive. Why don't we compensate Rosie for missing out on her skating trip by accepting Squire Kentmore's invite to his village fête?'

Ellie looked at him suspiciously. They heard the front door open and Tig's barking rise to a crescendo.

'Let's put it to She-who-must-be-obeyed,' said Ellie.

9

the decisive moment

Kilda Kentmore stood at her bedroom window and watched the cars bumping across the field to the side of her house. This was the overflow car park. Not yet midday and already the main car park must be full. The fine weather had brought the crowds out. Happily the same fine weather meant the ground surface was hard and firm. Last year it had rained, resulting in the double whammy of fewer visitors and the parking fields churned into a quagmire.

She yawned. For a long time after she'd been widowed, she hadn't been able to sleep except when completely exhausted and even then her terrible dreams had usually brought her cold and shaking back to the dark reality of life after very few minutes.

Well, she was over that now. Drink had helped, no denying that. But she was in control. There was a bottle of vodka on her dressing table. She could take a drink from it, or pour it down the loo, or just walk away from it.

That's control. Running from it isn't control, and hiding from it definitely isn't.

Empty words she'd judged them when first she heard them, but they kept coming back till she acknowledged their truth. And the truth of the words that followed.

You need something, pointless denying it. But find something better. I'd guess you've got real talent. Use it.

At first this had come across as a clumsy nudge towards sex. Instead she now saw it as a clever nudge towards . . . not survival, she doubted if survival had ever been an option . . . but towards meaning, with the bonus en route of her first twelve-hour dreamless sleep from which she'd woken as fresh and bubbly as when she was a girl, with none of that back-of-the-eyes dullness which was the price she paid for punching herself unconscious with alcohol.

She picked up the photo of her husband which stood next to the bottle on her dressing table. In it he looked incredibly young and boyish, blond hair blowing in a stiff breeze as he stood in swimming trunks on the beach at Scarborough. Sometimes you had to wait an age for the Cartier-Bresson *moment décisif* but occasionally it just happened. Not that she'd had any pretension to being a Cartier-Bresson, but she'd been making some headway out of the shallow waters of fashion photography when it happened. Maybe I should try photo-journalism, she'd said to him when he told her the squadron was posted to Iraq. I could specialize in combat photography. Then I wouldn't have to stay at home. No way, he'd replied, laughing. One crazy in the family's quite enough. Go for grainy realism if you like, but no way do I want you within a hundred miles of a war zone.

She had photos of him in uniform, standing by his helicopter, and he'd even smuggled her on board during a training flight and she had shots of him, very focused and professional, at the controls.

These she could not bear to have around her. In fact, until the last few weeks she hadn't felt the least urge to use her camera equipment. But life – even pointless, unwished-for life – is movement, one way or another.

She let her gaze drift from the photo to the mirror. She hadn't put back on all the weight she'd lost in those first few months, but she was no longer the skeletal figure she had become for a while. OK, a lot of the restored calories might have come out of a bottle, but now this lean taut body simply looked stripped for action.

She poured herself a glass of vodka. Her choice, her breakfast. Maurice had asked if she would be present at the fête's official opening on the lawn in front of the big house. She'd replied with a cool *no. In fact,* she'd gone on, *I doubt if I'll be in the mood for bucolic jollity at all.* They were unbreakably linked by tragedy, but just because she shared a name with him and had not yet found the energy to break away from this grace-and-favour existence on the family estate didn't mean she had to stand by his side at every public occasion. It was time he got himself a wife anyway. Someone like that Pascoe woman, strong, intelligent, passionate. It was a type he clearly admired. She might not be available, not for the moment anyway, but there must be plenty more like her swimming around, waiting to be trawled in.

She glanced through the window again, and lo and behold, there she was, Ellie Pascoe herself, climbing out of a dusty saloon, with her slim sharp-eyed husband getting out of the driver's door, and a young girl and dog spilling out of the back.

Now this was interesting. The woman had looked at her and not much liked what she saw. It had been fun to tease her by feigning to find her husband fuckable. As she'd said good night, she hadn't thought there was a cat in hell's chance of Maurice's stupid suggestion being acted upon. What had happened to bring this about? Which of them had the impulse come from?

Unexpected things come in threes, whether good or bad. You break a cup at breakfast, there'll be another couple of breakages before supper. You hear from a lost friend in the morning post, another two will emerge out of the mist before the day is out.

A green Skoda with a noisy engine nosed into the same row as the Pascoes. Out of the driver's door slid a young woman in jeans and a belly-exposing top. Kilda recognized her as Kalim Sarhadi's fiancée, Jamila. They'd met before the show the previous night, then sat around talking for what seemed an age while they waited for the police to take statements from the two men and Ellie Pascoe. The identification was confirmed when Sarhadi emerged from the passenger door. Presumably it was her car. He was a poor student, he'd told them last night, making enough money from helping with his father's taxi business to pay for his fees at Bradford University. She was a secretary in the university registrar's office, which was how they had met.

Kilda had listened to their self-revelations with the minimum effort necessary to conceal total uninterest, but Maurice had visibly basked in the Jamila's gratitude at his intervention during the threatened attack on Sarhadi. The young couple had also been invited to attend the Haresyke Fête, but Kilda would have given even longer odds against their appearance than the Pascoes'.

As she watched, Ellie Pascoe spotted Sarhadi and called out to him. He turned, looked blank for a second, then recognized her. The two groups joined, Pascoe was introduced. The child also. Jamila looked ready to make much of her, but the girl quickly spotted neither of the newcomers was particularly enthusiastic about the attentions of the small dog and responded with indifferent politeness.

Takes after her mother, judged Kilda. Quick judgments, doesn't much care if they show. Unlike her husband, whose judgment was probably as keen if not keener but who knew how to mask its conclusions with smiling courtesy.

So, two unlikely events in a morning. She could either sit around and await the third, or forestall fate by creating it.

Only Maurice would know how unlikely it was that she'd appear at the fête, but that ought to be enough. It might be interesting to see the slim cop again. While she'd done the cool flirtation thing to irritate his bossy wife, there had definitely been the whisper of a connection there.

She walked through her shower, dressed, breakfasted on crisp-bread and black coffee, and made for the door.

Here she paused, then turned and ran lightly up the stairs and took her favourite Nikon off the top shelf of the wardrobe where it had been gathering dust ever since . . .

She pushed the thought from her mind and checked the battery. It was long dead, but she had plenty of spares in her dark-room.

A fly had buzzed in through the open window and was perched on the rim of the untouched glass of vodka.

'Have this one on me,' she said, and a few moments later left her dark-room to go out into the sunshine.

10

queen of the fête

Saturday got off to a bad start. Not all my fault, thought Ellie Pascoe, but you certainly didn't help. What you need's a long PIN you've got to enter before you can punch the explosion button!

Rosie's return had brought truce and when the child had made it clear that whatever they did that day didn't matter as long as they all did it together, going to the Haresyke Fête began to seem not such a bad idea.

Within half an hour of arrival, it began to seem a very good idea indeed.

As they wandered round the stalls in the warm sunshine, she saw her husband relaxing into a condition as close to his old self as he'd been since the Mill Street explosion. Meeting Sarhadi and his fiancée had helped. He seemed to take to the young man and, as for Jamila, the company of a bright and attractive young woman rarely failed to regress him to the lively laughing student he'd been when Ellie first met him.

Ellie was able to enjoy the transformation with no hint of jealousy. She liked the girl herself and, more importantly, it was clear the girl thought the sun shone out of her fiancé's big brown eyes. Jamila, she discovered, was third-generation British and in her speech and dress was so indistinguishable from her Anglo-Saxon co-evals, that Ellie wondered how this went down with traditionalists at the mosque.

A firm believer that the first step to finding answers was to ask questions, she said casually, 'God, I wish I still had the figure to wear a top like that.'

'You look great to me,' said Jamila with a pleasing sincerity.

'Thank you kindly, but once you get a bulge, even if it's still bike tyre rather than the full Michelin, I think it's best to keep it under wraps.'

'Maybe, but a lot of the oldies down the mosque would reckon I'm far too skinny. They love a bit of bulging.'

'So you don't get any aggro for the way you dress?'

'Oh yes,' she said. 'All the time, but not from my family, and that's all that matters to me. Of course I wouldn't go near the mosque looking like this. Next week I'll be wearing the full trad kit for my wedding. That should take the bangers by surprise.'

'The bangers?'

'Head-bangers. That's what I call these lads who creep around Sheikh Ibrahim like he's a prophet or something. Kalim says I shouldn't provoke them, but they don't bother me. Anyway, they're all blow. They rattle on about how I ought to be disciplined for the way I dress and talk, but the Sheikh keeps them in order 'cos I'm Kalim's girl.'

'So Kalim and the Sheikh are close?' probed Ellie, remembering the young man's defensive attitude to Al-Hijazi on *Fidler's Three*.

'Sort of,' said the young woman hesitantly. 'A lot of the time they're right in each other's face about politics. He's funny, the Sheikh. Sometimes he sounds like he wants to set a torch to most of the West, other times he's even more laid-back than my dad.'

'So you don't think there's anything in what some of the papers say about him encouraging his followers to commit terrorist acts?'

The girl did not reply straight away and Ellie thought she'd overstepped the mark, but it seemed Jamila was only getting her thoughts together.

'I think what Kal says about him is likely right. He doesn't encourage the bangers to break the law, but some of them are brain-dead enough to imagine he does, and mebbe he ought to take more care of that.'

'Ellie,' called Pascoe. 'Do you know where Rosie's got to?'

'I thought you were watching her,' said Ellie. 'Sorry, Jam, we'd better find her.'

'She can't come to much harm here,' said the girl reassuringly.

282

'It's not her I'm worried about,' said Ellie. 'We'll probably see you two later.'

It didn't take long to locate their daughter as the fête wasn't all that extensive. The set-up was deliciously old-fashioned, not in any self-conscious retro fashion but because this was the way they'd been doing things for years and no one saw any good reason to change. A crowd of kids had attracted Rosie to a stall where for twenty pence you got three chances to precipitate one of the village schoolteachers into a trough of water by hitting a wooden lever with a well-aimed rubber ball. Rosie's daily routine of hurling Tig's ball as far as possible for at least an hour had built up a good throwing action. Her first success won rapturous cheers from the watching children, redoubled when Tig, imagining this was all for his benefit, plunged into the water alongside the drenched pedagogue. By the time her parents tracked her down, she had repeated her success twice, and her many new friends were ready to elect her Queen of the fête.

She didn't want to be parted from them and sent her parents on their way, having made it clear she found their concern agonizingly embarrassing.

'Reminds me of you,' said Pascoe as they walked away. 'Wilful, loud-mouthed, anti-authoritarian . . . ouch!'

They made no special effort to seek out Maurice Kentmore but a little later, as they paused before the bottle stall, Ellie did wonder aloud if maybe he wasn't there.

'Probably declares the show open, then retreats for a sherry in his library leaving a couple of mastiffs at the front door to repel the malodorous peasantry,' said Pascoe.

'Did I hear the word sherry? There was a rather nice bottle of amontillado somewhere. It's great to see you both again. I'm so glad you decided to come.'

Kentmore in his shirt sleeves emerged from beneath the stall flourishing a large bottle of Windsor Sauce, which he handed to a small woman who examined the sell-by date with a jay's beady eye before paying an absurdly small sum and moving off.

'Now, that amontillado,' he said. 'Ah, here we are. I can recommend it, as I donated it myself. It's marked up at two quid. At that price I'm tempted to buy it back!'

Pascoe was no great fan of amontillado but he felt guilty that Kentmore might have caught more of his comment than the word sherry.

As he paid he said, 'Are you on here all day?'

'Neglecting my squirely duties of twirling my mustachios and ogling the milkmaids, you mean?'

So he had heard. Oh well. At least he was smiling about it.

'Nothing so responsible, I fear,' the man went on. 'I am the lowest of the low, a general dogs-body. I wander around and, whenever a stall-minder wants a break, I step into the breach. Out of which I am about to step as I see Miss Jigg returning. You two fancy a sit down and a snack? Our local ladies could bake for Old England.'

They followed him to a refreshment tent. He sat them down at a table in the open air, vanished inside and returned with a small tray on which rested a teapot, milk jug, cups and saucers. Behind him came a pretty girl, well worth an ogle, carrying a much larger tray with sandwiches and cakes.

Pascoe sampled the cakes. Kentmore hadn't oversold the baking ladies. They were delicious. Then a hand rested lightly on his shoulder and Kilda's voice said, 'Peter, Ellie, isn't this nice? Maurice, I see they've worked you off your feet already.'

'Kilda, you've surfaced,' said Kentmore. 'I was just thinking about sending a search party down to your house.'

The woman gave Pascoe's shoulder a last little squeeze then slipped on to a chair, putting her camera on the table.

Your house, Pascoe noticed. Ellie too, but she liked her assurances double sure.

'You live in the village, do you, Kilda?' she said.

'No. On the estate. You'd have seen the cottage as you drove into the car park. They call it the Gatehouse, but the gate's long gone. Maurice was kind enough to offer it to Chris and me when we got married. Inertia has kept me there since I became a widow. I keep thinking I must move on, but it will probably take an eviction order to shift me.'

Kentmore said, 'You know the house is yours as long as you want it, Kilda.'

There was an awkward pause of the kind Ellie was expert at filling when she felt like it. This time she just sat quietly and waited to see how far it would stretch.

Not far, was the answer. There were two interruptions in quick succession. First an anxious matron summoned Kentmore to deal with some crisis. Then Rosie appeared followed by a dripping Tig with the news that she wanted to enter him in the terrier race but the stupid organizers required adult supervision of each entrant in case of trouble.

Trouble, thought Pascoe looking at Tig, who was clearly in a state of delirious excitement, is what they were likely to get.

Ellie looked at her husband who held up a wedge of lemon meringue pie as evidence he was otherwise engaged.

'All right,' she said in response to Rosie's impatient tug. 'I'm coming.'

Pascoe watched them move away then pushed the cakes invitingly towards Kilda.

She smiled and shook her head.

'You can't be dieting,' said Pascoe.

'I could be wearing a very tight corset,' she said.

'I don't think so. That's the first thing they teach us to spot at detective school.'

'What's the second?'

'That's it, the whole curriculum in a nutshell, guaranteeing what the great British press tells the great British public we are: a bunch of hopeless plods.'

'That sounds bitter.'

'It was meant to sound funny,' said Pascoe.

'I'd understand bitter. Being blown up in the line of duty and no one getting arrested for it would make me bitter too. How's your friend in hospital doing?'

'Just the same. I should go to see him some time this weekend.'

'You don't sound keen.'

'He's in a coma. It just seems, I don't know, like going through the motions.'

'At least you get to see him,' she said.

He recalled what had happened to her and felt a little pang of shame. At least Andy was alive. To be told you were never going to see again someone you loved . . . he recalled once more his feelings when the TV screen went blank last night and shivered.

'So will you go?' she asked.

'Probably. There is another of our guys in there I ought to look in on.'

'Not another in a coma, I hope?'

He smiled and said, 'Well, there are different opinions about that. Happily our Constable Hector is notoriously a hard man to inflict serious damage on and I gather that he is conscious and reasonably well and likely to make a full recovery.'

'It's a dangerous profession,' she said. 'What happened to this one?'

'Nothing exotic. Accident. Hit and run. We're still looking for the bastard.'

'And will you get him?'

'I expect so. We've a pretty good idea about the car, and as it's a black Jag and it's bound to have a large dent in it, that makes things easier.'

She picked up the camera and asked, 'Mind if I take your picture?'

'Not in the least. That looks an expensive bit of kit.'

'Never stint when it's your livelihood. No, don't pose, just carry on scoffing.'

All the time as she talked she was taking snaps.

'So you're still shooting for the rag trade then?'

'Not really. But I may sell this to the *Police Gazette*, "What the well-dressed copper is eating this season". Do you like being a policeman?'

'Yes, I suppose I do,' he said. 'Do you like being a photographer?'

'It's OK.'

'That doesn't sound terribly positive.'

'No? What I mean is, yes, I like doing it well enough. But you need more, don't you? I think you implied that. You feel being a cop's a job worth doing, right?'

'Yes, I do.'

288

'And you like doing it. That's what makes life worth living, isn't it? Finding something you feel's worth doing, and something you get a kick out of doing.'

'I hope you find it.'

'I think I'm moving in the right direction,' she said with a smile. 'There, that will do for capturing your likeness. Now I think I might be tempted to a sliver of apple tart.'

'Good choice,' he said.

They sat in silence for a while, one of those silences which can steal upon two people unawares, not a universal silence but one peculiar to them alone and their situation, a silence not broken but intensified by the totally separate existence of background noise, music playing, people laughing, and which for a moment seemed to encompass the whole of the sunlit field where the fête was taking place. The silence might be called companionable, but there was nothing sexual in it, at least nothing which would require action and the expense of energy and sweat. Indeed, the feelings Pascoe felt rising within him had less to do with erotic fantasy than sentimental patriotism.

This is England, he found himself thinking. This is what Englishness means. Sitting at a village fête on a warm day of summer in pleasant company, eating Victoria sponge beneath a blue sky spotted with little white clouds, this is worth fighting for . . .

And then the idyll was shattered by a distant cacophony of barking and the din of human voices upraised in alarm and in command.

'What on earth is happening?' wondered Kilda.

'I think,' said Pascoe, sinking lower in his chair and reaching for another cream éclair, 'I think that my daughter's terrier may be introducing his fellow competitors to his totally original handicap system.'

11

forgotten dreams

Pascoe awoke suddenly.

There was a hooded figure standing over him, one hand on his shoulder, the other swinging a gleaming cleaver at his vulnerable neck.

He closed his eyes and tried to roll away. The hand held him more firmly. He opened his eyes once more, and this time found he was looking up into the anxious face of his wife. The bedside clock said it was five to two.

He struggled upright and said, 'What?'

'You were rolling around and muttering.'

'Was I?'

He realized he was hot and sweaty and nauseous.

He rolled out of bed and just made it to the bathroom before he was sick.

'Pete, are you OK?' said Ellie in the doorway.

'I'll survive. Must have been something I ate.'

'Like all those cakes,' she said. 'And how much did you drink with Wieldy?'

When they got home from the fête and he

recalled he'd promised to meet the sergeant for a drink, he hadn't wanted to go. But Ellie, who was very protective of Wield, had stopped him from ringing to cancel, saying, 'Half an hour while I make the dinner won't hurt.'

He should have followed his instinct. It hadn't been a very successful meeting.

He'd laid out his theories about what had actually happened in Mill Street with what had seemed to him pellucid eloquence and irrefutable logic. Instead of applause, what he got from Wield was the blank stare a probationer might have received who'd just made a botched report.

'So what do you think?' he'd demanded.

'Let's be clear,' said Wield. 'Your theory is that these Templars who murdered Mazraani and Carradice were responsible for the Mill Street bang. They were interrupted by Hector after one of them fired a gun, presumably to put the frighteners on the Arabs. They then made their escape via the roof space to the end house, Number 6. They knew the police were in the vicinity because of Hector's intervention. Nevertheless they recklessly detonated by remote control the bomb they'd left in Number 3. But when they heard that you and Andy had been hurt in the explosion, they decided to keep quiet about their involvement because they didn't want to start their campaign with a botched op that could turn out to have killed a copper.'

'Right,' said Pascoe, wondering why his recent lucidity now seemed so opaque.

'And you're also saying that these Templars who made such a cock-up aren't just a bunch of gung-ho vigilantes but a well-organized cell of conspirators who have probably got someone in CAT feeding them info and running protection.'

'That's how it seems to me,' declared Pascoe. 'Look at the evidence! The bullet, the post-mortem reports, the cover-up of Freeman's surveillance op, the reaction from CAT when I seem to be stirring things . . .'

'Pete, if you heard one of our DCs reaching for conclusions like yours from evidence like this, you'd slap him down and send him to bed without his supper. Even if there's more to Mill Street than CAT are letting on, maybe they're simply keeping quiet about their suspicions because it gives them a bit of an edge in the investigation. Maybe they found a lot more stuff when they were running the crime scene there and they just don't want to let the perps know they're coming at them from that particular direction.'

Pascoe considered this. There was a disturbing amount of sense in it.

'So why keep me on the outside?' he asked.

'Because that's what you are, Pete. An outsider. They're worried about you, not because there's stuff to hide, but because after your own experience and with Andy lying in a coma, you're a loose cannon. Likely that's why Glenister got you attached to her team in the first place, so she can keep a close eye on you.

You said yourself you'd been given a non-job.'

He'd had another couple of drinks with the sergeant to show he wasn't put out at this demolition of his carefully constructed hypotheses. And he was nearly an hour late for his dinner, which he didn't fancy anyway but which uxorial diplomacy made him eat.

And this had been the result. A nightmare he couldn't, or wouldn't recall. And a stomach like the Red Sea after the application of Moses' rod.

He immersed his head in cold water, brushed his teeth, gargled, and felt a little better. By the time he emerged from the bathroom, Ellie had made a hot milky drink.

She'd also unearthed the tablets prescribed by John Sowden when Pascoe left hospital. He'd stopped taking them after a few days and had left them at home when he went to Manchester. Now he looked at them with distaste.

'They make me drowsy,' he objected.

'You're in your pyjamas, it's two o'clock in the fucking morning,' said Ellie. 'Take them.'

Pascoe's fairy godmother had been more generous than poor Hector's, but they did to some extent share the gift of survival, though the Pascoe version was rather more specialized. He knew when not to argue with his wife.

He climbed back into bed.

'Feeling a bit better now?' she asked.

'Yes. Much. Thought I might go along to visit Andy in the morning. And Hector too.'

'I think that's a good idea,' she said.

She leaned over to kiss him. He turned his mouth away because, despite the toothpaste, gargle, and milky drink, he still had a faint after-taste of vomit at the back of his throat. But she kissed him on the lips anyway.

Then they both lay there, side by side, simulating sleep while their open eyes stared uncertainly into the dark.

12

the man of my dreams

Next morning when Rosie heard about the proposed hospital visit she said, 'I'll come too.'

'No,' said Pascoe, more shortly than he'd intended. 'I don't think that's a good idea. Uncle Andy's very ill. Very ill indeed.'

'That's why I want to see him.'

'But he still hasn't woken up, he won't know you're there.'

'He won't know you're there either and that doesn't stop you from going.'

But it didn't make it easy, thought Pascoe. Was he just transferring to Rosie his own unhappiness at the prospect of sitting at the Fat Man's side, murmuring a few awkward self-conscious phrases in his ear, but with growing conviction that if this unresponsive hulk could hear anything, it was only the melancholy, long, withdrawing roar of that same tide of life which had beached him here?

'OK,' said Pascoe. 'If Mum says it's OK, you can come.'

He looked at Ellie. She gave him the look she usually gave him when he wished a decision about Rosie on to her, but her voice was even and pleasant as she said, 'Of course you can go, darling, if that's what you want.'

'Yes, that's what I want,' said the girl. 'What time shall I be ready?'

She spoke with great aplomb, but as they approached Dalziel's room, Pascoe was able to gauge from the increased pressure of her fingers around his that she was as nervous as he was.

When he pushed open the door, it was a relief to see Cap Marvell sitting by the bedside.

She was talking to the recumbent figure, naturally, easily, with none of the self-consciousness of his own attempts. Indeed, as if in the middle of a real conversation, she gave them a welcoming smile but didn't break off till she'd finished what she had to say.

'. . . and the bastard said I was trespassing and if I didn't get off his land, he was in his rights to throw me off, and I asked if he could drive a tractor one-handed because if he laid a finger on me I'd break his arm. Then I rang the RSPCA. Had to wait an hour till they got there, but I didn't trust him not to blow the poor beast's brains out and drag it off and hide the body if I left. Now here's Peter and Rosie to see you. Hello, you two. Rosie, how are you? It's been an age since I saw you. You're still awfully thin, my dear. I hope you're eating properly. How's school?'

297

Amanda Marvell had shed much of the conditioning of her upbringing, but in her attitude to children the spirit of nanny and nursery still clung close.

'Fine,' said Rosie.

She began to walk slowly round the bed as if determined to get the fullest possible view of the Fat Man.

Cap had a small bottle in her hand which she now held beneath Dalziel's nose.

'Smelling salts?' enquired Pascoe.

She smiled and moved the bottle beneath his nose.

A peaty spirituous aroma floated out of it.

'Lagavulin,' she said. 'Very distinctive.'

'Good Lord. Do you think it does any good?' said Pascoe doubtfully.

'Watch this.'

She produced another small bottle, removed the stopper and held that under Dalziel's nostrils, which immediately crinkled in seeming distaste.

'Gin,' said Cap. 'Which Andy thinks is only fit for disinfecting urinals.'

'What do the staff here think of your . . . treatment?'

'The staff?' she said puzzled. 'How on earth should I know?'

She was truly formidable. Pascoe wasn't absolutely certain how much he liked her, and though always friendly towards him, he occasionally got the feeling that she regarded him as a

Leporello to the great Don. In build she was Wagnerian rather than Mozartian, in this at least a fit consort for the Fat Man. In background (landed gentry), education (St Dorothy's Academy) and beliefs (animal rights, Greenpeace, Friends of the Earth) she was a Scots mile away from him. In bed . . . the collective imagination of Mid-Yorkshire constabulary had become considerably overheated fantasizing on their carnal relationship. 'Whales do it,' PC Maycock had said. 'Yes, but they do it in water,' PC Jennison had responded. On land or in sea, the Fat Man and his buxom leman seemed to be managing very well, thank you.

Rosie meanwhile had settled herself on a chair on the other side of the bed, leaning forward over Dalziel. Her eyes were wide open and fixed unblinkingly on his face.

Pascoe said, 'Any change?'

'I got the impression he was getting bored with the Big Bands, so I've changed the tape,' said Cap. 'Thought he'd like this.'

She showed him a cassette box which advertised it contained the perfect music to turn your dull Anglo-Saxon New Year into a hootenanny Hogmanay ceilidh.

'Good, good,' said Pascoe, thinking, The world is full of seriously weird people. And I should know, living with two of them.

He said, 'Look, we won't interrupt. There's another of our officers in hospital. I think I'll pop along and see him. Rosie, you want to come and say hello to Constable Hector?'

The girl didn't respond. She was leaning so far forward now her face was almost touching the Fat Man's. She'd had to move some of his tubes and wires to get so close.

'Rosie?' he said, faintly alarmed. 'Be careful you don't get tangled in that stuff.'

Detective's daughter switches her dad's boss off. That would be a headline to set alongside the one about Cousin Mick.

'Rosie!' he said more sternly.

She stood up and came to the end of the bed.

'OK,' she said. 'Let's go.'

Pascoe felt a coward at his readiness to take off after such a very short visit, but at least he'd made an excuse, however feeble, whereas Rosie's response just sounded totally indifferent.

He glanced apologetically at Cap, who gave him an ironic smile as if she knew he was running for cover.

He said defensively, 'Maybe we can look in again on our way out.'

Rosie said, 'No need. We're done for now.'

This hardly improved matters.

'We?' he said sternly. As he spoke the word, it occurred to him it didn't feel as if it included him or Cap.

'Me and Uncle Andy.'

Was she saying she'd taken her farewell? Not a road to go down here and now.

He said, 'OK. Let's go then. Oh, by the way,

Cap. You'd better have this, for when he wakes up.'

He handed her a plastic bag containing Dalziel's dental plate.

To his horror, he saw her eyes fill. She doesn't really believe he's going to recover either, he thought.

'Thank you,' she said, taking the bag. 'Good of you to come. You too, Rosie.'

The girl looked at her thoughtfully then said, 'I think he'd like the Scottish music now. Bye.'

In the corridor Pascoe said, 'How did you know Cap had brought some Scottish music for Uncle Andy?'

'Didn't she tell us?'

'No. Perhaps you saw the box.'

'That must have been it. I'm going to get Uncle Andy to teach me the sword dance when he comes home. He's got some real claymores in his attic.'

This was true. Pascoe had seen them one night when he'd accompanied the Fat Man home for a night-cap after the enthusiastic celebration of a successful case. The night-cap had turned into a whole milliner's shop, and something had been said which provoked Dalziel into giving a demonstration of his prowess. For ten minutes his stockinged feet had performed intricate and athletic steps between the gleaming blades of the crossed claymores without a single mistake. Finished, he had essayed a bow and toppled over across a substantial coffee table which he reduced to matchwood.

Maybe Rosie had overheard him describing the scene to Ellie.

They got directions to Hector's ward from a nurse. As they approached, a man came from the opposite direction and began to open the door. He paused when the Pascoes halted, preparatory to following him into the room.

Through the half-open door they could see two beds, one with Hector's unmistakeable head, eyes closed, on the pillow, the other empty but looking as if it had been recently occupied.

'Damn,' said the man. 'He must have gone to the day room. I'll check it out.'

With a courteous smile he held the door open to allow them to pass, then closed it behind them.

They approached Hector's bed. Sleep had smoothed his normal waking emotions of doubt and concern from the constable's face and for a moment Pascoe saw him as he might have been if life hadn't set such ambushes in his path.

Then the eyes opened, the old bewilderment returned, followed after a little while by recognition and an attempt thwarted by his long legs to stiffen to attention under the sheet.

'At ease,' said Pascoe. 'Sorry to hear about your spot of bother, Hec. How are you doing?'

While the constable rifled his word-hoard for a suitable response, Pascoe's gaze drifted to the bedside locker. Its surface was bare except for a stub of pencil and a cheap writing pad. It stood in strong contrast with the locker by the other bed, its surface precariously crowded with a bowl of fruit, a vase of flowers, a box of chocolates and a pile of paperbacks. He recalled Hector's appearance at his sick bed with the custard tart and was annoyed at himself for coming empty-handed.

'Not so bad, sir,' said Hector.

'Good. Good. This is my daughter, Rosie. We've just been visiting Mr Dalziel.'

Hector suddenly looked animated.

'How is he? Has he woken up?'

'Not yet, I'm afraid.'

The animation faded.

Pascoe tried to find something optimistic to say but the words stuck in his throat.

Instead he asked, 'So when can we expect you back then?'

'Back?'

'At work. Everyone's missing you.'

Not a lie, just an ambiguity.

'That's nice,' said Hector. 'I'm looking forward to getting back.'

'Good. But make sure you're fit first. By all accounts it was a nasty knock you took. Have you remembered anything about the accident?'

'I thought maybe . . . I'm not sure . . . don't think so, sir.'

This was a truly Hectorian answer.

'Don't worry. We'll get him. The milkman who found you gave a description of the car and it's bound to have a dent in it.'

The door opened and a man in a dressing gown

came in. He didn't look pleased to see them and made straight for his bed.

As he climbed in, Pascoe called to him, 'Did your friend find you all right?'

'What friend?'

'There was someone looking for you. He said he'd try the day room.'

'That's where I've been, so he can't have tried very hard,' said the man indifferently.

He picked up a book and started to read.

Rosie said, 'Is this supposed to be Brad Pitt?'

She'd picked up the writing pad and opened it.

Hector said, 'No. It's not him.'

'That's all right then, because it doesn't look like him. The armour's good though.'

Pascoe, knowing how sensitive Hector was about his drawing, said sharply, 'Rosie, don't be rude. You've no right to be looking at that anyway.'

They both looked at him in a faintly puzzled way and he realized that in fact there hadn't been any rudeness intended nor any offence taken. It had been an exchange between children who feel no need to soften facts.

'It's all right, sir,' said Hector.

'Well, if you don't mind . . .'

He took the pad and looked at the drawing. It really was quite good. He could see why Rosie had thought of Brad Pitt. The chariot and the armoured figure were strongly reminiscent of the movie *Troy* which he'd seen on television recently.

But it wasn't the kind of film he'd ever let Rosie sit up to watch and when it came out a couple of years ago there was no way she'd been to see it. So how . . . ?

One of her stopovers with friends, he thought grimly. On Friday night they'd caught the big action moment on *Fidler's Three*. On other occasions where there was a DVD player built into the bedroom set, they'd probably dump the kiddy film and take a look at something 'borrowed' from the parents' collection. God knows what else Rosie had seen! He reminded himself to have a word with Ellie. Somehow his own well-honed interview techniques lost their edge when he tried to interrogate his daughter.

He gave her a promissory glower and asked, 'This one of yours, Hec?'

'Yes,' said Hector defiantly, as if he'd been accused of something.

'It's very good, though I don't recall many cats pulling chariots in the movie.'

'It's not a cat, silly,' said Rosie. 'It's a jaguar.'

'Is that so? I bow to your superior knowledge,' said Pascoe.

Apart from the weirdness of the beast between the shafts, there was something else about the picture . . .

He said, 'The charioteer, if it's not Brad Pitt . . .'

'It looks like the man at the door,' said Rosie, putting into words what he found almost too far-fetched to admit, let alone say.

But now it had been said, there was no doubt about it. The face staring out beneath the funny helmet was the man who'd been opening the ward door when they arrived.

He said, 'What made you draw this picture, Hec?'

The constable's eyes showed the beginnings of panic and Pascoe went on reassuringly, 'It's just that it's so good, it's almost like it was drawn from life. Could be really useful to someone in our line of work.'

The inclusion of Hector in the DCI's line of work did the trick.

The panic faded and Hector said, 'It was a face in my mind . . . someone in a sort of dream.'

'That's really interesting.'

He wanted to lean forward closer and urge Hector to talk about his dream, but he guessed that too much pressure might be counterproductive.

He leaned back in his chair and said, 'Isn't that interesting, Rosie? You have some funny dreams too, don't you? I bet you'd like to hear what Hec was dreaming about.'

Was it his imagination or did she look at him with a cool amusement which said clearer than words, OK, if I do this, does that get me off the hook about watching *Troy*?

It must have been imagination. No child could be as super subtle as that, not even Ellie's daughter. Could she?

She said, 'I sometimes dream about playing

the clarinet in a really big orchestra, and I'm doing a solo, and the conductor's someone really famous like Simon Rattle who I saw when Mum took me to Leeds once and in my dream it looks just like him. What did you dream about, Hec?'

Hesitantly, Hector began to tell her about his dream, making the point several times that it wasn't like an ordinary dream because he seemed to still have it when he was awake.

Pascoe thought, this is crazy. A man in a chariot pulled by a jaguar who deliberately runs him down . . . the milkman seeing a big car, maybe a Jag, pulling away at high speed . . . I rest my case, m'lud. Court collapses in helpless laughter.

He stood up and took the writing pad to the other patient, covering the distracting jaguar with his thumb.

'Excuse me,' he said. 'Do you recognize this man?'

The man raised his eyes from his book, said, 'Yes,' and went back to his reading.

This should have been a relief. Why the hell should Hector's subconscious mind be any more reliable than his conscious? And it was a relief insomuch as Pascoe, still smarting from Wield's demolition of his hypothetical construction last night, shuddered at the thought that he might have tried out this latest theory on any of his colleagues.

And yet it was disappointing too. No man likes to see his fantasy, no matter how far-fetched, destroyed.

He began to turn away, then, because he was famous for, as Dalziel put it, liking his eyes crossed and his teas dotted, he said, 'And were you expecting him to visit you today?'

The patient looked at him with irritation.

'Eh?' he said.

'Your friend, the one who was looking for you, were you expecting to see him today?'

'What the fuck are you talking about?'

'This man, the one in the drawing, the one you said you recognized, isn't he your friend?'

'What's up with you, mate? Yes, I recognize him. No, he's not a friend. Hang about . . .'

He leaned over to his locker and pulled a book from the bottom of the pile of paperbacks.

'There,' he said, thrusting it into Pascoe's hand. 'That's the fucker. Now can I get on with my reading?'

The book was called *Blood on the Sand* and sub-titled *A Novel of the Iraqi Wars*. Its author was John T. Youngman, formerly, so Pascoe discovered when he turned the book over, of the SAS. He also noticed the publisher was Hedley-Case, the same as Ellie's, but what really drew his eye was the photograph of the author beneath the blurb.

It wasn't very big, passport-size at most, but it was undoubtedly a picture of both the man at the door and Hector's charioteer.

13

no change

Pascoe moved fast.

No doubt Wield, and everyone else, would have rational explanations for all this, but he wasn't taking any chances.

He called up Hospital Security and got a man posted outside Hector's room.

'No one in unless they're known to you,' he commanded. 'Especially not this chap.'

He showed the photo on the back of the book which he'd confiscated from the grumpy patient whose name was Mills and who was in the Central for an haemorrhoidectomy, which perhaps explained his grumpiness.

Compared with the jacket photo, Hector's drawing gave a rather clearer picture of the man's features, but Pascoe felt the armour and the jaguar might be a distraction.

'I'll get one of our officers stationed here as soon as possible,' he told the security guard. 'Till then, don't budge.'

Two of the other three Security men on duty he set to checking waiting rooms and public areas just in case Youngman was still on the premises. The third he despatched to the car park to take a note of any Jaguars left there. But Pascoe had a feeling that his man was long gone.

He rang through to the Station and found Paddy Ireland on duty. When he enquired about spare bodies, the inspector began Uniformed's standard moan about shortage of manpower and deep cuts in the overtime budget till Pascoe silenced him with, 'Paddy, remember you got your knickers in a twist about Mill Street? Well, you were right then, I humbly admit it, and I apologize. But I'm right now.'

'In that case, I'll see what I can do,' said Ireland.

A car with Alan Maycock and Joker Jennison in it appeared on the scene within ten minutes. Jennison said, 'Got another firework display laid on for us, sir?' Maycock kicked him violently on the ankle and said, 'Mr Ireland says he'll try and get another couple of bodies along in the next half-hour.'

Pascoe said, 'Thank you for that, Alan. And for the kick,' and put them to work.

He was grateful to Ireland but didn't doubt he'd cover his own back, so it was no surprise when Chief Constable Dan Trimble showed up a quarter of an hour later, looking like a man who'd been snatched unwillingly from the bosom of his family.

'Peter, what's going on?' he demanded. 'Paddy

Ireland says you think someone might be trying to kill Hector. Why in the name of God should anyone want to do that?'

Paddy's told him what I think, thought Pascoe. But he wants to make me say it myself, and then he can bollock me for not ringing him straight away.

Trimble listened without comment till Pascoe concluded, 'I think that Hector's accident wasn't an accident, but someone deliberately ran him down for fear he might be able to identify the man he saw in the video shop on Mill Street. And I think the same man came here today to try and have a second bite at the cherry.'

Now the chief spoke.

'I thought I made it clear that I was to be kept apprized of anything that could have a connection with the Mill Street explosion,' he said coldly.

'Yes, sir. And I was going to ring you just as soon as I got things sorted on the ground here. When an officer's at risk, practicalities come before protocol, that's what Mr Dalziel always says.'

In fact he couldn't recall Fat Andy ever saying any such thing, but if he hadn't, it was only because it was too sodding obvious to need saying.

It certainly gave Trimble pause.

'Right, then. Let's hear about these practicalities.'

Pascoe filled him in on what he'd done, concluding, 'I did a quick check with the ward staff. A couple of them recall seeing the man around the ward earlier, and one of them spotted him sitting

311

in the day room reading a paper, about an hour ago.'

'I haven't had much truck with hired assassins. Is that normal behaviour?' interrupted Trimble.

'He's not going to go around with a homburg pulled down over his eyes, carrying a violin case,' said Pascoe with some irritation. 'Mr Mills, that's Hector's room-mate, recalls the door to their room being opened earlier this morning. Someone looked in – he didn't see who it was – then went away. I think it was Youngman. When he realized that Hector had someone else in the same room, he went and waited quietly in the day room till he saw Mr Mills come in. Then he headed back to the ward, only to find myself and Rosie arriving to visit Hector at the same time. He probably kept an eye on things till he saw Mr Mills return and realized that this wasn't really his day. Like I said, I've got Security looking for him, but I reckon he's gone. He could come back though.'

If he'd had to give a rating to his report, it would have been Beta minus at best. He'd started with a heavy handicap. In Mid-Yorkshire anything with Hector at its centre needed a supporting affidavit from the angel Gabriel. And he couldn't blame the chief for looking shell-shocked when he heard about the constable's vision, nor for his uncontrollable twitch when the charioteer sketch was produced as supporting evidence.

But Trimble was a man who liked to give his officers leeway. Anyone with Andy Dalziel under

312

his command soon learned that the likely alternative was to find yourself high and dry on a sandbank.

He said, 'All right. Leave someone on watch here. I don't suppose you've had time to contact Superintendent Glenister yet, though of course you were going to ring her immediately after you rang me?'

'That's right, sir,' said Pascoe.

'Good. Well, just as Mr Ireland saved you the trouble of contacting me, I'll extend the same courtesy with regard to CAT.'

Meaning you don't trust me to do anything about it for the next couple of hours, thought Pascoe.

But Trimble was wrong. Locally Pascoe knew all the short cuts and short circuits. He'd been well taught. Getting after Youngman outside Mid-Yorkshire where he guessed the search would have to begin was another matter. Dalziel might have been able to manage it. He had strings to pull whose tar ends were tied to some very strange places. But for Pascoe that kind of network was still being woven.

In any case the quickest way to show CAT you didn't trust them was to act like you didn't trust them, and he wanted a far better hand before he made that play.

'Peter!'

He turned to see Ellie coming towards him with Rosie.

He'd got one of the nurses to look after her.

He'd suggested taking her to the hospital crèche at first but this had evoked such a furious response that he'd changed it to the canteen and offered as placation a tenner for refreshment.

Then he'd rung Ellie, said there was a bit of an emergency, and asked if she could come and pick the girl up.

Ellie as always had responded to the word *emergency* without question.

But now she was here, she expected to hear what was going on.

Her response echoed Trimble's.

'Someone wants to kill Hector?' she said incredulously. 'But why?'

She listened to his theory with the kind of expression Galileo probably saw on the face of his Chief Inquisitor.

'Pete, for heaven's sake, this is Quentin Tarantino stuff. I mean . . . *Hector*!'

'All right,' he said testily. 'One way to check is I'll cancel the guard on Hector's room and if he gets killed, then I was right!'

'Now you're being silly.'

He glowered at her, then turned his attention to his daughter, intending to short circuit the discussion before it became a row by asking for his change. How much refreshment could a girl ingest in forty minutes?

She regarded him with her mother's wide-eyed candour then, before he could speak, said, 'I think Dad's right. I didn't like that man.'

'You didn't?' said Pascoe, delighted at this unexpected support. 'Why was that?'

'Well, he smiled as he held the door open, but I could tell he was really pissed off,' said Rosie. 'I mean, a lot more pissed off than you'd be just because someone you'd come to visit wasn't in his bed.'

Do I reprimand her for saying 'pissed off' – twice! – or let it go because she's said it in support of my case? Pascoe asked himself.

Ellie had no doubt.

'Come on, my girl,' she said grimly. 'We'll get you home and on the way we'll have a little heart-to-heart about your special relationship with the language of Shakespeare. Any idea how long you'll be, Peter?'

Truce offered and accepted. 'Not long,' he promised. They kissed. Definitely accepted.

She said softly, 'Just in case you're right, which I don't admit, take care.'

He watched them go. She was right. If he was right, he should perhaps take care.

And of course the people he should take most care of weren't lying in a hospital bed but walking away from him.

At the door Ellie turned and called, 'I forgot to ask. How's Andy?'

Pascoe looked at his daughter who smiled at him complicitly.

He said, 'No change there. Either.'

315

14

the tangle o' the Isles

Andy Dalziel is on his way to Mairi's Wedding.

Step we gaily on we go
Heel for heel and toe for toe

Proud to be a Yorkshireman, proud of all that his lovely Yorkshire mam had brought to his being, proud to belt out 'On Ilkla Moor baht'at' with the best of them, it has always been the music from his father's side of the family that plucked at his heart strings and squeezed the tear out of his eye.

Arm in arm and row on row
All for Mairi's wedding

Who he is arm in arm with he is not certain, nor indeed whether in any strict sense the arms in question are arms at all, but the feelings of joy and lightness which the song inspires are real enough, and he's never been a man to look a gift horse in the mouth.

Unless of course it's donated by Greeks. Or Lancastrians.

> *Over hillways up and down*
> *Myrtle green and bracken brown ...*

No real hills of course. No greens or browns. Just effortlessly floating on a highway of music as he recalled doing years ago, squashed in a corner of some tiny bothy with his Scottish cousins when big Uncle Hamish got his fiddle out.

> *Plenty herring plenty meal*
> *Plenty peat tae fill her creel*

Peat. The sweet smoky reek of it. And better still when it's coming off the surface of a golden pool set in a crystal tumbler ...

> *Plenty bonny bairns as weel ...*

Now young Rosie Pascoe was a bonnie bairn and she'd grown into a bonnie lass and would, if God was kind, which so far he'd not been given any reason to doubt, turn out a stunning woman. And what was more important a kind and caring one.

> *Cheeks as bright as rowans are ...*

He'd always been able to depend on the kindness of women. Even his wife had been kind . . . in her way . . . Some women before they left cut up their husbands' suits or poured their twenty-year-old single malts down the bog and substituted vinegar. His had left a note . . . *Your dinner's in the oven on the low burner* . . . He'd gone to the kitchen and opened the oven.

There it was, gently crisping.

A plate of ham salad.

It still makes him laugh all these years on.

Women, women . . . perhaps it is their arms that he feels in his now . . . all those kind women . . .

And one above all . . .

The last? Who can say that?

But a star . . . more than a star . . .

> *Brighter far than any star*
> *Fairest of them all by far* . . .

Cap. Ms Amanda Marvell. Mrs the Hon. Rupert Pitt-Evenlode. Call her what you will. The sense of her presence sends him soaring even higher than the music.

> *Over hillways up and down*
> *Myrtle green and bracken brown*
> *Past the shieling through the town*
> *All for the sake of* . . .

Cap.

The music dies away but still he floats.

But what's this? The pace slackens to a crawl, the mood changes. Oh no!

The Flower of Scotland.

Dear God! What a doleful dirge. He has always been persuaded that the only thing keeping Scottish rugby from World Cup glory is their pre-match anthem. How can those fine young men be expected to march forward to fight the auld enemy with this turgid tune clogging their feet? It makes 'God Save the Queen' sound like a cavalry charge!

But at last it drags its weary weight to a close.

And now thank God he's out of the mire again and soaring high once more as the pipes and drums explode into the song which is his signature tune at the Police Christmas Party.

> *Sure by Tummel and Loch Rannock and*
> *   Lochaber I will go*
> *By heather tracks wi' heaven in their wiles*
> *If it's thinking' in your inner hairt the*
> *   braggart's in my step,*
> *You've never smelt the tangle o' the Isles.*

Here's the truth of it. Though his feet have always been firmly planted in the rich earth of his native Yorkshire and on the hard pavements of its great cities, the heart is for ever Highland.

And when a man is hovering between this world and the next, it takes a music as seductive as that of the far Cuillins to pull him away, though whether its call is to heaven or to earth Andy Dalziel as yet cannot and indeed does not care to know.

15

a shot in the dark

As far as Peter Pascoe was concerned, you could take heather tracks and stick them up your reeking lum.

There was heather beneath his feet now and he was being bitten to death. OK, Scotland didn't begin officially for another dozen miles, but nobody had bothered to tell this to the midges which were assailing his face with a Caledonian ferocity. Perhaps their native reiving instincts had been alerted by the rancid smell of the CAT camouflage make-up that Glenister had insisted he smeared on his cheekbones and brow.

It was her suggestion too that he should wear a flak jacket. No, *suggestion* was the wrong word. The jacket had been a *sine qua non* of his inclusion in the raid.

Pascoe was confident that both jacket and camouflage were unnecessary.

If, as he suspected, the Templars had a mole in CAT, then the chances of John T. Youngman being inside the small white cottage the CAT hit squad was presently surrounding were nil.

Glenister was full of bounce, in strong contrast to her rather weary and harassed demeanour last time he'd seen her at the Lubyanka. The prospect of crawling around in the dark in pursuit of a dangerous suspect seemed to have perked her up. Pascoe had seen plenty of male officers turned on by the prospect of physical danger, but never a woman.

Perhaps he ought to get out more.

Though if this was what getting out entailed, perhaps not.

The reaction to Trimble's phone call had been swift.

First Freeman had turned up at the hospital.

In reply to Pascoe's, 'You must have been close,' he had given that irritating enigmatic smile. Then he'd asked a few questions, very sharp and pertinent Pascoe had to admit, before interviewing Hector. What he got out of that he didn't reveal. Finally he had approved all the measures Pascoe had taken and vanished with the charioteer sketch.

At no point had he hinted a doubt of Pascoe's interpretation of events.

Despite this, even with every possible precaution in place, an irrational fear that the moment he left orders would be given countermanding all he'd done made it hard for Pascoe to leave. It took an anxious, irritated phone call from Ellie wondering if he was the only police officer on call that weekend to give him the impetus to head for home.

Ellie did her best to make the evening as normal as possible and Pascoe did his best to respond. He tried to conceal his restlessness, but he knew he wasn't being very successful and it was a relief when, about eight o'clock, the phone rang. Somehow they both knew it was to do with the case.

Ellie answered it.

'I'll get him,' she said.

Handing the phone to Pascoe she said, 'Mrs Sinister,' loudly enough to be heard at the far end of the line.

'You've been at it again, laddie. Go on like this and you'll put us all out of work.'

This sounded like a sort of compliment.

'What's happening?' he said.

'We've got a possible location for Youngman and we're going to try and pick him up tonight. Want to come along? Thinking is, you've earned it.'

Earned the right to leave his home and family in the middle of the night to go chasing around after a suspected killer! What would they reward him with if he did something really amazing? Two weeks undercover work in Afghanistan?

He said, 'Yes.'

'Good. Knew you'd be up for it. Thing is it's a bit distant. He's got a cottage up in Northumberland, near the Kielder Reservoir. Can you make Hexham by ten o'clock?'

'Yes,' said Pascoe, not bothering to try and work it out.

'Great. Here's a grid reference.'

She gave it only once.

'Fine. If you're not there by ten we won't wait.' A pause, then she laughed softly and said, 'It's about ten miles north of Hexham along the B road to Bellingham. Me, I'm an old-fashioned A to Z lassie.'

He told Ellie where he was going because there wasn't any point in lying.

'Why?' she said with genuine amazement. 'It's not your patch. It's not your kind of work. And if you're right, and he's been warned off, there's not a cat in hell's chance of this Youngman fellow being there anyway. So why?'

He said, 'Because they want me there, and I want them to go on wanting me around till I get some answers. Also it might give me the chance to poke about in Youngman's stuff before it all gets classified and locked up somewhere out of reach.'

He went and got changed before she could pick his response to pieces.

When he reappeared, Rosie, who'd been on her way to bed when the phone rang and who'd naturally used the distraction to snatch an extra half-hour, said, 'Are you going bird-watching, Dad?'

Pascoe glanced down. He'd put on his heavy walking boots and hiking trousers and had his binocular case draped round his neck.

'Not if I can help it, darling,' he said, smiling.

'When could you last help anything, Pete?' said Ellie.

'I'm just doing what I get paid for,' he said.

'No, you're not. No one's paying you to think you're Superman!'

It wasn't a note to part on but there was no choice. Even with light Sunday-night traffic, he was going to have to move fast to keep his rendezvous.

It was almost ten as he passed through Hexham. The sun had just set and there was still plenty of residual light. Before he left he'd marked the grid reference carefully on his map. He had it in his head that the CAT hit squad would have pulled off the road and set up camouflage and he was determined he wasn't going to give them the satisfaction of seeing him drive by.

He needn't have worried. As he approached the rendezvous point, he saw a car parked at the roadside with Sandy Glenister leaning against the boot, smoking a cigarette and talking to Freeman.

She gave him a welcoming wave as he drew in behind them.

As he went to join them, he saw that she was wearing slacks and trainers, whereas Freeman was dressed in a sharp Italian suit and what looked like hand-made shoes.

His eyes ran down to Pascoe's hiking boots and he twitched an eyebrow.

'Hi, Pete. Good timing,' said Glenister. 'Lovely evening, eh? I really like it round here. Gorgeous countryside and not too many tourists. Pity we didn't hang on to it after giving your lot a kicking at Otterburn. Let's hope we're not in for another moonlit battle.'

'Any reason to think we might be?' said Pascoe.

'He seems to fancy himself as a hard man, this Jonty Youngman,' she said. 'I'll fill you in as we drive. Leave your car here, we'll go the rest of the way in Dave's.'

'So Youngman's cottage isn't close?' said Pascoe as he climbed in the back of the other car.

Glenister twisted round in her seat and said, 'Pete, you don't really think our hit squad would arrange to meet you within a couple of miles of a target, do you? They'd be worried you'd get lost and end up knocking at Youngman's door to ask for directions.'

'Well, I'm glad not to have worried them,' said Pascoe coldly.

She laughed and lit another cigarette as Freeman sent the car racing along the narrow road.

'Not just that,' she said. 'They didn't want to stop alongside a public road. Even round here where there's more foxes per square mile than people, half a dozen men in black with hard hats and assault rifles might draw attention.'

She puffed out a jet of smoke which Pascoe waved away.

'Run out of Smarties?' he said.

'No, but there are times – after sex, before action, in serious midge country – when My Lady

Nicotine's charms are still irresistible. So, Peter, that was some sharp work you did at the hospital. And it seems you were right about Constable Hector. There's more to him than meets the eye. That other thing he said – "a bit funny, but not a darkie", was it? – maybe we should get him to do a drawing. Always listen to the man on the spot, eh?'

For the first time it occurred to Pascoe that perhaps it was because someone had listened to his loyal defence of Hector that the Templars had decided not to take risks but get rid of him.

He pushed the idea aside and asked, 'What do we know about Youngman?'

'Apart from his military record, not a great deal,' she said. 'Ex-SAS. Rank sergeant. Real name is Young, known as Jonty, so not much change to John T. Youngman. Served in the Balkans, Afghanistan and Iraq. Not the most popular member of the unit, kept himself to himself, but was noted for his reliability and efficiency. Marked down for advancement till an incident in Iraq when several prisoners were blown up in unexplained circumstances put a question mark on his record. Left the army in 2005. He'd already got Hedley-Case, the publishers, interested in his first book *Death in the Desert*. There's been one more since that came out, *Blood on the Sand*, I think it's called, and I gather there's another in the pipeline. You read any of his stuff?'

Pascoe shook his head.

'Me neither, but Dave's had a glance through them. What did you think, Dave?'

'Interesting,' said Freeman. 'Claims to be faction, real stories rejigged to give a strong narrative thread, and with some names and details altered for security reasons. Makes it hard for the War Office or anyone else to raise objections without tacitly agreeing that they recognize the individuals or incidents described. Clever, really.'

'So he's a clever arrogant murderous bastard,' said Pascoe.

'You've taken against him, I see.'

'I take against any bastard who goes around trying to kill my officers,' growled Pascoe. 'These books of his, are they big sellers?'

'Moderately so,' said Glenister. 'But the Hedley-Case website says they've got high hopes for a breakthrough with the next one. The bastards will be delighted when they get a whiff that we might be taking a professional interest. Man writes about the Gulf Wars then the Security Services go after him, you can see how that plays in terms of free publicity.'

'You don't seem very concerned.'

'It's business, laddie. And when it comes to my turn to write my memoirs, it's always nice to know how the publishing mind works. Maybe I should have a word with your wife. Nice bit of publicity she got on the box the other night. She's OK, is she?'

'She's fine.'

'I was sure she would be. Struck me as a tough lady.'

Her mobile sounded. She listened, said, 'On our way. Ten minutes tops.'

Just under the ten, Freeman slowed from the steady fifty mph he'd been doing and bumped off the road along a rutted track between soaring pine trees. After a couple of hundred yards, he came to a halt alongside a large black van with the Forestry Commission logo on the side. He killed the lights.

Glenister said, 'Stay here,' and got out.

It took Pascoe's eyes a little while to adjust, but when they did, he realized that, even here among the crowding trees, some residual light from the long summer day still managed to filter through. He looked for signs of life but couldn't see any. Then a figure detached itself from the bole of a tree. Clad in black combats and carrying a short-barrelled weapon, he looked like something out of an action movie.

What the hell am I doing here? Pascoe asked himself.

Glenister and the man talked. Pascoe managed to pick out another couple of armed figures crouched among the trees. Glenister came back to the car.

'We're about a mile away from the cottage,' she said. 'Gordon, the team leader, has sent a couple of men ahead to reconnoitre. So let's get ourselves kitted out, Peter.'

He got out of the car. Freeman didn't move.

'You not coming?' asked Pascoe.

'I've not been invited to the party,' said Freeman. 'So I don't need to wear the fancy dress.'

He gave that smile again as he spoke. He didn't look put out at missing the fun.

Perhaps, thought Pascoe, because like me he knows there's no chance of finding anyone at home in the cottage.

Glenister led him to the van, and that's where the nonsense with the face paint and the flak jacket began.

The superintendent grunted as she squeezed herself into her jacket.

'No one's bothered to update our equipment buyers on equal opportunity legislation,' she said. 'These things just don't take big tits into account.'

Gordon (whether this was his first or second name never became clear) joined them as they completed their preparations. Pascoe couldn't get a clear picture of the man's face behind his black-up, but the gaze that measured him was cold and unfriendly.

'You ready?' he said to Glenister. 'OK, let's move. Sullivan's with you. Do everything he says. Everything.'

The last *everything* was almost spat at Pascoe.

'Don't think he likes me being here,' he said when Gordon had retreated.

'At least you're a fellow,' said Glenister. 'From now on, no talking. No sound at all.'

'What happens if I sneeze?' asked Pascoe, determined not to be sucked into their game. 'This chap Sullivan shoots me?'

'Of course not,' said Glenister. 'Far too noisy. He'll probably slit your throat.'

In fact within a short time of setting off, Pascoe began to feel very pleased to be in the care of the man called Sullivan. Without his careful guidance, communicated by tugs and touches and simple unambiguous hand-signals, progress through the forest would have been certainly slow and noisy, and probably painful and wet.

As it was they advanced at a rate not much below his normal hill-walking pace.

Gradually the trees thinned till at last they came to a halt in a ditch alongside a narrow roadway whose once tarmacked surface had deteriorated into eczemous patches.

On the far side of the road at a distance of about fifty yards was the cottage. It stood in a rectangle of tumbledown wall which presumably had once enclosed a garden, but the tussocky grass and moorland bracken had long since reclaimed the lost ground.

Not satisfied with this victory, nature also had the actual building in its sights.

An almost full moon had risen as they advanced and in its light the cottage looked new painted, but when he studied it through his binoculars, he saw the pebbledash of the once white walls was flaking and stained with water and lichen. So much for moonshine.

How long would they hang around here before deciding what he was already sure of, that the place was empty? Not long, he hoped. The midges which had started taking a few *amuse-bouche* nibbles as soon as he got out of the car had now decided to make a main course out of him. Perhaps like Glenister they had fond memories of Otterburn.

Gordon materialized beside them.

He spoke into Glenister's ear then moved away.

'What do we do now?' asked Pascoe. 'Hang around in the hope he'll show up?'

She looked at him in surprise.

'But he's here already, Peter, or someone is. They've seen a light inside and their heat-scanner things confirm there's somebody there.'

Pascoe looked at her like a man who has just seen his self-assembly bookcase collapse under the weight of the first paperback.

'But there's no light showing,' he protested, unwilling to accept what he'd heard.

'Round the back there is. Oil lamp, they think. There's no electricity. Fan of the primitive life is our Sergeant Jonty.'

Somewhere close an owl hooted.

'OK,' said Glenister. 'They're going in.'

'That was a signal?' said Pascoe.

'No,' said Glenister. 'That was an owl. This is the twenty-first century.'

She patted the side of her head and Pascoe saw she was wearing an ear-piece.

There was movement around the cottage, dark

shadows flitting across the moon-white walls. Then sound. An explosion. A crash. A cry of pain. Voices.

'That sounds interesting,' said Glenister. 'Let's not miss the fun.'

I'm right, thought Pascoe. She does get turned on by this stuff.

He followed her across the rough grass, crouching low. He was no expert, but the explosion hadn't sounded like the crack of an assault weapon. Maybe a stun grenade? Except there was no sign of disturbance within the cottage. Whatever was going on, the wise move would have been no move. Stay in the ditch till the professionals gave the all-clear. But here he was again, following his superior officer towards the enemy line. Last time he'd done that . . .

He put the thought out of his mind. Also the thought of Ellie's reaction if she could see him now, scuttling into danger like some Hollywood action hero.

They reached the cottage and Glenister headed down its windowless side.

At the rear corner crouched two figures. One of them was Gordon.

He looked round and saw them.

'Told you to stay put,' he snarled.

'And very insubordinate it sounded,' said Glenister. 'What's happening?'

'The bastard had set a booby trap. Simple trip-wire, set off a charge, probably a small amount of explosive in a can packed full of earth. Not life-threatening, just meant to frighten and warn. But one of my men got a gobful of pebbles and fell against a dustbin.'

'And Youngman?'

'He'll be ready now. Makes it that much harder to get him out in one piece.'

'Hard's OK,' said Glenister sharply. 'Impossible is what I don't want to hear.'

Pascoe peered round the corner. In the moonlight he saw a garden area which a couple of shrubs and a tree made appear a little more organized than the wilderness at the front. But the shrubs were gorse and the tree looked like a sycamore, so hardly the remnants of cultivation.

His shoulder was seized and he was dragged roughly back.

'You trying to get yourself killed?' demanded Gordon.

'Not as such,' said Pascoe. 'What's the problem with a locked door? I thought you people just kicked them down or smashed windows and threw grenades inside?'

Gordon said, 'You're watching too much television. Our Mr Youngman's gone to a lot of trouble to make his cottage secure. Kind of doors and windows he's got, we'd need to set a charge that would bring half the wall down with it. And if he's got weapons in there to match, I'm not taking any chances with my men.'

'So what do you propose doing?' said Glenister.

'Let things settle for a while, then start negotiating. Hold on.'

Something was coming over his head-set. But
presumably not over Glenister's ear-piece, observed
Pascoe. She might be in charge on paper, but on
the ground Gordon was determined to be king.

'What?' demanded Glenister impatiently.

'Upstairs window open. Gun barrel showing.'
He spoke into his mike. 'Room to get a stun
grenade in?'

He listened, then addressed Glenister.

'Too small a gap to be sure of a grenade, but
my sergeant reckons he can put enough rounds
through it to take out anyone inside. Your call,
ma'am.'

'Suddenly I've got my rank back,' the woman
murmured. 'I told you, we want him in a fit state
to talk, so let's try and start the process now, shall
we?'

But they didn't have to try very hard. Without
any prompting a voice came shrilling from above.

'You people out there, go away! I've got a gun,
see. And I know how to use it.'

There was a bang. Pellets whistled through the
foliage of the sycamore.

'Next one's for you! Now go away!'

Gordon and Glenister looked at each other in
surprise.

The superintendent said, 'Either that's a
woman or Sergeant Young got a very serious war
wound he doesn't like to talk about.'

Gordon said, 'Man, woman, makes no difference. Weapon discharged puts the next move down to me, I think, ma'am.'

'Only if your men are under real and imminent threat,' said Glenister. 'That sounded more like a shotgun than a Kalashnikov. How threatening is that, Mr Gordon?'

Then Pascoe, who'd been struggling with the old problem of identifying the familiar in an unfamiliar context, suddenly put two and two, and two more, together. The same publisher as Ellie . . . a trip to the north-east . . . that familiar Celtic lilt . . .

'For God's sake!' he said. 'Forget about the gun. The poor woman sounds terrified! And no bloody wonder. Has anyone bothered to tell her who we are?'

He pushed past Gordon, stuck his head round the angle of the wall and called, 'Ffion!'

Silence, then the voice with its unmistakable Welsh accent said, 'Who's that?'

'It's me, Peter Pascoe. Ellie's husband. Eleanor Soper. It's the police out here, Ffion. Open the door and let us in. These midges are eating me alive!'

'Peter? Is that really you? Step out where I can see you.'

'No!' said Glenister. 'You stay where you are, Chief Inspector. Do I gather you know this woman?'

'Yes! She works for Hedley-Case, my wife's publishers, who also happen to publish Youngman's books. She was up here to look after one of her writers who should have been on *Fidler's Three*. But he had to cancel and this woman got my wife to do the show instead. Damn damn damn. I should have asked. Fidler was clearly after guests with a terrorist connection. It's so bloody obvious!'

'Most things are,' murmured Glenister. 'In retrospect.'

'Peter, I'm not doing anything till I see it's really you!' came the woman's voice.

Pascoe began to move forward, but both Gordon and Glenister grabbed him.

'No,' said the superintendent. 'We know nothing about her and she may not be alone.'

'Of course she's alone!' exploded Pascoe. 'Doesn't the heat scanner show there's only one person inside? And I know enough about her to know that, while she's pretty ruthless in getting publicity for her authors, she won't go as far as killing their husbands.'

Gordon's grip slackened. He'd probably worked out that the worst that could happen was he'd lose someone he found a bit of a pain and at the same time get an excuse to deploy maximum force.

Pascoe gently disengaged Glenister's hand, squeezing it reassuringly, and stepped out on to the ground at the rear of the cottage.

Something impeded his progress at shin height. He looked down and made out an axe embedded in a log. The video from Said Mazraani's flat came into his mind. These were seriously dangerous people. Perhaps he should have listened to Gordon.

But he wasn't going to give him the satisfaction of seeing him go into retreat now.

Looking up he could see the bedroom window opened just sufficiently to allow a shotgun barrel to protrude. Behind the glass he could see a dim figure.

'Ffion!' he yelled. 'See, it's me, Peter.'

He spread out his arms and moved backwards to give her a better angle to view him.

A better angle to shoot him too, the thought slipped into his mind.

He discarded it with irritation. This was no mad terrorist up there, no fugitive killer. This was a frightened young woman who'd somehow got caught up in this crazy business. He was safer here than driving down the by-pass in the rush hour.

Calling, 'Ffion, just leave the gun there and come down!' he took another step backward.

He saw the protruding gun barrel move.

Then there was a loud explosion and he felt a dull blow on the left side of his neck just above the protection of his flak jacket, and as he dropped to his knees, waiting for the pain which must surely follow, he thought, I can't keep on getting things wrong like this!

16

the word of an Englishman

Ffion Lyke-Evans was a very lucky young woman.

Normally when the door of a besieged building is thrown open and a suspect comes running out wielding a shotgun, what follows is a remake of the closing scene from *Butch Cassidy and the Sundance Kid*. Happily the CAT Armed Response Unit, responded to Sandy Glenister's directorial scream of, 'Don't shoot!' by holding both their discipline and their fire.

When Peter Pascoe saw Ffion rushing towards him brandishing a shotgun, he presumed she was intent on finishing the job. So sure was he that he was dying anyway, he hardly felt relieved when he saw two of the men in black bring her crashing to the ground and remove the weapon from her unresisting hands. As she lay there, she shouted something which he had difficulty in hearing through the ringing in his ears. But if he'd got it right and what she was shouting was, 'Peter! Peter! Are you all right?' this struck him as a pretty cheeky attempt at spin even for a publicist.

By now, however, most of his attention was focused on the terrible pain he expected any moment, on the life-draining gush of arterial blood from the wound in his neck.

But for some reason the pain didn't come, and when he put his hand up to his wound, the spurt of hot blood felt surprisingly like a smear of cold earth.

The truth, revealed to him by Officer Sullivan, who turned out to be a soft-spoken Ulsterman of amiable disposition, was both a huge relief and a slight embarrassment.

He hadn't been shot. He'd backed into another of Youngman's tripwires, and the explosion had hurled a clod of earth that had struck him on the neck.

The only medication required was also provided by Sullivan in the form of a water bottle full of whiskey, which the gentle Irishman administered only after extracting a promise of complete confidentiality.

It could have been a lot worse, thought Pascoe as he accepted a second dose. Especially the embarrassment. At least as he sank to his knees, he hadn't dictated any dying messages. Indeed on this occasion as in Mill Street all the elegant valedictory epigrams he had collected over the years had quite gone out of his mind.

By the time he was fully back in the world he'd feared he might be leaving, there was no sign of Ffion or Glenister. When he tried to get into the cottage, Gordon, who'd set his men to combing the environs for other warning devices, barred his passage.

'Can't go in there,' he said. 'Crime scene. You should know that.'

Pascoe, disappointed at missing a chance to have a poke around among Youngman's things, thought of arguing the toss. But never pull rank with a man who pulls triggers is a good maxim. Also he had no idea what Gordon's rank was, nor indeed whether he belonged to the police or the spook faction of CAT.

He said, 'Where's Ffion, the Welsh girl?'

'Sandy Glenister's taken her to your car. Watch how you go. Don't want you falling over any more tripwires.'

He found the two women in the back of the car. Freeman must have driven up as soon as the action was over. He got out of the driving seat as he saw Pascoe approach.

'Best leave them be a little while longer,' he murmured with the smile. 'Girl talk.'

'Which it's all right for you to hear but not me? What's that make you? The palace eunuch?'

This seemed to tickle Freeman who laughed out loud, then enquired solicitously, 'And how are you, Peter? After your little shock, I mean.'

'I'm fine,' said Pascoe.

As with Gordon and entry to the cottage, there was nothing to do but sit on his frustration and

341

wait for whatever crumbs of information fell his way, which seemed unlikely to compensate for a row with Ellie and the loss of a quiet Sunday night at home.

At last Glenister got out of the car and came to join him.

'So what's she say?' he asked impatiently.

'A great deal, but very little to the point,' said the superintendent. 'She claims to have strayed into all of this just following her hormones.'

Ffion's story as told to the superintendent was fairly straightforward, starting with an admission that, while doing publicity on Youngman's last book, she'd slipped into a relationship with him.

'Nothing serious, she says,' said Glenister. 'But she did spend a weekend up here in the wilds last spring, which suggests that it was more than just a fling. On Friday afternoon she got the train up north and just as she was getting into Middlesbrough she got a call from Youngman saying he couldn't do the TV show after all, family illness. She was pretty pissed off but calmed down a bit when he said he didn't think it would make any difference to their spending the weekend together as planned. He'd ring her later. Which he did, Friday night, after the show. He picked her up and drove her out here. Spent the next twenty-four hours shagging themselves witless. This morning he said he had to go off again. Gave her a choice. Either get dropped off at the nearest mainline station or hang around waiting for his return, which he anticipated would be mid afternoon.'

'What was his story this time?'

'Same as before. Hospital visiting. She recalls he grinned as he said it.'

'Really funny,' said Pascoe. 'So she decided to wait. He must be good value.'

'Sounds like it. Also she'd cleared herself till Tuesday morning in anticipation of this bonking break, so there was no rush. By tea-time she was getting annoyed. Then the phone rang. It was Youngman saying his relative was too ill to leave. Now you'll like this bit. He told her that if he wasn't back by dark, she should lock all doors and windows and load up his shotgun. There was this bunch of local yobs he'd been having a running battle with ever since he bought the place. That's why he had the booby traps . . .'

'She knew about the traps then?'

'Oh yes. Last time she was here, he'd shown them to her, so she would take care to steer clear of them, he said. She says he never missed a chance to remind her he was a hairy-arsed survivalist, which she freely admits she found a turn-on.'

Freeman, who'd been listening, said doubtfully, 'You believe her when she claims she's a complete innocent? I mean, how many women know how to use a shotgun?'

'Sometimes you are almost Neanderthal, Dave,' said Glenister pityingly. 'Apart from bonking, their only other activity during her previous stay had been a bit of rough shooting, which, incidentally, she seems to have been doing since she was six. It was either that or start playing rugby.'

'So he told her there might be intruders,' prompted Pascoe.

'You're getting there. He said if she did have any bother, just to open the bedroom window a crack and fire a warning shot. That would send them running.'

'Jesus!'

'Yes, lovely guy, isn't he? When things went pear-shaped at the hospital, thanks to you, Pete, the last place he was going to head was home. He knew we'd be on to this place eventually. And he must have thought it would hold things up a bit if there was someone on site, armed and ready to resist boarders.'

'My God. The poor woman could have been killed!'

'Which would have left us with egg on our face and probably muddied up his tracks even more.'

Freeman said obstinately, 'I think she should still be treated as a suspect.'

'Is that right? Opinion noted, Dave,' said Glenister. 'Now why don't you run along like a good little spook and see if they've secured the cottage yet? And you might tell Gordon I'd like a word.'

Freeman moved away. Pascoe had enjoyed seeing him squashed but wished he'd wriggled a bit more.

'I'm glad for Ffion's sake he's not in charge,' he said. 'I think he'd be booking her a room in the Tower with the Full English Execution laid on for the morning. What will you do with her, by the way?'

'She'll need to sign a statement, then we'll cut her loose, I expect.'

'Good,' said Pascoe. 'All right if I have a word with her now?'

'By all means. The poor child's naturally a bit strung out. A familiar face would probably be a comfort to her.'

Giving Glenister house-points for humanity, Pascoe opened the car door and slipped in beside the publicist. She looked haggard and weary but her face lit up when she saw who it was.

'Peter,' she said. 'Are you OK? God, I was so worried when I saw you go down!'

She leaned towards him and he put his arm round her shoulders and drew her in.

'I'm fine,' he said. 'Really. How are you, that's the important thing. This must have been a terrible shock.'

'You're not wrong there! It's a nightmare? What happens now?'

'You'll need to make a written statement, then we'll get you back to civilization.'

'You sure?'

'Of course. What else did you imagine might happen?'

'I don't know. It's all been so crazy. When I

345

heard that first bang and looked out and saw those guys running around all tooled up, I thought, this is it for you, girl! I slammed everything shut and said a prayer of thanks that Jonty had got the place so well protected. But I thought those guys out there look like they've come for serious business and they're not going to let a bit of stainless steel and reinforced glass keep them out for long. When you appeared I was never so glad to see anyone in my life! But what's happening anyway? What's Jonty supposed to have done?'

Pascoe said cautiously, 'It's a security matter. We think he might have got mixed up with some rather unsavoury people.'

'Is this anything to do with that Templar gang who chopped the Arab's head off and poisoned Carradice?'

She was sharp, perhaps too sharp for her own good. Of course the possible connection was not too hard to make, especially if she had a radio. The airwaves had been full of debate about the origins, identities and intentions of the so-called New Knighthood, most of it pure speculation, and ranging in tone from absolute condemnation, through various versions of understanding-the-impulse-while-deploring-the-deeds, to the near open approval of the *Voice*'s editor. Interviewed on one of the news programmes he had repeated the burden of his editorial rant:

If the Security Services can't catch the terrorists,
and the Law is powerless to punish the few who
do get caught, it's hard to blame anyone who looks
for a better way. If the question is, Do the Templars
make me feel safer now than I did before, the
answer is a resounding, Yes, they certainly do!

Pascoe thought of warning Ffion about putting her speculations in the public domain but decided that would only come close to confirming them.

He said, 'Look, we need to talk to Youngman, for his own good as much as anything. The sooner we can eliminate him from our enquiries the better. So if there's any way you can give us a line on him . . .'

There was something, he felt it. But she was hesitating, maybe because she was in the media business herself and hated to give up a possible story, or maybe because she was recalling her own terror at the sight of those armed men coming at her across the garden. He thought of drumming home his conviction that Youngman had deliberately set her up to take the brunt of the likely assault on the cottage. But he decided she'd been terrified enough tonight without piling on more.

He said gently, 'Listen, Ffion, if there is anything, I'll do my best to get to him by myself, just to talk to him, none of this guns-at-midnight nonsense. We want to talk to him, that's all, to let him have his say. So if there's anything you can tell me that might help me reach him before the Wild Bunch out there, now's the time. It won't go any further.'

He felt her relax against him and she said, 'It's probably nothing, but when I toured his second book in February, there were a couple of times he spent the night away from our hotels. Nothing wrong with that, he never missed a promotional meet, not until Friday, that is. I probably wouldn't have noticed he was away, except that we'd sort of got together by then, so him not being around at night impinged, if you follow me.'

'Did you ask him where he'd been?' said Pascoe.

'Too bloody right I did!' she said with sudden force. 'OK, he's not the kind of guy you expect exclusive rights on, but no way was I going to play second fiddle to some randy reading-group woman. Some of these writers are forever on the make when they do a signing, see. It's a small step from fan to fanny, that's what one of them once said to me, and him what they call a literary novelist and on the Booker shortlist that year!'

Pascoe made a note to tell Ellie that Ffion clearly expected a higher standard of behaviour from serious novelists than mere genre fiction writers.

He said, 'But he convinced you he hadn't just availed himself of a better offer?'

'Oh yes. First time he said he'd dropped in on an old military friend and been persuaded to stay the night. That was when we were staying in Sheffield. Same thing a couple of nights later when we were doing Leeds. I said, "Another old military friend?" He laughed and said, "In a way, though not so old." I didn't get that, but I did get the impression that if I started acting like I had some sort of right to know what he was up to, I'd soon get the dusty answer. So I shut up.'

'Because you liked him a lot?'

'Because I liked him quite a lot, yeah. Also I like my job, and if a successful author says he wants to dump a publicist, people start asking questions. Talking of jobs, you sure I'll get away tonight? I really need to be back at my desk some time tomorrow.'

Forgetting that you've already told Glenister you're not expected back till Tuesday, thought Pascoe. But he couldn't blame her for wanting to be back in bright-light land as quickly as possible, especially not with a story like hers to tell. No doubt they would try to persuade her to keep quiet for a while at least. Well, good luck. It wasn't his job, thank heaven!

'Yes, sure,' he said. 'But you ought to take things quietly when you get home. You've had quite a weekend. First that thing on the Fidler show, now this. Maybe you should pick your authors more carefully.'

'Will you tell Ellie or shall I?' she riposted.

Smiling he got out of the car and went to join Glenister.

'Nice work,' she said.

'What? I haven't told you anything yet,' he

replied. And he still wasn't certain how much he was going to tell. Feed information into CAT and you never knew where it was going to come out.

Then he saw her remove her ear-piece, and the implication of her compliment struck home.

'You've been listening!'

'Of course,' she said. 'Told you a friendly familiar face would do the trick, didn't I? You played it well, laddie. That stuff about wanting a little heart-to-heart with Jonty, no nasty guns, that was the perfect line. We've got his military record already, of course. Now we'll do a deep trawl to see if we can pick up a link around Sheffield or Leeds.'

There was no way to express his indignation without giving away his doubts.

He said, 'We try to please. So if we're done here now, shall I send her on her way?'

She gave him the schoolmarm stare.

'You're joking,' she said.

'But I practically gave her my word . . .'

'She's Welsh. You know what they think of the word of an Englishman. Get real, Peter. You don't think I'm letting someone with her press connections loose, do you? At least, not before two Appeal Lords and a whole coven of Amnesty lawyers make me!'

'But surely if we explain to her, she'll promise to co-operate.'

'Of course she will. She'll promise you her bonny Welsh body if it means getting somewhere she can start haggling with the *Voice*. After that trick she played on your wife, I'm amazed you can even contemplate trusting her.'

'So what's going to happen?'

'She's going to be invited to accompany us back to Manchester for further questioning. If she plays up, I'll arrest her.'

'For what?'

'Come on, laddie! Earn your pay! She had a rendezvous with a man suspected of being complicit in several serious crimes. She held stuff back when she talked to me, God knows what she's still holding back. And she fired a shotgun at my men.'

'But you know she's innocent!'

'Innocent? You sure of that, Peter? We need to be absolutely certain. Anyway, innocent, guilty, the important thing is it will be a couple of days before anyone starts asking questions about her, so why let her run round shooting off her mouth before then? You know it makes sense. Do you want to be the one who tells her or shall I?'

Pascoe looked towards the car. Ffion was watching them through the window. She smiled at him. He smiled uncertainly back.

God knows what all this is going to do for Ellie's literary career, he thought gloomily.

'She's all yours,' he said. 'Now, please, can I go home?'

'Of course,' said Glénister. 'I've sent someone to fetch your car. Didn't think you'd want to sit with the fair Ffion again! Thanks a lot, Peter. You've been a great help.'

This sounded a bit final.

He said, 'So, see you tomorrow.'

She looked at him blankly, then said, 'Here, help me get out of this torture machine before I swoon away like a Victorian maiden.'

She doesn't know what to do with me, he thought as he gave her what was quite unneces sary assistance in removing her bullet-proof vest.

'Thank God for that,' she said, joggling her liberated bosom. 'I've lost all sense of feeling. I could suckle a warthog and not feel a thing.'

He said, 'And tomorrow?'

'I hope normal service will have been resumed by tomorrow,' she laughed.

'I meant me, tomorrow. Shall I report to the Lubyanka?'

'No. Take a day off, Peter,' she said. 'You prob-ably came back to work too soon anyway, and this weekend was meant to be an R-and-R session for you. Didn't really work out that way, did it? You have a long lie-in with that lovely wifey of yours, and I'll give you a bell, OK?'

I shouldn't have asked, he reproached himself. I should just have turned up in Manchester. Now they can cut me right out of the loop.

He felt as if he were on the edge of seeing things plainly but was powerless to stop the lights being turned off.

He said, 'I'd like to go on helping. I think I can contribute.'

He tried to keep it tight and professional. Any

hint of a personal plea could be counterproductive. He knew from his own experience that having someone on your team whose motives were too up close and personal was generally a bad idea.

'Of course you can,' she said reassuringly. 'But only if you're fully fit. And Peter, a word. If I ring you at home and find that you're not at home because you've gone into work, that's it. I don't like laddies on my team who can't follow instructions. Watch how you drive now.'

Was she his friend or not? He didn't know, but he had to act as if she was.

'I will,' he said. 'And you watch out for warthogs.'

Her laughter as he walked away sounded genuine enough.

But then it would, wouldn't it?

Part Five

For God is like a skilful Geometrician, who, when more easily and with one stroak of his Compass he might describe or divide a right line, had yet rather do this in a circle or longer way, according to the constituted and fore-laid principles of his Art.

Sir Thomas Browne, *Religio Medici*

1

a free lunch

For the next few days the papers were full of Templar and terrorist stories, but by mid-week even the speculative fecundity of the tabloids was finding it difficult to create the appearance of novelty without hard facts.

The weekend security alert at Mid-Yorkshire Central Hospital got a good airing, but on the whole it was a blank white sheet that flapped in the wind. The gentlemen of the press, desperate for copy, soon seized upon the fact that two policemen linked to the Mill Street bombing were patients there. But only the *Voice*, which in matters of pure fabrication always went the extra mile, for once got close to the truth with its theory that an attempt had been made on the life of one of the officers, though they could offer no hard evidence to support it. The official spin was that the alert had been sparked by an attempt to steal drugs from the dispensary. While no one believed it, no one could disprove it either, and a lie unchallenged is very soon stronger than a truth unsupported.

Knowing that *Voice* jackals would have been padding round the hospital corridors waving bundles of banknotes under every nose that came their way, Pascoe wondered how CAT had managed to sit on the grumpy Mr Mills who shared Hector's room.

Perhaps they'd locked him up with Ffion Lyke-Evans.

When Ellie heard that Ffion was being held *incommunicado*, she grew indignant on her behalf, which at least took the heat off Pascoe for a while.

On his return from Northumberland, he had opted to tell Ellie everything on the deplorably sexist grounds that simple facts could never be as bad as female fancy.

Unhappily he quickly discovered that parity of information does not necessarily lead to parity of conclusion. While it was obvious to him that he had (a) never been in any danger during the assault on Youngman's cottage and (b) that the only way he was going to discover what had really happened to put Fat Andy into a life-threatening coma was to stick as close to CAT operations as he could, to Ellie it was just as clear that if his conspiracy theories had any merit at all, his persistence in nosing around unofficially could only put his own health, physical and professional, at serious risk.

'Go and see Trimble,' she urged. 'Or write to

the Commissioner. Get it in the open so you're
not a solitary target.'

'You think that would help,' he retorted, 'when
I've no idea how high this goes, how many blind
eyes are being turned at top level to these so-
called Templars?'

To which she replied, 'And you think that's
going to comfort me?'

But what did comfort her was his strong suspicion that his ad hoc secondment to CAT was going
to be terminated.

On Monday, he'd wanted to go into the Station
and see how things were there but, recalling
Glenister's injunction, he stayed at home, jumping
every time the phone rang.

It was never Glenister and by mid-afternoon
he was convinced that she wasn't going to call.
Then at five o'clock, it rang again.

'Pascoe,' he said.

'Peter, hi. It's Dave Freeman.'

His heart sank. She wasn't even doing her own
dirty work.

Then what Freeman was saying sank in.

'Sandy's sorry she can't ring herself, but she's
busy busy. How're you feeling?'

'Fine. Well rested. Ready for work.'

'Excellent. But let's not rush things. Sandy
thought you were looking a bit peaky on Sunday.
Why don't you meander across here tomorrow
evening, settle back in your hotel, then report for
duty at the Lube on Wednesday.'

His first impulse was to say he could be there tonight, but he resisted it.

'Yes! Fine,' he said. 'I'll be there first thing Wednesday.'

He must have sounded keen.

'At least wait till sun-up,' said Freeman.

He laughed as he spoke, but it was a sharing friendly laugh rather than his usual knowing fricative.

When he told Ellie, she wasn't pleased but, seeing it was pointless to argue, she held her peace. *Never part mad*, had been one of their early marriage resolutions, never broken without subsequent regret, and her goodbye kiss as he left the following day was as passionate as a man could wish for.

Next morning she was sitting glaring in frustration at the recalcitrant third chapter of her new novel when the phone rang. The number in the caller display was unfamiliar, and she answered with a snappy 'Yes?' ready to cut off any attempt to sell her anything.

'Ellie?' said a man's voice cautiously.

'That's right. And you are?'

'It's Maurice. Maurice Kentmore. I'm sorry, is this a bad time?'

'Maurice!' she said. 'Hi. No, it's fine, really. For some reason I thought you were trying to sell double-glazing. Sorry.'

He laughed and said, 'No, not selling. The opposite, in fact. I had to come over here on business this morning, and I just wondered if I could buy you – and Peter, of course – lunch? Sorry it's so last minute, but I got my business done much quicker than I expected, and I have to hang around as I'm picking up Kilda later – she's visiting a friend – so what I mean is, I thought I'd have a bite to eat somewhere, and I tend to bolt my food when I'm eating alone, which gives me indigestion . . .'

'So this is a medical emergency rather than a social call?' said Ellie, amused for once rather than irritated at the polite Englishman's inability to say, Fancy some lunch?

Kentmore said, 'Sorry, I'm going on, aren't I? Look, it would be nice to see you, but if you're busy or have made other arrangements or . . .'

Now Ellie did let herself sound a little irritated.

'Maurice,' she said, 'I'm quite capable of finding my own excuses. If I wanted any. Which I don't. So when and where?'

'I really only know the Keldale Hotel,' he said. 'The restaurant is pretty reliable. What do you think?'

Reliable, in this case, meaning dull, stodgy and pretentious.

'If you're seriously asking, I think I'd rather grab a burger in the park,' she said.

'Oh well, if you really wanted to do that . . .'

'I'm joking, Maurice. But not the Keldale. How about the Saracen's Head, Little Hen Street, twelve thirty? You'll need to book. Or would you like me . . . ?'

This was a challenge too far to his masculinity.

'No. I'll do it. Look forward to seeing you.'

Was I rude? thought Ellie, putting the phone down. Maybe. But I'm not going to reorganize my day to lunch in the fucking Keldale!

It occurred to her that she hadn't mentioned she'd be alone. Ah well, it would be a pleasant surprise for him. She hoped. Whoops. Why did she hope that? Because she was assuming it was her company he wanted, not Peter's.

To what end? she heard her husband enquire. *For your sparkling conversation? Or your lily-white body?* 'How should I know!' she said to her reflection in the mirror. *OK, but you should know why you said yes,* came the retort. 'Because he seemed to expect me to say no,' she replied briskly as she stood in front of her wardrobe, wondering what to wear. *But couldn't that be exactly the reaction he was looking to provoke?* asked her husband. *Men, as you have from time to time pointed out, can be devious bastards, especially in pursuit of l-wb's.* 'Speak for yourself,' she retorted.

And found herself wishing yearningly that he was here to do that.

She closed the wardrobe and looked at herself in the mirrored door. For a casual pub lunch, what was wrong with the M&S jeans and checked shirt she was wearing?

Nothing, came the answer.

Nothing at all.

*   *   *

362

The Saracen's Head was an old coaching inn which Peter and Ellie often used if they met at lunchtime. It was old and dark and could have done with a bit of tender loving care from a sympathetic decorator, but the dining room was clean and airy with well-scrubbed deal tables not too crowded together and a short menu of good plain food cooked from scratch on the premises. Another advantage was that it was a good mile from the Black Bull, CID's favourite pit-stop, so there was little chance of an overspill.

It occurred to Ellie as she walked towards the ancient sign which had been creaking over the cobbles of Little Hen Street for at least two hundred years that in light of Kentmore's sad family history it wasn't perhaps the most diplomatic of venues.

The inn sign showed the eponymous head looking a touch pop-eyed, which was perhaps not surprising as it had evidently just been severed from its body.

A Lib-Dem councillor with more sensibility than sense had mounted a campaign to have the sign removed on the grounds that it was likely to cause offence to non-Christian faith groups. The local paper had produced an editorial which seemed to be supporting the campaign until you reached the paragraph listing other signs the councillor might like to put on his hit list, such as Men on public toilets (sexist), Help the Aged over a charity shop (ageist), St George's Church (dragonist), and Posy Please (florist).

Ellie had laughed even though the councillor was a friend of hers. She too had taken a while to learn that sometimes perception is the better part of principle.

Kentmore was already there.

He's keen, thought Ellie as she saw him rising from his chair and stepping forward to greet her. She was prepared for anything from an air-kiss to the touch of warm lips, but all he offered was a brisk handshake. They sat down. The table was only set for two. Did this mean he'd guessed or presumed that Peter wouldn't come? Watch out for your lily-white body, girl! she admonished herself as she ordered the poached salmon salad and a small glass of white wine. He did the same. He said it was his first time here and asked if she knew anything of the history of the place. To an ex-lecturer, it's always pleasant to be given an excuse to deliver a short lecture, so she did, watching carefully for the first sign of eye-glaze but not detecting any.

'So,' she concluded, 'though the building is seventeenth century, it could be the name was inherited from a medieval pub that once occupied the same site. Or it could be that some Yorkshire entrepreneur cashing in on the buoyant market for cakes and ale after the Restoration thought a nice bit of retro-design would be just the job. Probably had lances on the wall, Crusader ale in the cask.'

'Steak and Coeur-de-lion pie on the menu,' he contributed, smiling.

He had a very attractive smile. Apart from the table for two, nothing in his demeanour or conversation suggested he had l-wbs on his mind, but she recalled once hearing the Great Guru Dalziel say that getting a confession and getting laid had much in common – you had to be willing to listen to a lot of crap en route without falling asleep.

The salmon came. It was delicious. She refused a second glass of wine, not through fear of weakening her resistance but because she was picking Rosie up from school later. Kentmore made no effort to persuade her.

She asked after his sister-in-law, Kilda.

'She's fine,' he said. 'She keeps herself busy. She has lots of friends.'

Most of whom she meets at AA sessions, thought Ellie. Then slapped herself mentally for being a bitch.

'Is she working again now? She was a photographer, wasn't she?'

'I hope she'll get back to it,' he said. 'On Saturday at the fête, that was the first time I've seen her using her camera since Chris '

He tailed off and she came in quickly, 'What about family? Any kids?'

'No.'

'That's a pity.'

'Why do you say that?'

'I just thought, losing her husband, kids might have been a comfort. I know if anything ever happened to Peter, I'm certain I'd be even gladder

than I am to have my daughter, Rosie . . . Sorry.
Not my business.'

'Kilda's got me. After it happened we had each
other.'

'It's good you're so close,' she said.

'Yes, it was really handy that she and Chris
had a house on the estate.'

She almost said she didn't mean that, but
stopped herself. Of course he knew she didn't
mean that. How close they were, what comfort
they had sought in each other, was their business. And she recalled her instinctive feeling,
which she'd passed on to Peter, that they weren't
in a physical relationship.

She said, 'I'm sorry. I didn't mean to pry. Grief,
sharing a death, that either brings people together
or thrusts them apart . . .'

'Are you speaking from experience?'

She said, 'Sort of, I suppose. Before we got
married, we lost some friends, people we'd been
at university with, in circumstances . . . well, we
don't need to go into that. And I wasn't certain
at the time where it was going to leave us.'

'But it brought you closer?'

'Oh yes. Then later, there was a time when
Rosie was seriously ill and I really didn't know
what might happen to us if she didn't make it . . .
still don't . . .'

His hand rested on hers and he said, 'I think
you'd have been OK. But it's hell, no getting away
from it. They say time heals, but that moment

when I realized Chris was dead, that's left a wound that nothing can heal.'

His fingers were digging into the back of her hand.

She said, because it felt necessary to say something, anything, to stop him from reliving the experience, 'How did you hear? Letter, or did they contact you direct?'

'What? Oh yes, eventually. But I knew already. I heard him die, you see.'

Oh God, she thought. Was this going to be one of those mystic experiences she usually mocked as a retrospective rearranging of the furniture? *And when I heard he'd died at two o'clock on Thursday, I remembered that it was just about then that I broke one of my best crystal glasses . . . just fell apart . . . He always loved those glasses . . .*

She drew her hand away from beneath his and said, 'Heard . . . ? In what sense?'

'In the sense of *I heard*,' he said. 'He rang me. That's right. I was in bed and the phone rang and when I picked it up, it was Chris. His helicopter had been shot down and he got taken prisoner. He was injured already and the bastards who took him decided they weren't going to waste medical supplies on him but they might as well extract any useful information they could before they dumped him. So they tortured him.'

'Jesus!' exclaimed Ellie. 'But this phone call you say he made . . .'

'A rescue party turned up and sorted out the

bastards who were torturing him, but it was too late for Chris. He knew he was dying. There was a satellite phone. Chris begged the chap in charge to let him use it. Strictly against the rules, I imagine, but what use are rules when a man's dying in front of you?'

He fell silent.

Ellie said, 'And he rang you?'

She tried to keep the note of puzzlement out of her voice, but didn't succeed.

He said, 'And not Kilda, you mean? Of course he tried her first. But she was away. So he rang me. We spoke only a few seconds. And then he fell silent. After a moment a voice said, "Sorry, sir, he's gone. I'll be in touch." Then the phone went dead.'

'Oh my God. And what did you do?'

'What do you think I did?' he demanded savagely. 'Dialled 1471 and tried to get reconnected? Sorry, that was rude. I don't know what I did. It felt like a dream, a nightmare. Eventually of course it became official. That was better, marginally. Official you can deal with. Official gives you things to do, decisions to make, papers to sign.'

He emptied his glass, pointed at Ellie's.

She shook her head.

He said, 'Probably wise. The bottle was a temptation back then. In the end I resisted it. But let's have some coffee.'

When it came he said, 'This was meant to be a jolly sociable lunch. Sorry to off-load all this stuff on to you, especially when you've got troubles of your own.'

'Troubles?' she echoed, unsure which of them he might be referring to.

'Peter's boss, I get the impression he means a lot to you both . . .'

'Andy? Yes, he does. A lot.'

'So if he doesn't make it, you're going to be hit hard?'

It occurred to her that, if this was his idea of getting the lunch back on jolly sociable lines, he ought to go on a course.

She said, 'Yes, we are. It will be . . . I think earth-shattering's the only way to put it. Most people we love, kids, parents, spouses, you feel their vulnerability, you worry about them, often too much maybe. But Andy . . . imagine going to the Lake District and finding that Great Gable wasn't there. I keep telling myself the prognosis isn't good, that it's time to start letting go. But inside I can't get close to accepting it.'

He squeezed her hand again. It felt like genuine sympathy rather than a move.

He said, 'Incidentally, I was reading in the paper about an alert at the hospital on Sunday. There was some speculation that an attempt had been made on the life of a policeman who was a patient there and I wondered if it might have been your friend.'

Ellie looked at him curiously. The only paper which had come that close to the truth was the

Voice, and she wouldn't have put Kentmore down as a reader.

He misread her hesitation and said, 'Look, I'm sorry, I shouldn't be asking you about police matters. It was crass of me. And as I only saw it in some rag I glanced at in the hairdressers, it's probably a load of rubbish anyway.'

'No,' she said. 'You're right, there was an incident. But it didn't involve Andy, not directly that is. Another officer who was a witness in the Mill Street case. Look, I really don't know anything more than that.'

And Peter would tell her she shouldn't have said even as much as that. But by comparison with what she wasn't saying, about her crazy husband running around the Kielder Forest with a bunch of heavily armed madmen, it was the tiniest of indiscretions. And whatever else Kentmore was, she couldn't see him as an under-cover *Voice* reporter!

His hand was still on hers. He gave what felt like a farewell squeeze, poured more coffee and asked how Tig and Rosie were after their triumph at the fête.

As they left together, Ellie said, 'Thanks for the lunch. I enjoyed it.'

'Does that mean you'll want to come again if I call again?'

'If? That's not very flattering,' she said.

'It just means I'm far too old-fashioned to be presumptive enough to say "when".'

This rang a bit arch. Or maybe that's what old-fashioned flirting sounded like.

'In that case, goodbye. Or *au revoir*,' she said, offering her hand.

She could do archness too.

He took her hand. This time however he did not shake it firmly but used his grip to draw her towards him and brushed his lips against her cheek.

'I've really had a good time,' he murmured. 'Thank you.'

For a moment she thought his lips were coming round to her mouth. Then over his shoulder reflected in the glass of one of the pub windows on the far side of the road half hidden by a parked car she saw a figure she recognized.

'There's Kilda,' she said, breaking away. 'She must have come looking for you.'

She turned to wave, and felt her face adjusting into an expressive mode she couldn't immediately identify. Then she got it. This was the look of wide-eyed innocence she used to adopt whenever her mother almost caught her reading a magazine that didn't have the parental seal of approval. Jesus! she thought, forcing her features into a neutral mask. It isn't like I had my hand down the guy's trouser front or something!

For a second the woman behind the car didn't move and Ellie thought, Maybe it isn't her. Or maybe she's had a few and doesn't care to meet me.

Then she moved forward across the road towards them.

If she'd been hitting the bottle, there was no sign of it in either her appearance or her speech. She flashed a brief formal smile at Ellie then said, 'Maurice, I finished earlier than I expected so thought I might still catch you here. Hello, Ellie.'

'Hello,' said Ellie. 'We were just saying goodbye.'

'That sounds a bit final,' said the woman.

Ellie detected a note of mocking satisfaction which she found provocative.

'Not really,' she said. 'In fact, I was just going to ask Maurice here if he fancied coming to lunch with us at the weekend? Peter will be back by then and I know he'll be sorry to have missed you. You too, of course, Kilda.'

There you are, dear, thought Ellie, feeling back in control of the situation. Let's see just how possessive you are!

The Kentmores looked at each other, deciding which of them would formulate the refusal, guessed Ellie.

Then Maurice said, 'It would have to be Saturday for me.'

'Fine.'

'Then that would be lovely. Wouldn't it, Kilda?'

'Great,' said the woman.

'Oh good,' said Ellie. 'I'll look forward to seeing you then. Shall we say round about twelve? Thanks again for lunch, Maurice.'

'Thanks for coming. I enjoyed it. See you Saturday then.'

The pair of them walked away, close but not touching. As soon as they were out of earshot an animated conversation broke out between them. It didn't look too friendly.

Just what is the relationship between them? wondered Ellie as she watched them go.

And how the hell am I going to explain to Peter that I've asked them for lunch?

2

promotion

Back in the Lubyanka, Pascoe found that attitudes had changed.

The first person he'd seen when he arrived at eight forty-five was Freeman, who'd glanced at his Patek Philippe watch with a smile and said, 'What kept you?'

'My ten-mile run before breakfast,' said Pascoe. 'Is Sandy in yet?'

'Of course she is. You know the old Jacobite tradition: no breakfast till you've killed an Englishman. But you'll have to wait. She's upstairs with Uncle Bernie.'

'Killing him?'

'I hope not. I'll let her know you're here, shall I? Where will you be?'

Pascoe said, 'In the cellar, I suppose. I don't want to get myself arrested by showing up anywhere else.'

Freeman seemed to find this very witty.

'Good to have you back, Pete,' he said, sounding as if he meant it.

Pondering these things, Pascoe descended to the room where he'd worked so boringly the previous week. Here he found Tim and Rod already engaged in their seemingly endless task of record trawling.

When they saw him, they both rose with expressions of delight and greeted him like a returned prodigal. News of his role in the Youngman affair had clearly reached them and they were eager for details. Suspecting some kind of confidentiality test, he only confirmed what they already knew. Unsatisfied, they insisted he join them in the staff canteen for further debriefing and morning coffee. The few people already there and others who came later also gave him the big welcome, confirming what he'd already begun to feel, that he had moved, or been moved, from outsider to one-of-us.

Still he looked for hidden motives, for mocking irony. But quickly he began to realize how much his sense of being kept out of the loop and his suspicion that the Templars had an informant in CAT had coloured his feelings about the whole of the unit. Now he was reminded what he shouldn't have forgotten, that these people too – even the spooks – were policemen, and cops don't like vigilantes. If, as occasionally happens, there is dirty work to be done, then you consult your conscience and, if you get a green light, you do it yourself. What you never do is let civilians trespass on your turf, even if they seem to be giving you a helping hand. And when the vigilantes in question not only blow up a cop, but then compound what was presumably an accident by trying to kill another who might be a witness, any ambiguity about their status evaporates completely.

As a natural team-player, it was good to feel that at last he was truly in the squad. This sense of belonging saw him return to the basement full of confidence that Glenister wouldn't let him fester down here for long. He offered to help Tim and Rod in their work but they said, 'No no, this is only for us menials. You take the weight off your feet, Peter, and rest up till you are summoned.'

He sat at his desk and opened *Death in the Desert*, the first of Youngman's books, both of which he'd bought on his way to the Lubyanka that morning. It was hailed by its publisher as a new form, the docu-novel, in which a factual skeleton was fleshed with fiction. Bugger new forms, what they needed was a new copy-writer, thought Pascoe. It was dedicated *To Q, leader of men*. Its back cover was crammed with snippets of praise extracted from reviews of the hardback. Pascoe was unimpressed. He and Ellie, finally realizing that two paragraphs in the local evening paper and three lines in the 'Other New Books' section of a Sunday national was all the notice her novel was going to attract, had spent a tipsy evening extracting from this critical molehill an encomiastic mountain.

He started to read.

Youngman's narrative style was raw and unsophisticated but Pascoe could see its appeal. His hero was, unsurprisingly, an SAS sergeant. Called William Shackleton, universally known both by his officers and his men as Shack, he was brutal, amoral and pragmatic. His motto was *Make it happen*. His men didn't like him much but followed him unquestioningly because he got them through. When someone in his hearing said the problem with guerrilla warfare was identifying the enemy, he said, 'No problem. They're all the fucking enemy.' He referred to the population of the Middle East in general as 'Abdul'. When he needed to individuate, he called them 'Abs'. His sexual philosophy was as basic as his military. He made no pretence of the nature of his interest. If a woman didn't respond, he moved on. If she did respond, she got no promise of commitment. But most of his conquests remained as loyal as his men. In a rare moment of openness he explained his technique to one of his few friends. 'If you fuck a woman five times in a night, she knows she'd be crazy to imagine she's going to be the only one. Most of them don't mind not being the only one so long as they think they're the best. When I'm with a woman I make no secret there's plenty of others. But I tell her, honey, whenever I'm fucking them, I'm thinking of you.' Shortly after this conversation, as usually happened to any man he got close to, the friend got blown away.

Was all this wishful thinking, or did Youngman actually practise what he preached? wondered Pascoe as he worked his way through the book. Maybe he should have asked Ffion, wherever she was. The thought made him feel guilty.

He'd just finished the last chapter and was thinking of lunch when the phone rang.

Rod picked it up, listened, and said, 'Big Mac would like to see you.'

'Big Mac?'

'You know, the North-British lady with the knockers,' he said, cupping his hands.

In Glenister's office he was slightly taken aback to find not only the chief superintendent but Bloomfield and Komorowski. They were drinking coffee. Perhaps they'd had lunch already. His stomach rumbled as if to say, Well, I haven't!

'There you are, Peter. How nice,' said Bloomfield, as if this were a chance encounter. 'Just talking about you. Read your wife's book over the weekend. Jolly good. You must be proud of her.'

'Yes, I am,' said Pascoe, wondering where this was going.

'And she of you, I don't doubt. Not without cause. That was a sharp piece of work at the hospital. Very sharp. So what did you make of it all?'

As if Sunday's events hadn't been analysed down to their quarks, thought Pascoe.

But he replied in measured tones, 'I think that these Templars, though they have not laid claim to it, were responsible for the Mill Street explosion. Concerned that PC Hector might be able identify one of them, they decided to take him out. The first attempt with the hit-and-run having failed, they planned to complete the job in the hospital.'

'Sounds about right to me. Lukasz?'

Komorowski said in his chalk-dry voice, 'Their reluctance to claim Mill Street because Superintendent Dalziel got seriously injured doesn't quite fit with their apparent readiness to murder Constable Hector.'

'Down to perceptions,' said Glenister. 'Mill Street was their opening salvo, so to speak, and they didn't want the bad press associated with injuring a policeman. On the other hand offing Hector to protect themselves is fine, so long as it looks accidental. Which makes them almost as ruthless as the bastards they're killing.'

'So it does,' said Bloomfield. 'They right to worry about this man Hector, Peter?'

Pascoe, still uneasy that somehow his previous defence of Hector might have triggered the attack, shook his head.

'No,' he said firmly. 'I don't think we're going to get anything more from him.'

'But it was his drawing of his attacker that put you on to Youngman, wasn't it?'

'Yes, by an indirect route,' said Pascoe. 'But

he'd had a clear view of him in the car, whereas the man in the video shop was deeply obscured by shadow.'

'Still, to capture such a good likeness from a face glimpsed only for a split second moving towards you at sixty miles an hour takes a special talent,' said Komorowski. 'Which, incidentally, I don't find any reference to in Constable Hector's file.'

Been studying that, have you? thought Pascoe.

He said, 'Probably because no one was aware of it.'

'Ah,' said Komorowski, in a tone so neutral it said clearly, If he'd been one of mine, I'd have been aware of it.

'Ah, indeed,' rejoined Pascoe, in a tone which he hoped conveyed just as clearly that Komorowski, not having to deal daily with the loose amalgam of incompetences which was Hector, was talking through his arsehole.

'We are well pleased with the work you did here, Peter,' declared Bloomfield somewhat regally, bringing this polite confrontation to a close. 'How do you feel about following it up? Strictly speaking, it's not within our brief, which is counter-terrorism. To be frank, we're pretty over-stretched as it is, and it would be a great help if you could take this on. I can spare Chetwynd and Loxam to work with you. What do you say?'

Pascoe was momentarily dumbstruck. To be offered the chance to do officially what he was in fact trying to do surreptitiously seemed too good to be true. Already his suspicious mind was suggesting that making his unofficial activities official was the perfect way for the Templar mole to keep close track of what he was up to.

Whose idea was it? he wondered. Pointless asking. It could well be that the person who thought it was his or her idea had had it planted there by someone else anyway.

He said, 'Chetwynd and Loxam . . . ?'

'Tim and Rod, the guys you've been doing such sterling work with in the cellar,' said Glenister, frowning as if surprised he didn't know their surnames, which indeed she was right to be. 'Dave Freeman will help you settle in and act as your link to me.'

That cleared up one thing, thought Pascoe. Freeman's sudden friendliness was presumably explained by foreknowledge of this promotion, it that's what it was.

But, promotion or not, he could hardly say, No, I'd prefer to carry on sneaking around behind everyone's backs.

He said, 'To do this properly, I'd need to have full access to all available records and other material.'

'Of course. On tap. Not, I suspect, that an ingenious chap like you would have any problem finding less conventional modes of access,' said Bloomfield, smiling.

Shit, thought Pascoe. Somehow the old sod

knows that last time I was in this office, I was rifling through Glenister's desk in search of information!

'So we can take it that's settled?' said Bloomfield.

'Yes, sir. Thank you.'

'Good. Sandy, you'll see Peter gets everything he needs? Excellent. Come on Lukasz. Work to do.'

He headed for the door, where he paused and looked up at the ceiling.

'Sandy, that security camera, you ever get it fixed?'

'Yes, sir. It's working fine now,' said Glenister.

'Good. Place like this, you need to be able to see what's going on everywhere, Peter. Downside is, you get to know who picks their nose a lot.'

He looked at Pascoe as he said this, and smiled, and it might have been that his left eye-lid drooped in a slow wink or it may have been just a natural blink.

3

melodious twang

Cap Marvell was not a devout woman. Her father
was a tribal Anglican who regarded the Church
as God's way of affirming the Tories' right to rule
even when Labour was in power, while her
mother was a devout Roman Catholic who made
sure little Amanda was brought up in all the
proper Romish observances and insisted she went
to her own old school, St Dorothy's Academy for
Catholic Girls, which she regarded as the only
doctrinally sound school in the country.

Yet despite all these attempts to establish lines
of control from the Holy See, it was the dear old
domestic C of E which retained a niche in Cap's
affections when mature scepticism swept all other
religious debris away, a fondness based almost
entirely on childhood memories of her father's
insistence that his pack of assorted hounds, terriers,
pointers and retrievers should join him in the
family pew at the village church. She hated the
use they were put to, but she loved their company,

and a heavenly kingdom without animals was not one she had any interest in entering.

Andy Dalziel reckoned that if there were a God, He should be done for dereliction of duty, letting His Creation get into such a mess and relying on folk like A. Dalziel Esq. to pick up the pieces.

This did not prevent him from being on good terms with the odd cleric, particularly if they shared his interest in the really important aspects of the human condition, such as where do you find the best whisky, and who would you pick for your eclectic all-time XV?

Such a one was Father Joe Kerrigan, a parish priest of indeterminate age, with a creased and crumpled leathery face like an old deflated rugby ball. Sport and whisky had brought them together, and once they'd established the ground rule that Kerrigan didn't try to solve crimes and Dalziel didn't try to save souls, they had become good friends who many a night tired the moon with talking and sent her down the sky.

Cap, true to her own unbelief, and knowing Dalziel's considered view that most religious ceremonies were balls, and them as weren't balls were bollocks, had placed a strict interdict on admission to his room of any of the pack of spiritual predators who roam the corridors of modern multi-faith hospitals looking for their defenceless prey.

Joe Kerrigan, however, was an exception. His distress at Andy's plight was personal rather than professional, and he won her imprimatur as a friend, not as a priest.

But the leopard cannot change his spots, and that afternoon Father Kerrigan, visiting the Central to administer the last rites to a dying parishioner, was very much in professional mode when he decided to look in on Dalziel on his way out.

The guardian constable placed outside the room since the events of Sunday recognized the priest and let him in without demur. For the first time Father Joe found himself alone with his friend, and now the prayers which previously in deference to and, it must be said, in fear of Cap Marvell, he had offered silently from within now poured spontaneously from his lips, 'Dear Jesus, Divine physician and Healer of the sick, we turn to you in this time of illness . . .'

As he spoke the priest's words, through his mind ran the friend's thought, 'Where are you, Andy, me dear? Is it living you still are, or am I talking to a lump of flesh in which the heart still beats but out of which the mind and the soul have long fled?'

In fact, Dalziel is both closer than Kerrigan can guess and further than he can imagine. Living he still is, but that point of awareness in which his being is now entirely focused has drifted back to the far edge of darkness, close up against the wafer-thin membrane which separates him from the white light of elsewhere.

He's here partly through necessity in that, whenever the will to survive grows weary, this is where he automatically drifts, but also in some part through choice, because he is essentially a social animal and while his comatose limbo is filled with shadows of his consciousness, he is unable to truly communicate with any of them. Here, however, just beyond the membrane, there is possibly something distinct from himself.

'I know you're in there,' says Dalziel. 'We've got you surrounded. If you come out with your hands up, we can all go home.'

This approach is as unsuccessful as it was in Mill Street.

'If my lad Pascoe were here,' says Dalziel, 'he'd soon talk you out. He's been on a course.'

There is a something. Not a response. Something like that lightest breath of wind in a forest on a still day which reminds you of the huge canopy of foliage under which you stand. But it is enough for Dalziel.

'You are there then,' he says triumphantly. 'Grand. Now we're getting somewhere. Next off is find a name, that's what the manuals say. I'm Andy. What shall I call you? God, is it?'

Again the breeze in the trees, and this time he thinks he gets a meaning.

Why don't you come through and see for yourself?

'Nay,' says Dalziel. 'Last time I tried that, I got blown up. Hang about. What's going off?'

Apart from his brief out-of-body experience,

which had come to a sudden end when his unexpected glimpse of Hector lying in bed had driven him back to the security of his coma, he has no sense of external context. All he knows is that at the end of the darkness furthermost from the membrane separating him from the white light of Elsewhere lies another Elsewhere from which derive those fragments of sensation which still have the power to call him back.

What is coming through now is a sort of monotonous mutter which gradually he starts to break up into words.

Omnipotent and eternal God, the everlasting salvation of those who believe, hear me on behalf of Thy sick servant, Andrew . . .

'Bloody hell!' says Dalziel indignantly. 'Some bugger's praying to me!'

To *me*, for *you, I think you'll find, corrects the forest breeze.*

'Same difference. You must get a lot of this stuff in your line of work. How the hell do you put up with it?'

C'est mon métier, says the breeze.

'Right. Like me having to listen to scrotes telling me they were somewhere else on the night in question, ladling out soup to the poor.'

Something like that.

'So what else do you do, apart from listening to this drivel? There's got to be something else your side that keeps you too busy to take care of things my side.'

You still think of yourself as being part of what you call your side?

'Why shouldn't I?'

Come through and we'll talk about it.

'Nay, you don't catch me like that. This is as close as I'm getting. In fact, it's a bit too close for comfort. I'm off back there. Ta ta.'

See you soon.

'You sound very sure of that.'

I am. You will be back. And each time you come back you will find it more difficult to retreat.

'Is that right. Not so clever telling me then, is it?'

I tell you because you will not be able to help coming back. And I tell you that because of course you know you already know.

'No one likes a smart arse,' says Dalziel as he retreats.

But he has to admit the breeze-like Presence is right. It's bloody hard and if it weren't for the help offered by that thread of sound he might never have made it.

This doesn't make him any the less resentful when he gets close enough to confirm that the mournful muttering is indeed nothing less than prayer. All he knows about prayers is that most of the ones he's felt constrained to utter, particularly the one asking for a widow's cruse of single malt or the ones suggesting a thunderbolt might be good response to some particularly irritating piece of official idiocy, have remained unanswered. But now he thinks he recognizes the voice. Surely those rough raspings can only emerge from the smoke-and-whisky-corroded larynx of his old mate, Joe Kerrigan? If anyone deserves an answer, it's good old Joe.

He concentrates all the power still at his command on finding a fitting response.

Father Joe paused in his prayer. He thought he detected a movement of the great bulk on the bed. Yes, he was right. Something was stirring down there. Dear Lord, he thought. Is it possible that just for once you're giving me a quick answer to my prayers?

From beneath the bed sheet drifted a sound which put the scholarly Father Joe in mind of John Aubrey's account of that spirit who vanished with 'a curious perfume and most melodious twang'.

When it died away and the body once more lay, a sheer hulk on the bed of an unfathomable sea, Father Joe stood up.

'All right, you fat bastard,' he said, 'I can take a hint. But God bless you anyway.'

4

red mite and greenfly

Pascoe was having lunch with Dave Freeman.

It had been Sandy Glenister's idea.

'With Dave acting as liaison, it's time you two started hitting it off a bit better. You've a lot in common,' she'd said.

So she'd noticed the antipathy, thought Pascoe. Sharp eyes she had, though what they'd spotted he and Freeman had in common he couldn't imagine.

Or was it his own eyes which were developing a squint through looking at everything connected with the Lubyanka sideways?

As he and Freeman moved from the counter of the staff canteen and started unloading their trays, he noticed that they'd made almost identical choices. Perhaps Glenister was right.

Or perhaps Freeman had deliberately echoed his choices . . .

There I go again! he thought.

But certainly as they picked over their salads,

it became apparent that Freeman was making a real effort at rapprochement.

He talked to Pascoe freely about CAT's resources and the quickest way of tapping into them, then invited questions. Pascoe asked for some background on Tim and Rod.

'I like to know the people I'm working closely with,' he said.

'Me too,' smiled Freeman. 'I'll send you my CV later. OK. Tim and Rod . . .'

By the time he'd finished talking, Pascoe's initial image of the pair as young Work Experience students, already considerably modified, had vanished completely. Freeman talked of them as equal colleagues, with their feet firmly on the Security Service career ladder.

Tim Chetwynd was in fact twenty-seven, married, with three young children. Rod Loxam was twenty-three, unmarried but rarely unattached.

'If,' said Freeman dryly, 'you can call the kind of relationships Rod usually has attachments. He is what is called in the vernacular, I gather, a babe-magnet. Among our canteen staff I understand he is known as Hot Rod.'

'Good Lord,' said Pascoe, conjuring up a picture of the young man. Amiable, attractive, yes, but a babe-magnet . . . ?

'Introduce your wife to him and you'll soon see what I mean,' said Freeman, observing his doubts. 'It is a talent not without advantage in our line of business, if only because long-term relationships often cause real problems.'

'Tim seems to have managed.'

'It was an in-house romance,' said Freeman. 'Nice if it happens, but we're a bit short on available tottie at the moment, unless dear Sandy takes your fancy. Tim came up the conventional route: university, spotted by a talent scout and recruited before he'd done his finals. Rod left school in the sixth form, drifted for a couple of years, did casual work, got a job with a gardening firm who did maintenance on Lukasz's garden . . .'

'Komorowski? Yes, he was telling me that gardening was his hobby.'

'Was he now?' Freeman regarded Pascoe as if impressed by the revelation of an unsuspected talent. 'You could do worse than brush up on your bedding plants, Pete, Lukasz is a good man to have on your side. I've never seen his garden – he's got this place with a couple of acres out near Guildford – but I gather it's really something. Impossible for one man to look after, even if he didn't have a job like ours, hence the maintenance firm. So Rod delved, Lukasz was impressed, did a bit of delving of his own, and eventually recruited him.'

'Romantic,' said Pascoe, using the word broadly, but Freeman misinterpreted and said, 'Wrong tree. As I told you, Rod's definitely a fig-and-melons man and from all accounts Lukasz was never short of a bed warmer in his younger days. No, he just saw potential and snapped it up.

Now, is there anything else I can help you with, Peter, before you apply your nose to the grindstone?'

'What's the situation with Lyke-Evans?'

'Oh yes. Ffion, the Silurian Circe. I believe she's still watching daytime telly in Safe House 4, which is one of our more comfortable hideaways. Why do you ask?'

'Just wondered if they'd got anything more out of her.'

'Not that I know of. Seems that her connection with Youngman was exactly what she said, professional with generous side-helpings of sex.'

'So when will she be released?'

'Once we're persuaded she won't be heading straight to the *Voice* with her exclusive.' said Freeman.

'How will you manage that? By appealing to her patriotic loyalty?'

'You're joking! No, in such cases, which are more frequent than you might imagine, the conventional alternatives are bribery and threat. We have a little specialist team we call the Fitters who work out the details. That bugger in the hospital – the one sharing a room with your man, Hector – now he was easy. The Fitters checked his background and it turns out he's got three Child Support payment orders outstanding against him, each with a different woman. The last thing he wants is his details splashed all over the front page. Could make his next visiting day very interesting!

Unfortunately, though it's hard to believe, Silurian Circe seems to have led a pretty blameless life.'

'I think my wife would give you an argument there,' said Pascoe.

'I'm talking about things a publicist might be ashamed of,' said Freeman. 'I'm sure the Fitters will come up with something. Of course, if they don't, it may be poisoned umbrella time. Quicker, cheaper, and a lot more certain.'

He spoke very seriously. Then he grinned and said, 'So it's down to you, Pete. Get us Youngman and the fair Ffion can be let loose to talk to the tabloids all she wants.'

'I presume she's been interrogated again? Could I see the transcripts?'

'No problem. Anything else?'

'I'd like to talk to someone in the SAS who'd be able to fill me in on Youngman.'

Freeman said, 'I'm sure you'll find his service record in the large pile of bumf Tim and Rod are doubtless already sorting through on your desk.'

'I was thinking something a bit more impressionistic than that. The kind of stuff you'd really like to know about a man you may be crawling through a minefield with.'

'Ah. Getting that kind of stuff may not be all that easy.'

'Why?' said Pascoe. 'Surely they'll be keen to help?'

'About as keen as we would be to drop our knickers if they got in touch to say they thought one of our agents had gone rogue. I doubt if you or I would get very far if we approached them direct. Lukasz is your man. He worked closely with them when he was with Six. Knows how they think. I'll have a word. Now let's get you to work.'

Any hope that his upgrade might have raised him to an office with a window was quickly shattered as Freeman led the way back down to the basement.

At least the computers down there were now all at his disposal, and there was a new arrival: a state-of-the-art coffee machine.

'A welcome prezzie,' said Freeman. 'If you need anything else, just ring me.'

'Thanks a lot,' said Pascoe, the old tag about Greeks bearing gifts drifting across his mind. But instantly he dismissed the thought as ungenerous. And illogical.

If they wanted to keep tabs on him, they already had computers, telephones and security cameras at their disposal. Why gild the lily with a bugged percolator?

As Freeman had forecast, his desk was covered with files and folders which Tim and Rod had already started putting in order.

Pascoe looked at the stacks without enthusiasm then turned to the percolator.

'First things first,' he said. 'Which of you two can work this thing?'

As usual at the beginning of an enquiry the main task was clearing away the brushwood so you could see the bare earth beneath the trees.

By mid afternoon, they'd made positive progress. On the Hedley-Case website Rod found a filmed interview which Youngman had done to publicize his second book. In it he assured his readers that every significant incident in the story was based on fact.

Perhaps I should tell Uncle Bernie that our best way forward is to wait for the next book, which should read like a confession, thought Pascoe.

Without waiting to be asked, Rod had sent a copy of the interview to AV, asking them to compare it with the voices on the Mazraani tape. Half an hour later, it came back with the ninety per cent conclusion that Youngman was the man calling himself Andre de Montbard, the one who'd done the actual beheading.

'Well done,' enthused Pascoe. 'Now let's see if we can tie him in with the Mill Street explosion and the Carradice killing.'

He had some hope that this might be possible in the former case. A CAT search team had taken Youngman's cottage apart, finding several automatic weapons and traces of Semtex which proved to be of the same type used in the Mill Street bomb.

'Great!' said Pascoe. 'Now all we need to do is put the bastard close to Mill Street on the Bank Holiday.'

Since Sunday, a lot of hard work had already

gone into correlating possible sightings of Youngman. One which looked pretty definite was that
of a man turning up at a car body shop in Bishop
Auckland on Friday morning and paying over the
odds for rush job tidying up the nearside wing of
his black Jaguar. He'd left the car with them for a
couple of hours, which was going to make it pretty
well impossible to get down to Nottingham for
Carradice's acquittal. It would have been possible
for him to be involved later in the actual killing of
Carradice and placing the body on the reservoir
which, as a note from Bernie Bloomfield suggested,
could explain why he'd backed out of *Fidler's Three*,
but Pascoe found this unpersuasive. To him the
Carradice business looked carefully planned, and
if Youngman were directly involved, why would
he have headed back north instead of south after
his attempt on Hector?

As for Mill Street, that looked a real possibility
when news came that the team trawling through
A1 speed-camera tapes had picked up a black Jag
heading south into Mid-Yorkshire on the Bank
Holiday afternoon. Confirmation that it was
Youngman's quickly followed, but the timing was
wrong, an hour or more after the explosion.

'Could be he was on his way to do a debriefing,'
said Rod.

'The Semtex traces suggest he might have acted
as quartermaster too,' said Tim.

'Which makes him a really important player,'
said Pascoe. 'It's looking as if this isn't just a

two-man band. There have to be at least two teams out there, possibly three.'

There could of course be even more, but Pascoe doubted it. The more people involved, the greater the security risk. And, if his suspicions were right, there was someone behind the Templars who would be very *au fait* with security risks.

He was reading the transcript of Ffion Lyke-Evans' interrogation when Tim coughed a discreet Jeevesian cough behind his hand. It wasn't the sound itself but its repetition a few moments later that attracted Pascoe's attention.

He looked up to see Chetwynd pointing at the wall clock, which read five thirty.

'I didn't realize spooks kept office hours,' said Pascoe.

'Whenever we can,' said Tim. 'To compensate our nearest and dearest for the innumerable times we can't. Of course, if there's something urgent . . .'

He recalled that Tim had a wife and family. There'd been plenty of times when, sidetracked by Fat Andy into the Black Bull, he'd promised himself he would never let anything but professional necessity make him put an obstacle between a man and his home.

'No, nothing. Off you go. See you bright and early tomorrow. Thanks for helping me hit the ground running. You too, Rod.'

'I'm not in a hurry,' said Rod. 'Shift doesn't start till eight.'

'Sorry?' said Pascoe, puzzled. 'You do shift work?'

'He means the husband's shift,' said Tim from the doorway. He sounded disapproving. Married man with three kids knows where his loyalty lies, thought Pascoe.

'In that case,' he said to Rod, 'you can spend a couple of hours in church, praying for salvation. Now bugger off before I find you something really nasty to do!'

Just because he wouldn't do a Dalziel and keep them hanging around didn't mean he had to forget all the lessons he'd learned!

He worked on for another half-hour till he found that his eyes were beginning to glaze. To be caught on video sleeping at his desk would be a cause of at least amusement so he slipped the interrogation transcripts into his briefcase and set off upstairs. As he checked out, he noticed Lukasz Komorowski in the foyer, meticulously examining the plants in the trough and giving them an occasional shot from an insecticide spray.

'Red mite and greenfly,' he said as Pascoe passed. 'Like most mindless terrorists, persistent, fecund, and deadly.'

'But susceptible to a quick squirt from a spray can,' said Pascoe. 'Pity we can't say that about them all.'

Komorowski said, 'You sound as if you might have some sympathy with direct action, Mr Pascoe. A dangerous ambiguity in your new job, I should have thought.'

'No. No dangerous ambiguity,' said Pascoe. 'Just harmless fantasy.'

'I'm glad to hear it. We have to play by the rules we are trying to defend.'

'That sounds very English.'

The man smiled at him.

'But I am English, Mr Pascoe. Born and bred here.'

'I'm sorry. I didn't mean . . .'

'I know you didn't,' said Komorowski. 'It's the name, of course. In America it would pass unnoticed, but here anything un-Anglo Saxon still gets people speaking very slowly in a loud voice. But I'm glad my family ended here not in the States. They have no rules over there, just laws. By the way, Freeman said you would like to talk to someone about this man Youngman's military service. You might try this number.'

He took a scrap of paper out of his pocket and handed it over.

'Thank you,' said Pascoe. 'Is there a name?'

'No name. Ring any time you like. They don't keep office hours. Ah, there's one. Got you! Have a pleasant evening, Mr Pascoe. At least that's one good thing our rules provide for by making it difficult for us to take work home.'

His gaze flickered to Pascoe's briefcase.

Oh shit, thought Pascoe. I should have got authority to remove the transcripts of Ffion's interrogation. But he can't know they're in there. Can he? What the hell's it matter anyway? It's not like

I'm stealing the plans of the latest Star Wars system!

'Good night,' he said, and went out into the rich fumid air of a Manchester summer evening.

5

no-name

Instead of going straight back to his hotel, Pascoe diverted to Albert Square where he found himself an empty bench. He took out his mobile phone and the scrap of paper Komorowski had given him. He looked around. No one in overhearing distance. But that meant nothing in these days of audio-guns.

Jesus, I really am getting paranoiac! he told himself as he keyed in the number.

'Hello,' came a response almost instantly.

'Hello, my name's Pascoe, I'm . . .'

'Yes. Fine. This is about our friend, Sergeant Jonty Young, right? Or Mr John T. Youngman as we ought to call him now. What would you like to know?'

The voice was deep baritone with a faint West Country burr. You could imagine it giving a powerful rendition of 'The Floral Dance'.

'Anything you can tell me that I can't find out somewhere else,' said Pascoe.

'Nice to know there's still places you bastards can't get,' said No-name with a chuckle. 'All I can tell you is I knew him as a serving soldier and I've kept tabs on him since he left. We take a close interest in any former colleague who takes to writing. There are some cats that need to be kept in the bag. Anyone who looks like stepping over the line we drop on from a great height.'

'You mean you take out an injunction against publication?'

'Sometimes,' said No-name. 'Sometimes we just drop something on them from a great height. Joke.'

'Ha ha,' said Pascoe. 'Did Youngman need to be dropped on?'

'No. From our point of view his stuff was harmless.'

'He claimed much of it was fact-based.'

'And he was right. Lots of recognizable incident, some of which he was involved in himself, most of which was general knowledge in the Service. We're a close-knit bunch. We like to share our adventures. But he never gave anything away that we wanted kept quiet. If anything, his books gave us a lot of rather good publicity.'

What would these people regard as *bad* publicity? wondered Pascoe.

He said, 'So he didn't have an axe to grind?'

'Not against the Service. But he really hated the people he was fighting against. That comes across loud and clear in his books, and it was even louder and clearer when he was out there, fighting them. Sounds like he didn't lose it when he got out. Absolutely wrong, of course, but there'll be a lot of sympathy for him both in and out of the Service.'

For trying to kill a cop? Then Pascoe recalled that as far as No-name was concerned, their interest in Youngman was solely as a suspect in the Templar anti-subversives activities.

He said, 'Would this sympathy go as far as giving him a helping hand when he is a fugitive from justice?'

'In the Service, no problem. You look after your mates first, ask questions afterwards. And as I say, if all he's been doing is reaching parts that the Law can't reach, I don't imagine he'll be short of support.'

This was more or less what Pascoe had expected, but it didn't make him happy.

He said, 'Does that include you?'

'Good Lord, what a question for a loyal servant of Her Majesty and the State! But I dare say I might be tempted to give him a sporting start before I blew the whistle.'

That at least was honest.

'What about going further than just not turning him in? I suspect his first port of call if he set out to recruit people to the Templars would be people like himself. Any likely names you can give me?'

A pause, then the man said, 'Look, it's one thing helping you out with Young who, I gather, you can definitely tie in with criminal activity. I don't see it as part of my job to give you names on spec just so you can go about harassing them and their families.'

'Very loyal of you,' said Pascoe. 'Naturally I

already have a list from the MoD of all personnel who have left the SAS in the past ten years. We'll just have to work our way through it alphabetically and harass the lot of them.'

In fact he was lying. Such a list could no doubt be obtained, but he guessed it would be extensive and any meaningful checking would probably involve more man-hours than he would be able to squeeze out of Bloomfield.

'All right,' said No-name. 'I'll see what I can do. But if you talk to anyone whose name I supply, your source is the MoD, right? And it's part of a general check-up.'

'That's how I'd play it anyway,' said Pascoe. 'I'll be very grateful for your help. You're the expert here, we're just grafting away, collecting information. For everyone's sake, we need to find Youngman as quickly as possible. If you were in my shoes, how would you set about it? You know what his training will have taught him. More importantly, you know the man himself. So I'd really appreciate any tips you could give.'

When it came to what he called 'flarchery' (by which he meant flattery laid on with a trowel but so lightly recipients hardly felt a thing), Andy Dalziel was happy to give the palm to Pascoe. 'Yon bugger could flarch for Hollywood,' he used to say proudly.

No-name was clearly susceptible.

'Well, he won't be living rough,' he said, 'that's for sure. In a civilized country, you live rough, eventually you get spotted. So he'll be somewhere out of sight but not out of doors. What you need to ask yourself is, first, what might lead you to him, and second, what might bring him out. First is easy. Sex. You've read his books?'

'One of them.'

'Well, believe me, the sex scenes are definitely based on experience. He enjoys it, he needs it, and he has an insatiable appetite for it. Me, I wouldn't leave him in a room with a female cat I was fond of. So *cherchez les femmes*, plural. Along with sex, he loved soldiering. Just writing about either was never going to do it for him. He really needs action. He tried to re-enlist after we let him go, did you know that?'

'No. When you say "let him go", I gather there was some trouble with Iraqi prisoners?'

'He murdered them,' said No-name flatly. 'Couldn't be proved, of course, far too clever for that. But we knew, so that was that. Got to draw a line somewhere. Pity. He was a good soldier.'

'But not so good you wanted to let him back in?'

'No one's that good. Surprising how often it happens. In the past probably a lot got away with it, but in this day and age, cross-checking identities is that much cleverer. So he didn't make it. Anyway, as I was saying, he's clearly been back in the action or you chaps wouldn't be after him. But being blown doesn't mean he's going to stop. Unless he's ordered.'

'Ordered? You wouldn't expect him to be the man in charge?'

'Of these Templar people? Well, you'll know more about them than I do, but if there's a complex strategy level, no, I wouldn't expect the sergeant to be at that. Where the beautiful trumpets sound, that's where you'll find him. That it?'

'One thing more. Don't you chaps refer to your quartermaster as Q?'

'Occasionally, though it's a bit naff since the James Bond movies. Why?'

'It's just that Youngman's first book is dedicated to Q, leader of men.'

No-name laughed.

'Not a quality much looked for in a quartermaster, I think. Hoarder of duff might be nearer the mark. No, I rather think that would be Major Kewley-Hodge, DSO. He was Young's section leader. Everyone called him Q. Tipped for the top was poor Luke.'

'Poor . . . ?'

'Yes. Got a nasty one in Afghanistan. Ended up paralysed from the waist down.'

'I'm sorry,' said Pascoe.

'Indeed. But it's part of the deal. The moving finger writes and all that. And at least he can still move his fingers and push his own wheelchair. We done now?'

'I think so. Thank you.'

'Pleasure. Hope you get him, but I wouldn't put money on it! Bye.'

Wouldn't put money on it, eh? thought Pascoe. SAS veteran versus PC Plod. A mismatch on Youngman's terrain, perhaps. But I get choice of weapons! One of which was, or ought to be, the terror of the criminal world.

He punched in another number.

'Wield.'

'Wieldy! It's Peter.'

'Pete! How're you doing?'

'Fine. Listen, could you do something for me? Major Kewley-Hodge, DSO, ex-SAS. Present location, if you please. And anything else you can find.'

'What's up? Don't them funny buggers have computers?'

'Yes, but I've left the building and I don't want to attract attention by going back in. Also you're like that beer that reaches places other beers can't.'

'But cheaper.'

'No. Beyond price. Can you help?'

'I'll try. But not till tomorrow, OK? Edwin's going off at the crack. Book fair in Ghent then a little tour around the Netherlands. He'll be away for nearly a week, so we're having a nice meal in and an early night.'

'Tomorrow's fine. As long as it's before eight a.m.'

'Oh, that's all right then. As long as it's not a rush job.'

They talked a little longer. Pascoe didn't ask after Dalziel. He knew that any change good or bad would have been retailed to him straight away.

When he got back to his hotel he ran a bath and, as he lay back in the scented waters, he rang Ellie.

'Hi,' he said. 'Missing you.'

'Are you? Easily remedied.'

She didn't sound as if her reaction to his decision to return to Manchester had mellowed.

'So what are you doing?' she went on. 'Apart from making the world safer for George Bush?'

'Actually I'm in the bath and I could do with someone to scrub my back.'

'I thought CAT would supply Oriental body servants to its top agents.'

'If that's the case, mine should be on her way,' he said rather smugly.

And he told her about his elevation.

She didn't react with unconfined joy.

'So what's that mean, Peter? They've put you in the tent so you can piss out?'

This was too close to Pascoe's own suspicion for him to react indignantly.

He said, 'You could be right. But at least I'm in the tent and when the time comes, I'll piss any which way I like.'

There it was again, thought Ellie, that harshly defiant note which came so natural to Fat Andy Dalziel but which from her husband sounded like bravado.

She said, 'Listen, love, you will take care, won't you? You're in unknown territory over there, and I don't just mean Lancashire. There be dragons, and there's nobody to watch your back, let alone scrub it.'

'Yes, I could do with Wieldy beside me. Sight of that face would make most dragons run a mile.'

Now it was Pascoe's turn to detect and deplore a Dalzielesque note. He went on hastily, 'But there's a lot of upside. At least I'm really getting to know the people I'm working with.'

He gave her an entertaining account of his new insights into Tim and Rod.

'You'd like them,' he assured her. 'They're bright young guys making their way. Even Dave Freeman, now that he's been told off to be my buddy, is good company.'

He always liked to be a member of a team, thought Ellie. His strength, but maybe his weakness too? Then she thought of all the times that his single-minded sense of purpose had surprised her.

'But that's quite enough about me,' he went on. 'How's your day been?'

'Thought you'd never ask,' said Ellie brightly. 'While you were busy being promoted, I was being chatted up.'

'Doesn't surprise me,' said Pascoe. 'And which of your many still-hopeful admirers is taking advantage of my absence?'

'Got myself a new one,' she said.

She gave an account of her lunch with Kentmore.

Pascoe said, 'How odd. What's his game, I wonder?'

'Peter, it would be nice if occasionally you reacted like a jealous husband rather than a suspicious copper,' she said.

'OK, OK, I'll challenge him to a duel next time we meet. Seriously, did you get the impression his interest was purely, or rather *impurely* carnal? Or were you really persuaded that, on the basis of your previous encounters, he decided, hello, here's a woman who could share my lifelong interest in breeding pigs?'

'Maybe he just felt it would be nice to see me again. Anything wrong with that?'

'Nothing at all,' said Pascoe. 'Hey, I thought you wanted me to act jealous.'

'Nice readjustment,' she said. 'Maybe wrong verb, though.'

'Sorry. *Feel* jealous. Which of course I do. So what did you talk about? Apart from the price of pork, that is.'

'It wasn't what you call flirtatious stuff,' she admitted. 'He asked how Andy was and how I'd feel if he didn't make it. From there we got to talking about loss and grief . . .'

'Jesus!' interrupted Pascoe. 'He's not one of those weirdoes who get off on death, is he? Watch him if he suggests a rendezvous in a graveyard.'

'That might be interesting,' she said. 'But no, I just think he's a man who's not really got over the death of his brother. I can understand why. It's so unbelievable you couldn't invent it. He actually heard him dying.'

'Sorry? I thought he got killed in Iraq.'

Ellie told him the story.

'God, that must have been rough,' he said when she finished. 'Poor bastard. Bet that took the edge off your appetite.'

'I managed. The grub's too good at the Saracen to leave on your plate.'

Pascoe laughed. His wife's healthy appetite was something Andy Dalziel always put at the top of a list of her good qualities. Sometimes when they were particularly at odds, it was the only item on the list.

'So, having softened you up with his sad story, did he weep on your shoulder and suggest another meeting for the next instalment?'

'No,' she said brightly. 'I did.'

'Sorry?'

'Yes. You see, your fan Kilda turned up as we were leaving, and knowing how struck you were by her boozy charms, I thought I'd let you have your chance to shine. I've invited them to lunch on Saturday.'

'You've what?'

'You heard. Is there a problem?'

'I was looking forward to a quiet weekend with my family,' he said gloomily.

'Like the one we had last weekend?' she said. 'Sorry. At least it sounds as if you're planning to come back this weekend.'

'Of course I am,' he retorted.

'Even if your country needs you?'

He was too honest to assure her that he'd be home whatever, but she'd long ago come to accept that being married to a cop meant you couldn't demand assurances, so she didn't leave him hanging but said, 'Look, love, it was just one of those invitations that sort of slipped out. I don't think they were all that keen, at least not her. It'll be the easiest thing in the world to ring and say you can't get back from Manchester so lunch is off.'

'That's sounds like tempting fate a bit,' he said.

Like most policemen, he had a broad superstitious streak, though like most policemen he would have denied it.

'OK,' said Ellie. 'Let's wait till we're absolutely sure you can make it home before I tell them you can't.'

After all these years, her pragmatism still had the power to leave him breathless.

'Sounds good to me,' he said. 'But if they did come, you weren't planning to let your common interest in pig breeding persuade you to give them roast pork, were you?'

'No. Why?'

'It's just I thought I could hear a pig being slaughtered in the background.'

It took a second for Ellie to catch on.

'Pete! She'd be mortified if she heard you!'

'She'd be Wonder Woman to hear anything over that din. Do you think Benny Goodman could bear to be dragged away from practice to talk to her old dad?'

'Only if you hold the jokes,' said Ellie sternly. 'I'll get her in a minute. So how do you intend to pass the rest of the evening in swinging Manchester?'

'You know me,' said Pascoe. 'Grab a bite to eat, then do the clubs, sink a couple of bottles of bubbly, snort a few lines of coke. Or maybe I'll just settle down with a good book.'

The reading matter he actually settled down with as he ate his excellent dinner in the hotel restaurant was Ffion's interrogation. There'd clearly been several sessions, but it seemed to him that at an early stage the interrogation team had decided they'd got everything useful and were concentrating on frightening the shit out of the poor woman.

After the meal and a stroll round the block to get some air, he went up to his room. He wasted an hour watching a TV cop-shop show that had more holes than an election manifesto, then decided it was time for the good book he'd mentioned to Ellie.

The choice lay between two sagas of struggle and sacrifice and brutality and destruction against a desert background, to wit, *Blood on the Sand*, the second of Youngman's novels, and the Gideon Bible.

Well, he told himself, what you want's a soporific not something of riveting interest.

He made the right choice. After two chapters of *Blood on the Sand*, he fell fast asleep.

6

wake-up call

Edgar Wield was woken by hot lips nibbling his ear.

He lay there enjoying what was a rare treat. Edwin Digweed, who admitted to being at least ten years older than his partner, had made it clear at an early stage that his vital juices ran sluggishly till the sun stood high in the sky, so matutinal dalliance was rarely on the menu at Corpse Cottage.

Then Wield recalled that they'd said their good-byes last night and only half an hour ago he'd heard his partner's car cough to life and drive away.

He sat bolt upright to check whose hot lips they were.

'Jesus, Monty!' he said. 'You'll get me shot if Edwin finds out you've been here.'

Monty drew his lips back and grinned his indifference.

He was a marmoset whom Wield had 'rescued' from a drug company lab in somewhat dubious circumstances. Digweed had put up with his presence till a dietary experiment with old books had

415

led to an edict of banishment. Happily Wield had been able to find a new home for the beast in the small wildlife compound at neighbouring Enscombe Hall. But Monty never forgot his old benefactor and from time to time returned, though he had the wit to keep out of sight when Edwin was around.

It was not yet six o'clock but with the sun already flooding Eendale with gold, it was pointless trying to get back to sleep, even if Monty were in the mood to permit it. He made himself three slices of white toast, doubled their thickness with butter and raspberry jam, put two spoonfuls of instant coffee and an equal amount of sugar and milk into a mug, filled it with boiling water, and sat down in the sunlit garden. There were some compensations for Edwin's absence. Breakfasts like this, for instance, with a guest like Monty who accepted a slice of toast gratefully and retired to an apple tree to eat it.

This was Eden before the Fall, thought Wield, not usually a religious man. But the outside world still lurked and, never afraid to face up to reality, he decided to use the borrowed time to perform his promise to Pascoe.

Happily a wireless connection enabled him to use his laptop in the garden and soon he was winging his way through the vast inane of cyber-space.

It proved a relatively easy journey. After an hour he looked at what he'd got, then at his watch, smiled, and took out his mobile.

It was some time before he heard Pascoe's sleep-slurred voice.

416

'Wieldy, what the hell's happened?'

'Nowt. Just ringing in with that stuff you wanted. You did say before eight o'clock, and it's nearly seven now.'

'Jesus! I'll get you for this. Hold on while I get a pen. OK, shoot.'

'Here we go,' said Wield. 'Kewley-Hodge, full name John Matthew Luke, only son of Alexander John Kewley-Hodge, deceased, and Edith, née Hodge. Well-known Derbyshire Catholic family, hence perhaps the choice of names . . .'

'I wonder what Mark did to miss out?' said Pascoe.

'Mebbe he interrupted his friends trying to do him a favour,' said Wield.

'Ouch. Go on.'

'Educated Ashby College and Sandhurst. Not married. Served with the SAS in Northern Ireland, Bosnia, Iraq, and Afghanistan. Rose to the rank of major. Badly injured by a mortar shell in Afghanistan. You want the gory details?'

'At this hour in the morning? The outcome will do.'

'Paralysed from the waist down. Permanent. No hope of recovery. Now lives with his mother at the family home, Kewley Castle, near Hathersage, Derbyshire.'

'Lives with Mummy in the family castle, does he?' said Pascoe. 'Shouldn't he have a title or something?'

'No, there's no title. Family never amounted to much and their castle wasn't exactly state of

417

the art. Took the Roundheads less than a day to overrun it during the Civil War so the Kewleys didn't get a lot of loyalty points to cash in after the Restoration. Being RC didn't help either, what with the Popish Plot and all. Settled for being gentlemen farmers, declining eventually to genteel poverty with the option of bankruptcy, till the major's father, Alexander, did a rescue act by marrying Edith, elder daughter of Matt Hodge of Derby, founder of Hodge Construction UK, and worth a bob or two. Tagging the Hodge name on to Kewley was presumably part of the deal.'

'Where are you getting all this stuff?' said Pascoe, impressed.

'Mainly from a local history group's website.'

'Oh yes. I know the type,' said Pascoe. 'Bunch of incomers angling for an invite to the castle with the real peasants. You've probably got one in Enscombe.'

'Edwin's the chairman,' said Wield. 'He'll be interested in your analysis. But as it happens there ain't no real Kewley Castle to get invited to. Seems the original building was already falling apart by the end of the eighteenth century. The family took over what had been their factor's house, seventeenth-century farmhouse with improvements. But they kept their old address. There's little to see of the original castle except a few stones and half a gate tower. Doesn't even get a mention as a visitor attraction.'

'Might have attracted one visitor I can think of,' said Pascoe. 'Anything more?'

'Bit of detail if you're interested. Real *Boy's Own* stuff. Our laddo was top cadet at Sandhurst, commissioned into his local Yorkshire regiment but rapidly transferred to the SAS, awarded DSO for something he did in Bosnia. Bright, too. Good linguist, fluent in main European languages, gets by in the rest. Rapid promotion. Looked like he was on track to becoming one of the youngest lieutenant colonels since World War Two, then bang! the wheels came off in Afghanistan. Literally.'

'Farewell the plumed troops, and the big wars,' murmured Pascoe.

'Sorry?'

'I was just wondering what a man does when his occupation's gone,' he said. 'Thanks, Wieldy. As always, you are a wonder.'

'No problem. Oh shit.'

A movement by the open bedroom window had caught Wield's eye. He looked up to see Monty emerge and perch on the sill. In his paws he held what looked like a very old, very pricey vellum-bound volume.

'What?'

'Got to go. Take care, Pete.'

He switched off the phone. Pursuit he knew was counterproductive. In the marmoset's eyes, it just became a game. But a clever detective knows that sometimes the name of the game is Softly, Softly . . .

He went into the kitchen to make some more toast.

7

safe house

Pascoe sat in the hotel dining room and thought about what Wield had told him as he toyed with the Continental Breakfast at £12.50, patriotic parsimony having made him decline the Full English at £32.

Ffion had mentioned that on one of their northern book tours Young had gone walkabout when they were doing Sheffield. Visiting an old military friend, had been his excuse. Kewley Castle near Hathersage fitted the bill very nicely. Another word with the Welsh witch would be useful, especially now that he'd read the interrogation transcript. And this Kewley-Hodge character was definitely worth having a chat with.

His instinct was to strike out alone, but simply not turning up at the Lube was just as likely to alert the suspected CAT mole as putting all this on an official basis. On the other hand, keeping his plans to himself at least meant no one could officially veto them.

In the end he took out his phone and rang Rod's mobile.

'Morning, Peter.'

Sharp boy already had him entered in his phone book.

'Morning, Rod. Sorry to disturb you, but when you get to the Lube, could you book out one of those nice stealth cars you lot use and pick me up at the hotel?'

'Right on it. I'm just walking into the building now.'

Pascoe looked at his watch. Ten to eight.

'You are keen,' he said. 'Bad night?'

'Good one, but all good shifts come to an end.'

The weary and unwitting cuckolded husband returning home . . .

'I see. Well, I hope you're not too weary to drive.'

'No, I'm fine. Where are we going?'

'Into the country to chat with an old army buddy of Young's. Leave Tim a note to that effect, will you?'

That should cover his back, he hoped.

'Sure. See you in half an hour, OK?'

'OK.'

At half past eight on the dot, he was climbing into a Ford Focus in a suitably ambiguous shade of bluey green. Rod certainly looked bright enough.

He smiled and said, 'Morning, Chief. Which direction are we heading in?'

Pascoe thought for a moment then said, 'For a start, let's visit Safe House 4.'

If Rod now said, 'And where is that?' then he was stymied. But the young man merely checked his mirrors, signalled, and moved slowly away from the kerb. Ten minutes later, even with the central rush-hour traffic behind them, they were still moving through the quiet outer suburbs with a legal stateliness that Pascoe was about to remark upon when the car turned into a narrow cul-de-sac and came to a halt.

'Here we are,' said Rod.

Pascoe's picture of what a Security Service safe house looked like derived mainly from television. While he certainly hadn't been expecting something like a mini Colditz with barred windows and a portcullis, this small suburban bungalow with whitewashed walls and a wisteria growing around the door came as a surprise.

As he walked up the short drive, he found himself wondering how on earth they keep someone in a place like this who didn't want to be kept.

He got at least part of the answer when the door was opened by a middle-aged woman built like a London bus. She greeted Rod with evident pleasure, but glowered at Pascoe and refused to remove the security chain till she'd checked his ID.

'She's not up yet,' she said after she'd let them in. 'You'd best wait in here.'

She'd opened a door into a kitchen designed by a myopic optimist. Its walls were canary yellow with cupboards and work surfaces to match. On the hotplate of the yellow oven, a yellow coffeepot bubbled.

'She'll likely need waking up,' said the woman.

'Well, coming in here should certainly do the trick,' said Pascoe, blinking.

The woman looked at him blankly and said, 'I'll get her.'

The idea of Ffion not wanting to be got clearly did not enter her calculations.

Pascoe said, 'I think I'd better talk to her alone, Rod.'

'You sure?'

'Oh yes. It'll make her feel more at ease. I've known her some time,' said Pascoe with more confidence than he felt.

'OK,' said Rod. 'I'll be in the sitting room with Dolly.'

Dolly!

A couple of minutes later the door opened and Ffion Lyke-Evans came in.

Her hair was uncombed and she wore no make-up. She was wearing a towelling robe loosely tied around her narrow waist. What she wore underneath it, Pascoe did not care to let himself speculate.

She didn't look at him but went to the stove, poured herself a cup of coffee.

'Hi, Ffion,' he said. 'Everything OK?'

She sat down at the yellow kitchen table and made a face.

'I've been banged up here since Sunday with Grendel's mother,' she said. 'What do you fucking think?'

'Look,' he said sitting down. 'I know it's a pain, but these Security people think everyone's as devious as they are. They need to check and double check, then check again. I'm sure you'll be out of here in no time.'

'Oh yes? Last time we talked you said I'd be sleeping in my own bed that night.'

'Yes. I thought you would be. I'm sorry.'

'That's all right then. So long as you're sorry.'

She leaned back in her chair, her robe opening far enough to show him she had nothing on above the waist at least. Dalziel would have got himself an eyeful and passed an opinion. Pascoe stood up, went to the stove and poured himself a cup of coffee, giving her the chance to adjust her robe. She didn't bother.

'This a social call, is it?' she said as he resumed his seat. 'Or have you just come to practise your lying technique?'

'Just wanted to get a couple of things clear,' he said. 'Let's go back to last Friday. You say that Youngman rang you on the train to say he was ducking out of the show just as you were arriving in Middlesbrough, right?'

She didn't answer and he said, 'Look, Ffion, I know you're pissed off with me, but I really did think they'd be turning you loose on Sunday. And I'm doing everything in my power to get you out of here, all right?'

Coming from a man who had next to no power, it wasn't absolutely a lie.

She shrugged and said, 'If you say so.'

'Well, I am, I promise you. So Youngman rang you on the train . . . ?'

'That's right.'

'Was that the first time you'd spoken to him that day?'

'No. I'd rung him earlier in the journey, just to confirm the arrangements. It's best when you're dealing with writers and the media to double check everything all the time.'

'So before you rang Youngman, you'd already checked with the *Fidler's Three* producer to make sure everything was going ahead as planned?'

'Yes.'

'*Fidler's Three* doesn't advertise ahead who's going to be on, does it?'

'No. That's part of the gimmick,' she said. 'Clever, really. They don't use big names with a lot of pulling power, see, so Joe makes *not knowing* the hook.'

'How about the people he invites on the show? And the people he passes the invite through, like you? Do they know in advance who the other guests are?'

'No. That's part of the deal too.'

'So you didn't know that Kalim Sarhadi was going to be on?'

She hesitated and leaned forward. This time when she caught the involuntary flicker of his gaze to her breasts, she drew the robe more tightly around her.

'Not before Friday,' she said.

'Meaning the producer told you when you spoke to him from the train?'

'That's right. I asked him straight out.'

'Any reason?'

'Not really. It's not like Jerry Springer or something. They don't dig ex-wives or bastard kids up just to embarrass people.'

'But they do like to get some kind of connection going, right? Like in this case, the Middle East and terrorism. Which was how you were able to sell them Ellie when Youngman pulled out, right?'

He hadn't meant to get personal. Perhaps he was just trying to work up a bit of uxorial indignation to compensate for the stirrings of lust caused by his glimpses of that lithe brown body.

She grinned and let the robe relax once more.

'Look, Ellie and I talked about it after. OK, she was pissed, but I told her, wait till you see next month's sales figures. Her book got more hype from Friday night than we could have bought with a publicity budget twenty times as large as hers.'

'I don't doubt it,' said Pascoe dryly. 'Twenty times a fiver doesn't get you much these days. So when you rang Youngman, naturally you'd mention to him that Sarhadi was going to be on the panel?'

'Yes, I think I did.'

He cocked his head and raised his left eyebrow quizzically, a trick it had taken many hours in front of his shaving mirror to master.

'All right, of course I did. I'm there for my writers, that's what I get paid for.'

You were certainly there for Youngman, thought Pascoe.

She glared at him defiantly as if she'd caught the thought and he said quickly, 'Before he told you he was going off to visit this alleged sick relative on Sunday, had there been any indication that he might be planning to leave?'

'Like what?'

'Like, say, a phone call which he might have claimed was from the hospital?'

She thought then said, 'No.'

'Or did he ring anyone?'

'Not that morning,' she said. 'His phone did ring the previous evening while we were . . . busy. One of those rings like it does when you get a text. He checked it after . . . we'd finished. Then he went off with it into the bathroom and I think I heard him talking in there, so likely he'd rung someone.'

'Did he seem agitated at all when he came out? As if he'd had bad news?'

'No,' she said, shaking her head. 'Just the same as when he'd left the room. Or not quite the same. Unlike most men I know, he had a very quick recovery time.'

'Sounds as if he needed it,' said Pascoe dryly.

He immediately regretted the gibe. A flush spread across her face, then she stood up abruptly with her cup in her hand and turned towards the stove. As she moved forward her bare foot caught against the table leg and she stubbed her toe. She cried out, letting the cup fall to the floor where it shattered against the hard yellow tiles. Her other foot came down on one of the shards which dug into her instep. Now she shrieked in pain and fell back across the table. Pascoe jumped up and started to pull her upright. Her robe had opened wide and the full length of her naked brown body was pressing against him when the door opened and Rod and Dolly came rushing in.

In such circumstances explanation is usually vain and often counterproductive. Better to let the situation speak for itself to the disinterested ear. But Pascoe heard himself babbling defensively, 'She was going to get more coffee and she dropped her cup, I think she may have cut herself.' Ffion wasn't helping matters. Sensing his embarrassment, she was treating this as payback time, pressing ever closer and looking up into his face with moist parted lips.

Dolly regarded him with a neutral stare worse than accusation and said, 'Best if you sat her down till I get this lot swept up.'

Pascoe was only too pleased to oblige. He resettled her on to the kitchen chair, pulling the robe shut over her body.

'Thank you, Ffion,' he said stiffly. 'Hope you get out of here soon.'

She said, 'Give my regards to Ellie.'

Outside he looked at Rod and said, 'Don't say a word.'

'What word would that be, Peter?' said the young man, grinning. 'And is that the entertainment over for the day, or are we going on somewhere?'

'Oh yes,' said Pascoe, recovering a little. 'The fun is just beginning.'

8

to the castle

An hour and a half later they were approaching the village of Hathersage.

With anyone else driving it might have been just an hour later, but Rod seemed to think there was an eleventh commandment which read *Thou shalt not overtake without a clear mile of empty road ahead*, and all speed limits were meticulously observed with a good two per cent safety margin.

'Do a lot of driving, do you, Rod?' Pascoe had enquired after a while.

'Not since the big pile-up,' said the young man tremulously.

Jesus Christ! thought Pascoe in alarm. Then he saw Rod was grinning and realized he was being sent up.

'I know everyone says I'm a bit slow,' said Rod. 'But when I got recruited into the firm, I got told that sometimes getting a job done might mean having to break the law, but if I started breaking laws for personal convenience, then I was no good to anybody. Sticking to the Highway Code seems a good way to keep that in mind.'

Pascoe digested this, then said, 'Lukasz Komorowski?'

'That's right. How did you guess?'

'I heard he recruited you. And it sounds like the kind of thing he might say.'

'Yeah, I was really lucky, not just with catching his eye, but because that's more or less the way he was recruited too. I think it pleased him to be offering someone else the chance that he got.'

I was right, thought Pascoe. Despite Freeman's objection to the word, it really was romantic.

'Wasn't there a Komorowski who was some thing to do with the Warsaw uprising?' he said.

'General Tadeusz, C-in-C of the Polish Home Army,' replied Rod promptly. 'Lukasz's dad was a half-cousin. There were a lot of reprisals against the family. Lukasz is surprisingly unbitter. He says war does things to people so the trick is to avoid war.'

'Seems a nice guy,' said Pascoe.

'Yes,' said Rod, nodding vigorously. 'He is.'

So are they all, all nice guys, thought Pascoe. Lukasz and Bernie and Dave and Sandy and Tim and Rod and probably all of the others who worked in the Lubyanka.

But one of them, if his guess was right, believed that 'getting the job done' gave the Templars licence to ignore lesser laws such as the one against murder. In the world of Security, reaching that

431

position probably took only a very small step. Deception, betrayal, assassination, torture were, after all, the tools of their trade, only usable perhaps as last resorts in circumstances of dire necessity, but even admitting that possibility put you on a downward slope.

The police world was very different. You were there to uphold the Law. OK, on occasion you could stretch it, twist it, bend it, even tie it in knots, but once you broke it you weren't on a downward slope, you were off the edge and falling.

These musings, and others more precise, occupied his mind till Rod brought him back to the world with a triumphant, 'This looks like it.'

He looked up to see that they were turning through a gateway which bore a sign reading *Kewley Castle 2 miles – unfenced road – please observe 10 mph speed limit*, which Rod certainly did, from a considerable distance.

At least, thought Pascoe, it gives me time to enjoy my passenger's perk and take in the view, which was of attractive moorland, a-glow with gorse, and rising into shapely hills, good walking country.

The castle itself, however, was as disappointing as Wield had forecast.

Little more than a line of rubble lying behind a modest declivity which had presumably once been a moat, only the broken arch of its ruined gatehouse took the eye, but even that did not hold it long as Pascoe spotted a movement through the trees of a small copse just beyond the ruin.

A man on a white horse emerged. When he saw the car he came to a halt framed against the broken arch. It made a lovely picture, fit for a tapestry woven with bone needles in an older age, a more innocent time.

Then he resumed his advance at a stately canter. Only the fact that the horse had further to go allowed them to beat it to the house which stood a few hundred yards behind the ruined castle whose name it bore.

Pascoe got out of the car with some relief. Not the kind he felt when he got out of a car driven by, say, DC Shirley Novello, who believed that time spent driving from *here* to *there* was wasted time which would have to be accounted for on Judgment Day, but a sense of pleasure at being back in the dangerous world of standing on his own two feet.

He stood for a moment and took in the house, a severe looking three storied building in dark grey stone entirely without adornment, apart from a battlemented portico presumably added on to justify the appellation *castle*. They were in a tar-macked yard formed by a two-storey stable block and a barn converted into a triple garage.

'An Englishman's home,' said Pascoe.

'Probably a lot more convenient than the real thing,' said Rod.

The door of the main house opened and a woman appeared. She was in her late forties, with short dark hair and a classically oval face. She had a full rounded figure and she held herself like a gymnast. She wore a plain grey dress which, though not positively a uniform, had something of a uniform about it. Too young to be the mother, judged Pascoe. Housekeeper maybe. Or serving wench? He flashed her his boyish smile and got no response either of expression or word. But when Rod called out, 'Hi there,' as if addressing some girl he'd bumped into in a club, he noticed an immediate thawing of her chilly expression under the warmth of the young man's grin.

Before he could try to take advantage of this, he heard the clop of horse's hooves behind him and a voice said, 'Can I help you?'

He turned to look up at the rider. He was a man of about thirty, his fine black hair tousled by the wind, his skin weather-beaten. Dark brown eyes regarded Pascoe unblinkingly.

Estate manager, he guessed. Certainly a man of authority. Or maybe that's just because I'm looking up at him. Someone had said that a man astride a beast is always ridiculous, unless he's fucking it, in which case he's disgusting as well. Probably Dalziel. But Pascoe always found horsemen a bit intimidating and this one sat with a straightness of back which somehow suggested a superiority more than physical.

'We're here to see Major Kewley-Hodge,' he said.

'Mister Kewley-Hodge,' corrected the man. 'Is he expecting you?'

'No,' said Pascoe.

'So how do you know he is going to be in?'

To say, I don't, but it's a risk I was willing to take in order to catch him unprepared, was not an answer Pascoe felt he could give.

He said, 'Is he in?'

'In fact he's not,' said the man. 'I dare say you thought, being wheelchair-bound, he can't get out much.'

'No. In fact I didn't think that,' said Pascoe evenly. 'I understand he is suffering from para-plegia. I have heard nothing of agoraphobia.'

The man smiled and nodded as if approving the answer.

'So if I see him, who shall I say he wasn't expecting?'

'I'm Chief Inspector Pascoe of Mid-Yorkshire CID, currently attached to the Combined Anti-Terrorism unit. And you, sir, are . . . ?'

'I'm not in,' said the man. 'On, girl.'

The grey moved forward obediently and came to a halt by one of the barns with an opening on the first floor from which protruded an iron bar, presumably intended for a hoist to raise hay into the loft.

From his leather jerkin the man took what looked like a TV remote control and pressed a button. Out of the loft along the metal bar ran a square metal box from which depended what looked like a pair of nooses for a double hanging.

Another touch on the remote brought the

nooses down a foot or two. The man eased his arms through the loops, which Pascoe now saw were part of a harness. The rider fastened a retaining belt across his chest, used the remote to lift himself a fraction and take the weight off the saddle, then spoke to the horse, which moved forward, leaving the rider dangling in air.

He must have used the control again for out of the open barn door rolled a wheelchair. It came to a halt directly beneath him and he lowered himself into it, released the harness and sent it back up into the loft.

Then he turned the chair to face Pascoe.

'Now I'm in,' he said. 'Good day, Chief Inspector. Luke Kewley-Hodge at your service. Shall we go inside?'

9

armour

As they advanced towards the front door, Pascoe was wondering how to indicate to Rod that he should stay outside and see what his charms could winkle out of the woman.

He needn't have worried.

The woman came forward to take the horse's reins. Rod moved quickly towards the stable door saying, 'Let me give you a hand there.'

'You any good at rubbing down horses?' asked the woman in an upper-class voice.

'No, but I'm a terribly quick learner,' said Rod with a grin.

You are indeed, thought Pascoe as he followed the man in the chair through the main entrance.

'That's a clever bit of kit you've got back there,' he said.

'Yes, I'm quite pleased with it,' answered Kewley-Hodge. 'I got the technology from our bomb-squad remote-control units, but the original idea came from the Middle Ages. Knights' armour

437

became so heavy that they had to use hoists to get them into the saddle, and of course their mounts were very like our shire horses, chosen for strength rather than speed. Modern movies which show knights charging at each other as if they were in a two-furlong race at Kempton are quite misleading. To the modern eye, a real joust would probably look as if it had been filmed in slow motion. But I mustn't knock Hollywood, not when I go jogging around like Charlton Heston at the end of *El Cid.*'

He glanced up at Pascoe and smiled, as though inviting him to share a joke. The hall they were in was well this side of baronial, but it was large enough to accommodate two suits of armour which stood in opposing corners.

'The proof of the pudding,' murmured Pascoe.

'In two ways,' said Kewley-Hodge. 'The one on the left is twelfth-century European and weighs about fifty pounds. The one on the right, if you look closely, has a great deal more leather about it, and the metal is much thinner. It weighs less than half as much. That was brought back from the Second Crusade by one of my ancestors. The crusaders found out the hard way that heavy armour and slow horses were no competition for smaller, faster Saracen mounts ridden by men carrying so much less weight in metal, especially in the desert heat. The smarter ones adapted. The slower ones died.'

'Fascinating,' said Pascoe. 'You are a military historian, are you, sir?'

'A historian of survival, perhaps,' said Kewley-Hodge. 'Through here.'

He sent his chair towards an inner door that opened ahead of him, presumably at the breaking of a magic eye. Pascoe followed him into a medium-sized sitting room, sparsely furnished, with no pictures on the wall and a fireplace in black slate, which gaped like a back door to hell. On the broad mantel-shelf rested a packet of cigarettes, a lighter and an ashtray. Pascoe calculated the height and worked out that, if the fags belonged to his host, the man would need to summon a servant every time he wanted a smoke. Perhaps he was trying to give it up.

'Coffee, Mr Pascoe? Or something stronger?'

He looked down at the man in the wheelchair and recalled his feelings when he'd looked up at the man on horseback. Was that the way Kewley-Hodge felt a dozen times a day as people loomed over him?

And was his reference to El Cid a reminder that, even dead, the body of the Spaniard bound to his saddle had power to strike terror into the hearts of the Moors?

'No thanks,' said Pascoe, lowering himself gingerly into a leather armchair which turned out to be more yielding than its appearance promised. 'I don't want to take up more of your time than necessary.'

'Be my guest. Time is a commodity I'm not short of. So how can I help you?'

439

'I believe that during your military service you knew a man called Young. Sergeant John Young, known as Jonty.'

'Now, like me, a plain mister, and making a name as a popular author: John T. Youngman. Yes, I remember him.'

'How well did you know him, may I ask?'

'Very well indeed. I'd say we were as close as you can get without being bent.'

Pascoe let his surprise show.

'Despite the fact that you were an officer and he was an NCO?'

'I think you're confusing class and rank, Mr Pascoe. David Stirling, the Regiment's founder, stated categorically that in the SAS there should be no distinction of class. All ranks belong to one company. It makes good sense because it means good soldiering. I leaned heavily on Jonty, and I like to be sure that what I'm leaning on isn't going to give.'

'I see. And he was clearly dedicated to you. In every sense.'

Kewley-Hodge smiled appreciatively and said, 'Yes, that tickled me somewhat. So what has Jonty done to arouse your interest, Mr Pascoe? Inciting racial hatred, is it?'

'What makes you say that, sir?'

'Well, I don't imagine they send chief inspectors to deal with a traffic offence.'

'I meant, do you have any reason for thinking that inciting racial hatred is a crime more likely to be committed by Youngman than, say, burglary? Or rape? Or peculation?'

'Now let me see . . . Burglary? No that wouldn't be Jonty's cup of tea. I could see him as a pirate or a highwayman, maybe, but crawling in through a kitchen window to steal the candlesticks? No way. Rape? He always seemed to be able to get his wicked way with the ladies without needing to resort either to violence or indeed to paying hard cash. I once asked him his secret. He said, letting them see you want them more than anyone's ever wanted them before, and making no promises. I tried it and got my face slapped, so there has to be something else. As for peculation, what the hell's that?'

'Embezzlement,' said Pascoe.

'Is that so? Interesting. Add an "s" and it becomes the legal and acceptable basis of most activity in the City. What a flimsy divide there is between crime and respectability, Chief Inspector.'

'So, not Youngman's bag then? But incitement to racial hatred might be?'

'Sometimes it's possible for a soldier to develop some kind of respect for the people he's fighting against. And of course it helps a great deal if he's got a great deal of respect for the people he's defending. Out in the Gulf, Sergeant Young, I fear, had neither. He hated the enemy with an absolute hatred which permitted no quarter. And he despised the local citizenry that we were supposed to be there to protect. I have heard him say that there was nothing in the whole Arab world worth shedding one drop of a British soldier's blood to preserve. So, yes, I imagine, if he still holds this point of view, and if he were foolish enough to promulgate it in the wrong company, he could well lay himself open to the charge of inciting racial hatred.'

Pascoe shifted on his chair. The cushion had flattened to deceive, drawing him down through its yielding softness to a bed of sharp-edged rocks.

He said, *'If he still holds this point of view . . . ?* You haven't seen him then since he left the Service and started writing?'

'Good Lord, yes, several times,' said Kewley-Hodge. 'Whenever he's in these parts, he drops in. We chat about old times. But either he's mellowed or he doesn't feel it necessary to trot out his old views, perhaps because he assumes that my present condition means I must automatically share them.'

'And do you?' asked Pascoe softly.

'Is that a trick question?' asked Kewley-Hodge, smiling. 'Have you got a blank space on your warrant waiting to slip my name in?'

'Hardly, sir. And I have no witness anyway.' Pascoe smiled back.

'That's true. Wonder what's become of your sidekick. Working his charms on Mama, I would guess.'

'That was your mother?' said Pascoe, unable to conceal his surprise.

'Yes,' said Kewley-Hodge, amused. 'Sorry, I didn't introduce you, did I? But she likes to keep her roles separate, the chatelaine and the maternal. I'm sure your young man will bring out the motherly side. She bakes a mean seed cake. I hope he gets a slice for his trouble.'

'I hope so too.'

So the woman was that Edith Hodge whose money had kept the Kewleys solvent. She must have given birth young. Even making allowances for the ageing effect of pain, there couldn't be more than twenty years at the very most between them.

He said, 'Now, you were going to explain your views on Muslim extremists, sir?'

'Well, I go along to the village church about once a month and I try to get in the forgiving vein, sometimes I even get close, but you know, when everyone else stands up and walks out at the end of the service, somehow the forgiving vein dries up and I hate the bastards who did this to me as much as ever. We go out to these places to help, but in the end who are we helping? We talk about extremists but, given the chance, they're all bloody extremists. Look at what's happened in Iraq since we gave them back their miserable country. Where were all these brave freedom fighters, these suicide bombers, these well-armed resistance groups, when Saddam was in power? Skulking in their caves, of course, because they didn't dare take up arms against a tyrant who'd give them back ten blows for every one they struck, who'd make sure that every suicide martyr was accompanied to his reward by a couple of hundred of his friends and family. Suddenly they've found their courage, have they? The courage to murder their rescuers! I piss on such courage! The lesson of history is that people get the dictators they deserve. We should have left them to rot until they came begging for help, then left them to rot a little longer.'

He fell silent. He was breathing hard. Had he let himself be carried away further than he intended? Somehow Pascoe doubted it. This was a man who felt so secure behind whatever armour he'd built for himself that he had no compunction about speaking his mind.

Which might mean he had no involvement with the Templars.

Or perhaps that he was so certain of his rightness, he didn't give a damn about being caught. In fact he might even look forward to sitting in his wheelchair in the Old Bailey, defying a jury not to admit they felt some sympathy for him.

Pascoe said, 'When did you last see Sergeant Young?'

'I believe it was in February. He was doing a promotional tour and when he got to Sheffield, he popped along to pay me a visit.'

'Did he stay the night?' asked Pascoe.

'Yes, he did. I recall asking him if he wouldn't be missed. I gather these publishers like to keep their writers to a pretty tight schedule. He laughed and said his minder would cover for him, that's what she got paid for.'

'And did he give you any hint that he might be involved in any activity which might reflect his extreme views on the Middle Eastern situation?'

Kewley-Hodge leaned forward and said, 'Good Lord, is that what this is all about? Not just inciting racial hatred but doing something about it? You think he could be mixed up with these Templars the papers are going on about, don't you?'

'If I did, would you be surprised, Mr Kewley-Hodge?'

'Not in the slightest,' said the man, without pausing for thought. 'Skulking in the background urging others to act was never Jonty's way. My problem on ops was stopping him from always putting himself in the most dangerous position.'

'Seems to me these Templars are doing a deal of skulking,' said Pascoe dryly.

'I don't think so. Skulking is not the same as using local cover and subterfuge to avoid falling into the hands of the enemy.'

'Not much chance of that when you're in the UK and murdering the enemy piecemeal,' said Pascoe.

'I think you're missing the point, Mr Pascoe. The people getting killed are criminals who have been condemned to death by every court of natural justice in the land. In this case, it's people like yourself trying to interfere with the process who are the enemy these Templars need to evade.'

'Would that mean it's OK to injure us then?'

'Of course not. But, alas, one of the many perils of modern warfare is friendly fire. If you're in the zone, you need to be very careful indeed.'

'I'll remember that, sir. So, to return to my question, has Youngman, that is to say, ex-Sergeant Young, ever said anything directly or indirectly that would indicate he is actively involved with the Templars?'

This time Kewley-Hodge did give himself time to think. He pressed a button that sent his chair rolling forward till it came to a halt alongside the fireplace. Then suddenly the seat of the chair began to rise, at the same time pivoting at its front edge, while the chairback moved forward to form a vertical with it. And from being a man in a wheelchair, Kewley-Hodge became a country gent, standing against his fireplace, lighting a cigarette.

He had his right elbow fixed firmly on the mantel, and there was, Pascoe noticed, a narrow supporting ledge that had emerged at buttock height in the wheelchair's vertical face, like a monk's misericord, but the physical effort needed to maintain the pose must have been immense. Yet as he now smiled down upon the seated Pascoe, he gave out nothing but an impression of negligent ease.

'Can't say he did, Chief Inspector. And of course I've no idea whether or not he's involved with these people. But if it turns out he is, then I say good luck to him! And I think you'll find there are many thousands of our fellow citizens who are saying exactly the same.'

Pascoe stood up abruptly. Dalziel, he thought, would probably have offered his hand to see if the bugger would fall over.

He said, 'Thank you for your co-operation, sir. I'll leave my card, if I may. I'd appreciate it if you could give me a ring should Mr Youngman get in touch with you.'

'Of course,' said Kewley-Hodge. 'Could you see yourself out? Have a look around first, if you want. Not much to see by way of ornament, but the house itself is not without interest to a student of vernacular architecture. And you might bump into your good-looking young assistant, if he's survived Mama's ministrations.'

He spoke with a faint hint of mockery as if to say he knew exactly what Rod was up to.

'Let's hope he's saved me a slice of seed cake,' said Pascoe.

10

mother love

In fact by the time Rod had finished, there wasn't much cake left. One of the consequences of getting up so early had been he missed breakfast and Pascoe's summons hadn't left any space to fit it in.

'Sorry,' he said, looking at the sparse remains of a once-bulky seed cake.

'That's all right,' said the woman with a smile. 'Young men need to keep their seed level high. And you did help me with rubbing down my son's horse.'

He smiled back at her. He had rapidly sussed two things that Pascoe on his admittedly briefer contact had missed.

One look at her eyes had told him she was undoubtedly related to Kewley-Hodge, a relationship she'd just confirmed. The second thing he'd assessed instantly was that she was a very sexy woman, and after a few minutes in her company he added bright, lively, with a sense of humour. And a great baker.

So he relaxed and prepared to enjoy himself. If information came, well and good. But instinct told him it would be useless to try to force the game. Also he knew from experience that, when he relaxed, it was often infectious.

'I'm Rod, by the way,' he said.

'Edie. So how long have you been in the Service, Rod?'

'How do you know I'm not a copper?' he asked.

'You didn't say "Hello, hello," and rock back on your heels.'

'Inside I did when I saw you,' he said boldly.

'Think I'm in the market for a toy-boy, do you?' she said, smiling. 'I'll need to know a lot more about you first. So how did you become a spook? And don't tell me you answered an ad in the *Church Times*.'

He saw no reason not to tell her the story of the way he'd been recruited, though he was careful not to mention Komorowski's name. She seemed genuinely interested and ten minutes later he realized he was still talking about himself in answer to her questions, whereas it should have been the other way round.

'Time out,' he said. 'Now you know everything interesting there is to know about me, it's your turn. Fair's fair.'

'You want everything interesting?' she said. 'That could take a long long time or a couple of seconds. Depends what interests you.'

'You do,' he said, meaning it.

'OK. I'll give you the full history, shall I? Only slightly expurgated because you're so young.'

She was as good as her word. Most of the early stuff he'd heard from Pascoe as they drove from Manchester, but hearing it from the woman's own lips gave him a charge which meant he didn't have to feign interest. She told him about her father, Matthew Hodge, the construction king; about growing up as the swinging sixties merged into the sybaritic seventies; about going to boarding school; about marrying Alexander Kewley at an age when most of her friends were planning university careers. She didn't say she was pregnant when she married, but that was the implication.

Whatever her intention had been when she embarked on this voyage through her past, she seemed borne along on an irresistible current and needed only the gentlest of interlocutory zephyrs to keep her on course.

She told him of her joy and pride in her son, and her father's pride in his grandchild who he hoped would grow up to take over the family business. But before he could do so, Hodge Construction, a victim of its own success, was taken over by a huge American conglomerate, which was perhaps just as well as the teenage Luke showed little sign of wanting to become anything but a soldier. So off he went to Sandhurst, and passed out with huge distinction.

Here a pause. Knowing the rocks and reefs ahead, Rod offered his gentle zephyr.

'Edie, this must be so painful to you, I'm sorry, I didn't mean that you should . . .'

'It's OK,' she said. 'You get used to pain. You've still got that to discover, Rod. My boy went into the army and his career continued as it had begun, a real *Boy's Own* story. Till the day the news came that he'd been hurt.'

And now the story changed from *Boy's Own* to dark tragedy.

The news that Luke had been injured had been a huge shock. But so used had his friends and family become to the with-one-mighty-leap-he-was-free sequel to all his perils that hope remained high till they got confirmation that the effects of the injury were going to be permanent.

This news was even more devastating than the first report.

On hearing it, Edie's father, Matt Hodge, collapsed with a coronary thrombosis and was dead before the ambulance arrived.

Alexander Kewley-Hodge was himself just out of hospital where he'd been receiving treatment for bowel cancer. How much his condition was affected by the news no one could say, but, subsequent to hearing it, he deteriorated rapidly and within a fortnight he too was dead.

'That's awful,' said Rod, genuinely moved.

'Yes, it was,' said the woman in a matter-of-fact voice. 'And it would have continued to be awful if it hadn't been for Luke. From the start he refused to be pitied. Help that sprang out of

love he would accept, but let him get the slightest
waft of pity and he'd throw it back in the helper's
face. That applied to me and others close to him
as much as anyone. As you've seen, his aim is
maximum control, of his own life that is, not
other people's. I'm here as his housekeeper, not
his nurse.'

'And his mother too!' protested Rod.

'That goes without saying,' she said. 'So there
you are, young man. Now you know everything
interesting there is to know about me. Do finish
what remains of that cake. In your job, heaven
knows when your next meal may turn up.'

11

a change of direction

'And was she right?' asked Pascoe.

They were driving away from the castle. Having to report on his encounter with Mrs Kewley-Hodge as he drove cut Rod's speed by half and they were moving so slowly that pheasants crossing the road were able to pause and check the surface for nibbles before getting out of the way.

'Up to you, Pete. Are we going back for lunch or shall we stop somewhere on the way?'

'I mean about knowing everything interesting about her, not about your cuisine,' snapped Pascoe.

'Of course. Sorry,' said Rod, grinning. 'No, I shouldn't imagine so. I suspect she told me exactly what she wanted me to know. But most women do.'

'And she showed no curiosity about our reasons for turning up here?'

'None whatsoever.'

'Didn't you find that odd?'

'Not particularly. I reckon she's got so used to

453

her control-freak boy calling the shots that she reckons he'll tell her if he wants to, and if he doesn't, then she doesn't need to know.'

'You think he has that amount of control?'

'Oh yes. She worships the ground he doesn't walk on,' said Rod. 'What about you, Peter? What did you make of the galloping major?'

Pascoe looked at him reflectively and said, 'You didn't take to him, did you?'

'Hardly saw him,' said Rod negligently. 'But from what I did see, and certainly from what I heard about the guy, I got the impression he might make a big thing about being master of his fate and all that stuff while he's at home in a controlled environment, but once he's away from here, he's just another poor sod in a wheelchair, right? Is it really possible he could be involved with the Templars?'

Pascoe said, 'Know what I think, Rod. I think rubbing down that horse with Edie has turned you all chivalric. You're pissed off with Luke because you reckon he's mucking his dear old mum about. You're sorry for the poor old bird. Unless . . . don't tell me you fancied her?'

The young man grinned.

'A bit maybe. Think it was mutual,' he said. 'That's why we got on so well. She's taken care of herself, you can see that. Must have been a real stunner. Yes, I liked her and I wouldn't have said no. What about you? No, sorry, of course you go for the young stuff like Ffion.'

Rod laughed, inviting Pascoe to join in the fun.

When he didn't, the young man said seriously, 'You really think he could be involved, don't you?'

'Oh yes,' said Pascoe. 'Up to his fucking neck.'

Rod was so surprised by the force of the affirmation that his gaze momentarily flickered from the road to Pascoe's face.

'Careful,' said Pascoe. 'You'll have us in the ditch. Eventually.'

To tell the truth, he too was a little surprised by the positiveness of his own response. Maybe Ellie was right and, because the Fat Man wasn't around, he felt it necessary to speak his lines. But having spoken this one, he realized he believed it absolutely.

'But Edie . . . I mean, if she was mixed up in something like this, she would hardly have been so forthcoming. Would she?'

'You mean just because she has something to hide doesn't mean she'd try her damnedest to persuade you she hasn't? That's an interesting view of criminal psychology. I must remember to put it into my next CID seminar paper.'

Rod flushed rather becomingly and Pascoe pressed on.

'As for her son being just another poor sod in a wheelchair, as you so sensitively put it, first off, there's sods in wheelchairs running everything from their own businesses to the London Marathon. And if there are times when, like all of us, they require a little help from their friends, where better to look for it than from a devoted mumsy who thinks the sun shines out of your paralysed arse?'

For the next minute, which meant rather less than the next half-mile, they drove in silence. Then Rod said, 'Yes. Of course. I'm sorry.'

'No need. You did really well,' said Pascoe, feeling guilty that he'd gone over the top to score points and put the youngster back in his place. But there was one more point it was necessary to make. 'Stop the car.'

The young man checked his mirrors, signalled, and carefully drew into the side of the road, which was empty as far as the eye could see in both directions.

'Now get out,' said Pascoe.

Rod hesitated, then obeyed.

Pascoe slid over into the driver's seat and looked up at the youngster's anxious face. Maybe he thinks I'm going to make him walk home, he thought.

'Don't just stand there,' he said wearily. 'Get in the passenger seat. There are only twenty-four hours in the day, so I'm going to drive. You can cover your eyes if you like.'

Rod climbed in and fastened his seat belt with showy precision. He didn't cover his eyes but sat in a stiff silence till they reached their junction with the main road.

He glanced towards Pascoe as he gunned the engine to propel the car into a rather narrow gap in the traffic.

'Peter,' he said. 'I hate to tell you this, but I think you just turned the wrong way.'

'You think so? What if I was taking a short cut back to Manchester via the M1 and M62?'

'I don't think you'll find that's a short cut,' said Rod.

'It is if you want to visit Bradford,' said Pascoe.

12

prison

'Hugh.'

'Bernard.'

'De Payens.'

'De Clairvaux.'

one thousand two thousand three thousand

'Bernard, it would have been a kindness to warn me that PC Plod was going to pay a visit.'

'Ah. That's where he is. I wondered. But I didn't worry. Should I have worried?'

'Whether I'd be able to deal with a country bobby? I hope you know me better than that.'

'Don't underestimate him. I thought we had corralled him, but I see we have not. Don't worry, I'll deal with it. So how did it go?'

'He asked me about Andre while his acolyte chatted up Mummy.'

'And?'

'And he went away as he arrived, which is, I'd say, uncertain but extremely suspicious. I could find nothing to say to allay his suspicions. In fact, to have attempted to be other than I am would itself have been suspicious, don't you think?'

'You're probably right. He's no fool, and he's been an irritation since he first appeared. And of course it's through him that the hunt is on for Andre.'

'Yes. Maybe I should have sent Andre after him rather than the moron.'

'No. That was a mistake, *my* mistake, which has already proved costly. Let's not make any more. So far, unless the one in a coma dies, our hands are clean of our own side's blood. Andre is still holed up with Geoffrey O, I take it?'

'Yes. I spoke to him yesterday. He was still keen to go ahead with taking the Sheikh out. He seemed amused when Omer admitted to having taken that pot-shot and said he'd like to demonstrate how the job should be done.'

'I hope you told him that's a definite no. After Omer's stupidity, Sheikh Ibrahim is going to be particularly difficult, and the last thing we want is Andre exposing himself. It's too great a risk.'

'He enjoys risk. And surely now he's been blown, he's the one we could afford to keep active? The others have been signalled to go to earth for the time being. And if the worst happened and he was taken, he is at the same time completely loyal and completely unbreakable.'

'No one is unbreakable.'

'I am, Bernard. OK, Andre *could* lead them to me, but I don't believe he ever would . . .'

'He has already.'

'Not directly. That was that smart Alec cop. Anyway, my point is, even if I did get blown, there's no way I would ever lead them to you, if that's what's worrying you. Sorry. I shouldn't have said that.'

'Why not? Of course it worries me. And it should worry you too. You may not mean to do it, but as our persistent Mr Pascoe has demonstrated, these people are no fools. And if Andre did crack, then they'd have you in their chosen environment. Don't imagine your wheelchair will keep you out of prison.'

'Where do you think I am now?'

'I assume you're sitting on that horse of yours? No riding in prison. No filet mignon and fine wines, no hi-tech to smooth your path, no loving hand to smooth your brow. Think about it.'

'I'll think about it. But whatever happens, I wouldn't give you up any more than I think Andre would give me up. We were trained in the same school, remember?'

'But not one that Geoffrey B went to.'

'Forget Geoffrey B. At the worst he might think of giving himself up, but he can't do that without giving O up too, which, being a true English gentleman, he will hardly do.'

'I prefer not to rely too heavily on the code of the Woosters. Worst-case scenario – if he snapped, what damage can he do?'

'Nothing, except point them to Andre, and

they're after him already. But why should it happen? So let's forget Geoffrey B and concentrate on keeping up the momentum.'

'Momentum is what a hand-cart heading down to hell has. For the time being, let's just keep things on an even keel, at least until I get Pascoe out of the way. Tell Andre he needs to keep his head down till arrangements are made for him to get out of the country. It may be short notice. He needs to be available at all times. Make that clear to him. We do things my way.'

'Without you, Bernard, it would hardly be possible to do anything all.'

13

girls and boys

They stopped for a sandwich at the Woolley Edge
service station on the M1. Pascoe went off to the
loo and when he came back to his table, Rod was
on his mobile.

He finished his call as Pascoe sat down and
said, 'Thought I'd better let them know we'd be
keeping the car longer than I said.'

'Do they charge by the mile or by the hour?'
said Pascoe, gently mocking. 'Never answer questions till they're asked, didn't they teach you that
at Hogwarts?'

Hogwarts, he'd picked up, was their generic
term for training courses.

He ate half a sandwich, washed it down with
coffee, which wasn't at all bad, and said, 'Can't
sit here enjoying ourselves all day. Come on.'

On his way back from the toilet he had popped
into the shop and picked up a Bradford *A to Z*. In the
car, he handed this to Rod and said, 'We're looking
for a suburb called Marrside – 16 Blackwell Road.'

Rod studied the map closely for the next fifteen minutes or so, then set it aside and gave crisp incisive directions as they turned off the motorway.

Marrside had probably once been a small village, but at least a hundred years had passed since Bradford had reached out and buried its rural identity under a grid of long terraces, many of which opened straight on to the pavement. But for the most part these terraces had avoided, or recovered from, that sense of dereliction which had hung over the house in, say, Mill Street. They looked well kept, there were cars parked along the kerbs, the small shops were bright and busy, and where there were buildings boarded up or half destroyed, it was because of the ongoing reconstruction programme advertised, with apologies for inconvenience, on billboards.

Sarhadi, according to Pascoe's information, was a part-time student who paid his way by sharing shifts on his father's taxi cab. Unmarried, he still lived at his parents' house in Blackwell Road, which Rod brought them to with no hesitations or diversions.

There was a taxi parked outside the house. Pascoe drew in behind it and sat for a moment taking stock.

Always have a good look at a door afore you kick it down, was one of Dalziel's more useful tips. *You can tell a lot from a door. Like, is it going to break your toe?*

This door looked solid enough to do just that.

He told Rod to stay in the car while he got out. Closer inspection revealed the door to be not only solid but freshly painted, with a gleaming brass letter box and a matching knocker buffed to such a high degree of shine he found himself wiping his fingers on his trouser leg before he grasped it.

There are many types of knock a policeman uses. The dawn-raid knock which sends a thunderous summons through a house, the gentle knock which wouldn't disturb a nervous cat but counts in evidence as a genuine attempt to gain conventional admittance before you kick the door down, the reluctant knock which presages sharing of bad news, and the polite but firm knock which just means you'd like a friendly chat.

Polite but firm did the trick here. The door was opened by a round-faced woman, middle-aged, comfortably built, in loose black slacks and a waist-length blouse patterned with enough red and brown and orange leaves to choke a Vallambrosan brook.

'Mrs Sarhadi?' he said.

'Who's askin'?'

He could see he was being weighed in the balance, salesman or council. Policeman didn't figure. There was a certain tightening round the eyes which affected most people when they realized they were being door-stepped by a cop.

He said, 'Is Kalim at home?'

'No, he's not. What do you want him for?'

'Just a chat.'

'You a journalist then?'

Kalim's fame must have accustomed her to journalists.

'No. I'm police.'

He saw the eye-tightening and hastily added, 'Nothing serious, just a tidy-up really. Kalim knows me. I met him and his fiancée last Saturday. And my wife was on the TV show with him the night before.'

'Oh aye? *Her*. Here, that mad woman who tried to shoot my lad, what's going off with her then? Slap on the wrist and two hours' community service, is it?'

'I think the CPS are still working out charges,' he said.

'What's to work out, 'less you're brain-dead?' she demanded.

Pascoe, feeling some sympathy with this response but not caring to incriminate himself, nodded.

'Tottie!' came a plaintive cry drilling down the stairs. 'Where's me clean pants?'

'In the fridge where I always put them! Where do you think? In the airing cupboard, you daft bugger,' Mrs Sarhadi yelled back. 'Men. You'd not know which way was forwards without we told you.'

Tottie. The name rang a bell somewhere with Pascoe. She was, he recollected from Joe Fidler's interview with Sarhadi, a local convert who clearly had not found that accepting Islam meant giving up being an independent Yorkshire lass.

He said, 'If you could tell me where I might find Kalim . . .'

'He's down the mosque. Here, what's your rush?'

This was addressed to a slim middle-aged Asian who came rushing down the stairs tucking his shirt tails into his waistband.

'I told you, I'm picking Mrs Atwood up from the station this afternoon. You should have woken me earlier.'

'What with? A cannon in your ear? Have you forgot – I'm meeting Jamila down the Grange and you said you'd drop me off.'

'Did I? Sorry, no time no time.'

'What do you mean, "no time"? Mrs Atwood can't wait, but your own wife can walk? Any road, when did you ever know a train to be on time?'

Pascoe could see that Mr Sarhadi was in that position much favoured by Yorkshire wives – between a rock and a hard place.

Self-interest and male solidarity combined to make him say, 'Perhaps I could give you a lift, Mrs Sarhadi.'

The man's eyes, which had run over him questioningly, now brightened with grateful relief.

'Well,' said Tottie doubtfully. 'We'd have to pass the mosque on the way, so I could show you where to go.'

This was ur-Yorkshire. Never let yourself be put under an obligation if you could see a way to turn it back on the giver.

'There,' said her husband. 'Problem solved. See you later.'

He pushed past Pascoe and got into his taxi.

His wife yelled after him, 'You don't even know who he is. Could be my fancy man for all you care!'

But she said it in that tone of exasperated affection which is the hallmark of a Yorkshire marriage.

'That's my car,' said Pascoe, pointing to the Focus. 'As soon as you're ready . . .'

'I'm ready now,' said the woman, seizing a broad silk scarf from a peg behind the door and draping it over her head. 'Let's be off.'

Pascoe opened the rear door of the car for her and she slid in. Rod turned round and gave her a smile and said, 'Hi. I'm Rod.'

'And I'm Tottie. Glad to meet you,' she said, returning the smile with interest.

I should have sent him to the door, thought Pascoe. Except that he'd have probably been inside by now, drinking tea and eating fresh-baked parkin.

He got in the driver's seat, started the engine.

'You not the boss then?' said the woman.

'Sorry?'

'Thought, with coppers, it were always the boss who sat in the passenger seat.'

'That depends. You've been in a lot of police cars then?'

'You'd be surprised,' she said knowingly, with a wink at Rod.

Suddenly Pascoe recalled where he'd heard the

467

name Tottie. It was Andy Dalziel, that day a lifetime ago when they'd squatted together behind the car in Mill Street. The Fat Man had reminisced about an old dancing partner of his, Tottie Truman from Doncaster, a girl remarkable for her spirit, her body, and her tango.

Could this be the same woman, who'd continued the journey from one Mecca towards another? Hadn't Dalziel said she'd got religion? He must check it out with him . . . if he ever got the chance . . .

'Left,' said the woman loudly. 'Are you deaf?'

His auto-pilot, which had stopped the car at a junction, clearly didn't have audio.

He said, 'Sorry,' and turned.

'Up to the lights, then right,' she commanded. 'The mosque is fifty yards on.'

'Where?' he said as he turned.

'There!' she said. 'Can't you read?'

Now he looked and saw not the white dome and tall minaret his auto-pilot had been looking for, but a large sign in English and Urdu telling him they'd arrived at the Marrside Mosque, which turned out to be an old red-brick building with the words MARRSIDE BOARD SCHOOL 1883 carved on the lintel of its forbidding main door.

He brought the car to a halt.

'Why've you stopped? The Grange is half a mile on, by the bypass.'

'The Grange Hotel? Yes, I noticed it as we drove by earlier,' said Rod. 'It looks very nice.'

'Aye, mebbe, but looks aren't everything,' said

Tottie grimly. 'It's where we're having the *Walima* after my lad's wedding. What you'd call the reception. I'm meeting my daughter-in-law there to make sure their dozy catering manager's on top of the job. At least I would be if young Lochinvar here would get his finger out.'

'Tell you what,' said Pascoe, 'Rod can drive you on to the hotel. I'll drop off here and see if I can find Kalim.'

He got out of the car. Rod followed suit to transfer to the driving seat. As they passed, the young man paused and said, 'Peter, do you think you really ought to be doing this? Without consultation, I mean.'

'Doing what? Having a friendly chat with a friendly witness? Nothing in my book which makes that a hanging offence.'

He moved across the pavement towards the building.

From the rear window, Tottie yelled after him, 'Make sure you go in the right door. And I hope your missus darns your socks!'

Both remarks seemed a little enigmatic till he noticed that to the right of the main entrance, which didn't look as if it had been opened in a decade, was a door with *Boys* carved in the stone lintel. On the other side was a corresponding door marked *Girls*.

Might have been purpose-built for conversion from school to mosque, he thought as he went through the *Boys* door.

He found himself in a long porch lined with shelves bearing many pairs of shoes, and the woman's second comment made sense. As he slipped his slip-ons off, the entrance door opened behind him to admit a young Asian man who regarded him with unfriendly curiosity.

Finally he spoke in a broad Yorkshire accent.

'Can I help thee wi' owt?'

'I've come to see Kalim Sarhadi,' said Pascoe.

'Oh aye? And what do you want with him then?'

This, Pascoe guessed, must be one of Jamila's head-bangers who did not look as if the revelation that he was talking to a cop was going to lighten his mood.

'Hey, I'm just a friend. It's about the wedding,' said Pascoe smiling.

He didn't get a return smile, but at least the man grunted what he took as an instruction to follow and led the way out of the entrance porch down a long corridor.

It became apparent to Pascoe as they walked along that, though to outward appearances the old board school had scarcely changed in the past century and a half, inside the new occupants had really made their mark. Though there was still evidence in plenty of the old institutional dull browns and drab greens, it was being overlaid with a new brightness of colour and ornament. Ceilings were painted in a rich gold, in places the old cracked wall tiles had been replaced with intricately

470

patterned ceramics, and areas of flaky old plaster had been smoothed over and inscribed with flowing Arabic letters which he guessed spelt texts from the Koran. Many of the windows were glazed with stained panels through which the summer sun poured a torrent of rainbow hues, and his stockinged feet sank into deep-piled intrinsically patterned carpet.

His guide halted, grunted, 'Wait,' and entered a classroom. closing the door firmly behind him, but not before Pascoe glimpsed a group of men sitting cross-legged on the floor. One of them, a tall bearded man with piercing eyes, he recognized as Sheikh Ibrahim Al-Hijazi whose activities were a source of such virulent speculation for *Voice* journalists.

After a moment the door opened again and Kalim Sarhadi came out.

'Hello, Mr Pascoe,' he said.

'It was Peter at the fête,' Pascoe replied, smiling.

'This not official then?'

'Well, sort of,' admitted Pascoe.

'Aye, I didn't really think you'd be wanting to talk about my wedding.'

'I just didn't want to trouble your friend. But it's not official in any official kind of way,' said Pascoe. 'Can we talk somewhere?'

'Along here,' said Sarhadi, leading him into a small office. 'So what do you want?'

His attitude was polite but restrained.

Pascoe who knew when to go round the houses,

when to be direct, took a photograph of Youngman out of his pocket and put it in front of Sarhadi.

'Do you recognize this man?' he asked.

'Aye.'

Pascoe felt that tremor of pleasure that comes from a hypothesis proven.

'So how do you know him?' he asked.

'Didn't say I knew him. But he's the guy who writes them SAS books, right?'

The tremor of pleasure fizzled out.

'That's right,' said Pascoe. 'You've never actually met him?'

'Why should I? Some of the lads wanted to go over to a reading he were doing at a bookshop in Leeds earlier this year.'

That must have been the tour Ffion had told him about.

'To demonstrate?' he asked.

'Well, they weren't planning to buy his book, that's for sure. Have you looked at the stuff he writes? Don't mind a good thriller, superhero killing all the baddies, but in Youngman's books that's everyone who's not white plus anyone who is who doesn't agree with him. It weren't just Saddam and his supporters that was the enemy, it was every Iraqi, bar none. And he gets on the bestseller lists. Makes a lot of our lads think, if this is your multi-cultural society, you can stuff it.'

'So off they go and train as suicide bombers, because someone's written a bad thriller?'

Sarhadi said, 'That's a jump. I'm not talking

killing people, just a bit of a demo. Mind you, doesn't take much to make some folk think it's right to take the law into their own hands. I know, I got beaten up to prove it. And these Templar loonies going around murdering people, what did it take to push them over the edge? Not much, probably.'

'So why didn't the demo take place?' asked Pascoe, not wanting to get on to the topic of the Templars.

'What's the point? Would likely have ended in a ruckus with us getting all the bad publicity.'

He paused and regarded Pascoe shrewdly.

'This writer guy, Youngman, you don't think he's one of them Templars, do you? Is that why you're here?'

He was bright, thought Pascoe. Bright enough to be playing a double game? Could the woman waving the air pistol on *Fidler's Three* have been right after all?

'Just part of a general enquiry,' he said. 'I'm sorry to have troubled you.'

But Sarhadi wasn't finished yet.

'But if you're after Youngman 'cos he's a Templar, why do you think he might have spoken to me? Hang about! You're not thinking he might have tried to recruit me 'cos I'm on the record as saying Al-Quaeda extremism's the wrong way? Bloody hell, you must be desperate! You're really reaching, aren't you?'

It was true, thought Pascoe. Freeman's scepticism he'd been able to dismiss as partial and prejudiced, but Sarhadi's open mockery made him feel the absurdity of what he'd been suggesting. If there really were someone in the Lubyanka pulling the Templar strings, then they must be laughing their bollocks off watching him running around like a blue-arsed flea. Whoops, there he went, slipping into Fat Man terminology again.

He was saved further embarrassment by the door opening and the tall bearded man coming in.

'Here you are, Kalim,' he said in a pleasantly musical voice with just the slightest hint of guttural continuo. 'Won't you introduce me to our visitor?'

'Of course. This is Chief Inspector Pascoe of Mid-Yorkshire CID, isn't it?'

Pascoe nodded. And Sarhadi went on, 'And this is our Imam, Sheikh Ibrahim.'

The Sheikh put his hands together and inclined his head.

Pascoe said, 'Glad to meet you.'

'And I you. Is there any particular reason for your visit, Chief Inspector? Or are you just seeking after truth?'

'That's my particular reason and my general profession,' said Pascoe.

The Sheikh smiled.

'Then I hope you may find it. Peace be with you and the mercy of Allah.'

He turned and went out.

'So that's the famous Sheikh Ibrahim,' said Pascoe.

'Aye, that's the famous bogeyman that's going to eat you all in your beds.'

'You must read the *Voice*,' said Pascoe. 'My paper just says he preaches from a rather extremist viewpoint. Which makes me wonder about your relationship with him.'

'Why's that?'

'Well, if as you say, you're anti-demonstrations and anti-Al-Quacda, then you don't seem to have a lot in common.'

'He's our Imam, so we've got our faith in common. Anyway, you want he should only deal with people who agree with everything he says? One thing I'm sure of, if you lot had owt on him, you'd arrest him. Here, is that the real reason you're here? To see if you can dig up some dirt on the Sheikh?'

'If I wanted to do that, where would you suggest I dig?'

Sarhadi shook his head and said, 'I've told your lot already: I'll not turn into a spy on my own people.'

'Not even if you see one of them heading off towards the town centre wearing a Semtex corset?'

'I hope I'd act like I hope your lot would act if they saw someone trying to take another shot the Sheikh. By the way, it were him that stopped the lads demonstrating against Youngman, not me.'

'I'm glad to hear it,' said Pascoe. 'Kalim, I'm

sorry to have troubled you. Many congratulations in advance for Saturday. I hope you have a long and happy married life.'

'Ta,' said the young man. 'Give my best to your missus. How's that poor woman with the gun, by the way?'

'She's receiving treatment, I believe.'

'Hope it turns out OK for her. Losing someone like that must be hard to get over.'

Then his face split in a very attractive smile.

'Still, out of bad comes good. When she shot Joe Fidler in the bollocks, that must have made a lot of people think there has to be a God, eh?'

Pascoe was still grinning as he got back into the car which was waiting outside.

Rod, who was on his phone, didn't return the grin. He put his hand over the mouthpiece and said, 'Bernie. And he's pissed off.'

Frowning, Pascoe took the phone.

'Hello, sir,' he said.

'Peter, what the hell are you playing at?'

'Don't follow you, sir. I'm just doing the job you gave me.'

'Then I must brush up on my communication skills. I don't remember giving you *carte blanche* to be a one-man band!'

'I'm sorry, sir, but if you could be a little more specific . . .'

'You want specificity, do you? Right. Item, you do not interrogate detainees in safe houses without clearance from a senior officer. And you

476

certainly do not subject them to sexual harass-ment. Item, you do not remove confidential files from this building without clearance, and you certainly do not sit reading them in a public place. Item, you do not invade the privacy of distin-guished ex-officers in Her Majesty's armed forces without preparing the ground very carefully. Item, you do not descend unannounced on a location which a moment's thought should have told you we have under close surveillance. Is that specific enough for you?'

'Yes, sir. Look, I'm sorry but . . .'

'Save your excuses. Get yourself back here as quickly as possible. And that means don't stop on the way, not even if the angel Gabriel appears to you with yet another brilliant idea!'

The phone went dead.

He handed it back to Rod who said miserably, 'Peter, I'm sorry. I did try to say . . .'

'That we shouldn't be doing this? Yes, you did. And I'm sure it's already on tape if not on video,' said Pascoe wearily. 'Sorry. It's a lot more than that. And none of it is down to you, I'll make that clear. So let's head on back and face the music, shall we?'

14

a wee deoch an doris

To start with, the music seemed less discordant than he'd expected.

Back at the Lube, he expected to be wheeled in before a court-martial consisting of Bloomfield, Komorowski and Glenister. Instead he was met by two men he didn't know who introduced themselves without a flicker of a smile as Smith and Jones.

Their job, they said, was to debrief him, which they did with great courtesy but at considerable length. And when they had finished taking him through his activities in minute detail, they went back to the beginning and started again. After a couple of hours, they offered him coffee and sandwiches. Then they started again.

By the time they announced they were finished it was after ten p.m. He felt as if he'd been in the interview room with them for days. It seemed impossible that it was only yesterday

478

morning that he had returned to the Lube and taken up his new job.

He stood up and said, 'Any chance of a word with the commander now?'

They looked at each other, then Smith (he'd got them distinguished by the colour of their eyes) said, 'I'm sure you'll be contacted if it is felt necessary.'

Pascoe digested this, then said, 'You mean this is it?'

'As far as we're concerned, yes.'

'Then I'll bid you goodnight,' he said, stretching. 'May I have my briefcase?'

'It will be waiting for you at Security.'

They walked down the stairs with him. The foyer was dark and empty. Komorowski's plants looked as if they'd curled up for the night.

At the security check-out, as he handed over his badge, the duty officer said, 'May I have your pass too, sir?'

His sense of relief began to wash away.

'But I'll need it to get in tomorrow morning,' he said.

'Sorry, sir. If you could just hand it over . . .'

So this was how it was done, he thought disbelievingly. Not even a kangaroo court. One strike and you were out. If he'd ever really been in.

'I suppose it's better than the poisoned umbrella,' he said, handing over the pass.

'Your briefcase, sir. And your mobile phone.'

He took them and walked across the foyer. Nobody said goodnight.

Back at the hotel, he wouldn't have been surprised to find his bag packed and waiting at reception. He sat down in his room and tried to think things through.

He'd crossed a line, and he was out. The question was whether he was out because he'd broken a few of their stupid fucking rules or because he'd started to get too close to the Templar mole.

Not that it mattered. He had done everything he could. Should he have been more subtle? Perhaps. But if you were dropped blindfold into a snake pit, it surely made more sense to follow your instinct and make a mad rush to where you thought the exit might be, rather than crawl around, trying to feel your way out?

He was tempted to ring Ellie, but he suspected he'd be bugged and anyway to ring her so late with talk of snake-pits and blindfolds would add to her fear that he was heading for the funny farm.

Maybe she was right and maybe what he'd been doing wasn't conducting an investigation but running round like a headless chicken in a superstitious effort to distract whatever judgmental deity held Andy Dalziel's life in the scales.

He opened the mini-bar. A distaste for people who were profligate with public money had kept his demands on it to a minimum, but now he felt he'd earned what Dalziel would probably have called *a wee deoch an doris*. He plucked out a couple of miniatures of single malt and poured them into a goblet. They went down very smoothly, and he replenished his glass with another two. That left the mini-bar empty of whisky. He'd have to move on to cognac, or liqueurs.

What would Andy have done at such a juncture? Tipped the lot into a jug probably, given it a shake, then taken it to bed with him.

Each to his own. He set the goblet on the bedside table and went into the bathroom where he showered, then climbed into bed.

His mind was still working too hard to make sleep an imminent prospect. The alcohol should kick in eventually, but meantime he needed some other soporific.

Blood on the Sand lay beside his whisky glass.

He opened it and began to read, and for a while it seemed set to do the trick.

He was reading a chapter in which nothing much happened.

Shack's patrol had been sent out to check an enemy MSR. They found themselves in a stretch of empty desert watching a length of empty road along which nothing moved for twenty-four hours. The chapter was full of authenticating acronyms and cant terms and the characters seemed to be competing to decide who was the most boring and limited. Shack's authorial voice was at pains to point out that life, even in a 'glamorous' unit like the SAS, could be tedious and uninvolving. Pascoe felt that he overdid the demonstration but it was perfect for a reader in search of rest.

481

The chapter ended with them packing up to rendezvous with the Chinook that was taking them back to base. Then a call came through on the radio telling them to stay put and await further orders. No reason, but this wasn't surprising. Radio traffic was always kept as brief as possible to make it harder for the enemy to get a fix.

Finally they got the bad news. Their helicopter had been brought down by enemy fire en route to the rendezvous. A reconnaissance over-flight had spotted the downed machine still more or less in one piece, but there was no sign of its three crew members. When the Search and Rescue choppers got there, they confirmed that, though there was blood in the cabin, the crew and all portable equipment had vanished, which suggested they'd been taken prisoner. The Iraqis would not have bothered to remove corpses.

The only significant centre of population within a radius of fifty kilometres was a substantial village which an SAS patrol had recce'd a fortnight earlier, finding no sign of enemy occupation. Tracks from the downed machine led here and when one of the S and R helicopters did an over-flight, it drew ground fire. Normally the response would have been to pump in a few rockets and call up a Tornado strike, but the possibility that captured crew members might be held here gave pause. Shack's patrol was less than an hour's journey away. They were instructed to approach with caution, check on the enemy disposition and, if possible, confirm the presence of prisoners.

By now Pascoe was drifting away, but the day's events still lurked at the far end of his mind, ready to emerge, so he stifled a yawn and began the next chapter.

Ten minutes later he was as wide awake as he'd been all day.

15

a call in the night

It was dark when we reached the village.

There's a lot of crap written about working behind enemy lines. Truth is, they had no lines. You could waste a whole day the way we'd just done hanging around in the middle of a lot of emptiness. And if you stumbled across a village, it didn't matter what it said on the map. Sometimes you could stroll in, sit at a table in the local café, order a coffee and watch while the locals ripped the Saddam posters off the wall and set fire to them for your approval. Other times the whole fucking place was a rats' nest that the fly-boys would need to sanitize before our lads moved in.

There was a half-moon, and in its ghostly light the place looked almost picturesque. We hardly needed our kite-lights to spot that Abdul was certainly here now, mainly because he was making no effort not to be spotted. This was because they were packing up to pull out. Not many of them either, just two armoured trucks being loaded up and a couple of jeeps outside the only substantial house in the village. We went in closer. If they'd had perimeter guards, they must have called them in prior to the withdrawal.

My job was to check out whether they were holding prisoners. If I decided not, I'd wait till the trucks were on the move, then call in their direction so that the fly-boys could take them out on the road. Result, dead Abdul, a clean settlement and us on our way without anyone knowing we'd been around, which was the way we liked it.

The troops were climbing into the trucks. So far we'd seen no sign of anyone under restraint, and when the Abs were on the move with prisoners, they weren't shy of showing them, reckoning that this lessened the chance of a blanket air attack.

Then Ginger said, 'Shack, there's a guy there wearing a fly-boy's headpiece.'

I checked it out through my bins. He was right. There was this Ab prancing around like a hairy Biggles. Got himself a nice trophy to impress the houris with. But still no sign of the poor sod he'd taken it off.

'Maybe they're still in the house,' said Ginger.

I'd been thinking the same.

If they were, and if they weren't brought out in the next couple of minutes, it meant one of two things. I knew for certain these bastards wouldn't be leaving living prisoners behind. So either they were dead already, or they would be before long.

All the lads had reached the same conclusion and were looking at me for orders.

Well, I had mine, which were, observe, don't make contact.

I knew that I should sit it out till I was certain they weren't carrying prisoners with them, then call in an air-strike to take out the column on the move while we went in to check out the village.

But I was ninety per cent certain if I did that all I'd find were bodies.

I said, 'Ginger, three minutes, you and Lugs take out the trucks. The rest with me.'

We left them setting up the anti-tank guns and moved forward.

It was impossible to get close without being spotted by locals, but those we saw faded rapidly away and made no effort raise the alarm. Wise move. Sit it out, see who comes out on top, then start cheering – the formula for civilian survival since wars began.

We were less than fifty metres from the house when one of the trucks started up. At the same time two Ab officers who'd been standing by the jeeps talking went inside.

I didn't imagine they'd gone to kiss their prisoners goodbye.

'Where the fuck are you, Ginger?' I began to say. But I needn't have worried.

Next moment there was that familiar whoosh! and the nearest truck went up like a curry fart across a candle. Figures spilled out, many on fire. The second truck began to move. Another whoosh! Another exploding fart. We were already running forward, shooting at everything that moved. No one was in much of a state for shooting back and I left the lads to mop up and kept on going right into the building. There were two men and a woman in the first chamber. They didn't look military but this was no time for introductions. I blew them away without breaking stride, went through another empty room and out into a small central courtyard.

In the middle was a bronze fountain in a sunken basin. It must have looked pretty when water was sprinkling from the jets into the pool below. But no water flowed now and the basin was dry and dusty.

But it wasn't empty.

There were three figures sprawled in it. I didn't pay them much heed to start with. I was more concerned with the two Abs who were in the courtyard.

One of them was standing on the edge of the fountain basin looking down, an automatic pistol in his hand. The other had an AKK which was pointed towards me. If he'd started firing as soon as I appeared, that would have been it. But the fact that I was wearing a burnoose over my desert kit made him hesitate a fraction and that was enough. I dropped them both with a single burst.

When I looked at the figures in the fountain I hoped I'd only wounded the Abs. Their exit deserved to be a lot slower and a helluva lot more painful.

One of them was wearing full flying kit. He looked as if he'd been badly injured when the chopper came down and had died by the time they got him in here.

He was the lucky one, I'd say.

The other two men in the basin were naked. They'd been bound with wire to the fountain. The wire had been so tightly twisted round their calves that the blood had stopped flowing to the flesh below which was greeny white. OK, they'd probably suffered some damage in the crash as well, but that was nothing to what had happened since. Their bodies bore the signs of beating, cutting and burning. One of them was already dead, which was just was well as his eyes had been half gouged out. I thought the other was gone too, but he suddenly raised his head. He still had one good eye which took me in, then his mouth opened but he couldn't speak. I poured some water from my canteen into the palm of my hand and moistened his lips. Then I started to untwist the wire that bound him but I could see that it was pointless, and so could he.

He spoke, a low croaking noise, but I could make out what he said.

'Shouldn't bother, old chap.'

I gave him some more water and this time he was able to drink.

I said, 'Don't worry, mate, you're safe now,' and he made a sound which I think he intended as a laugh.

When he spoke again, his voice was stronger.

'Told these chaps I was entitled to a phone call, but they didn't oblige. Any chance now?'

I thought he was delirious then I saw what his one eye was looking at. The Ab with the pistol who'd been about to shoot him had a satellite phone in a pouch on his belt.

I bent down to remove it. The Ab opened his eyes. His mate was clearly dead but this one still had a spark. I gave him a promissory smile and took the phone. It was Eastern European, I think, but basically the same as the ones in use back at base. I switched it on. The battery was charged.

I said, 'Who do you want to ring?'

He said, 'My wife,' and whispered a number.

I punched it in. I'm not a fanciful man but my mind was painting pictures now. It would be midnight back home. The phone would probably be ringing in a dark house. She'd hear it, sit up in bed, get up and set off downstairs. She'd be part irritated, part concerned. Who could be calling at this time of night? It couldn't be good news, that was for sure. Then she'd reach the phone and pick it up and . . .

'Hello?' said a woman's voice in my ear.

I held out the phone but his fingers were broken and most of them had the nails ripped out so I had to hold it to his ear.

'Hi, darling,' he said.

To me his voice sounded like glass crackling under a rolling pin, but there had to be enough there to recognize.

'Oh God,' she said. 'Is that you?'

This was a conversation I didn't want to listen to, but I had no choice. I tried to direct my mind away, but when two voices a thousand miles apart are speaking the last words they'll ever speak to each other, it's impossible not to listen.

I won't write their words here.

They wouldn't look much if I did.

But at that time, in that place, with him knowing he was dying, and her beginning to understand it, they were so moving they blotted out for a moment the noise of gunfire and explosions in the street outside.

But it couldn't go on for long. It was a miracle he was still able to talk at all.

He stopped in mid-syllable. And the din of battle returned.

And for me love stopped, hate returned.

I spoke into the phone.

'Sorry, love, he's gone.'

What else was there to say? Nothing, Not then.

Maybe when I got home, I'd find this woman and tell her everything I knew about her husband's death. She deserved that at least.

But for now I had more urgent business.

I bent over the Ab and gave him a drink from my canteen. He looked at me gratefully. Then he stopped looking grateful.

He only lasted a couple of minutes, which was disappointing.

I gave him one last kick and went to see if my lads had left any more of those murdering bastards for me to kill.

16

the full English

Next morning Pascoe rose early and had a cold shower to wake himself up.

He hadn't slept well.

A second reading had been followed by a third.

Then he got up, had another drink from the mini-bar and tried to recall all that Ellie had told him about her lunch with Maurice Kentmore.

Once more Dalziel's deep distrust of coincidence was upmost in his mind.

OK, it hadn't been his wife but his brother that Christopher Kentmore had spoken to as he lay dying. But in terms of drama, and of novel sales, a dying man speaking to his wife from the battlefield made a much better story.

He'd riffled through the pages to the end of the book. In the short last chapter, Shack returned to England. It consisted mainly of descriptions of energetic sexual encounters with various old and new flames, and equally energetic encounters with various anti-war protesters. After the last of these, in which he consigned a trio of what he called 'bearded leftie dickheads' to Intensive Care, he drove north, thinking,

> *Now it was time to go and talk to people who knew from experience what war was really about and why there could be no compromise with the enemy we were fighting. The desert makes you see choices simply. We win or we die.*
> *Me, I intend winning.*

If the episode in the book were based on a real incident in which Sergeant Young helped Christopher Kentmore to speak to his brother, what more natural than that Youngman should have called on Maurice to fill him in on the background?

Then later when he had joined or even founded the Templars to take the fight to the terrorists in the UK, perhaps memory of Kentmore's reaction had made Youngman think of him as a possible recruit.

Was Kentmore the kind of man who'd get involved in such madness? On the surface, perhaps not, but that's what surfaces are for, to hide beneath. From his record during the foot-and-mouth crisis, and his actions on *Fidler's Three*, he seemed to be the kind of man who had no trouble moving forward from belief to action.

Which didn't mean he was equipped to deal with all the consequences of action.

Military experience might inure soldiers to the

concept of collateral damage and friendly-fire casualties, but a civilian who got involved, especially outside the supporting framework of the concept of a just war, could be devastated at the thought that his actions in no matter how good a cause had shed innocent blood.

Which would explain Kentmore's interest in maintaining contact with Ellie and through her getting information about the progress of both the injured cops.

Also, how worried might he have been when tabloid speculation about the alarms last Sunday in the Central Hospital made him suspect an attempt had been made to take out Hector? Meeting Ellie for lunch could have seemed a good way to get confirmation or contradiction of this.

And finally, his own theory about Youngman's reason for backing away from *Fidler's Three* could be just as valid if it were Kentmore not Kal he wanted to avoid.

It all fitted together very nicely.

Like Patrick Fitzwilliam and William Fitzpatrick, the Irish queers, he heard Dalziel say. *They fit together very nicely, but they're not going to give birth, are they?*

In other words, don't believe in coincidence, but don't jump to conclusions either!

He finished his drink and climbed back into bed. If he didn't get some sleep he'd be a wreck in the morning. When sleep didn't come, he picked up the Gideon Bible and opened it at random.

Hear my voice, O God, in my prayer; preserve my life from fear of the enemy. Hide me from the secret counsel of the wicked; from the insurrection of the workers of iniquity. Who whet their tongue like a sword; and bend their bows to shoot their arrows, even bitter words: That they may shoot in secret at the perfect: suddenly do they shoot at him, and fear not.

But who is the enemy? And who is the perfect? he found himself asking.

And still pondering these questions, he'd fallen into a fitful sleep.

The phone was ringing as he stepped out of the shower.

'Hello,' he said.

'Pete, it's Dave Freeman. Sandy and I are downstairs. Can we talk?'

'Why not? Stay for breakfast. I'll be down in a few minutes. Order for me, will you? The Full English. Might as well fill my belly before my credit's cancelled.'

As he dried himself, he tried to work out why they were here. Not, he guessed, to tell him all was forgiven and invite him back into the fold. Anyway, he'd had enough of the fold.

He picked up his mobile and rang home.

'Hi,' said Ellie. 'I was getting worried. I tried to ring last night but you were switched off.'

'Sorry. I was otherwise engaged.'

'Not running around playing at Action Man again, I hope?'

'No. In fact I was very sedentary. I'll tell you all about it when I get home.'

'Home?' Her voice filled with a hope which touched his heart. 'You're definitely getting back for the weekend?'

'No,' he said. Paused. Then went on, 'Bit longer than that. I'm finished here. We can get back to normal.'

'Peter, that's marvellous! When shall I expect you?'

'Well, you weren't planning to go out for lunch, were you? I mean, no unexpected summons to appear on television to accept the Nobel Prize for Literature or something like that?'

'No! And if there were, I'd cancel it. Talking of which, I'll give Maurice Kentmore a ring and tell him tomorrow's off, shall I?'

He said, 'Kentmore? I'd forgotten that. No, it's a bit late to cancel, isn't it? And now I'm going to be back permanently, not just for a couple of days, it doesn't matter so much. Let him come.'

In his own ears his words rang false as a TV soap star upgrading to Hamlet.

'You mean, let *them* come. It's not the prospect of seeing lean and hungry Kilda again that's made you change your tune, is it?' mocked Ellie.

'Could be. You'll just have to make sure I'm too exhausted to take an interest. Now I'm off to

495

eat my last all-expenses-paid breakfast. Love to Rosie. Bye.'

He felt guilty at deceiving her, but the knowledge of how very much he was looking forward to getting home salved his conscience. And the deceit element wasn't so significant, was it? All he wanted to do was have another close up look at Kentmore for himself. Nothing wrong in that. Probably his suspicions would evaporate in a cloud of conversation about Yorkshire cricket and prize pigs.

He went down to the oak-panelled breakfast room where he found Freeman and Glenister sitting at a table, drinking coffee.

Freeman greeted him with a smile. Glenister looked more serious.

She said 'Peter, I didn't want you to go without speaking to you.'

'So I'm definitely going?' he said.

'The commander says he has no choice. Believe me, as a cop he understands the value of playing it by ear now and then. He says he'd have been surprised if someone who'd flourished under Superintendent Dalziel didn't take a strong independent line from time to time. But our work is such a web of complexities, there are some rules you can't break. Shoot off by yourself and you never know what damage you may be doing.'

'You're a cop,' he said.

'Yes, and I learned the hard way.'

'But you don't think I can?'

'Peter, I'm sure you could. But you were never going to be anything but a temporary attachment,' she said gently. 'So what's the point of prolonging things? You've trodden on sensitive toes, that's all.'

'So whose sensitive toe is it I feel up my back-side?' he asked, looking at Freeman. 'Sounds as if it's definitely spooky. You, Dave? Lukasz? Were Tim and Rod asked for their assessment?'

Before Freeman could reply, Glenister said, 'It was a unanimous decision. There are no sides here, Peter. We all have the greatest respect for you. At a personal level, I haven't encountered anyone at the Lube who hasn't liked you.'

'I can second that,' said Freeman.

'Well, I'm touched,' said Pascoe. 'So is this what you've come to tell me, that I'm a nice guy, much loved by little children everywhere? Or are you going to hang around to see me safely off the premises?'

His sarcasm seemed to bounce off them.

A waiter approached and set a huge plateful of breakfast down before Pascoe.

'You two not joining me then?' he said.

'I'm a muesli man myself,' said Freeman. 'Just looking at that clogs my arteries.'

'So we'll leave you to enjoy it,' said Glenister. 'Peter, my main reason for coming this morning was I wanted you to know, nothing that's happened over here will leave the slightest mark on your record. I understand your deep personal interest in parts of this investigation and I'll make sure you are kept in the loop. Mainly though, I didn't want to miss the chance of saying goodbye to you personally. I hope we get the chance to work together again. You're my kind of cop. A real blue Smartie. Thanks for everything.'

'I'll second that, Pete,' said Freeman. 'It's been really good working with you. You'd have made a great spook. Any time you think of changing career, be sure to let me know. In the meantime, the very best of luck to you.'

The two of them pushed their chairs back from the table as though preparing to rise, and regarded him with warm smiles.

They're waiting for me to say something, thought Pascoe.

Despite himself, he felt quite flattered by their unsolicited testimonial. The courteous and the sensible response would be to accept their praise modestly, then confirm its accuracy by telling them about his discovery of the possible link between Kentmore and Youngman. Unless there were a broad conspiracy in CAT to support the Templars, the fact that there were two of them should ensure his suspicions got acted on. So, let it be someone else's job to check out the connection. He could then ring Ellie again, tell her he was on his way, and say he'd changed his mind about having the Kentmores to lunch. That way he could really get his life back.

That would be the sensible and the courteous

thing to do, the natural response one would look for from the famous silver-tongued, blue Smartie, rope-dancer, Detective Chief Inspector Peter Pascoe.

His blunt and brutish ringmaster, Detective Superintendent Andrew Dalziel, on the other hand, would probably have ruined the friendly almost sentimental moment by saying something totally inappropriate like, 'Get fucked.'

He looked down with patriotic pride at the Full English before him, picked up the sauce bottle, gave it a St George's cross of ketchup, stabbed a sausage and began to eat.

Now they rose from their seats, still smiling, though a trifle uneasily.

He looked up at them, chewed, swallowed and said, 'Get fucked.'

17

one last decision

It's crisis time for Andy Dalziel.

Despite all his efforts of will and attempts at distraction he is back in the deep darkness, pressing against the fragile membrane between himself and white-light Elsewhere.

Into his mind drifts a zephyrean greeting.

Welcome back.

'You don't fool me.'

Don't I?

'Nay. I've been thinking about thee and I know what you are.'

Indeed? May I presume that knowing that means you are ready to come through?

'No, it bloody well doesn't! 'Cos what I know is you're nowt but summat I've invented. You're a figment, that's what.'

You mean you are talking to yourself?

'That's it, sunshine.'

Sunshine . . . I remember sunshine. One of my better ideas. But this is very interesting. So how would you describe yourself? As an Existentialist, perhaps? Or merely a Pyrrhonist?

'Eh?'

Oh dear. That's a bit of a problem, isn't it? If you are talking to yourself, surely you should be able to understand what you are saying to yourself?

'Not necessarily, clever clogs. I'm forever surprising myself.'

That must be very disconcerting. But if you do not believe in me, why would you take the trouble of inventing me?

''Cos I like a chat and there's no other bugger to talk to here.'

And where do you think here *is?*

'Not there.'

And where is there?

Dalziel tries to think but finds he has nothing to think about. The weight of darkness presses heavy upon him. There's no familiar voice, no big band brass, no ceilidh skirl, not even an irritating skein of prayer to lead him back to that universe of sound and colour and smell and texture which he can no longer imagine let alone recall.

The darkness is on him, soon it will be in him. The only way out is to exert that drachm of extra pressure which will explode him through the gossamer membrane into the glory of light that waits beyond.

Better to make the decision yourself than have it made for you.

Was that me or it? he wonders.

501

But there is no *it*, he reminds himself. Just me.
Which is likely why *it* sometimes makes a bit of
sense.

One last decision and then we're done.

He'd never been afraid of making decisions so
why was he hesitating now?

One last decision . . .

He made it and burst through the membrane
into the light.

Part Six

And that dismal cry rose slowly
And sank slowly through the air,
Full of spirit's melancholy
And eternity's despair;
And they heard the words it said –
'Pan is dead! Great Pan is dead!
Pan, Pan is dead!'

Elizabeth Barrett Browning, *The Dead Pan*

1

the very worst

'Ellie, I'm late and I'm alone and I'm devastated,'
said Maurice Kentmore. 'Kilda's had to pull out.
A migraine. She's been getting them ever since
. . . you know. They come on like lightning and
lay her low. The doctors have tried everything but
in the end there's nothing for the poor girl to do
but lie in a darkened room for six or seven hours.
I thought of ringing you, but what was the point?
Nothing you could change at such short notice,
so better to hurry on here and offer apologies face
to face. Which I do. Sorry.'

He finished, out of breath and out of words.
If, thought Ellie, he'd spiked everything after *you
know*, it might have been more convincing.

'Poor Kilda,' she said. 'Maurice, don't just stand
there, come on in.'

Kentmore stepped into the hall. Pascoe was
standing in the living-room doorway.

'Peter, Kilda can't make it. A migraine,' said
Ellie.

'I heard. Poor woman. Maurice, nice to see you again. Let me get you a drink. White wine OK?'

'Fine.'

Pascoe stood aside to let his guest pass through the door. Ellie made a wry face at her husband and headed for the kitchen. Kentmore accepted the glass poured for him, tasted it and said, 'This is nice. Where do you get it?'

'Sainsbury's, I expect,' said Pascoe. 'How goes it with the piglets?'

'What? Oh yes. Fine, they're fine.'

'Good. Here you are. Must be hard when the time comes to kill them.'

'No. Not hard. I'm a farmer. You breed animals for meat, it's part of the job.'

'And you don't actually slaughter them yourself, of course.'

'Only in extremis, to put them out of pain.'

Ellie came back in and poured herself a glass of wine.

'What are you talking about?' she said.

'Pigs,' said Pascoe. 'And whether you can have a relationship with them before you kill them.'

'Ugh. Luckily we're having trout and it's hard to get attached to a fish.'

'I don't know. Remember Goldie? Goldie was our daughter's goldfish,' he explained to Kentmore. 'When it went belly-up, Ellie would have given it a nautical send-off down the loo, but Rosie insisted on the full C of E service and she still puts flowers on the grave when she remembers.'

'On the site of the grave,' corrected Ellie. 'Tig dug the box up a few days later while Rosie was at school. Didn't seem worth putting it back, and it was bin day.'

'You never said. Ellie, as you see, is not sentimental, Maurice. She would have made a good farmer's wife.'

'I don't doubt it,' said Kentmore with an effort at a smile. 'Is your girl at home?'

'No, she's gone skating. Should have gone last week but she missed out.'

'And came to our fête instead. A poor substitute.'

'No, no,' said Ellie. 'She thoroughly enjoyed herself, and Tig had a really great time. He's not so hot at skating. Pete, take Maurice into the garden. We thought we'd cross our fingers and eat outside. Ready in about five minutes.'

She went out and Pascoe said, 'Meaning, if you want the loo, now's the time. She gets seriously pissed with people who wait till the gong sounds, then disappear.'

'Not my intention,' said Kentmore, following Pascoe through the French window on to a raised patio. 'So this is how a policeman lives. Nice garden.'

In fact, the narrow rectangle of lawn showed signs of the depredations of an active daughter and an even more active dog, but the well-tended borders were rich with shrub roses creating a corridor of colour which drew the eye down to the fine magnolia grandiflora against the high south-facing wall. Birds sang in its branches, bees buzzed among the roses, and the light summer wind twitching the white cloth on the garden table was heavy with the sweet scent of both tree and shrubs.

'Yes, it is,' said Pascoe with the complacency of one whose wife did most of the actual work. 'Not exactly a landed estate, but we try to keep up appearances and of course the bribes help.'

'What? Oh yes. Like a Jewish joke, only funny when a Jew makes it. So how were things in Manchester?'

'Oh, you know, Lancastrian.'

'Sorry, I wasn't trying to pry into your work.'

'And I wasn't being coy,' said Pascoe. 'I felt a little out of my element over there. Also it was a bad time to be away with my boss out of commission and all that.'

'Any news there?'

'No. Nothing. There's still evidence of brain activity so we're a still long way off the switching-off option, but it's been nearly three weeks now.'

'Nineteen days.'

That was very precise, thought Pascoe.

'That's right, nineteen days. For Andy Dalziel, that's a long time between drinks. It's going to be hard going in on Monday and finding he's not there. I suppose if I'd been back in my own office continuously since I got signed off the sick list,

I might have made some adjustments, but this will be like starting all over again . . . Sorry. I'm getting maudlin.'

'No, no. He sounds like a very special man.'

'Oh yes he was. I mean, he is. Very special. Irreplaceable. When he goes, it will feel like the end of things.'

Ellie's voice broke the silence that followed.

'Grub up!' she said, stepping on to the patio with a laden tray. 'Maurice, grab a seat. Peter, could you bring the wine?'

As he passed her she hissed, 'Lighten up, for God's sake!'

At the table she moved smoothly into lively hostess mode and Kentmore relaxed into the guest having a good time role with well-bred ease. But it seemed to Pascoe that his mind was elsewhere.

Or is it just my mind that's elsewhere? Pascoe asked himself. In Mill Street, to be precise. Have I become so obsessed by what happened there that I want to see connections everywhere? Perhaps instead of looking at my ejection from CAT in terms of conspiracy theory, I should be booking a few sessions with a good counselling service.

Ellie kicked him under the table and he realized he'd drifted off into an introspective silence.

He said brightly, 'Are you a cricket fan, Maurice?'

'I keep an eye on the test score, but I haven't played myself since school. Too busy farming, I suppose.'

'Oh yes. And riding, and climbing mountains. That must fill the day.'

It was meant to come out as admiration that one man could pack so much into one life, instead it sounded to Pascoe's own critical ear not far short of a social sneer.

Kentmore said, 'I still ride when I can, but I've rather given up on the climbing. How about you two?'

Ellie said, 'We do a bit of hill-walking but when it gets so steep you need a rope, we head down to the nearest pub.'

'Each to his own,' said Kentmore.

'Yeah, a man's gotta do what a man's gotta do,' said Pascoe.

There I go again! What the hell's getting into me?

Ellie opened her mouth but whether it was to issue a stinging reproof or to ask if anyone wanted seconds remained a mystery as the door bell rang.

Pascoe began to rise but she said firmly, 'No, you sit and talk. I'll get it.'

She went out.

Pascoe poured more wine.

'This is nice,' said Kentmore. 'Where do you get it?'

Poor sod was repeating himself. Pascoe felt a little better about his flirtation with rudeness. Socially this guy was on auto-pilot, his mind was definitely elsewhere.

But where?

Don't reach, Pascoe warned himself. Let reason be your guide.

'Sainsbury's, I think,' he said. 'Well, look who's here.'

A figure had appeared at the French window. It was Edgar Wield. His face was, as always, unreadable but there was something in his posture which said he wasn't about to ask if anyone fancied tennis.

Behind him stood Ellie, looking faintly puzzled.

'Peter, I need a word,' said Wield in a rough peremptory tone.

'Sure,' said Pascoe.

He stood up and as if the movement had triggered it, let out a tremendous sneeze.

'Sorry,' he said, pulling out his handkerchief. 'Hope I'm not getting a summer cold. Wieldy, would you like a glass of wine?'

'No thanks,' said the sergeant.

He took a step on to the patio, his eyes fixed on Pascoe.

Something about the way he held himself, a stiffness across his shoulders, a rigidity in his arms, was alarming Ellie.

'Is everything OK, Wieldy?' she asked.

He didn't respond. His gaze stayed fixed on Pascoe.

'Pete,' he said.

It sounded like a preliminary, but nothing followed.

Pascoe said, 'For God's sake, Wieldy, what is it? Is something wrong? Oh shit. Is it Andy?'

'Yes,' said Wield. 'It's Andy. I've just come from the hospital.'

He was having difficulty speaking. His voice sounded hoarse and unfamiliar. Whatever it was he had to say, he clearly didn't want to say it.

'What? Spit it out, man! Is he worse?'

Wield shook his head, but his answer was affirmative.

'Worse, aye. The very worst.'

He looked round at Ellie as if he didn't want her to be there. Then his gaze returned to Pascoe and he sucked in a deep breath as if the heavy words he had to speak needed a torrent of air to float them out.

'Pete, he's dead,' he said brokenly. 'I'm sorry. He's dead. Dalziel is dead. Andy Dalziel is dead.'

2

wheel of fire

Some news is so tremendous that silence is the only possible response.

Everything went still, the breeze in the table cloth, the bees in the roses, the birds in the magnolia, the earth on its axis, the stars in their courses.

Then, as it will, as it must, life went on.

Ellie threw back her head and let out a sob which came close to a scream, Pascoe shook his head like a man betrayed and cried, 'No, Wieldy, no!' Wield looked from one to the other, saying, 'I'm sorry, I'm sorry.' And from the table came a crash as Maurice Kentmore slumped forward, his head in his hands, toppling the wine bottle into the sauce boat from Ellie's best china set.

Pascoe turned to look at him, then turned back towards the doorway and said, 'Wieldy, take care of Ellie.'

And to her evident surprise, Ellie, who was moving towards him, her face full of love and

514

concern, found herself caught up in the sergeant's strong arms and urged irresistibly across the lounge and out of the door into the hallway.

Pascoe sat down heavily next to Kentmore.

After a while the man raised his head and looked at his host with anguished eyes.

Neither man spoke. It was as if they were waiting for a sign.

It came in the form of another high-pitched cry from inside the house.

To the untutored ear this sounded very like its predecessor, springing from the depths of some divine despair, but Pascoe recognized in its long wavering note the tremolo of a far from divine rage.

The sound unlocked Kentmore's tongue.

'I prayed this wouldn't happen . . . I really prayed . . . not selfishly, at least I don't think so . . . for him, not for me . . .'

Then he paused and fixed his gaze on Pascoe, and after a moment nodded as if a question had been answered.

'You know, don't you?' he said.

'Yes. I know.'

'Peter, I'm so sorry. It wasn't meant to be like this. I'm so very sorry.'

'Well, that's all right then, so long as you're sorry,' said Pascoe with a controlled vehemence. 'But sorry's not going to bring Andy back, any more than murdering people was going to bring your brother back. What were you thinking about, for God's sake?'

'I was . . . I don't know . . . I owed it to him . . . the blood debt . . . *I owed it to him!*'

He put his head between his hands again as if trying to hide from Pascoe's cold unblinking gaze.

I owed it to him.

The repeated phrase echoed again in Pascoe's mind.

It spoke of something more than simple revenge, an eye for an eye and a tooth for a tooth. There was nothing Old Testament about Kentmore, no hint of Italianate emotionalism or even a Celtic nursing of old resentments. He was English through and through . . . and in your true-blue Englishman loss paralyses . . .

But guilt energizes!

I owed it to him.

Not simple revenge, but expiation!

It had to be sexual . . . English guilt was always sexual.

'It was Kilda, wasn't it?' said Pascoe.

'Yes. Kilda.'

He removed his hands but kept his head bent forward, his eyes fixed on the ruined table cloth, as he began to speak in a low harsh monotone.

'She was in bed with me that night when the phone rang. Youngman told me he'd tried the Gatehouse number first. Then, when there was no answer, Chris asked him to ring me. Youngman said he could see it was only will power that was keeping him alive. He should have been long dead, but he wanted to speak to Kilda before he went. Instead he spoke to me. And Kilda was by my side, her warm naked flesh close against mine, and he gave me words of love and farewell to pass on to her and I wanted to say she's here and let him hear her voice, but I couldn't, I couldn't let my kid brother die knowing that, while he lay dying, I was fucking his wife.'

Pascoe felt a pang of sympathy, quickly suppressed. Sympathy was not on today's agenda.

'How much of this did Youngman know?'

'I've no idea. I never told him. I don't know about Kilda. He came to see us when he got back to the UK. It was, I believe, a simple act of kindness, of duty even, one soldier looking out for another. He came back several times. We wanted him to. Sometimes he saw us together, sometimes separately. Gradually he passed on more and more detail of what they'd actually done to Chris. Whatever his motives were originally, I think at some point he started assessing our readiness to be recruited to the Templars.'

'And you passed the test with flying colours,' said Pascoe. 'Maurice, what the hell were you thinking of? This is crazy stuff! This is torchlight processions and master-race mythology! From what I've seen of you, it's just not your sort of thing at all!'

He'd picked the right tone. Kentmore raised his head and looked straight at him.

'You're right,' he said. 'I was a bit crazy, I think. It was Kilda. No, I'm not blaming her. After Chris's

517

death, she went very strange. Started drinking heavily, practically stopped eating. In fact, if it hadn't been for the bit of nourishment she got from the booze, I think she may have starved herself to death. Last thing Chris said to me was, "Look after Kilda," and pretty soon I was thinking that, just as I'd betrayed him while he was alive, I was going to let him down now he was dead. Then things began to change.'

'After Youngman came?' Pascoe guessed.

'Yes. Not at first, but eventually, as he became a fairly regular visitor, she seemed to get herself together. Didn't stop the drinking, but started taking on board enough food to pull herself back from the brink. He broached this Templar stuff with her first and she mentioned it to me. I was furious, but when she saw that she clammed up. Things had been strained between us since it happened. We never . . . did it again. There was no way either of us could think of each other in that way after what happened. But somehow we were bound closer than we'd ever been . . . bound on a wheel of fire . . . don't know why that came into my mind . . . something I read at school . . . but now I knew what it meant . . . and at the same time I think we hated each other for being part of the pain. Then when she started on about the Templars, for the first time in a long time she opened up like she'd done in the old days. And I cut her off short.'

He shook his head as though to dislodge the memory.

'So next time it came up, you listened, because you'd promised your brother to take care of her,' prompted Pascoe, keen to get beyond naked souls to naked fact.

'Yes, I listened. And I listened to Youngman. Look, I'm not saying I got involved simply because of Kilda. I was off balance myself, and I'd felt for a long time that politically we were pretty wishy-washy in our response to the terrorism, and the idea of fighting fire with fire had a lot of appeal. Also to start with it seemed like a game. Secret names, special ways of contacting each other, it was . . . I don't know, it was sort of fun.'

'Like Stalky and Co, you mean?' said Pascoe savagely. 'Like being back at boarding school? And when you discovered your particular mission was to blow up a video shop in Mill Street and murder the men who ran it, did it still seem like fun?'

'It seemed unreal. It was a step-by-step thing. At first it was just a matter of leaving a small bomb in the shop and doing a lot of damage. This was a terrorist operations centre, Youngman said. People came here to get instructions, to discuss targets, to plan attacks.'

'How did he know this? Why did you believe him?'

'He was convincing. He showed us photographs and documents, copies of Security Service reports.'

'Where did he get these?'

Kentmore shrugged.

'There was a contact inside the Service, he said.

He implied this came close to unofficial official approval.'

'Any name?'

'He just referred to him as Bernard.'

'*Bernard*?'

Bernie Bloomfield? Could it be that simple?

'Yes. After St Bernard. He was the big religious name behind the Templars, I gather. The one who provided their moral justification.'

'Ah yes, that Bernard,' said Pascoe.

So not that simple. Unless of course this was a CAT joke. Not much different from Freeman using Wills and Croft.

He said, 'So the plan was . . . ?'

'First to get into the video shop. There was a window open on the side of the end house of the terrace. Once in, we got up into the roof space and worked our way along.'

'Were you expecting to find anyone in the shop?'

'Possibly. It was Bank Holiday, but terrorists don't keep Bank Holidays, said Youngman. So like boy scouts we should be prepared. He provided us with guns.'

'And a bomb.'

'Yes. And a bomb. It didn't look like much. Just a small plastic box. The kind of thing you'd put sandwiches in. Youngman said it would wreck the room it was placed in. I said, what if there were someone in the room? He said anyone in there would be the kind of bastard who'd tortured and murdered my brother, so where was my problem?'

'And you said?'

'I said I didn't have one,' replied Kentmore in a low voice. 'And I didn't. But I still hoped the place might be empty.'

'But it wasn't.'

'No. When we got into Number 3, we found two men there already. They were totally flabbergasted when we appeared. They offered no resistance. I tied them up and gagged them. As I was finishing the job, we heard a noise downstairs. Kilda said she'd take a look. A little later there was a shot. I nearly died of shock. I went to the door and was just going to call down when I heard voices. I stood there, not certain what to do. But eventually Kilda came up the stairs with another Asian and told me to tie him up too.'

Which you did, thought Pascoe. Probably relieved to have someone telling you what to do. In a crisis, everyone finds their level.

He said, 'What did Kilda say had happened?'

'She'd found this other man in the shop and pointed her gun at him and told him to go upstairs. When he realized she was a woman, he'd laughed and said he wasn't frightened of a replica, human or mechanical. So Kilda fired a shot past his ear and asked him if he still wasn't frightened. Then the door opened and your man came in.'

Hector. Who'd said the 'man' with the gun *looked funny*. Why didn't I pay more heed to Hector? Pascoe asked himself savagely.

'Kilda said he didn't seem at all certain what to do,' continued Kentmore. 'She moved back into the shadows and lowered the gun, but kept the other man covered. Knowing what was stowed away in the shop, he wouldn't have been keen to involve the police anyway. Probably he thought there was a burglary going on. Last thing terrorists expect is to be terrorized, that's what Youngman said. So when the constable asked if everything was all right, he said yes, it was, and your man left.'

'And your reaction was?'

'To get away from there as quickly as possible. After I'd tied the third man up, I looked out of the window and nearly died when I saw a police patrol car outside. I told Kilda we had to get out, which we did, via the roof space again.'

'But you left the bomb behind?'

Kentmore sighed and rubbed his eyes and said, 'I simply forgot all about it. Kilda had been carrying it. When I asked her, she said she'd put it down as planned.'

'And then you sent the signal that exploded it?'

He said, 'Not straight away. Kilda wanted to, but I said no, not while there was any chance that a policeman could be on the premises.'

'That was kind of you,' said Pascoe.

The sarcasm slipped out. He didn't want to antagonize Kentmore, not till he'd got all he could out of him. But he needn't have worried.

'We argued,' said Kentmore, as if he hadn't heard the interruption. 'I insisted we talked to

Youngman. There was this silly procedure with texts and code names. When we finally spoke, I told him what had happened. He told me to wait and rang off. About half an hour later he rang back and said it was OK, all taken care of, there would be no policemen in the building, and any outside would be a safe distance away. I was still doubtful, but Kilda said I was being stupid. And without further ado, she sent the signal.'

'Ah,' said Pascoe. 'So it was Kilda's fault, not yours.'

This time the sarcasm got through.

'If you imagine I am trying to dilute my share of responsibility, you're a fool,' said Kentmore wearily. 'If anything, I'm much more guilty. From the start, Kilda has been in a very disturbed state of mind. I make no such claim. Everything I have done I have done with my eyes wide open. Earlier you accused me of treating it like a game. That was how it felt. Now I can see what a stupid, pathetic game it was. I saw it from the moment I heard about the extent of the explosion, and the injuries to you and your colleague. Since then I've gone about my business as normal, as if by so doing I could help make come true what I prayed for every morning and night. That your friend, Superintendent Dalziel, would make a complete recovery.'

'That's nice. Pity God's choosey about whose prayers he answers.'

'Mr Pascoe, believe me, there's nothing you can say that can match what I feel about myself.

I was stupid. He paid the price. But even though I know how wrong I was, I still believe there are questions that need to be asked. If, as I believe, the invasion of Iraq was justified and men like my brother died fighting a just war, then, as a citizen of the country he died to defend, aren't I right in expecting our security forces to attack the enemy who killed Chris with every weapon at their disposal, within or without the law?'

Curiously this stilted expression of a right-wing tabloid viewpoint touched Pascoe more than anything else he'd heard from the man. How many nights had the poor bastard lain awake desperately trying to formulate a defence which played better than *I was fucking my brother's wife so when she said, 'Let's kill some Abs,' I went along with it?*

'Needs a bit of work on the syntax,' he said. 'But once the *Voice* has reduced it to tabloidese, you could have the jury waving Union Jacks and singing "Land of Hope and Glory". Mind you, the same flag-wavers will probably be screaming for your public execution. Juries, God bless 'em, don't like cop-killers.'

He paused, judged that Kentmore was as softened up as he was going to be, and moved into direct interrogation mode.

'So who do you know besides Youngman?'

'No one. He was our only contact. Referring to others he always used Templar names. The one pulling the strings was called Hugh, after Hugh de Payens, the first Grandmaster of the Order.'

'When did you last see Youngman?'

'On that Bank Holiday afternoon. We had a debriefing meeting arranged in Charter Park. I was very angry. I'd heard about the results of the explosion by then.'

'So no contact since?'

'I talked to him on the phone on Wednesday night, after I'd lunched with Ellie.'

'Why?'

'Because of PC Hector. Kilda had already told me he was in hospital. I believe she got the information from you at the fête. When she saw how agitated I was by the news she told me not to be silly, it was just a traffic accident. But I think she knew more.'

She knew it was a black Jag because I told her, thought Pascoe. And she knew Hector was making a good recovery. And she probably passed on this info to Youngman, which was why he decided to finish off the job in the hospital. Shit! I have not been a friend to poor old Hector in all this!

Kentmore was still speaking.

'Then at the start of the week, the papers, the *Voice* anyway, were hinting that an attempt had been made on a policeman's life in the Central. Now I was seriously concerned. This wasn't collateral damage, this was attempted murder. I arranged to see Ellie in the hope that I could get some details. When I told Kilda, she seemed to approve the idea. Probably she was hoping to pick up more information useful to Youngman.'

525

'And did you find out anything?'

'Don't worry. Ellie was very discreet. But I was able to work out from what she said that an attempt had been made and the target was PC Hector. Afterwards I tried to contact Youngman. But his mobile wasn't responding. Kilda said he'd probably dumped it because he was on the run as a result of what happened at the hospital. She also said I should be grateful rather than angry. Hugh had decided Hector had to be dealt with because he might be able to identify her, and once he'd done that, the police would be on to me in no time.'

'And were you grateful?'

'No. I've told you, I was horrified.'

'So horrified you did . . . what? Sent yourself to bed without any supper?'

'No,' said Kentmore. 'I went about my business. Things were out of my control. In fact I could see they'd never been in my control. But at least Hector and Mr Dalziel were still alive. And with Youngman on the run, surely the men behind the Templars would call their campaign off? Above all I told myself I still owed it to Chris not to let Kilda down. I just wanted to immerse myself in Haresyke, to cut all links with what had happened. Several times I picked up the phone to cancel lunch with you and Ellie.'

'So why didn't you?'

'Because, no matter how I rationalized everything, part of me still said I had to act. I came along today half believing I could tell you everything.

But it's so hard. It had been such a nice lunch, it seemed a shame to spoil it – funny what banalities we use to divert us from unpleasant duties. And then your friend arrived. Oh Jesus, Peter, believe me, there's nothing that has happened that I can use to dilute my responsibility for Mr Dalziel's death. There's no punishment you can impose which will make me feel worse.'

It was an outburst to make a jury cry, but Pascoe was not in a tearful mood.

'Yeah, yeah,' he said. 'So do you have any idea where Youngman might be now?'

Kentmore hesitated then said, 'No. How could I? I presume, if he's got any sense, with you people on his tail, he'll have got out of the country.'

Sometimes a thing is so obvious it has to be pushed in your face at least three times before you notice it.

Pascoe said, 'How do you know he's on the run? Hang on . . . You said before that when you couldn't get through to him on Wednesday after your lunch with Ellie, Kilda said he'd probably dumped his mobile because he was on the run, right? So how did *she* know? It hasn't been in the papers or on the news.'

He leaned forward to bring his face close to Kentmore's.

'He's holed up at the Gatehouse with Kilda, isn't he? That's why she didn't come today. Not a sodding migraine, she's too busy giving shelter and comfort and God knows what fucking else to that madman. Did she tell you to keep the date, though, to see what you could find out? Is that why you're here?'

Kentmore shook his head and said, 'No . . . I don't know . . . I mean, I haven't seen him, but when I called at the house earlier in the week she didn't ask me in and I got to wondering . . . We've spoken on the phone since. I put it to her and she said I didn't want to know. Maybe she was trying to protect me . . .'

'You really think she gives a toss about you?' said Pascoe.

'Perhaps not,' said Kentmore wearily. 'But when you're bound together on a wheel of fire . . . The truth is, I think I've been deluding myself for a long time that I could understand Kilda, that I could help save her from herself. The only spark of life that exists in her was lit by Youngman – that's one of the reasons I went along with his crazy scheme. I was wrong. God forgive me. Now I have to pay for it.'

'Great. OK, let's go and start you paying the first instalment, shall we?'

He stood up, pulled Kentmore to his feet, and urged the man off the patio, across the living room and into the kitchen.

Wield and Ellie were sitting opposite each other at the breakfast table. They both clutched glasses of whisky in their hands. Ellie leapt to her feet when she saw him. He had seen her angry before but never like this. She came at him so violently he brought his forearm up to ward off a physical attack, but she stopped a couple of feet away and hissed, 'You bastard!'

Then she threw the contents of her glass into his face.

The raw spirit stung his eyes. He rubbed at them with the back of his hand and gasped, 'I'm sorry.'

'Not yet, you're not. What if Rosie had been here? Would that have made any difference?'

'Yes. No. I don't know . . . we'll talk later . . . I'm sorry, I don't have the time now . . .'

'You don't have the time . . . ?' she yelled, but he wasn't paying attention.

'Wieldy, take this one in to the factory, book him in and lock him up, and don't let anyone near him till I say so, OK?'

'Sure,' said Wield. He didn't look very happy.

'So your little trick worked?' snarled Ellie. 'And that makes everything OK?'

'I don't know,' said Pascoe. 'Not yet.'

Kentmore was looking from one to the other in bewilderment.

'What's going on?' he said. 'What trick?'

'Oh, sorry, bit of a mistake,' said Pascoe. 'Wires crossed. Seems Andy Dalziel's not dead after all, right, Wieldy?'

'Right,' said Wield. 'In fact, like I was just telling Ellie, the news is a bit better. Seems he actually opened his eyes, looked at the nurse who was giving him a bed bath, said, "You missed a bit, luv," and then went to sleep. But they reckon that's what it is this time, sleep, different brain patterns from before or summat.'

For a long moment Kentmore looked stunned, as if this news were harder to take in than the lie about Dalziel's death.

Then he sagged down on to a chair and said brokenly, 'Thank God. Thank God.'

'Right response,' said Pascoe. 'Make sure he gets a cup of tea and a chocolate digestive, Wieldy. Now I've got to go.'

Ellie's anger was still there but now it was joined by concern.

'What's going on?' she cried. 'Why are you doing this? Where are you going?'

Pascoe shook his head. Every impulse but one urged him to put his arms around her and beg her forgiveness. The single exception told him he was running out of time. To do what, to prevent what, he wasn't certain. But it could not be denied.

'I don't have the time,' he said. 'I really don't.'

He headed into the hallway and out of the front door.

As he slid into his car, Wield called, 'Shall I contact Glenister?'

'No!' shouted Pascoe. 'Definitely not. No one at CAT. Not a single one of them!'

He saw Ellie standing behind Wield, her face wracked with a conflict of emotions.

He dragged his gaze away and sent the car hurtling down the drive.

3

singles

'Hugh.'

'Andre.'

'De Payens.'

'De Montbard.'

one thousand two thousand three thousand

'Everything all right?'

'Yeah. I'm very comfortable.'

'Don't get too comfortable. You're on your way. East Midlands zero six thirty hours, singles holiday to Alicante so you won't stand out. Room booked at the EM Hilton tonight, package to pick up at the desk with passport, tickets, euros.'

'And then?'

'Head down for a while. No long-term problem. Bernard says eventually you'll be recruited. Once you're on the books officially, the slate's wiped clean.'

'Nice. So this means our mad mullah gets an extension?'

'I thought I'd made that clear. Bernard says let

the dust settle. You've got Geoffrey O under control?'

'Absolutely.'

'Good. Bon voyage then.'

'Cheers.'

Jonty Youngman switched the phone off and looked at Kilda.

'That's it confirmed,' he said. 'I'm off to brown my knees in the sunshine, everything here stays cool. Orders.'

'Do you always obey orders?'

'Oh yes.'

'You didn't when you went in after Chris.'

'That was different.'

'No. Nothing's different. Everything's always the same.'

He regarded her thoughtfully. Normally women didn't baffle him because he wasn't interested in what they were thinking. They were soft machinery, a pleasurable arrangement of moving parts. But, maybe because he'd never managed to get hold of any of Kilda's moving parts, he found himself from time to time trying to get a grip on her thought processes.

'You want I should tell you what I did to that Ab again?' he asked.

When first he told her the details of how he'd killed the man who'd tortured her husband, he'd thought she was finding it a sexual turn-on, but she'd soon disabused him of that notion. It certainly did something to her though.

She shook her head.

'No. I'm beyond that,' she said. 'So Hugh says you've got to go, and you've got to go quietly, is that it?'

'That's it.'

'He must be a pretty scary guy to make someone like you jump.'

'Scary enough, but it's not Hugh who bothers me here. This guy Bernard, don't know who he is but I do know a slap on the wrist from him would likely take my hand off.'

'Did Hugh pass on any instructions from scary Bernard about me?'

'Says I should kill you before I go.'

He usually found it hard to get a reaction from Kilda, but that did it.

He let her think he was serious for a moment then laughed.

'Only joking.'

'You're sure?'

'Yeah, if I killed you then I'd have to off your bro-in-law too, and I don't have the time. Anyway, I told Hugh I had you under control.'

'He believed you?'

'He thinks I'm shagging you rotten.'

'You told him that?'

'Didn't need to. Just assumes anything shaggable comes my way, I'll have a slice.'

He grinned and went on, 'Should have thought of that when he introduced me to his mam. Many a good tune played on an old fiddle.'

'He didn't mind?'

'He didn't know. You don't think of your old mam as shaggable, do you? Not unless you're seriously bent.'

She looked at him over her coffee cup.

'I can honestly say I don't think I've ever met anyone like you, Jonty.'

'You're pretty unique yourself,' he said. 'In two ways at least.'

'Which are?'

'One, you hate Abdul even more than I do. And, two, you're the first woman I fancied fucking that I didn't.'

She smiled coldly and said, 'Into every life a little rain must fall. Which reminds me, I should be on my cloudy way.'

'Don't forget your camera,' he said.

She picked the Nikon up from the table.

'It's all fixed, is it?'

'You're the photographer. You just point and click.'

'Will you get into trouble for this?'

'You really bothered?'

'Not really.'

'Thought not. So why bother with something that doesn't bother you?'

'What bothers you, Jonty?'

'Not a lot.'

'So why did you get involved?'

He shrugged.

534

'Needed something to do when the Service dumped me. Till then, skirt and offing Abdul had been enough. Now I just had skirt. Man needs more than skirt.'

'You could have joined the BNP.'

He laughed derisively.

'Bunch of wankers. All mouth and beating up kids and women. Let them get a sniff of real action and they'd shit themselves.'

'Is that why you started writing your books? Because you missed the real action?'

'I suppose. Don't reckon much to that analysis stuff. But when I saw the chance to get back into the action, no, I didn't hesitate. So that's me. How about you?'

'What about me?'

He said, 'Normally I'm not much interested in what goes on in a tart's head, 'cos it's like chasing a gnat in a dust storm. But you've been the one exception, so you might as well be another. You were so crazy about Chris that losing him's driven you a bit crazy, right? So why did you fuck his brother?'

For a moment he thought she wasn't going to answer. She rose, picked up the camera and went to the door. Then she paused and without turning said, 'It was my wedding anniversary. Maurice had been best man. He said I shouldn't be alone on that day and he took me out for a drive to the coast, then we had a meal together and when we got back we had a couple of drinks at the Hall, and looked at some photos and talked about Chris and who said what at the wedding. I think we both had a bit more to drink than we were used to. I realized how much when I went to the loo, but I bathed my face in cold water and thought I was OK. Then I came out of the bathroom and a little further down the landing Maurice was just coming out of his bedroom. It was a trick of the light, or a trick of the drink, or a trick of the imagination overheated by all that talk of my wedding day, whatever, it all combined and for a moment he was Chris, or so like Chris it seemed to make no difference. From us grabbing hold of each other to him rolling off me and us lying there naked realizing what we had just done seemed like the blink of an eye. And I hadn't had time to really start feeling guilty when the phone rang. Later it felt like what I did made it ring. I know that's stupid. The phone would have rung just as surely if I'd gone straight home. But at least I'd have been there to answer it . . .'

Now she turned to look at him.

'There,' she said. 'That make you happier?'

'No,' he said. 'I don't do happiness. Just oblivion. Sex and offing Abdul does that for me.'

'I need something a bit longer lasting,' she said.

'I know. Good luck.'

'You too. You won't hang around here too long, will you? They'll come looking.'

'Not for an hour or so. I'll be long gone. Kilda,

536

you sure about this? You could come with me, no strings . . .'

'There's always strings, Jonty. I just want to cut the last of them.'

'Sure?'

'What else do I have to be sure about?'

She left.

Not even a goodbye kiss, thought Youngman.

What the hell. There was no shortage of available women, especially if you were going on a singles holiday.

He finished his coffee and then went upstairs to start putting his gear together.

4

snapshots

As he headed west, Pascoe shouted a number into his voice-activated car phone.

God was good to him. He knew most of the officers on Harrogate CID but the voice which answered was the one he most hoped to hear.

'Harrogate CID, DI Collaboy speaking. How can I help you?'

'Very good, Jim,' he said. 'Very user-friendly. You must have been on the etiquette course.'

'Who the fuck's that?'

'Oh dear. Think we may need a refresher. Pete Pascoe here.'

'Thought I recognized that poncy voice. How do, Pete? How're they hanging?'

'Low and swinging free. Listen, Jim, you may have a situation. You know Haresyke Hall. Well, it's the Gatehouse . . .'

He gave a brief outline, ending, 'Hopefully you won't need it, but I'd rustle up an ARU if you can.'

'Jesus. I'd seen something asking us to keep our eyes skinned for this guy Youngman, but I didn't realize it was that serious.'

'CAT policy, they don't want to scare the shit out of the citizens.'

'So they keep honest cops in the dark? Great thinking. This woman, the sister-in-law, who lives there, she's in the frame too? So no hostage situation.'

'She's in the frame, sure, but that doesn't mean Youngman won't threaten to slit her throat. He's an ex-SAS hard case, so be very careful.'

'You're on your way, you say?' replied Collaboy. 'In that case I'll be so fucking careful, I'll do nowt till you show your pretty face. That way, if it goes well, I can take the credit, and if it goes pear-shaped, you can take the blame. Talking of which, I've just brought this Youngman character up on my computer and it says any sighting, inform CAT before action. You got that in hand, have you?'

'This isn't a sighting, Jim. Just a vague possibility.'

'Which you want me to vaguely support with some vaguely armed back-up? You pulling my plonker, Pete?'

'You never complained before. Look, leave CAT to me, OK? I'll see everyone who needs to know gets to know.'

'OK,' said Collaboy dubiously. 'But I'll need that in joined-up writing when you get here. My ex will be very unhappy indeed if I lose my pension.'

'Not all bad then,' said Pascoe. 'Cheers, mate.'

Cheers, mate, he echoed in his mind as he switched off. Soon as he'd heard Collaboy's voice he'd slipped into a saloon-bar modality, no conscious decision necessary, just a simple sound trigger.

Truly, he thought, I am the great chameleon. Fat Andy and Wieldy are themselves whoever they speak to, but me, I change shape and colour and idiom according to my company. Which is very useful, but does make it difficult to put your finger on the real me. Was it, for example, the real me who'd cruelly deceived Ellie into thinking Dalziel was dead? And does it make it better or worse that I knew her pain would not be so much at losing the Fat Man, though that would be painful enough, but the greater and more intense part would derive from her empathy with my imagined sense of loss?

Worse, he decided without much debate. It makes it much worse.

When this is over I'm going to change, he assured himself. It's Mill Street that has done this to me. I'll take the tablets, go on a counselling course, turn back the clock, be *me* again.

Which brings me back to the first question. Who is *me?*

He pushed these introspective musings to the back of his mind and concentrated on finding the quickest way through the Saturday-afternoon traffic which, though lighter than on a weekday, made up in unpredictability what it lost in intensity. What did these people do with their cars for the rest of the week? he wondered as he aggressively overtook a yellow Beetle holding the centre of the road with all the unconcerned assurance of a Panzer troop rolling into an undefended Belgian village.

His trip to the fête had taught him the quickest route. Out of Harrogate he took the Pateley Bridge road. As he passed Burnt Yates, the name slipped his mind back to A-Level English. *Human kind cannot bear very much reality.* That's why they have policemen, he thought. To bear the reality for the rest of the sods!

Now he was off the main road and, after passing through the village of Haresyke, he rolled up to a *Road Closed* sign with an attendant constable. Jim Collaboy gave an impression of comfortable inertia, but he didn't hang about.

Pascoe identified himself and the officer told him that the DI and his team were round the next bend about three hundred yards short of the entrance to Haresyke Hall.

The ARU team had parked a couple of hundred yards down the track. As Pascoe pulled in behind the ARU vehicles, he was reminded of the previous Sunday up in Northumberland. How long ago that seemed! How furious Ellie had been at his involvement. She hated guns and everything associated with them. Now here he was again, in pursuit of the same prey, once more rendezvousing with armed men in visored helmets and bullet-proof vests.

Jim Collaboy came forward to meet him.

He looked older than his forty years, with grey receding hair and a pouched and patchy face which hung on his broad cheekbones like a badly fitting mask.

'How do, Jim,' said Pascoe, shaking hands. 'You've moved bloody quick for a fat old fart.'

'Less of the *old*,' said Collaboy. 'Thought I'd leave you to do the briefing as I'd only be showing my ignorance.'

'Fine,' said Pascoe.

The sergeant in charge of the ARU was polished chalk to Collaboy's blue-veined cheese, with features which would not have looked out of place on an Elgin Marble. Even his name, Axon, had a Greek ring.

Pascoe spoke to him with crisp authority, thinking, Here I go again!

'Possible occupants, two persons, a man and a woman. The man is SAS-trained, a war veteran, expert in small arms and explosives. He should be regarded as potentially very dangerous. The woman has no weapons background that I know of, but she is possibly unstable and has shown herself ready and able to use violence. It is almost certain that the man will be armed.'

'Likely level of resistance, sir?' asked the sergeant in a surprisingly soft and gentle voice.

Pascoe hesitated, rehearsing what he knew of Youngman.

'I'd guess the man will be reluctant to get involved in a fire-fight. Firstly, because his quarrel is not with the police. Secondly, because realistically he knows he can't win.'

'And the woman?'

'Less capacity to resist, but less realism too.'

'Any chance he'll try to make her a hostage?'

'Possibly. But we shouldn't forget she is no innocent bystander,' said Pascoe. 'She is his accomplice. We do not negotiate with criminals because they are threatening each other.'

'Yes, sir. Procedure?'

This was the moment of choice. Hit the house hard and take them by surprise, or open up lines of communication?

If he was right and Youngman would be realistic enough to assess the odds and act accordingly, it had to be the latter.

Also, he admitted to himself, in these situations he was always reluctant to order other men to take risks he wasn't sharing, and if Youngman did decide not to come quietly, the risks could be great. ARU training was hard but it was kindergarten stuff compared with what you needed to get into the SAS.

'Dispose your men so that the building is completely covered, then I'll talk to him,' said Pascoe. 'No shooting except on my command.'

'Except if life is threatened,' said Sergeant Axon, wanting to hear him say it.

'Naturally.'

'Right,' said the sergeant and went to join his men.

Ten minutes later he returned to say, 'All in position. Some movement inside. So far only confirmation of one inmate.'

'Male or female?'

Axon shrugged.

'OK. Lead on.'

Pascoe followed the sergeant into a small beech copse. When the cottage came in sight, they halted behind a tree broad enough to absorb rounds from most small arms.

Collaboy gave him a field phone with a recording facility. You never knew how long a negotiation might take and it was as well to be able to check what both sides had said.

'Number?' he asked.

Collaboy gave it to him. Good old efficient Jim.

He punched it into the keypad.

The insistent shrill of the phone came floating out of the cottage's open windows.

On the fourth ring it was answered.

'Hi. Youngman here.'

He sounded very relaxed.

'Mr Youngman. This is Detective Chief Inspector Pascoe.'

'Thought it might be. Real early bird, aren't you?'

That was interesting.

Pascoe said, 'Mr Youngman, I'm ringing to tell you that the cottage is surrounded by armed officers . . .'

'I know,' the voice cut in. 'Been watching them

get into place for the last twenty minutes. Way those lads move, they're not going to win many prizes on *Celebrity Come Dancing*!'

'Perhaps not, but they are all expert marksmen, and they have instructions to shoot unless my instructions are carried out to the letter.'

'Fair enough. Instruct away.'

'First of all, is Mrs Kentmore there with you?'

'Kilda? No, sorry. She was, but she went off earlier. Had some shopping to do, I expect. You know women. If it's not sex, it's shopping. Any excuse. Sales, birthday, something for a wedding. I told her that she ought to stay put, but you're a married man, Chief Inspector, you must know that once a woman gets an idea in her head it would take an M19 to knock it out. Us servants of the Crown, we just follow orders, but a woman does whatever fucking well takes her fancy.'

The tone was mocking. Was he simply taking the piss or was he actually lying about Kilda's departure?

Why would he lie? Pascoe asked himself. So that he can show his face and lure us into the open, then Kilda springs an ambush?

Not likely, not unless Youngman himself was looking to go out in a blaze of glory, and from what Pascoe had read about him, he didn't sound like the suicidal type.

'OK. Here's what you do,' he said. 'I want you to remove your shirt and your trousers. Open the front door and come out with your hands on your

545

head. Advance six paces, then halt and wait for further instructions.'

'Don't want my Y-fronts off too? Folk have been surprised what I've got hidden down there.'

'No. Keep them on. But I hope you don't find uniforms a turn-on,' said Pascoe. 'You get twitchy, my marksmen could get twitchy too.'

He was doing his chameleon act again, slipping into the mode which seemed best suited for getting the job done.

Youngman laughed and said, 'I'm on my way. See you soon.'

The phone went dead. A few moments later, the front door opened.

'Coming out,' called a voice.

Then Youngman emerged, hands on head, stripped down to his underpants. He marched forward six paces and did a parodic military halt.

'OK, Sergeant,' said Pascoe. 'Over to you.'

There was the usual yelling and shouting and kicking open of doors and clatter of running feet which ended with Youngman lying on his face, his hands cuffed behind his back, and Axon reporting to Pascoe, 'Cottage clear, sir. No one else present.'

'Good work, Sergeant,' said Pascoe. 'Jim, you and your boys start searching the place. No nasty surprises lying around, I hope, Mr Youngman?'

Youngman rolled over on his back, looked up at him and grinned.

'Wouldn't dream of it, Chief Inspector.'

'Good.' He stooped to whisper directly into the

man's ear. 'But if it turns out you're lying, I'm going to cut your balls off.'

'That's tough talk, Mr Pascoe. But could you really do it?'

'Oh yes,' said Pascoe, straightening up.

The recumbent man regarded him thoughtfully then said, 'Yeah, maybe you could, but we're not going to find out today. No nasty surprises. Apart from yourself, of course. Didn't think you'd get here for another hour at least . . . Hold on, I've got it. It's Maurice, right? You were having lunch with him and you got him to talk. Knew he was a bit limp, but didn't think he'd drop Kilda in it.'

'Sometimes a man's conscience speaks even more loudly than family loyalty,' said Pascoe, deliberately sententious. There was no way he could maintain the hard-man role once this got official, and he didn't doubt that Youngman had been trained to withstand interrogation techniques far beyond anything he could bring to bear. But let him think you were a bit of a pompous plonker, get him to feel superior . . .

But he saw instantly that wasn't going to get him anywhere either.

Youngman grinned up at him and gave him an exaggerated wink.

'Oh yes, I can see all the stuff I've heard about you's true, Mr Pascoe. You're a one to watch. So that's it from me, nothing more but name and number.'

'You're not a prisoner of war,' said Pascoe.

'Aren't I? In that case, shouldn't you be telling me something about the right to remain silent? Which is a right I'm fucking well exercising till I've got my lawyer present.'

For a man lying almost naked at the feet of his captor, who he must know had evidence enough to put him away for a very long time, he sounded surprisingly unconcerned.

He knows that CAT are going to take control of him as soon as they get wind of this, thought Pascoe. And he reckons that, once he's in their hands, he's going to get a much better deal than he can expect from me.

So, back to hard man.

He said to Sergeant Axon, 'Get him into a car, wrap a blanket around him. Any move he makes that you haven't OK'd should be treated as an escape attempt. Warn him, then shoot him. My authority.'

He went into the house where Collaboy and a couple of uniformed officers had begun their search. The DI wasn't happy.

'Should we be doing this, Pete?' he asked. 'Won't CAT want to have a clean scene when they show up? At least I ought to call up a SOCO team.'

'It's not a crime scene, Jim,' nit-picked Pascoe. 'As for CAT, I'll take full responsibility. I've been seconded to them since getting back to work, didn't you know that?'

'Heard something,' said Collaboy.

'Cheer up,' said Pascoe, not happy at trying to

mislead his colleague. 'Your patch, your collar. Now let's see what we can find.'

'Sir!' called a constable from upstairs.

He was in a small single bedroom. There was a grip on the bed in which Youngman had been packing his clothes. The constable had pulled open the drawers in a dressing table. In one of them lay a 9mm Beretta and several clips of ammo. In the other was a bundle of what looked to Pascoe's inexpert eye like detonators alongside a plastic box containing a quantity of grey clay-like material.

'Sex-aids?' said Collaboy.

'I think we'd better get the bomb squad out here,' said Pascoe. 'Close this room up, but let's carry on looking elsewhere.'

Next door was another, larger bedroom, clearly the woman's. There was nothing to suggest they'd been sharing a bed, which was interesting in view of Youngman's reputation. Further along the landing Pascoe found a door that was locked. He didn't waste time looking for a key but kicked it open with his heel. It turned out to be Kilda's dark-room. There were shelves lined with photographic materials and a variety of cameras. She was evidently technically as well as artistically proficient, for on a work surface by the sink Pascoe spotted the innards of a camera, removed presumably for modification or repair. But he didn't waste much time looking at this for, out of the corner of his eye, he glimpsed something strangely familiar.

And when he turned to look at the wall half-hidden by the open door, he saw it was covered by photo prints, half a dozen of which featured his own face.

A man frozen in the act of stuffing a wedge of Victoria sponge into his gob doesn't look his best, he observed critically. But they were good pictures and they'd caught the bright delight in his eyes that sprang both from the pleasure of eating and the pleasure of Kilda's company. For a brief moment he relived the magic moment that had followed, when they'd sat at the still point of the turning world in a silence more potent than music.

Then his gaze drifted to the other pictures displayed here and the moment was dispelled more completely than it had been by the terriers' distant cacophony.

There were other mementoes of the fête here. Ellie looking quizzical, Kentmore determinedly hearty, Rosie obstinate, Sarhadi and Jamila smiling and happy. And these fête pictures were surrounded by others less clearly focused as though taken through a long lens by a hand-held camera, pictures which showed the Marrside Mosque and a bearded man coming out and ducking into a waiting car.

Sheikh Ibrahim. And Pascoe did not doubt that this was the same day that someone had put a bullet into the rear light of his car, not the bullet of a professional like Youngman which would have been from a high-powered perfectly zeroed sniper's rifle.

No, this had been a bullet fired opportunisti-
cally, a bullet from a 9mm Beretta, the same kind
of pistol that they'd found in the cottage and that
Kilda had used in Mill Street.

Pascoe hurried out of the dark room and went
downstairs and out of the house. The phone he'd
used to ring Youngman rested where he'd laid it.

He rewound the tape and played it.

*Kilda? No, sorry. She was, but she went off earlier.
Had some shopping to do, I expect. You know
women. If it's not sex, it's shopping. Any excuse.
Sales, birthday, something for a wedding. I told
her that she ought to stay put, but you're a married
man, Chief Inspector. you must know that once a
woman gets an idea in her head it would take an
M19 to knock it out. Us servants of the Crown,
we just follow orders, but a woman does whatever fucking well takes her fancy.*

And he recalled what the man had said as he
lay on his back, smiling up at him.

*No nasty surprises. Apart from yourself, of course.
Didn't expect you till later . . .*

Why should he have been expecting the police
would turn up at the Gatehouse some time that
day?

'Oh shit,' said Pascoe.

He started to run towards his car.

Behind him, Collaboy yelled, 'Pete!'

He paused and looked back. The DI had his mobile to his ear.

'What?'

Collaboy lowered the phone and muffled it with his hand.

'I've got Bagshit here. He's heard about me calling up an ARU and he wants to know what the fuck's going on.'

Superintendent Bagshott of Harrogate was notorious for being a stickler for proper procedure as well as being a great snapper-up of other officers' credit.

'What have you told him?' yelled Pascoe.

'The truth, dickhead. What else would I tell him? He wants to speak to you.'

'Tell him the truth again,' cried Pascoe. 'Tell him I'm not here.'

'But you are . . .'

Then Collaboy realized that Pascoe wasn't asking him to lie.

The DCI had vanished from sight at a fast run and a moment later all that indicated he'd ever been there was the scream of an over-revved engine fading away on the rich summer air.

5

wedding gifts

So now I'm a married man, thought Kalim Sarhadi.

Throughout the ceremony he had felt curiously disconnected, more like a casual onlooker than one of the main participants. His even stronger sense of disconnection from Jamila hadn't helped. A few weeks ago she'd announced that she wasn't going to wear the white bridal gown usually favoured in marriages in the West, but a traditional *shalwar-qameez* outfit. He'd been amused, thinking her main motive was to take the bangers by surprise, but when he saw her, he'd been struck dumb. In Western white she would doubtless have looked beautiful, but in scarlet silk richly embroidered with heavy gold thread, she was an exotic jewel. He could not believe this lovely creature was his Jamila. In his sharp grey suit and brilliant white shirt he felt shabby and out of place. It was as if he had entered one of the old stories in which a young man affianced since childhood to some unknown girl approaches his wedding day with considerable trepidation only to discover he has been contracted to a princess.

But he didn't want a princess, he wanted his Jamila.

The feeling of not-rightness persisted all the way to the Marrside Grange Hotel where he found himself enthroned alongside Jamila on a sofa raised on a shallow dais so that the assembled guests could see them together and approach them with congratulation and gifts. He turned towards her and she turned towards him. For a second they looked solemn-faced into each other's eyes, two complete strangers wondering what the future might bring.

Then she grinned and murmured, 'Any chance we can skip the nosh?' and suddenly she was his Jamila again.

He relaxed and began to enjoy his wedding day.

It was, as most second- and third-generation marriages were these days, a mix of old and new, of East and West.

The *Nikah* in the mosque had naturally followed the old established pattern, but once they'd moved on to the hotel for the *Walima*, tradition had been considerably rearranged. This enthronement was taking place before the actual *Walima* rather than after, and the *Walima* itself, which back in Pakistan traditionally consisted of two separate banquets, one for the men, one for the women, was going to be mixed.

'Don't care what they do over there,' Tottie had declared. 'Over here, them as pays the piper calls the tune.'

Any mutterings from fundamentalists had been stifled by the Sheikh's ready agreement to all the arrangements Tottie wanted to make. When Sarhadi thanked him for not raising any objection, he had replied with a smile, 'Fundamentalism is about substance, not form. Preserving old truths does not mean we cannot learn new tricks. And I dare say many of the old traditions will still be observed, if only by accident. For instance the one which declares that, strictly speaking, the *Walima* should not take place till after the marriage has been consummated.'

This hint that he knew how far Sarhadi and Jamila had gone in their very untraditional courtship had come as a shock. More likely it was just an educated guess. Thanks be to Allah that the bangers were not so educated.

His mother had greeted news of the Imam's accord with typical directness.

'Grand,' she'd said. 'Not that it 'ud have made a ha'porth of difference if the old bugger had said owt else.'

While Kalim never doubted that his mother's had been a true conversion, it was quite clear that the spirit of Allah had supplemented rather than replaced the spirit of Yorkshire independence.

Tottie was standing alongside the sofa-throne now, taking care of the gifts of money, most of which came in the form of notes or cheques, though some of the guests, harking back to the days when the bride was showered with coins, gave all or part of their offering in the form of purses stuffed with golden coins. The gift received and thanks given, any guests who looked inclined to linger too long were soon chivvied into the dining room by this redoubtable lady. There was no doubt who was in charge here. When Farrukh Khan, one of the group of young men who formed the Sheikh's unofficial bodyguard, tried to station himself behind the sofa, Tottie tapped his shoulder and with a jerk of her head sent him packing to join the pair of bangers who were checking on the guests entering the lounge.

The officious manner of most of these self-appointed guards got up Sarhadi's nose, but there was no escaping the fact that some lunatic had fired a gun at the Sheikh's car, so any occasion which involved his presence meant you had to put up with the bangers too.

By now the flow of guests was dying to a trickle and Tottie was glancing at her watch with the satisfaction of someone whose timetable was proving atomically accurate. She frowned as she saw Farrukh's bulky frame once more approaching the sofa, but the young man ignored her and said to Sarhadi, 'Got a woman outside trying to get in. Says she's a photographer and she knows you. You not been arranging another photographer, have you? My Uncle Asif's got the job, right?'

'Yeah, sure. What's her name?' asked Sarhadi, puzzled.

'Kent, something like that, I think. I'll tell her to push off.'

'No, hang on,' said Jamila. 'Kentmore, could it be? Kilda Kentmore?'

'That's right.'

'Kal, you remember her? Last week – she's the sister-in-law of that guy who was on the TV with you. We met her again at the fête. I talked with her a lot. She's a real photographer, Kal, did fashion, knows all the top models. If she wants to photograph us, let's ask her in.'

'What about Uncle Asif?' protested Farrukh.

'What about him?' said Jamila with spirit. 'Everyone knows he's going blind in one eye and that's the eye he puts to the viewfinder. I say you let Kilda in.'

Farrukh looked at Sarhadi. Tottie was one thing, but he wasn't about to start taking instructions from this mouthy girl.

Sarhadi said, 'Yeah. Why not? Let her through.'

6

hi-yo, Silver!

To average fifty plus miles per hour driving through urban West Yorkshire on a Saturday afternoon in the height of summer requires a lot of luck and a total disregard of law. In Pascoe's wake the law was in tatters, but fortunately so far his luck had held. He knew he was acting irrationally but rationality involved time.

Across his mind like a blizzard over an inland sea raged everything that had happened since Mill Street blew up. Because he'd feared – because deep down he'd *believed* – that Andy Dalziel was going to die, he had ploughed forward in what to start with had seemed a simple inexorable search for certainties.

Oh, what a dusty answer gets the soul . . .

He had made things happen, and the things he had made happen had made other things happen, so that in the end it wasn't a simple trail that he had followed, but a track many of whose twists and turns he had actually created. In trying to trace a line back from an effect to a cause he had himself become a cause and did not know if the place he was at now was a place that would have existed if he hadn't started on his quest, whether he was the Red Cross Knight riding to the rescue, or merely a bumbling Quixote, creating confusion rather than resolving it.

He would have liked nothing more than to pull over into a quiet lay-by, relax and let everything that had happened, everything he knew, or thought he knew, or merely guessed at, play across his mind till the surface lay still and the depths became clear.

But he just didn't have the time.

The first cause, the death of Dalziel, was no longer a cause.

Of course he only had Wield's second-hand account to assure him not only that the Fat Man had woken but that he had woken in his right mind. But somehow he felt certain that all was going to be well.

But how often did it happen that the starting point of a chain of action becomes irrelevant long before the end comes in sight?

No point in saying that, if Dalziel had woken up the day after the explosion, he would not be here now, desperately driving like a madman towards what he fervently prayed would be nothing more than a rendezvous with a few harmless windmills.

As he got through Skipton, his car phone rang.

'Yes!' he bellowed to activate the receiver.

It was Glenister. Being pissed off made her sound even more Scots than usual.

'What the hell's going on? We've just heard that Youngman's been taken. Your name was mentioned. Peter, you were warned to keep out of this stuff. Are you still playing the Lone fucking Ranger?'

Her emotion had the homeopathic effect of quelling his.

'Hi, Sandy,' he said calmly. 'I was just going to ring you.'

It wasn't a lie. As he drove along he'd found himself worrying about the consequences if something happened at Marrside and he hadn't called his suspicions in. His conscience would find it hard to live with, his career impossible.

'Oh, good! So now I've saved you the bother. Fill me in!'

He said, 'Let's leave the details for later, OK? I'm on my way to Bradford. I've got reason to suspect a woman called Kilda Kentmore might be planning an attempt on Sheikh Ibrahim's life. She's five foot eight, slender, thin face, black hair. She may be carrying a side-arm, but that's unlikely, too difficult to conceal. No, if she's got anything, it will be a bomb, and I think it may be concealed in a camera. She's a professional photographer, and I think she's going to Sarhadi's wedding reception. She won't have been invited, but he knows her so it could be easy for her to blag her way in.'

There was a pause then Glenister said incredulously, 'You're telling me that there's a Western suicide bomber going to Kalim Sarhadi's wedding? Christ, Pete, these Templars are crazy, but surely they're not *that* crazy?'

'The others have been acting out of some half-baked notion of vigilante justice,' said Pascoe. 'This one is just plain nuts. I think she wants to die. Look, it's complicated. You need to get off the phone and alert your people. I'm pretty certain she won't go to the mosque but will head straight for the *Walima* at the Marrside Grange Hotel, so tell your people watching the mosque to get along there straight away. Tell them if they spot her to approach with very great care.'

Another pause, then one stretching so long he said, 'Sandy, you still there?'

Glenister said, 'Peter, we've got no people at Marrside.'

'*What?* But you said there was an observation team on site. That's how you knew I'd gone to see Sarhadi . . . Oh no. Don't tell me, this is Mill Street all over again, right? Low-scale surveillance. Don't run up overtime over weekends and Bank Holidays. Jesus, what kind of Fred Karno outfit are you people running?'

'Pete, my bonny lad, we're not the CIA. Those plonkers in Westminster huff and puff about national security, but when it comes to doling out the dosh, they find it more painful than passing gallstones. How close are you?'

'Ten, fifteen minutes,' said Pascoe.

'OK. I'll get some people mobilized, but you'll definitely be first. At least you'll recognize her. Kentmore? She related to the Kentmore your wife was on TV with?'

'Yes.'

'He mixed up with this?'

'Yes.'

'So where can we get hold of him?'

'He's in custody. In the Mid-Yorkshire nick,' said Pascoe.

He didn't anticipate congratulation and he didn't get it.

'Since when, for Christ's sake?'

'Since lunch-time.'

Again the silence, longer this time, but not ending in the expected explosion.

'Oh Peter, Peter,' she finally breathed. 'What have you been playing at?'

'I can explain, but not now, eh?'

'Of course not. After all, if you get to Marrside and find the hotel in rubble, there's no explanation you can give which will be of any interest, is there?'

She rang off.

She was, he knew, right. If you played the Lone Ranger too long, there came a time when not even your faithful Indian companion could watch your back.

He threw back his head, yelled, 'Hi-yo Silver, away!' and stamped on the accelerator.

7

gatecrashers

Kilda Kentmore stepped into the hotel lounge.

What she would have done if refused entry she did not know because what she planned had such an air of inevitability about it, alternatives were pointless. What did these people say? *It is written.* Well, they were soon going to find out that non-believers could write a fair hand too.

No sign of the Sheikh. Not a problem. Her new sense of fatalism convinced her he'd be along shortly. Meanwhile she'd get the others used to her presence.

She advanced towards the sofa-throne, smiling.

Jamila returned her smile, with added brilliance. The girl looked so happy that for a moment Kilda felt uneasy at what she was going to do to her wedding day. But only for a moment. OK, the girl's memory of her big day was going to have a shadow over it, but at least if all went well she'd be able to share many anniversaries with her husband.

Kalim said, 'Nice to see you, but what are you doing here?'

'I was in Bradford, taking some pictures. And I remembered Jamila saying it was your wedding day today, and when I passed the hotel on my way to the motorway, I thought I'd see if I could get a few shots of you arriving or leaving or something. When I realized that everyone was inside already, I should just have carried on home. Sorry.'

'No. That's fine. Look, we're just finishing off in here, so if you'd like to take some shots of us sitting on this silly platform, that 'ud be grand.'

Behind him, his mother viewed the newcomer narrowly, but said nothing as she continued to muster the few remaining tribute-bearing guests.

Kilda moved around the room selecting different angles and pointing her camera at the loving couple from time to time. Finally the last of the guests went into the dining room. Tottie pulled tight the drawstrings on the linen bag into which she'd been dropping all the envelopes containing cheques and notes as well as the pouches of coins, flourished it triumphantly to demonstrate its weight, and said, 'That's it, all gathered in except for a couple, and I've got them on my list. Who's this then, Kalim?'

Sarhadi introduced Kilda to his mother, who greeted her with a chilly politeness. She felt that family courtesy had necessitated inviting plenty of people she'd rather have seen far enough without welcoming gatecrashers.

Kilda said, 'Can I have one of you, Mrs Sarhadi? You look great in that lovely outfit.'

'This is for free, is it?' checked Tottie.

'Aye, Mam, it's for free,' said her son.

'She does the fashion photos in the glossies,' added Jamila.

'Oh, in that case,' said Tottie.

She placed the linen bag on the edge of the dais, patted her hair, then smiled widely at the camera.

'Lovely,' said Kilda. 'Now I'm done. Unless there's any chance of getting a shot of the bride and groom with the Imam who conducted the ceremony. Is he still around?'

'Aye,' said Tottie without enthusiasm. 'But you'll not get near him without a note from the Islamic Council and an intimate body search.'

'Mam!' protested Sarhadi. 'No need to be like that. Any road, you're wrong, here he is now.'

The Sheikh had come into the room and was approaching them, smiling.

Kilda stepped into his path, her camera raised.

Get within three feet and you'll blow his fucking beard off, Jonty had said.

What about anyone else? she'd asked.

He'd shrugged and said, *Well, I'd not want to be in good spitting distance.*

How far could he spit? wondered Kilda.

The Sheikh was about six feet away and still advancing.

Then Tottie, revealing the benefit of a good Yorkshire education, said, 'Here's another one barging in. It'll be the ancient bloody mariner next!'

Everyone's eyes turned towards the door except Kilda's.

In the entrance, arguing with the self-appointed guardians, stood Peter Pascoe, his police ID in his hand.

Tiring of talk, he shouldered them aside and strode forward.

'Kilda!' he called.

Now the woman with the camera glanced at him and smiled before taking a step towards the Sheikh, who had come to a halt, sensing something was going on.

'Peter,' she said in a firm clear voice. 'Stand still. And make sure everyone else stands still.'

She was right in front of the Sheikh now. The burly banger on the doorway started to advance into the room. Pascoe's arm swung out and caught him across the midriff with a thud that drove the breath out of his body.

'Everybody stand still!' he yelled. 'Dead still!'

Not his best choice of phrase perhaps, but it did the trick.

Everyone froze, the only movement the turmoil of expression on their faces, bewilderment, alarm, anger, all mingling, each striving for dominance.

And then he added the words which put all other emotions in their pigmy place behind Giant Fear.

'She's got a bomb,' he said.

8

it is written

'So you're the infamous Sheikh Ibrahim,' said Kilda Kentmore.

She'd seen his photograph many times, and of course she'd seen him through the viewfinder of her camera that day she had wandered aimlessly, or at least without any conscious aim, to the Marrside Mosque, then taken that crazy pot-shot at his car.

How she'd got away with it, she did not know, or care. She'd felt as so often she'd felt since Chris's death, like a wraith drifting silently and unnoticed through a world of meaningless substance. She felt much the same now. Only two people existed in this room: Kilda Kentmore and Ibrahim Al-Hijazi, the destroyer and the soon-to-be-destroyed.

She studied him with a disinterested curiosity. He was quite a good-looking man, though she'd never much cared for beards. Certainly it was a face bearing little resemblance to the crazed caricatures of evil which appeared in the tabloid cartoons.

He was returning her gaze with a gentle enquiring smile.

'Yes, I am Sheikh Ibrahim,' he replied. 'How can I help you, lady?'

'You can help me to be reunited with my husband,' she said.

'I should be pleased to do so, but I am not sure how you imagine I can.'

'Don't you tell your followers that if they die in the act of destroying the enemies of your religion, their reward will be translation to paradise and the company of I forget how many young virgins?'

'I believe that seventy-two is the conventional number,' said the Sheikh.

'That seems a bit excessive,' said Kilda. 'But by the rules of proportionality, it makes my own hope that by dying in the act of destroying an enemy of my religion I will be reunited with my own dear husband, seem very reasonable, wouldn't you say?'

'It's certainly a hypothesis worthy of examination,' said the Sheikh. 'Could we perhaps sit down quietly and talk it over?'

He's trying to get me not to hate him, thought Kilda. Silly man. Doesn't he realize that hate has nothing to do with it? Except the hate I feel for my life.

'Sorry,' she said. 'Time's up. For you. For me.'

She held her camera up, her forefinger poised over the button.

'Kilda!' cried Pascoe, taking a step forward. 'Do you want to kill all of us?'

'You saying this bomb's in the camera?' said Tottie Sarhadi. 'Bloody hell. And there was me smiling like a loon when she pointed it my way.'

The spell of petrifaction woven by the interchange between the Sheikh and Kilda was broken. Sarhadi drew Jamila close towards him and in the doorway the bangers began to chatter excitedly till Pascoe shut them up with a glance.

'You don't want to kill everybody, do you?' Pascoe went on, desperate to engage Kilda's attention. 'Did Jonty tell you how much explosive he put in there? Did he?'

He thought he'd failed. She didn't turn her head and nothing in her body language suggested she'd heard him. But the finger stayed poised and when she spoke it was in answer to his question.

'Enough,' she said.

'Enough for what?'

'To kill him and me.'

'In what circumstances? At what range? Ten feet away? Cheek to cheek? In the same room? Kilda, knowing Jonty, wouldn't he give you a good margin for error? It could be if you set that device off now, it would take out everyone in this room.'

Again a pause, this time to consider what he'd said.

'I don't think so,' she said.

'But you don't know! Do you really want to

kill or maim these two young people? They've just got married, for God's sake! They've got their whole life in front of them!'

'That's what I thought when I got married,' she said. 'At least they would go together.'

'I don't believe you want them to go at all,' said Pascoe with quiet urgency. 'Or Mrs Sarhadi. Or these other young men. Or even me.'

Now she glanced quickly his way before returning her attention to the Sheikh. It's working, thought Pascoe. Get them engaged in an apparently rational discussion, no matter how irrational it really is. Avoid anything that sounds patronizing or merely conciliatory, but persuade them you're taking their madness seriously.

'Frankly I don't give a toss about those young men,' she said. 'In fact, I suspect we'd be a lot better off without them. As for you, Peter, I nearly did for you once, didn't I? Perhaps it is written, as the Sheikh might say. Right, Sheikh?'

'Everything is written,' said Sheikh Ibrahim who'd been listening to the exchange with the alert interest of a tutor conducting a seminar.

Pascoe didn't want him involved. This had to be between himself and Kilda, but there was worse disruption to come.

'Written, is it?' exclaimed Tottie Sarhadi. 'Aye, well, I dare say it is, but if you've got a gun, Mr Copper, I reckon it's written that now 'ud be a good time to pull it out and shoot her.'

This was addressed to Pascoe, who tried by

force of will and expression to convey to the woman the lesson he'd learnt on his negotiators' course, that you didn't meet threats of violence with threats of violence. But now came a new diversion, the sound of distant sirens getting nearer, welcome in one way but in another merely screwing up the tension several notches.

And Tottie was all too ready to help the process.

'About bloody time,' she said. 'You hear that, luv? Talk time's over. Soon this place'll be full of boys in blue with pop-guns. And one thing I've learned is give a little boy a pop-gun and he'll not be happy till he's used it.'

Kilda glanced towards her and smiled.

'I agree with you, Mrs Sarhadi,' she said. 'Time's up.'

She held the camera up to the Sheikh's face.

'Kilda!' cried Pascoe. 'Think about the young people!'

'I've thought,' said Kilda. 'I'll count up to five. Anyone not out of the room by then will just have to take their chances. Except, of course, you, Sheikh Ibrahim. You stay still. It's virgin count-down time for you. ONE.'

Pascoe screamed at the young couple, 'Go! Go!'

'TWO.'

Sarhadi pulled his young bride to her feet, She seemed to have lost the use of her legs. The body-guards began to move uncertainly this way and that. In case any of them might be thinking the promise of virgins made a suicidal charge worthwhile, Pascoe turned and screamed at them, 'Get out! Now!'

'THREE.'

The guards turned and retreated. Sarhadi half dragged, half carried Jamila off the dais and headed towards the doorway after them. Behind him his mother stepped off the dais.

'FOUR.'

What am I still doing here? Pascoe asked himself. I have a wife and daughter. What's keeping me here? Concern for a crazy woman who wants to die and a religious fanatic whose death will cause rejoicing in high places? I must be mad!

He commanded his legs to carry him towards the door but they seemed to be functioning even less efficiently than the young bride's. Tottie Sarhadi was having difficulty dragging herself away too, but her motives were at least mercenary. She'd taken a couple of paces forward when she realized she'd forgotten the money bag. She turned and stooped to pick it up from the edge of the dais. As she took hold of the bag by its drawstrings, Pascoe could see the muscles across her back bulging visibly beneath the tautened silk of her dress.

'FIVE.'

Time to run! But he found himself hypnotized by the chunky Yorkshirewoman who may have worked her rough magic on Andy Dalziel in the Mirely Mecca all those years ago. Could such coincidences happen and not be significant? wondered Pascoe as he watched Tottie, still half crouched on her haunches, begin to spin round like a hammer thrower in the circle. She had space for one and a half revolutions. Her feet did a series of intricate little dance steps, her arms straightened out as she rose to her full height, and she brought the heavy money bag, moving centrifugally at a speed not even a mathematician could have calculated in the split second available, slamming into Kilda's pale slender neck, just below the right ear.

Pascoe had never visited an abattoir but he hoped that the effect of a humane killer was as final and instantaneous as this. There was no hint of stagger, no delay into which any form of awareness of what was happening could creep. Kilda just slid straight to the ground like a dress slipping off a hanger.

The Sheikh reached out and dextrously caught the camera as it dropped from her nerveless fingers.

Tottie slung the bag over her shoulder and, without even a glance at the fallen woman, headed for the door through which her son and his beautiful bride had just made their exit.

As she passed Pascoe she said in tone more pitying than scornful, 'Everything's written, right enough, but even Allah needs a pen. *Men!*'

Part Seven

So a cried out, 'God, God, God!' three or four
times. Now I, to comfort him, bid him a should
not think of God; I hoped there was no need to
trouble himself with any such thoughts yet.

Shakespeare, *Henry V* Act II scene iii

1

the end

'You told him I were dead and the bugger actually believed you?' said Andy Dalziel.

Peter and Ellie Pascoe were sitting at his bedside. A week had passed since his return to consciousness. At first his days consisted of short bouts of confused wakefulness interspersed with long periods of sleep, some natural, some drug-induced. But by day three the waking periods were longer and less confused. On day six he was moved out of Intensive Care and on day seven he demanded a gill of Highland Park and six bacon butties, which some of the staff took to be evidence of incipient dementia. Happily, John Sowden, who knew him of old, was able to assure his colleagues that what it actually demonstrated was that Dalziel had taken a large step on the road to recovery.

'But it's a long road and precisely how far along it he will move is impossible to say,' Sowden warned Cap Marvell. 'He is not a young man. Any return to work will only be possible after an extended period of convalescence. In fact, were he that way inclined, I could not see any problem about retirement on medical grounds . . . What?'

Cap, who'd let out a hoot of amusement, said, 'Why don't you suggest that to him, Doctor? But I'd have your crash team on alert.'

'No need for that,' Sowden assured her. 'There's no problem with his heart.'

Cap said, 'I know that. I mean on alert for you.'

During this period there'd been a ban on visitors other than Cap, but that night she rang Pascoe to tell him that Dalziel was finally visitable.

'I've told him all I could about what's been happening,' said Cap. 'But he's really keen to hear your own account, Peter.'

Which was a loose translation of, 'I want to hear this from the horse's arse.'

It was a shock to see him sitting up, and not a reassuring one. On his back, unmoving, and linked to life by tubes and wires, he had somehow remained himself. A beached whale maybe, but still Leviathan. Now sitting up, pale and frail, talking and moving with visible effort, he was more like a flounder, flapping its last on the deck.

But he still had strength enough to make it clear he wanted to know everything that had happened with regard to the Mill Street investigation, so, at first hesitantly then with accelerating flow, Pascoe told the story.

Dalziel's weakness made him a better listener than he normally was. Perhaps even more surprisingly,

Ellie scarcely interrupted at all. Peace had broken out between the Pascoes with his assurance that his flirtation with the murky world of CAT and all its works was definitely over. His transgression was forgiven, but not, he suspected, forgotten, and when he reached the point in his story at which he tricked Kentmore, he attempted to glissade over it, but the Fat Man was on it in a flash.

'You told him I were dead, and the bugger actually believed you?'

'Well, yes,' said Pascoe.

Dalziel shook his head, incredulously. Pascoe caught Ellie's eye to see if she shared his amusement that, in this long twisty tale of death and deceit, the one thing the Fat Man found it hard to credit was that anyone could believe he was dead. She stayed stony-faced. Forgiven, he might be, but it was going to be a long time before she found anything about the deception amusing.

'You must have been bloody convincing,' said Dalziel accusingly.

'Well, actually, it was Wieldy who broke the news,' said Pascoe.

'I suppose he's got the face for it,' said the Fat Man grudgingly. 'So, on you go.'

The climax at the Grange Hotel Pascoe precis'd considerably, as he'd done when describing it to Ellie, not caring or, to be fair to himself, not able to explain to her why, when Kilda started counting, he hadn't been the first person out of the door.

Tottie Sarhadi's heroic role he did full justice to,

however, watching Dalziel keenly to see if there were any reaction to the name, but nothing showed.

Maybe he was being diplomatic with Cap Marvell in the room. Not that there was much chance of Cap hearing anything. Dalziel was in a large comfortable room with all mod cons in the private patient wing of the Central. Pascoe guessed that Cap Marvell was picking up the bill. One of the world's great organizers, she'd walked all over hospital regulations and installed herself in the room also. At present she was sitting at a table by the wall, earphones on, working at her laptop, probably organizing some direct action of doubtful legality, thought Pascoe, as he brought his story to its conclusion with a fittingly upbeat flourish, implying that everything was neat and tidy.

But the Fat Man, who had always been able to spot a loose thread on a Black Watch kilt at fifty yards, said, 'So let's get things straight. We've definitely got the buggers who put me in this sodding bed?'

'Yes. The Kentmores.'

'Grand. I hope they lock 'em up and throw away the key.'

Pascoe nodded agreement. It wasn't the time or place to let out a hint of the growing ambiguity of his own feelings about the Kentmores. They had murdered three men in Mill Street, they had almost killed Dalziel, and it was only the intervention of *kismet* in the person of Tottie Sarhadi that had prevented Kilda from further slaughter.

Yet when he thought of the two of them, what came into his mind were images of Kilda, pale as a waif child and still unconscious, vanishing into the ambulance, and of Maurice's stricken face as he received the deceitful news of Dalziel's death. *Bound together on a wheel of fire.* Now permanently bound there. It was a hard way to come to the truth of poetry.

'And this mad SAS bugger, Youngman. You say you've got him, but I've not heard any mention of him on the news.'

'CAT have taken charge of him.'

'How'd you let that happen? You collared the bugger, didn't you? When I had a prisoner, no bugger took him off me 'less I gave the go-ahead.'

Pascoe winced at the unjustness of it all.

By the time he was done at Marrside, Youngman had been whisked away to the Lube where the mysterious Bernard was doubtless already air-brushing him out of the picture. There was nothing of substance to link him to the Mazraani beheading. As for the attempt on Hector, all they really had there was Hector's jaguar sketch. Which left the Kentmores. And how willing would they be to testify against the man who'd helped Christopher in his dying moments?

Without Youngman, Pascoe could see no way of getting to Kewley-Hodge. And the galloping major was the only possible line of contact to St Bernard.

Pascoe couldn't even be sure he'd actually met

the Templar mole during his time at the Lube. But a copper has to go with what he's got, and those he thought of as the likely suspects had all turned up at the Grange Hotel within space of a few minutes: Sandy Glenister and Dave Freeman in one car, Bernie Bloomfield and Lukasz Komorowski separately. Whether they'd all come from the Lubyanka, or whether they'd been dragged from their weekend recreation, he did not know.

They'd sat in the hotel office and listened to Pascoe's account of events.

'Pete, you're a very lucky man,' said Glenister when he finished.

'Yes, you are,' said Bloomfield. 'Didn't Napoleon try to surround himself with lucky men? I'm not sure if you deserve congratulation or reduction to the ranks, Peter.'

'It is like gardening, the only thing that counts is results,' said Komorowski. 'This could hardly have worked out better.'

'Except perhaps,' said Freeman reflectively, 'if Pete and Mrs Sarhadi had got out of the room with the others and Mrs Kentmore had blown up herself and the Sheikh . . .'

To Pascoe this sounded a cynicism too far, but when he looked at the other three, he saw that they were all examining the proposition and finding much to agree with.

'Jesus!' he said in disgust. 'If that's what you want, why not just send out one of your own terminators and get the job done, nice and tidy?'

'I think you have been reading too many thrillers, Peter,' said Bloomfield. 'We are not in the terminating business, as you put it. On the other hand, *Thou shalt not kill but needst not strive officiously to keep alive.*'

He smiled, but Pascoe ignored the attempt to lighten the atmosphere.

'Officiously keeping people alive was part of a policeman's job, last time I looked,' he said. 'As for thrillers, it was reading Youngman's books that put me on to the Kentmores. Maybe you people at CAT should do a bit more reading.'

Freeman raised his eyebrows and looked at Bloomfield as if anticipating a sharp riposte, but it was Komorowski's quiet pedantic voice that spoke next.

'For me, I think things have turned out well. We have smashed this Templar gang and we can put the fact that you were instrumental in saving Al-Hijazi's life to good use, Mr Pascoe. Most important of all, this time you have escaped injury. I say well done.'

'Quite right, Lukasz,' said Bloomfield. 'Well done, Peter. Now let's get out of here before the press become intrusive. We'll finish Peter's debriefing back at the Lube.'

They had started moving to the door when Pascoe said, 'No.'

The movement stopped.

Bloomfield turned and said, 'I'm sorry?'

'I don't work for CAT any more, remember?

Any further questions you want to ask, you'll find me back home in Mid-Yorkshire. In the company of people I trust.'

'Now you've lost me, I'm afraid,' said Bloomfield, his face a landscape of lugubrious uncertainty.

'I very much doubt that, Commander,' said Pascoe crisply. 'To say we've smashed the Templars is at the very least premature. How many more are there? The one called Archambaud, certainly. And the group who murdered Carradice. Is Youngman going to give you a list of names? I won't hold my breath. And finally, Commander, it must have struck you by now that the Templars couldn't have functioned without considerable help from someone in CAT. St Bernard, I believe his code name is. Like yours. Not that I'm casting aspersions. It could be any of you. Or, worse, all of you. Me, I'm heading back to Kansas. I've got an angry wife and a sick friend there.'

And he'd walked out.

As he drove away, the words of Bacon came into his mind. A man who has a wife and children and a pension scheme should be very careful who he gives the finger to.

Complete openness was the best road to survival, he decided.

He'd written a detailed account of his activities, conclusions and suspicions since the Mill Street explosion, and made three copies, one of which he'd given to Dan Trimble, one he'd sent to CAT, and the third he'd put into the hands of his solicitor.

Maybe he was being neurotic, but sometimes neurotic felt good.

It also felt good to be talking to Andy Dalziel again, even if the old sod seemed inclined to blame him personally for the problems he foresaw in making charges stick.

'I'm sorry, Andy,' he said finally. 'Though it hurts me to say it, there's nothing more I can do.'

'It doesn't hurt me to hear it,' said Ellie. 'The further removed you are from those people, the better. Andy, we want you back on your feet soon as possible. Since you've been in here, he's bounced from one lot of trouble to another.'

'Never you worry, luv,' said Dalziel. 'Couple of weeks and I'll be right as rain. Then Youngman and yon Kewley-Hodge wanker had better look out.'

There was the sound of a chair being pushed back. Cap Marvell had removed her headphones in time to catch Dalziel's last remarks.

'Right as rain?' she said scornfully. 'Andy, if in a couple of weeks you've reached the stage where you can wipe your own bum, you'll be doing well.'

The Pascoes grinned. Cap Marvell had a line in upper-class coarseness which was more than a match for the Fat Man's vernacular bawdry.

Cap went on, 'This Kewley-Hodge you mentioned, would he be one of the Derbyshire Kewley-Hodges, or Kewleys as were?'

'That's right,' said Pascoe. 'Of Kewley Castle, near Hathersage. You know the family?'

'If they live in a sodding castle, of course she'd

know the family,' said Dalziel, clearly stung by the bum-wiping comment. 'Had to have an op to get the silver spoon out of her mouth when she took up with me. On BUPA, of course.'

They were made for each other, these two, thought Pascoe.

'Not really,' said Cap, ignoring the Fat Man, which was another of her rare talents. 'But Edie Hodge, whose name got tagged on to theirs, was at St Dot's when I was there.'

'St Dot's?'

'St Dorothy's Academy, near Matlock.'

'I think we used to play them at rugger,' said Dalziel.

'She must have been a lot older than you,' said Pascoe.

Cap laughed and said, 'Ellie, you've trained your husband well. Yes, but only a couple of years. Of course that makes a lot of difference at that age, but she was a legend in her own lunch-hour. Our answer to Lady Chatterley.'

'That sounds interesting,' said Pascoe, recalling Hot Rod's assurance that Edie was a very sexy lady.

'It was. Kitbag – that's Dame Kitty Bagnold, our head – caught her bonking in the potting shed with the college gardener. Or rather with his son and assistant, who was, I recall, quite dishy. Sex-on-a-shovel, we used to call him.'

'Bloody male hamster wouldn't be safe in them places,' muttered Dalziel.

'So what happened?' asked Pascoe.

'Boy vanished. I think his dad sent him out on other jobs thereafter. As for Edie, it was pack your bags and never darken this doorstep again.'

'Working-class employee gets off scot free, rich fee-paying pupil is sent down the road. Bet the Tory tabloids loved that!' said Ellie, hoping to steer the conversation into more general areas away from anything no matter how distantly connected with CAT.

It didn't work.

Cap said, 'Kitbag must have decided that good gardeners were harder to come by than rich kids and Edie only had a couple of terms to go anyway. She was a real school heroine till she ruined her image a couple of months later by marrying Andrew Kewley.'

'What was wrong with that?' asked Pascoe.

'For a start he was nearly thirty years older than she was, and it wasn't as if he were stinking rich or had a title or anything. He was a trustee of the school and he'd show up at Speech Day and Founders Day and Sports Day – especially at Sports Day. Wherever young flesh was being flashed, there would Alexander the Great be also. He was always chatting up Edie – I think he knew her father – and she'd do her cock-teasing thing. But no one imagined she would ever let him get closer than teasing distance.'

'So why did she do it?' wondered Pascoe.

Why is he always so fucking curious? Ellie asked herself.

Cap smiled reminiscently and went on, 'Maybe so she could turn up at the next Founder's Day with doting hubby and gurgling infant and queen it over Kitbag. I remember at one point Edie gave her the baby to hold while she tucked into the buffet, and the brat immediately filled his nappy.'

There was a loud snore from the bed. Dalziel was pretending to have gone to sleep. Or perhaps the poor old sod wasn't pretending.

Ellie saw her chance and said softly, 'Peter, I think perhaps we ought to go.'

'Yes, of course.'

Cap pressed a button to lower the bed's backrest. Supine, he looked even paler and frailer. They moved quietly to the door. Cap followed them into the corridor.

'Thanks for coming,' she said. 'Bring Rosie next time. He's very keen to see her.'

'We practically had to lock her up to stop her coming today,' said Ellie. 'But we thought, best leave it till we saw how he looked. How do you think he's doing, Cap?'

'Fine,' said Cap. 'But not half as fine as he wants to pretend. It's going to be a long haul to get him back to where he was, and you know Andy, he's a one-mighty-leap man. But don't worry, we'll get him there eventually.'

Her breezy confidence was reassuring, and Pascoe needed to be reassured. While there'd been flashes of the old Dalziel, what had been disturbingly constant was the sense of change, his fear that something had happened inside to dilute the Fat Man's essence, perhaps that something was broken beyond repair.

He tried to dislodge the distressing notion from his mind by returning to the niggle provoked by what Cap had told them.

'Why do you think Alexander Kewley agreed to change his name?' he asked.

'Don't know. Maybe because he was seriously strapped for cash and the Hodges had it dripping out of their ears,' said Cap.

'That makes it sound like a deal,' said Pascoe.

Ellie said, trying not very successfully to hide her irritation, 'Stop being a cop!'

Cap said, 'I'm still in touch with old Kitbag. Could ask her about Edie Hodge, if you like.'

Ellie gave him her Gorgon glare and Pascoe began to mutter, 'No really, don't bother,' when a thin reedy voice called from within the room, bringing to all their minds memories of past Dalzielesque summons that could drown all church bells within an acre.

Cap pushed open the door and went back inside.

Ellie said, 'Peter, you are going to leave it alone, aren't you?'

'Yes, of course I am. Honest. Normal service resumed. I promised, didn't I?'

She looked at him distrustingly but before she could respond, Cap reappeared.

'He woke up and realized you'd gone and he

says there's something he wanted to say to you, Peter. Do you mind?'

'Of course not.'

As the door closed behind Pascoe, Cap looked at Ellie curiously and said, 'You two OK, are you?'

'Yes. Fine,' said Ellie shortly. Then she added, because she disliked prevarication, and Cap, though not close, was a friend, 'He promised me all this business with CAT was behind him. He's lucky to have got out of it as lightly as he did. I just think that he ought to give it a rest and settle back into things here.'

'It was Andy who wanted to hear all about it,' said Cap.

'That's what Peter said, but I can tell, it's stirred it all up again.'

'Ellie,' said Cap gently, 'one thing I've learned since I partnered up with Andy is we need to be linked together by a long and loose rope.'

'Peter's not Andy.'

'Of course he isn't. But the rope linking them is in some ways a lot shorter and tighter than ours.'

The two women found things to look at in the empty corridor. They knew they were in a minefield where even a cautious step might end in explosion, and so they stood in silence, waiting for rescue.

There was a saving silence too at Dalziel's bedside. To Pascoe it seemed that the Fat Man had gone to sleep again and he felt relieved, suspecting that anything said now was merely going to confirm his worst fears.

He began to turn away.

A sound from the bed stopped him and he leaned over the still figure.

The lips moved a fraction, letting out scarcely enough breath to stir a feather. Pascoe thought he heard his name on the breath.

He said, 'Yes?'

'Peter, is that you?'

This was marginally stronger but not so strong it would have done more than tremble a candle flame.

'Yes, Andy, it's me.'

The Fat Man's eyes opened. The pupils seemed cloudy and unfocused.

He said, 'Peter.'

'Yes.'

His left hand moved. Pascoe instinctively patted it and felt his fingers seized in a grip weaker than he recalled his daughter's when first he held her.

'Pete, mate, I thought you'd gone.'

'No, Andy, still here,' said Pascoe, thinking *mate!* Oh Jesus, this was bad.

'Something I need to . . . Cap told me . . . back in Mill Street when I got blown up . . .'

The voice failed. Were those tears in his eyes? Oh shit, this was very bad!

'It's OK, Andy,' he said. 'You rest now. We'll talk about it later, OK?'

'No . . . need to do it now . . . in case . . . you

know. In case. Cap said . . . if it weren't for you I'd like have . . . she said you saved me, Pete . . . you saved me . . .'

His voice choked as if the emotion were too much for his depleted strength.

'I can't recall much about it now, Andy,' said Pascoe, eager to get out of here before the Fat Man said something so cloyingly sentimental it would clog up their relationship for ever. But the grip on his fingers was too strong now for him to break away without it being quite clear that's what he was doing.

'. . . and what I want to say, Pete . . .'

The voice was getting fainter again, the eyes had closed. Perhaps the poor bastard's debility was going to save him! He leaned forward closer to catch the soft-spoken words.

'. . . what I want to say is . . .'

And the eyes snapped open and stared straight into Pascoe's, bright and tearless.

'Just because tha gave me the kiss of life doesn't mean we're bloody engaged!'

Now the great mouth opened wide to let out a bellow of laughter so strong Pascoe felt himself blasted upright.

'You rotten bugger,' he said. 'Oh, you rotten bugger!'

Grinning broadly, he made for the door.

The two women, attracted by the sudden outburst within, greeted him anxiously.

'Is he all right?' asked Ellie.

591

'I'm afraid so,' said Pascoe. 'Well, look who's here.'

Along the corridor, moving on a pair of crutches with a strange crab-like motion, came Hector. Tucked into the neck of his T-shirt was a bunch of lilies whose pollen had redistributed itself generously across gaunt features giving him the appearance of a man who had just died of some rare form of jaundice.

'How're you doing, Hec?' enquired Pascoe.

'Fine, thank you, sir. How's Mr Dalziel? Can I go in to see him?'

Cap began to say, 'No, he's resting . . .' when Pascoe stepped in front of her and opened the door.

'Mr Dalziel's fine,' he said. 'And he'd love to see you. In you go, Hec.'

The constable hopped sideways through the door, which Pascoe closed gently after him. There was a moment's silence then came a crash, presumably as Hector dropped one of his crutches in order to extract his bouquet, then a dull thud, presumably as he fell across the bed, followed by a great cry of shock or rage or pain.

'Why did you let Hector in?' asked Ellie curiously as they left the hospital.

'Why not?' asked Pascoe gaily. 'After all, in a way it was them two that started it all. Only fitting that they should bring it to an end, don't you think?'

'Yes,' agreed Ellie, returning his smile. 'The end. Only fitting. Now let's go home.'

2

really the end

But it wasn't really the end.

The following sunny Sunday Pascoe and Rosie and Tig had gone for a walk to a favourite spot by the river where Tig could swim, Rosie could paddle and Pascoe could lie in a green shade and think thoughts of whatever colour he pleased. Ellie had excused herself on the grounds of a woman's work never being done.

This was true, but the work in question was not in fact the implied mountain of ironing, it was work on her novel, which had reached a sticky patch.

Not admitting this was of course just silly. In regard to her literary ambitions, Peter had never been anything but a source of support, admiration and praise. Yet, until she could wave a very large royalty cheque at their bank balance, she couldn't avoid this absurd sense of guilt at the inroads into her family life made by the creative impulse.

She switched on the computer and as always checked for e-mail.

There was a small backlog which she dealt with swiftly. Peter had a couple also, one from Cap Marvell. After a moment's thought, she brought it up.

Cap embraced all new forms of technology and their idiom with a fervour which brought out the mad Luddite in Dalziel. As Ellie picked her way through the message she felt some sympathy with the Fat Man. If this is what she did to her e-mails, God knows what her text messaging looked like!

Hi! Wnt to see Ktbg at Sndytn ystrdy – rmmbrd ur intrst in E Hodge as I ws lvng – Ktty v trd by thn – sd shd thnk abt it – gt e frm her tdy whch Im frwdng – A mkng gd prgss – tlks of cming hme – dr sys nt 4 a cpl wkks at lst – thn cnvlsce smwhre lke Sndytn whre wrks nt on hs drstp! Luv 2El nd Rsi nd Tg Cap

Ellie turned to the forwarded message and was relieved to find that Dame Kitty had not followed her old pupil down the path of mangled language. To her, e-mail was simply a faster way of sending a letter.

The Avalon Nursing Home
Sandytown
East Yorkshire

Dear Amanda,
Thank you for your visit of yesterday. Buried in this necropolis, it is always pleasant to receive news

594

from the world of the living, despite the fact that, as you doubtless observed, I find even the vicarious sharing of a life like yours quite exhausting.

I am sorry I was too fatigued by the end of your visit to deal with your enquiry about Edie Hodge, but I woke up this morning feeling much refreshed and all the details of Edie's adventure came flooding back.

The story that it was I myself who caught them in the potting shed is in fact untrue. The truth is, as so often, both likelier and stranger.

It was in fact Jacob, the boy's father, who came across them. You might have thought that his concern would have been to keep things quiet for fear of the possible consequences for his son, but his reaction was as Old Testament as his name. The way he saw it, his son was not the seducer but the seduced, led astray and defiled by a Daughter of Satan!

While not able to go along with this completely, knowing Edie as I did left me with the suspicion that it was probably six of one and half a dozen of the other. At least after that onslaught from Jacob, dealing with Matt Hodge was relatively easy. Initially, of course, he was very angry indeed, such anger being the natural emotion of a good Catholic parent who feels that his child's welfare has been neglected by those paid to take care of it. But though he was a doting father, he was by no means blindly so, and I do not doubt he was well aware of Edie's *proclivities. Indeed, after his initial anger, I wondered whether he did not see this case of* in flagrante *as an opportunity to re-establish some control over his wayward child.*

So the withdrawal of Edie from St Dot's was a decision reached amicably on both sides. Jacob despatched his son to fresh woods and pastures new, and I kept an excellent gardener!

Once the dust had settled, I must confess I was much more surprised by Edith's rapid return to a state of grace than by her fall from it. I suspect her marriage to Andrew Kewley was a case of her father striking a deal while the iron was hot! The nature of the heat is a matter of speculation, of course. I have no firm facts, though the circumstantial evidence does come close to being a trout in the milk. When I was left holding the baby at the Founder's Day reception (much to the amusement, I do not doubt, of all you girls), I was able to examine the infant at close quarters. And my reaction was, if this is a Kewley, I'm the Queen Mother! The hasty marriage, its speedy outcome, the change in the Kewley fortunes and the Kewley name were all explained, or at least explicable!

But I have always been an addict of detective fiction, so perhaps I only saw what an overheated imagination inclined me to see, though the giving of her lost love's name to the baby does seem indicative. Of course, when I read all these years later in the newspapers of the poor boy's sad fate, such speculation seemed irrelevant, almost in-

*decent. Poor Edith. That her pursuit of pleasure,
and her father's pursuit of respectability, should
have brought them to this ambush! Indeed, as
flies to wanton boys are we to the gods.*

*But I am very pleased to hear that the
wanton gods have not put paid to your Andy.
May his improvement continue. He sounds an
interesting man. Perhaps I may meet him some
day? By way of hint, let me remind you that
the Avalon Clinic complex is not simply a place
where old tuskers like myself come to die. The
old house, for instance, is used for convalescence, and its inmates have been seen to leave
on their own two feet.*

*Whatever you decide, do keep in touch, if only
to remind me that our speculative astronomers
are right and there definitely is life out there!*

Yours affectionately,

Kittie Bagnold

*P.S. I almost forgot. You asked about the
background of the gardener. He was a Pole who
came here as a child in 1945 when his family
decided that, after five years under the Nazis,
they deserved more than a communist future.
He grew up, married a Yorkshire girl, and they
produced that remarkably dishy young boy (yes,
even in the staff room we remarked on such
things!) who caused all the trouble.*

*The father was called Jakub, which we turned
to Jacob, the boy Lukasz, which we turned to
Luke, and their family name was Komorowski.*

Ellie sat quite still for several minutes. She thought of many things, of truth and deception, of justice and revenge, of human savagery and human rights, of principle and pragmatism, of conscience and consequence. She thought of parents and children and how you lived through them and sometimes suffered through them too. She thought of fathers and sons, of pride and hope, of hope shattered and pride deformed. She thought of fathers and daughters, of Peter and Rosie, of them both waving goodbye as they left with Tig, of Peter looking almost young and fit enough to be the girl's elder brother rather than her father. She thought of him lounging by the river watching Rosie and Tig competing madly to see which of them could return home the wettest and muddiest. She thought of the troubled weeks after the Mill Street explosion, and she thought of the placid days since their visit to see Dalziel, and she thought of Peter's joy at the prospect of the fat old sod's eventual complete recovery.

The time might be out of joint, but it was someone else's turn to put it right.

Somehow the imagined world of her novel in which her characters moved in a tangled mesh of conflicting loyalties and moral choices was no longer a place she wanted to be just now.

She pressed *delete* and went downstairs to do some ironing.